Praise for the work of Alfred Silver

Where the Ghost Horse Runs
"Finely crafted . . . Has the grandeur and grace of endlessly rolling tall-grass prairie."
—*Winnipeg Free Press*

"Well-written and authentic."
—*Publishers Weekly*

Keepers of the Dawn
"It's about time someone wrote an eminently readable novel about an Indian woman leader, and Alfred Silver has done it in superb fashion with Molly Brant. . . . Wonderfully entertaining."
—ALLAN W. ECKERT
Author of *The Frontiersman*

"A rollicking read . . . The heroine Molly Brant would seem almost too strong, courageous, generous, and wise if I didn't know [my wife] Dark Rain and other Native American women."
—JAMES ALEXANDER THOM
Author of *The Children of First Man*

Books published by The Ballantine Publishing Group
are available at quantity discounts on bulk purchases
for premium, educational, fund-raising, and special
sales use. For details, please call 1-800-733-3000.

ACADIA

Alfred Silver

BALLANTINE BOOKS • NEW YORK

This book is for all the good people of Hants County who've made us feel at home. As for the not-so-good ones, they probably don't buy books anyway.

Copyright © 1996 by Alfred Silver

All rights reserved under International and Pan-American Copyright Conventions. Published in the United States by Ballantine Books, a division of Random House, Inc., New York, and simultaneously in Canada by Random House of Canada Limited, Toronto.

http://www.randomhouse.com

Library of Congress Catalog Card Number: 95-96243

ISBN: 0-345-37950-0

Manufactured in the United States of America

First Edition: May 1996

10 9 8 7 6 5 4 3 2 1

PROLOGUE

On a winter's night in 1670, a man with a long white beard sat scratching down words in a stockaded hut on the eastern tip of North America. Nicolas Denys knew he was no writer and had no literary education, but he did know the land of Acadia better than any scholar ever would. So he was writing a book. It was his last hope. After a lifetime of scraping his way out from disasters, his new fort had burned down—which was why he and his family were huddled in this rickety outpost. If he could sell his book in France, he just might be able to pay off enough of his debts to start again.

He suddenly let his quill drop, flopped back in his chair, and stuffed the end of his ink-stained beard into his mouth. The way he was writing his book was to voyage in his mind along the coasts of Acadia, describing each port of call and the events that had taken place there. He'd been working his way up the Baye Françoise—what the English now called the Bay of Fundy—and had come to something he didn't want to remember.

It had happened a quarter century ago, but he could see it as though he were there: a bonfire lighting the courtyard of a cannon-shattered fort, a line of men waiting to die, a woman with her arms bound behind her back.

He knew it had happened, but how to explain it to someone idling through a reading hour in France? For that matter, how to explain it to himself?

On All Fools' Day in 1636, the merchantman *St. Jehan* set sail for the New World. Among the cabin passengers watching the towers of La Rochelle sink behind the stern rail was a

1

twenty-year-old woman named Jeanne Motin. She was traveling to a land she'd never seen before, to marry a man she'd met two years before and hadn't seen since.

Jeanne's memory of her fiancé was of a courtly chevalier with flowing black hair and large, soft, chestnut-colored eyes. What else she knew of Charles de Menou, Sieur d'Aulnay et de Charnisay, was that he was twelve years older than she, the son of one of the oldest and noblest families in France, and had served with great distinction on the warships of His Most Christian Majesty. It was remarkable to her that a man like Charles d'Aulnay would want to marry someone who'd never been more than middling in every way: of middling height, with medium brown hair, the middle daughter of a family of the middle class. But she wasn't about to argue.

What Jeanne knew of the continent she was sailing to was that it was an infinite, unexplored wilderness with a handful of colonies clinging to its edge: Quebec, Acadia, and then the English settlements of New England and Virginia. The Sieur d'Aulnay was lieutenant to the Governor of Acadia. Acadia's name had been familiar to Jeanne before Charles d'Aulnay's. The dowry she carried with her was fifty percent of her father's shares in the private trading company that shored up the Acadian interests of the Hundred Associates of La Compagnie de la Nouvelle France.

As the coast of France faded to a charcoal sketchline, and the gulls who'd been following the *St. Jehan* turned back, Jeanne's sister Hélène latticed her arm through hers and murmured a prayer. On Jeanne's other side, her other sister, Anne, had a stronger arm to cling to: the sword arm of Anne's new husband, Nicolas Le Creux de Breuil. Jeanne's father would never have allowed his daughters to cross the ocean had they not been traveling under the protection of Nicolas Le Creux. Last year "Nikki" had suffered two sword wounds defending an Acadian outpost from a mob of sailors and *sauvages* stirred up by a renegade fishing captain, and had nonetheless delivered that captain in chains to La Rochelle.

The *St. Jehan* passed beyond the islands of Ré and Oléron and began to pitch and roll in the swells and surges of the open sea. Jeanne folded back the hooped hood of her cloak to let the wind blow through her hair and around her suddenly clammy neck. It seemed odd to her, given the freshening rush of salt air, that the back of her throat should be constricting. She disentangled Hélène's arm from hers and retired to their cabin.

The cabin she was to share with Hélène contained two narrow, cupboarded beds, one on top of the other. Because Hélène had one leg a little shorter than the other, Jeanne was to have the upper bed. But she didn't feel much like climbing at the moment, and didn't think Hélène would mind her borrowing her bed for just a little while. She hadn't lain down long, though, before she had a sudden urge to jump up and stick her head out the window.

The *mal de mer* held her in its grip all the way across the ocean—sometimes just toying with her and allowing her to hold down a few mouthfuls of solid food. During the times when it was at its worst, and she was inclined to rail at herself for accepting the Sieur d'Aulnay's invitation, she tried to keep in mind the facts of life. She knew that people had good reason to think her flighty and bubbly and too easily enthused, but that didn't mean she couldn't understand facts. The facts of life were that a woman born into the world she'd been born into had three choices: she could marry until death do us part, she could take holy orders—as poor, clumsy Hélène seemed fated to do—or she could live out her days as a burdensome spinster in her parents' home. Those were the general facts. One fact specific to her case, or at least one she suspected, was that her current misery was one of the reasons Charles de Menou, Sieur d'Aulnay et de Charnisay, had ever considered marrying himself to plain Jeanne Motin. No highborn lady would suffer through weeks of nausea just to make herself a marriage in some unknown wilderness.

The *St. Jehan* took a month crossing the ocean and then spent a week anchored at a place of fogs, called the Grand Banks, to fill her hold with cod. Jeanne didn't mind the delay—a week of riding at anchor in a relatively calm sea gave her a chance to put a little meat back on her bones. By the time the *St. Jehan* started tacking south along the Acadian coast, Jeanne had even begun to believe she just might live to see Port Royal, the Acadian *seigneurie* of Charles d'Aulnay.

On a day in late May she and her sisters stood on the quarterdeck to get their first glimpse of the Baye Françoise, where Port Royal lay. A finger of smoke was rising from the shore. Hélène said authoritatively: "Another fishing station."

"No." The voice had such a darkness in it that Jeanne had to look to make sure that it had, indeed, come from Anne's "Nikki."

Anne said: "*Les sauvages*, then?"

"No. We are rounding Cape Sable. There is a man lives there with his English wife. Claude La Tour."

Jeanne said: "Why does he live there?"

"Why indeed? If my ladies will excuse me," and Nicolas Le Creux took himself off toward the bow, as though to find something to divert his mind from the man who lived at Cape Sable. Jeanne looked to Anne to see if she had any explanation for her husband's peculiar turn. Anne replied with a mystified shrug.

The next afternoon was a giddy few hours in Jeanne's cabin, with her sisters helping her to dress in the clothes she'd only worn at the dressmaker's. The corset didn't fit nearly as snugly as it had in La Rochelle. But her breasts still plumped up nicely over the brim, and the padded pannier tied around her waist gave the illusion that there were still hips under her skirt. The skirt and blouse were both of pink brocade, to accentuate what highlights there were in her hair.

Anne stepped back and said appraisingly: "The color does suit you, but it is too bad the Sieur d'Aulnay's first sight of you can't be when you're at your best."

"My best?"

"Well, your hair may be a little mousy, and your nose a little snubby, but if he could see you in your shift or less, he'd know what a lucky man he is."

Jeanne blushed and Hélène clucked. "Anne!"

"Well, it is a fact, Hélène, and only fair: I got the hair and nose, you got the mind, and Jeanne got everything below. But perhaps it is best that the Sieur d'Aulnay not get his happy surprise until his wedding night."

Jeanne blushed deeper and Hélène positively squawked: "Anne!"

By the time the three of them had gotten done with her hair, and decided between the pearl necklace and the gold chain, the light slanting through her cabin window was turning amber. As Jeanne followed her sisters up on deck, climbing the steps sideways to fit her skirt between the gangway railings, she heard the anchor splash. She asked her heart not to beat quite so fast and stepped out into the sunlight to take her first look at Port Royal.

There was a broad river mouth flanked by pine-studded cliffs. There was nothing else.

Jeanne called up to the captain on the half deck: "You said we would reach Port Royal before dark!"

"And so we have, mademoiselle. That inlet is the harbor mouth. Port Royal is but a few leagues beyond."

"Then why do we stop here?"

"The tide goes out. There are no tides in the world like those of the Baye Françoise—or none *I* ever seen or heard of. The rush out that inlet is like a millrace."

"So we must sit here all the way till the next turning?"

"Not the *next*, mademoiselle. I'll not try that passage in the dark. Midday tomorrow we ride the tide in. Stern foremost, to slow us enough that we're not dashed against the shore rocks or run aground on the shoals—with luck. You there! Get aloft and lend a hand before I hoist you up there with my boot!"

There was nothing Jeanne could do but stand at the rail, showing off her finery to the seagulls. She stared for a long time at the storm-stunted, twisted growth along the shoreline and the cathedral-spire pines beyond, trying to imagine what lay but a few leagues deeper into that forest. She hoped Port Royal had a wall around it. There was something menacing about that forest, where no one had cut down a tree since the dawn of time.

The cliffs in front of her grew noticeably higher as the ebbing tide exposed barnacle-encrusted rocks fringed with purple seaweed. In the water cavorted a pair of the diving birds the sailors called sea parrots, because of their ludicrous, rainbow beaks that were bigger than their puffed-out, black-and-white chests. The sea parrots at least made Jeanne feel she wasn't the only one gaudied up for no reason, but it didn't help much.

She had just about decided to go back down to her cabin

and change out of her ridiculous ball gown when a longboat came skimming out of the inlet, rippling the sunset-reddened water. Between the ranks of straining oarsmen lounged a black-haired man wearing a red-plumed hat, glistening black thigh-high boots and sword baldric, and a suit of red leather, red velvet, and pink lace.

The boatswain of the *St. Jehan* ran to roll out a ladder made of rope and slatted rungs. Before the Jacob's ladder could descend, Charles d'Aulnay grabbed a dangling rope in his fringe-gloved hands, swarmed up the side, vaulted over the rail, swept his hat off as he made a leg in front of Jeanne, kissed her hand, and said in a velvet voice: "Mademoiselle Motin, I would be deeply honored if you would sup with me tonight in Port Royal. Along with your sisters and Monsieur Le Creux, of course."

She was still feeling the kiss on the back of her hand: warm, dry lips and a double tickle from his neatly trimmed mustache and teardrop-shaped chin tuft. She said: "I . . . I . . . Yes!"

"I do not have sufficient eloquence to thank you fittingly for being so kind as to accept my invitation to dine. All you need bring with you are the articles for your toilette, and a day dress for next morning—the remainder of your baggage can be taken off the ship tomorrow."

Jeanne wafed down into her cabin. Hélène had to make the decision of which day dress to pack. When they came back out on deck, the Sieur d'Aulnay had already returned to the longboat. He called up: "Forgive me for preceding you, mademoiselle, but it seemed to me not so very gallant to send you climbing down a swaying Jacob's ladder with no one waiting at the bottom to receive you."

Jeanne put her right hand on the left post of the gate in the railing to steady herself, turned around, and started backward down the ladder. Half of her was embarrassed that Charles d'Aulnay would be able to see up her skirt on the way down; the other half was hoping he liked what he saw. As her foot reached the last rung he said: "If you will permit," and took hold of her waist from behind to support her into the longboat.

Once Nicolas Le Creux and Anne and Hélène were settled on board as well, the Sieur d'Aulnay sat down beside her and waved his hand forward. The helmsman pushed off and the rowers bent their backs to their oars to fight the tide.

The inlet opened up into a lake with uninhabited, glowering shores. Monsieur d'Aulnay said: "This is Port Royal basin. One could anchor a fleet in here and they would float serenely while a tempest tore the Baye Françoise to tatters. As, you see, my little fleet lies anchored there." Three ships came into view in the lee of an island. "The two ketches are suited only for coastal waters, but the *Vierge* has crossed the ocean a dozen times. And ahead, you see, we enter La Rivière au Dauphin— although it is difficult to say with precision where the sea ends and the river begins, since the tide carries salt water ten leagues inland twice a day."

The river mouth had slick, wet, pink, rippled lips of mudflats, which seemed to be growing wider in front of her eyes. A little farther along the shoreline, the mud gave way to lush marsh grass, where a crew of barefoot men were frantically building a wall of earth and stones and logs. Jeanne said: "Are the ramparts because of *les sauvages*?"

"Ramparts . . . ?" He saw what she was looking at and laughed. "Forgive me my laughter, Mademoiselle Motin, for you are right—they *are* ramparts of a sort. The enemy, however, is not *les sauvages*, but the sea. Those marshes are under salt water at high tide. Once they are diked and drained, we will have there a pasture or wheatfield richer than any in France, without us having to clear so much as an alder bush. *Les sauvages* say we are 'making land.' But I should not prattle on in such detail. I forget at times that my enthusiasms can grow tedious to those who have not the same interests."

She said: "Our interests are the same," then wondered if that sounded too proprietary too soon. But she liked that he said "we" and "us."

Another, smaller river flowed into La Rivière au Dauphin from the south. On the point of land between their joining stood the first human habitation Jeanne had seen in two months: a craggy, palisaded mass of sloping earthworks, stone, and timber, with the cross-and-lilies of France floating above it. Beyond the fort, she could see thatched cottage roofs and a chapel bell spire. The setting sun behind her gilded Port Royal in a liquid glow.

The rowers banked their oars smartly as the boat glided up to the landing stage. Two dockmen came running to fasten the lines. Charles d'Aulnay put a hand on Jeanne's elbow to assist her out of the boat. With her sisters and brother-in-law bringing up the rear, she walked beside the Sieur d'Aulnay up the broad path to the gates of Port Royal.

She didn't walk very well. After all those weeks at sea her feet were confused by a surface that didn't move beneath them. Charles d'Aulnay said: "If you will permit me, mademoiselle," and offered her his arm. Within the velvet and lace was a forearm thick with muscle that went rock hard whenever she stumbled. Even after her legs stopped wobbling, she pretended to stumble once or twice, just to feel that change take place within that sleeve.

Flanking the gates were two pikemen with mirror-polished cuirasses and steel-crested helmets, who snapped to attention as the gates swung open. In the courtyard beyond were several ranks of armored musketeers, who pointed their muskets at the sky and crashed off a volley in perfect unison. She clapped her hands and dropped them a curtsy in thanks for welcoming her to her new home.

As the Sieur d'Aulnay escorted her across the courtyard toward a wide, tall building made of immense beams and plaster facings, he said gently: "That was a pretty gesture, Mademoiselle Motin, but there is no need to thank them for doing what they were bidden."

Off the entrance hall to the château was a dining hall steaming with food smells—some deliciously exotic, some deliciously familiar. With her *mal de mer* finally vanished, she gorged herself on shellfish and fresh vegetables and a meat that was dark and tender—with a woodsy, herbal taste in the blood—which Charles d'Aulnay said was the flesh of the moosedeer. In fact, she felt like she was stuffing all her senses. After her long confinement on the *St. Jehan*, Port Royal was a barrage of new things to see and hear and notice. Particularly Charles de Menou, Sieur d'Aulnay et de Charnisay.

At one point his chestnut eyes drifted down the table away from her and then froze. He lifted a finger: "Steward."

"*Oui*, monsieur?"

"That candle is guttering."

"Oh, monsieur, so it is. Boy! Trim that candle. Forgive me, monsieur, I had not noticed."

"Odd, that you whose business it is to attend to the table did not notice flares of foul smoke and spurtages of wax I could not help but notice."

"It shall not happen again, monsieur, I assure you."

"Well, if you assure me, then it must be so."

But other than that, the *seigneur* of Port Royal devoted his attention entirely to Jeanne, even brushing aside Nicolas Le Creux's eager questions as to how Acadia had fared while he was wintering in France. The last course had barely arrived, though, when the Sieur d'Aulnay stood up and said with exquisitely distant *politesse*: "Mesdames et messieurs, et mademoiselles, I must beg you to forgive me, but the mornings come early in Acadia—at least they do in the summer, when there is so much work to be done. Please continue with the cognac and good cheer. When you so desire, the boy will light you to your beds."

He did kiss Jeanne's hand good night. But then he kissed Anne's and Hélène's as well.

The narrow room Jeanne was lighted to contained a bed that was a cloud of soft down—almost *too* soft after the straw ticking of a ship's bed. After she'd blown out her candle, she lay awake wondering whether Charles d'Aulnay was having second thoughts, or what he imagined was the reason she'd crossed the ocean to Acadia.

The morning came with a trilling birdsong she'd never heard before. She put on the blue wool day dress Hélène had picked out for her and went downstairs, unsure of how she was supposed to approach the day. Anne and Hélène were sitting at breakfast. The steward said: "The Sieur d'Aulnay instructed me to extend his apologies, mademoiselle. He and Monsieur Le Creux must spend the first hours of the morning on matters of business."

Anne was showing her and Hélène the quarters she shared with Nikki when a servant appeared in the doorway. "The Sieur d'Aulnay wonders whether it might be convenient for Mademoiselle Motin to come down and have a word with him?"

Anne said mischievously: "I wonder which Mademoiselle Motin he means?"

Hélène sniffed. "Don't be silly."

The Sieur d'Aulnay was standing in the entrance hall studying a piece of paper while one of his officers looked on. As Jeanne came down the staircase, feeling a little guarded, the chestnut eyes glanced up at her. He handed the paper to the officer, dismissed him with a nod, and said: "I trust you slept well, mademoiselle."

"Yes, thank you."

"Last evening you expressed some interest in how we 'make land' at Port Royal. I thought perhaps you might care to walk out with me to see one of the fields that has already been diked and drained and planted."

"Yes, thank you."

He didn't offer her his arm this time. A short walk up La Petite Rivière behind the fort there was a bowl-shaped field of the biggest cabbages Jeanne had ever seen. Charles d'Aulnay escorted her along the path topping the grass-covered dike and explained to her the ingeniously simple wooden mechanism that allowed marsh water to drain out but kept tidewater from flowing in. Then he walked her back to the château and excused himself to see to the unloading of the *St. Jehan*.

It became the daily routine. He would set aside the latter part of the morning to show her another aspect of Port Royal, then leave her to her own devices for the afternoon. He would reappear for the evening meal and excuse himself the instant he'd finished his last course.

He toured her through the fur warehouse, the chapel and tenants' farms on La Rivière au Dauphin, and the gristmill on La Petite Rivière. He showed her the fort's defenses and the inside of every room in the château—except the *seigneur*'s bedchamber.

She grew adjusted to thinking of her immediate world as a transplanted pocket of France bounded by La Rivière au Dau-

ACADIA 11

phin and the green-and-black wall signaling the domain of *les sauvages*. She even became accustomed to the sight of *les sauvages* themselves, coming in to Port Royal to trade or paddling by in their canoes: people with coarse black hair and black eyes and coppery skin covered only by short, sleeveless leather dresses or a kind of skimpy leather diaper fixed to a waist thong. She found it indefinably disturbing that they should seem as much a part of the forest as any squirrel or deer and yet go about on two legs.

As the Sieur d'Aulnay squired her around Port Royal or presided over the supper table, he talked to her at length of why earlier attempts to colonize Acadia had failed, of the varieties of fish rife in the Baye Françoise, of the tide-marsh salt hay that fattened sheep and cows astoundingly—of everything but the matter that had induced her to suffer two months of vertigo in a wave-rolled wooden dungeon. After ten days of waiting she resolved that if he didn't speak of it by the time the *St. Jehan* was ready to start the return voyage, she would tell him that if he no longer wished to marry her, she might just as well go back to France on the ship that had brought her to Acadia.

That night the last course was cleared away from the château's vast dining table and the Sieur d'Aulnay stayed in his chair. Instead it was Nicolas Le Creux—usually the last one to retreat from an evening of cognac and chatter—who rose to his feet and yawned. "It is high time I started remembering that a man can't go on forever keeping Parisian nights and Acadian mornings without it catching up to him. Shall we retire, my dear?"

Anne stood up, saying to Hélène: "Remember, you and I have planned to be woken in time to see the dawn birds on the marsh."

"We have? Oh, yes—it but slipped my mind a moment. Yes, I'd best come with you now so I can get an early rest so I'll be rested when it comes time for us to be wakened before dawn to see the marsh birds, just as we planned."

After her sisters had kissed Jeanne good night, Charles d'Aulnay gestured the servants to refill his goblet and hers, then said: "You may leave us."

When they were alone, he took a sip of his wine, fastidiously ran a fingertip along the fringe of his mustache, and leaned across the table. "Mademoiselle . . ." he said.

"Monsieur . . . ?"

He took another sip of wine, rolling it around in his mouth, stood up and looked at the wall beyond her for a moment, then swallowed and lowered his eyes to her. "I believe you have now seen and learned as much of Port Royal as it is possible to know without living through the seasons. Now that you know my home in Acadia, and since your father has given his blessings, I believe it would be proper for me to ask you: Jeanne, will you consent to be my wife?"

"Yes, Charles."

He stooped down beside her chair and kissed her mouth for the first time, his down-soft mustache warm against the tender indentation between her nose and upper lip. He straightened up again and said: "I will have the banns posted tomorrow. We can be married within the month. I bid you good night."

It was a bit more matter-of-fact than she'd imagined. But then, it *was* a matter of fact now, and that was what mattered. She reminded herself that the aristocracy—of which she was about to become a member—didn't go about flinging their hats in the air.

When the day came, the chapel and the meadow in front of it were filled with all the citizens of Port Royal, come to see their *seigneur* be wed. There were even a few *sauvages* looking on curiously. The groom was dressed in a magnificent suit of silver brocade. Jeanne wore the pink she'd worn the first day he'd seen her in Acadia.

After the nuptial banquet Jeanne and her husband were lighted up into the one room in the château she hadn't yet seen. It was a very large room, with a bright fire in a very large hearth flickering on a very large, canopied bed and on two tapestried screens in opposite corners. The firelight also gleamed on the hilts of Charles d'Aulnay's scabbarded sword, which leaned against one bedpost.

He gestured toward one of the screens. "Your trousseau has been laid out there. Tomorrow you may have the servants bring the rest of your wardrobe and other belongings in here and arrange them as you so choose." He bowed and disappeared behind the other screen.

She carried her candle behind her screen, changed into her virgin bedgown, and brushed out her hair. She stalled a little while, rubbing her eyes with her fingertips and swallowing. She had a general idea of what was about to happen, but neither her mother nor her older sister could help her now.

When she'd nerved herself to step out, he was nowhere in sight. From behind his screen she heard the murmur of his prayers.

She guessed that the side of the bed his sword was leaning against must be the side he preferred, so she knelt down at the other side to say her prayers. When she'd done, he still hadn't come out, so she peeled open the envelope of bedcovers and crawled inside.

When he finally emerged he was wearing a lace-collared, snowy nightshirt that made his hair and eyes look even darker than usual. Its pleated front was stuck slightly out of line at one point, by something that seemed to be markedly different from what she remembered of her little brothers making water in the Seine.

He furled back the bedclothes on his side of the bed, not far enough to uncover her, sat down on the rim, and swiveled in beside her. She lay on her back, eager and terrified. He said nothing, just put his hand to the side of her face and kissed her slowly, moving his hand down her shoulder to cup her left breast before moving farther down. She parted her thighs slightly and felt his fingers moving between them—first through the curtain of her nightgown and then skin to skin as he furled the hem up to her hips. He spread her legs wider apart and then moved on top of her.

At first there was a darkly delicious sensation that she feared would have to figure in her next confession, and then a terrible pain that made her turn her head and bite the pillow to keep from crying out. When he was done, he shuddered and slumped across her.

It seemed impossible that such a powerful man could be lying limp and helpless on her breast like a weary child. She put

her hand up to the thick waves at the back of his neck and tentatively stroked them.

They drank a little wine and talked awhile and then did it
again. This time there was no pain worth mentioning.

When she awoke in the morning, his sword was no longer
leaning against the bedpost and he was gone. When she went
downstairs, only Anne and Hélène were still at breakfast.
Hélène looked up at her with an expression of grim commis-
eration; the look that came from Anne made Jeanne blush.

The steward came to ask "Madame" about the menu for this
evening's meal, bringing home to Jeanne that she was now the
chatelaine of Port Royal. She went with the steward for a more
detailed tour of her new cellars and kitchens. At supper that
night she found herself seated in the hostess's place, at the far
end of the table from the host. When she'd been merely "mademoiselle," she'd sat at his right hand.

She'd been married barely a week when her husband came
to her somberly and said: "I have had news from the other side
of the peninsula. Governor Razilly is gone to God."

She crossed herself and murmured: "Mercy on his soul."

"I have already arranged for Masses to be said for him,
though there was never a man had fewer sins to account for."
It didn't seem to Jeanne, though, that her husband's grief was
unalloyed. She was learning to read those subtle shadings that
outsiders mistook for unrufflable sangfroid. "We will have to
wait almost a year, at the soonest, before we know who's been
declared the new Governor of Acadia. I fear you will have to
grow accustomed to the fact that if Cardinal Richelieu went
Protestant yesterday, we would not know until next summer
brought our next supply ship."

The winter came on more fiercely than any Jeanne had
known in France. But she and her husband and sisters and
brother-in-law were snug and warm inside Château Port Royal,
and the table she presided over groaned under the moosedeer
and caribou that *les sauvages* found easier to hunt when the
woods were thick with snow. She began to adjust to the fact
that, like it or not, she was now the final authority on all the

mechanics of the household. Her badge of office was the ring of keys for the wine cellar and larders.

She began to notice, though, that there was something dark lurking below the pastoral surface of Acadia. It wasn't the stone dungeons underneath the château; as horrible as they were, they were only used for short stays by a sentry found asleep at his post, or a tenant farmer who'd sampled too much of his own cider. And it certainly wasn't *les sauvages*; for all the scare stories of their ferocity, Jeanne had found them to be as unobtrusive and peaceable a people as she could imagine.

What it was, was that name she'd first heard from Nicolas Le Creux as the *St. Jehan* was rounding Cape Sable: "La Tour."

Whenever a guest at the table mentioned that name, Charles would scowl and change the subject. Either that or launch into some convoluted complaint that had something to do with the Hundred Associates of La Compagnie de la Nouvelle France.

As her husband was getting into bed one night, Jeanne said: "Charles, who is La Tour?"

"La Tour . . . ?" He chewed on his front teeth for a moment, then got back out of bed and poured himself a cup of wine, as though to wash the taste of that name out of his mouth. He said crisply: "There are two La Tours, father and son. The father is a traitor and the son is worse. *Claude* La Tour is old and toothless now, and allowed to live out his days at Cape Sable—instead of ornamenting a gibbet, as he should.

"*Charles* La Tour is . . . not a pleasant subject for conversation. But, since you've asked—and I suppose you should know *all* about Acadia, pleasant and unpleasant.

"If I told you of every crime Charles La Tour has committed, we'd neither of us get any sleep tonight. He began his career a quarter century ago, when the English burned the first Port Royal. Instead of returning to France with the other colonists, Charles La Tour and his friend Biencourt took to the woods and lived among *les sauvages*, sending out cargoes of furs with the fishery captains in exchange for enough trinkets and brandy to convince *les sauvages* that these two ragged *couriers de bois* were great men whom their daughters should be prostituted to.

"When the English finally surrendered Acadia back to

France, Biencourt inherited his noble father's title of Governor of Acadia. So what do you think Charles La Tour did?"

"I don't know."

"If you knew La Tour, you would guess what he would do in that circumstance. He poisoned his old friend Biencourt and claimed that Biencourt had declared him his heir, so that *he* was now Governor of Acadia.

"When Cardinal Richelieu created the Hundred Associates and appointed Governer Razilly to rule Acadia—and Governor Razilly selected me as his lieutenant governor—La Tour elbowed himself in as yet another lieutenant governor. Not that the chain of lawful authority means anything to him.

"There was . . ." He paused to take a sip of wine. It seemed to Jeanne that he wasn't as much thirsty as that he'd caught himself rising toward a passion he would've considered unseemly. When he took up the thread again, he'd regained his sangfroid. "There was an English outpost on Acadian soil, which the Boston traders refused to surrender. So Governor Razilly appointed me to lead an expedition to evict them, with La Tour as my second-in-command.

"La Tour refused to serve under me. *Me*—who has commanded warships and regiments of land troops, while the only war La Tour has seen is skirmishes of pirates and *sauvages*. So I had to drive out *les Bostonais* with no help from La Tour. And then the Hundred Associates awarded that trading post to *him*.

"He now squats in his new fort on La Rivière St. Jean, across the Baye Françoise from us. He takes not a jot of interest in fulfilling the conditions set for La Compagnie's monopoly of trade—that we colonize the country and bring *les sauvages* to God. La Tour prefers Acadia remain a pagan wilderness where he can lord it over *les sauvages* and debauch their daughters. So I am left to shoulder the burden alone.

"No matter how many dispatches I send to Paris or La Rochelle, they still fail to see how that man cripples us. La Tour has been too clever to show himself openly. But I know him; now that Governor Razilly is gone, La Tour's arrogance will grow and one day he will go too far."

"And then?"

"Then I will send him back to France in chains. Or in a coffin."

As the snowdrifts in the orchard behind the fort were transformed into white drifts of apple blossoms, Jeanne found pleasanter things to occupy her attention than the name La Tour. She forgot it completely as the appearance of the first, embryonic fruits coincided with the first ripening of her womb. She didn't mind being the chatelaine of Port Royal, and married into one of the noblest families in France, but the only real ambition she'd ever had was to mother children.

She was sitting in the sitting room, feeling the baby move inside her, when Charles came in looking as if he was having some difficulty maintaining his sangfroid. He said: "I have been reading the dispatches the supply ship carried with her. As I'd anticipated, Governor Razilly's younger brother has inherited the title of Governor of Acadia. But I know Claude de Razilly is too timid to ever venture across the ocean. He will be content to sit in France and affix his seal to whatever reports I care to send him. Which means that, in all but name, I am now the Governor of Acadia."

"Oh, Charles!"

"And you, my dear, are now the Queen of Acadia. But it does mean I must go to France to arrange matters. I've already given orders for the *Vierge* to be readied for an ocean voyage. It is unfortunate you cannot come with me, but so the good God wills."

"Why can I not come with you?"

He looked pointedly at her ball-round belly. "I should think that would be obvious."

"You might have asked me."

The chestnut eyes suddenly became more red than brown. In a voice like cut glass, he said: "Would you wish, madame, to be storm-tossed all the way across the ocean in your state of advancing pregnancy, doing the good God knows what damage to my unborn child, and chance giving birth on shipboard or a roadside on the way to Paris?"

"No, but—"

"There. I have asked and you have answered. Now, if you will excuse me, madame, I have matters to attend to."

He left her feeling like she wanted to tear his child out of her, or take herself and her unborn child as far away from him as fast as possible. All she could see, over and over, was those chestnut eyes turn red. She'd never known that red could be an icy color.

She reminded herself of the facts of life. Of the three choices open to a woman, he had never given her reason to regret the one she'd made. Until that moment. But now that it had happened, all she could do was try to understand why and make sure it never happened again.

The worst of it was that he'd appeared to see her as a bourgeois little fool for whining about the fact that he'd made the only logical decision the circumstances allowed. And she couldn't shake the niggling feeling that he was right.

But when she stood on the parapet waving at the *Vierge* disappearing down Port Royal basin, the only feeling she had was longing. She wiped her eyes and stiffened her mouth and went looking for her steward, to tell him she had an urge for sheep's liver tonight. She found him in the kitchen, looking ill at ease. He was standing tautly near two scullery maids huddled together on the hearth ledge—one of them sobbing and the other one trying to comfort her. Jeanne said: "Whatever is the matter?"

The sobbing one choked out: "Oh, madame, it is—"

"No need," the steward cut her off, "to disturb Madame with—"

"*Madame* prefers," Jeanne cut him off, "to be disturbed by whatever it may be that disturbs her household, rather than letting it fester."

"Oh, madame!" the girl wailed. *"Les sauvages!* While the master is gone to France to become governor, *les sauvages* mean to burn Port Royal and murder us all in our beds!"

"Nonsense, my dear. *Les sauvages* would never do such a thing."

"They would if they were bribed and forced to, madame."

"And who could bribe or force them to do anything?"

"Who else, madame? La Tour."

PART I

ALWAYS TRUSTED

"The La Tours could always be trusted—to look after their own interests first."
—Samuel de Champlain,
Les Voyages de la Nouvelle
France occidentale . . . Paris, 1632

CHAPTER 1

In the village of Médard, along the road from La Rochelle to Paris, a man with a voluminous brown beard climbed down off his horse in front of Médard's only inn. The man was Nicolas Denys, agent for La Compagnie de la Nouvelle France. He didn't want to be an agent for La Compagnie. In fact, he didn't want to be in France at all. He wanted to be back in Acadia.

Denys was certain he knew the recipe that could transform all of Acadia into a thriving French colony overnight: fish mixed with trees. Instead of fishermen sailing back and forth from France every summer, they should build a permanent fishing establishment in Acadia. During the winters the fishermen could become woodmen, turning the monumental forests of Acadia into monumental timbers for export to France.

Denys had been well on his way to turning his vision into a reality, back in Governor Razilly's day, with a sawmill and a winterproof fort on Acadia's Atlantic shore. But just when Denys had accumulated enough beautifully seasoned planks and beams to make a first shipload to France, Governor Razilly died and Charles d'Aulnay politely informed him that he no longer had permission to export Acadian lumber. So Denys had loaded his ship with Acadian cod and sent it off to the markets of Lisbon. In Lisbon, the Portuguese navy conscripted his ship, and her cargo was stolen by Portuguese merchants whom the Portuguese courts refused to prosecute.

What with one thing and another, Denys had found himself with a great many debts and no assets, and a family to feed. So here he was running errands in France while tyro navigators

21

blundered along the Acadian coasts that he knew like he knew his own beard.

But at least the matter that had led him to dismount in front of Médard's sag-raftered inn wasn't that of an errand boy, but of a man doing a favor for another man who'd done him many favors in the past. Denys went into the inn and asked for bread and cheese and a flagon of wine. When the innkeeper brought them to his table, Denys said: "Do you know how I might find the home of Demoiselle Françoise Jacquelin?"

The innkeeper arched his eyebrows. The conversation at the only other occupied table ground to a halt, and the farmers sitting around it cocked their heads toward Denys. The innkeeper said: "Do you know Mademoiselle Jacquelin well, monsieur?"

"I have never met the lady. I was asked to deliver her a letter."

One of the farmers snorted: " 'Lady . . .' "

The innkeeper said: "No one in Médard knows her well. She lives alone, save for a servant girl, in a cottage apart from the town, and keeps to herself."

"They say," put in the farmer who had snorted, "she was an actress in Paris."

"Or worse," one of his companions added.

"Some even say she is a Protestant."

"She has visitors at strange hours," the innkeeper contributed, "who come from the good God knows where and never stop in here for even so much as a cup of small beer."

Denys said: "How would I find her cottage?"

"Which direction are you traveling, monsieur?"

"Toward Paris."

"Ah. Then carry on the way you are traveling, until you come to the woodcarver's at the far end of the village. You will see another road winding off behind it to the left. Down that road you will find a lilac hedge that has been allowed to run wild. Behind that hedge is the cottage of Françoise Jacquelin."

Yellow leaves were blowing across the road, but there was still enough strength left in the sun to have warmed the air considerably since Denys had stopped to break his fast. He

furled his cloak back over his shoulder and turned his horse toward the far end of the village.

The far end of the village wasn't very far. The lilac hedge
the innkeeper had described was more than "run wild"—twice
Denys's height in some of its unkempt crowns, and so thick it
was impenetrable to the eye even with half its leaves fallen
away. There was a little white gate with lilac boughs arching
over it. Denys opened the gate and stepped inside.

The cottage was a story and a half of stone and timber and
glazed clay roof tiles, with blown-out roses climbing the door
frame. Between the face of the cottage and the back of the lilac
hedge lay the autumnal remnants of a garden that looked surprisingly orderly, given the condition of the hedge. The servant
girl the innkeeper had mentioned was kneeling beside the path,
putting the garden to bed.

Denys would hardly have called her a girl. He gauged her to
be at least halfway through her allotted three score and ten, although the ringlets spilling out from her head scarf had a glow-
ing reddish-purple tinge where he would've expected gray. She
was small-shouldered and plumpish—in a way that suggested
there were dimples at every place she bent. There was mud on
her arms, mud on her bare feet, mud on her skirt, even streaks
of mud across the faces of the plump breasts swinging freely
in the low-scooped, coarse-clothed, peasant blouse. When she
looked up toward him, he saw that her eyes were too big for
her face—and her nose almost so—while her smallish mouth
and chin were crowded in and plumped outward by apple
cheeks.

Denys said: "I bear a letter for your mistress."

She leered at him impudently. "I have no mistress. Do
you?"

"My good woman!"

"I am nothing of the kind. I am Françoise Marie Jacquelin."

"Oh! Forgive me, mademoiselle, but when I saw you on
your knees I thought—"

"Perfectly understandable. My girl, you see, is a much better
cook than I am, so I leave her to tend the kitchen while I tend
the garden." Her hand came up in a gesture that somehow

made him naturally take hold of it and assist her to her feet before he knew it had happened. Her hands were impossibly small, and creased around the wrist like a baby's.

"Won't you come inside, Monsieur . . . ?"

"Denys. Nicolas Denys."

"*Enchantez*, Monsieur Nicolas Denys."

The first floor of the cottage was one room, with a hearth at either end: a large one hung with hooks and pots and blazing fiercely, and a smaller one that was unlit at the moment. The kitchen hearth faced a serviceable oak table; the smaller one, several padded chairs and a shelf or two of books.

A girl with black hair and gamin eyes was stirring a pot bubbling above the fire. Françoise Marie Jacquelin said to her: "Lorette, this is Monsieur Nicolas Denys." The girl gave him a perfunctory curtsy without interrupting her stirring.

Mademoiselle Jacquelin pulled out one of the chairs around the table, gestured Denys toward another, and said: "Lorette, I think we should have a bottle of wine. Perhaps the white Bordeaux."

The servant girl replied unconcernedly: "In a moment, Françoise," and continued stirring the pot a moment, then stirred the fire down to coals, lit a candle stub from one of the remaining flames, lifted a trapdoor, and disappeared into the cellar in no apparent hurry.

Françoise Jacquelin's mouth quirked up in the same lopsided smile she'd given him in the garden. "You are wondering, Monsieur Denys, why I allow such familiarity from her. Lorette is the daughter of a woman I once knew, so she is somewhat more than a servant." There was the same oddly unsettling impression of deviltry in her smile that he'd noticed the first time. Denys pondered on it and put it down to the fact that the canine tooth on the side she smiled with was oversized and slightly crooked. There was always a practical explanation for eerie phenomena if one but studied on them awhile.

The girl reappeared with a cobwebbed bottle that she wiped clean, uncorked, and poured generously into three pewter vessels, taking the third one back with her to her hearth and bouillabaisse. Françoise Jacquelin took a healthy quaff, so Denys didn't feel constrained. Although he'd lived too rough a life to ever call himself a connoisseur, he didn't need an educated palate to tell the difference between what the local innkeeper served out and this.

Mademoiselle Jacquelin said: "You said something about a letter, Monsieur Denys . . . ?"

"Oh! Yes—" He reached into the pocket of his cloak and handed it across the table to her. "It came on the supply ship returning from Acadia."

"From Acadia . . . ?" She broke the seal, said: "If you will excuse me," and began to read.

As she read, her expression altered from confused to bemused to astounded and back through the spectrum. Watching the emotions play across her face, Denys could well believe that she might once have been an actress, particularly given those oversized eyes that would communicate at any distance from a candlelit stage.

She raised those eyes to him from the bottom of the page, took another sip of wine, and said: "Do you know what is in this letter, Monsieur Denys?"

"I have a general notion. It is a proposal of marriage from Charles de Saint Étienne de La Tour."

Chapter 2

Françoise folded the letter back up, but kept it in her lap. She refilled her wine cup and Nicolas Denys's and endeavored to remember Charles La Tour. Five years ago or thereabouts, when she was still on the stage, Charles La Tour had come to Paris from Acadia, and they had passed a few evenings in each other's company. She had a vague recollection of a lean, sun-browned man with grizzled hair, who went clean-shaven in an age when even the humblest friar took pride in his mustaches. He had seemed to be of an amiable temperament, but she'd learned long ago that one shouldn't assume too much from the temperament of a man on holiday. He was certainly no *jeune première*—but then, she was no *ingénue*. And she did remember him as being fitter and harder than most Parisian dandies half his age.

She said: "Do you know Acadia, Monsieur Denys?"

"As well as any man living. Excepting *les sauvages*—and Charles La Tour."

"Have you read Monsieur Marc Lescarbot's book on New France?"

"Parts."

"Does Lescarbot tell the truth?"

"I am not the man to say. I have not the kind of education that can tell you whether or not the marriage customs of *les sauvages* resemble the ancient Romans'."

"If you did, you would be of no help to me. What I ask is: Does Lescarbot tell the truth in his descriptions of the land of Acadia?"

Monsieur Denys chewed on that. Françoise suspected that Nicolas Denys would chew on it if she asked him whether the sun were likely to set in the west tonight. He finally said: "Monsieur Lescarbot tells mostly truth about Acadia—though he was no navigator. He does exaggerate a very little here and there, but then, he was only there a year."

"Would you go back there?"

"I *will*—just so soon as I can dig my way out of the rubble that certain thieves and usurers collapsed upon me. Small disasters come to us all, but the man who perseveres will prosper in the end.

"Acadia is the gift of the good God to a France choked with beggars and hungry farmers. When Marc Lescarbot describes the beauty and bounty of Acadia, and its vastness, he does not exaggerate even a little."

What impressed Françoise wasn't so much Nicolas Denys's words as that such a prosaic drayhorse could light up when he spoke of Acadia. She said thoughtfully: "And Charles de Saint Étienne de La Tour is governor of it all . . . ?"

"Is that what he writes in his letter?"

"Yes. Is that not true?"

Nicolas Denys looked pained and kneaded his fingers in his beard. He said: "It *is*, but . . . He is *a* governor. The Sieur d'Aulnay also claims to be Governor of Acadia. After some rancorousness, the matter was thought to be resolved by a royal decree which drew a line down the Baye Françoise—La Tour to have the west side and d'Aulnay the east. But the king's wise councillors in Paris are not so wise about Acadian geography. They mixed up Port Royal and Jemseg—"

"Port Royal and . . . ?"

"Jemseg is the name of Monsieur La Tour's establishment, on the west side of the bay. Port Royal is the Sieur d'Aulnay's *seigneurie*, on the eastern shore. The decree granted La Tour the west side and Port Royal, and d'Aulnay the east side and Jemseg. The decree bears the royal seal in green, which means it cannot be altered."

Françoise whooped with laughter. Monsieur Denys said dourly: "It may seem a laughing matter, mademoiselle, but the good God knows what it may lead to. Acadia can be a violent land—"

"So can France."

"That is true. But at least in France we are not an ocean away from some semblance of a court of law. Monsieur d'Aulnay has demanded that Monsieur La Tour surrender Jemseg; La Tour replies that d'Aulnay must surrender Port Royal. And so they sit and glower at each other across the bay.

"There are those who say the decree was no accident. Cardinal Richelieu has had a habit of making sure that every headman of a French colony has a rival so they will be too busy squabbling with each other to ever grow too powerful. Accident or no, relations between the two governors of Acadia are not harmonious."

"So, Monsieur de La Tour's position is . . . precarious?"

"Precarious . . ." Monsieur Denys chewed on the word. "Mademoiselle Jacquelin, Charles de La Tour has lived in

Acadia for thirty years and more. For ten of those years Acadia was New Scotland, and no place for Frenchmen. He has fought off English armies led by his own father; he has seen his fort destroyed by betrayal—leaving him no shelter for the winter; he has faced down privateers who had more cannons on one gun deck than his entire arsenal; and he is still there. I have come to believe that if the earth was to open up and swallow Charles La Tour today, he would come loping out of the woods tomorrow.

"I have not the gift of speaking deceptively, mademoiselle, which other men practice to prosper quickly. Since you have asked, I cannot but tell you that Acadia can be a merciless mistress to those that do not know her. Charles de La Tour knows her as well as any man can who was not born in a birchbark tent. But he has not survived with her these thirty years by practicing the beatitudes."

She fingered the letter in her lap. "When does Monsieur La Tour expect my answer?"

"He cannot be expecting anything to come to him from France until next summer. His supply ship will sail from La Rochelle in March or April, depending on the wind and tides. I can tell you little more than I have now, but Monsieur La Tour's agent in La Rochelle is Monsieur Desjardins du Val."

After Monsieur Denys had gone, Lorette said from the hearth: "You can't be thinking of accepting, Françoise . . . ?"

"At my age, Lorette, one entertains all offers."

Françoise sat up long into the night after Lorette had gone to bed, turning it over in her mind as she turned her wine cup in her hand and stared into the fire in her hearth. By all reasonable expectations, the unmarried daughter of a Le Mans barber shouldn't have her own hearth to stare into, much less her own cottage in her own garden. But from very early in her career she had converted every gentleman's presents into banked *livres* the instant the gentleman moved on. She had dined extravagantly whenever someone wished to entertain her, and lived on week-old bread between times. She had known the day would come when she grew too old to play Columbine to even the most grizzled Scaramouche or Pierrot.

And Monsieur Corneille's new tragic queens weren't in her line.

She had managed matters well enough that she could now spend the rest of her life tending her own garden and growing fatter, while so many of the women she'd bounced across stages with were begging in the streets—too time-ravaged to sell themselves even to sailors. It seemed mad to consider sailing out of the safe harbor she'd fought so long to win, for an uncertain future with a man she hardly knew.

But then, one of the things she did know about La Tour was that he was a wealthy man. Although she was too old for Columbine, perhaps she was too young to curl up by the hearth just yet. Perhaps she wasn't even too old to start a family—to make up for the two occasions when she'd condemned herself and the life inside her to that horrible old woman and her knitting needles, rather than to a life of squalor.

She pulled the candle closer and read the letter again.

Chère Mademoiselle Françoise Marie Jacquelin,

Perhaps you do not remember me. I remember you. You may not think it, but you have traveled widely in Acadia. You have lain beside me in forest clearings where the smoke of our little campfire makes a thread to the stars. You have laughed beside me in a bark canoe rushing down cascades of white water. You have danced beside me to the music of a fiddle and a moose-hide drum.

The Hundred Associates of La Compagnie de la Nouvelle France have appointed me governor here. At the mouth of La Rivière St. Jean I have builded a fort that lacks for no comforts—save one. My situation here is now secure enough that I can finally ask you what I wished to ask you seven years ago: will you come to Acadia and marry me?

While it is true that there is more white in my hair than when you saw me last, the life I live here has kept me fit and active. There is much wealth in this country. My *seigneurie* of Jemseg has large deposits of coal and limestone, besides the products of our woods and waters. Last

year my returns from furs and hides shipped to France was
in round numbers thirty thousand *livres*.

The people of the country hereabouts—Micmacs and
Malaseets—are my old friends, and you need fear no more
harm from them than from any good neighbor. The table we
set at Jemseg would be the envy of any Parisian glutton. We
always keep on hand a two-year store of wine and other
necessary imports, in case some accident befall our annual
supply ship.

So, *chère* mademoiselle, that is my proposal. I ask you to
become the Queen of Acadia. In seven years I have not forgot you. If you accept me, no number of future years will
make me forget how much I have wished for you to be here
with me.

Your servant,
Charles de Saint Étienne de La Tour

In the morning Françoise said to Lorette: "I will be going to
La Rochelle for a day or two."

"Not to *accept* this madman?"

"To obtain more details from this madman's agent. But if I
do decide to go to Acadia, will you come with me?"

"Where else have I to go?"

The La Rochelle offices of Desjardins du Val Associates
weren't hard to find. Desjardins du Val himself proved to be a
short-legged man with a keg torso and thinning hair. He said:
"Monsieur de La Tour naturally assumed, mademoiselle, that
you would wish more thorough detail than in his letter. He instructed me to draft a marriage contract. Perhaps you would
care to bring in an attorney to interpret it for you; I know of
an honest attorney whose rates are reasonable and is—"

"Monsieur du Val, do you know much about the workings
of the theater?"

"Not so much. I like a good play if there ain't too much
singing in it."

"Every play you've ever seen was mounted as a joint stock
company, with the actors holding shares. I made my living on
the stage for twenty years. I know how to read a contract."

"Yes, methinks you would at that. Wait but a moment and my clerk will ferret it out."

It was several pages long, but Françoise stopped reading at the first sentence. "The name of the bride is blank!"

"Well, mademoiselle"—the keg-lid shoulders shrugged—"he could not be certain we would be able to find you, or even if you were still alive. . . ."

She went back to reading, wondering whether leaving the name blank had been du Val's idea or his employer's. After the first few paragraphs she muttered: "This will not do. . . ."

"It is but a draft, mademoiselle. An item for discussion. I have Monsieur de La Tour's power of attorney in this matter, so we can discuss."

"To begin with, it is perfectly natural—as set down here—that he and I should each be deemed to own half of all our property. But *our* property cannot possibly include the jewelry and other personal possessions I would bring with me, or any gifts he gives me. Those remain solely mine."

"Naturally."

"And although this contract states he is responsible for my passage to Acadia, I will incur many other expenses in uprooting myself from France. Were I to accept, I should be presented with a sum of money upon signing the contract, say . . . two thousand *livres*."

"Done."

Merde, she scolded herself, should've asked for three. "Another question this draft contract does not resolve is: What if I arrive in Acadia to discover Monsieur La Tour is not so fond of me as of his memories?"

"You need not trouble yourself about that, mademoiselle. Once Monsieur de La Tour's heart is committed, he does not change his mind."

"That would make him a very unusual man."

"He is in many ways, mademoiselle."

"Nonetheless, what if some accident should befall him while I were on my way to Acadia?"

"God forbid."

"God forbid. But I would feel more at ease if the contract

stated that if I voyage to Acadia and no marriage takes place—
for whatever reason—Monsieur La Tour or his agents will see
that I am delivered safely back to Paris. And pay me ten thousand *livres*."

"I should think *eight* thousand would be more reasonable."

"If you are so certain Monsieur La Tour will not change his
mind, what difference if the contract says eight thousand or
ten?"

"Eight thousand, five hundred."

They went on like that all afternoon. Françoise spent the
night at an inn in La Rochelle, and the next morning inquiring
at various merchants about the availability of various wilderness necessities, such as heavy woolen cloaks and a ten-year
supply of henna. When she went back to Desjardins du Val
Associates in the afternoon, she still hadn't made up her mind.
But the revised marriage contract was hard to fault. "Oh—
Monsieur du Val, you may be aware that there is a fashion de-
veloping in some quarters, of a woman taking her husband's
name. If Monsieur La Tour expects me to be known as Madame La Tour, he will be disappointed. I have worn my name
too long to change it to anything but Madame Jacquelin."

"I am sure he does not care if you choose to call yourself
Madame Banana."

"Monsieur Nicolas Denys made mention of a supply ship
that would set out for Acadia next spring. Would that be the
ship I would be traveling on—were I to agree to this contract?"

"I had assumed, mademoiselle, that what you would do—
were you to agree to this contract—would be to send a letter
on that ship, informing Monsieur de La Tour of your accept-
ance."

"And then I wait for his reply to my reply? And so another
year goes by? I am no longer of an age where I can toss away
a year so lightly."

"There are flowers who keep their bloom longer than others.
You need not worry, Mademoiselle Jacquelin, that another
year, or two, would make you any less a welcome bride."

"You are very gallant, Monsieur du Val for a man who

deals in matters of business. Gallantry aside—your client has
made me a proposal; if I accept, I accept. Is that not how business is done?"

"Would it were so in all cases. But if you sail on next
spring's ship, you will give him no notice to prepare for you."

"If he is not prepared for me by now . . ." She riffled the
edge of the contract with her thumbnail. "Among your other
dealings as a business agent, do you sometimes deal in real estate?"

"From time to time."

"I own a cottage in the village of Médard. . . ."

A woman's signature on a marriage contract wasn't legally
binding unless it was cosigned by her parents or guardian—
even a thirty-seven-year-old woman who owned her own cottage and garden. And even a proxy with power of attorney
couldn't sign for the groom without witnesses from the
groom's family. It took some doing to assemble all the interested parties in one place.

They all convened in the finest hotel in Paris on the eve of
the new year 1640. All except Françoise's mother, who had, of
course, found a last-minute reason not to be in the same room
as her daughter. It only meant that she would have to make her
mark on the contract at a later date, after the notary had carried
it to Le Mans and read it to her.

The chief witness for the groom's side was his stepbrother,
Godard de Rainville. He was a doll-like young man, barely
taller than Françoise, with silky blond hair, bright blue eyes,
and bones and sinews like a bird. Françoise found him curiously unsettling, and it wasn't just the fact that he was left-
handed. She also noticed that when Godard de Rainville and
Desjardins du Val spoke of Charles La Tour to the assemblage,
they referred to "Monsieur de La Tour," or even "the Sieur de
La Tour"; but when they murmured among themselves they
said "Charlot."

The final version of the marriage contract was a bound book
six pages long. When she signed "Françoise Jacquelin," the
New Year's revelers cheered and applauded. She flourished her
inky quill at them in one hand and her wine cup in the other.

Behind the Scaramouche bravado, a still, small voice was asking whether she'd completely lost what little wits she'd been born with.

CHAPTER 3

Jeanne bundled up Nicole de Menou d'Aulnay in her little blanket of woven rabbit skins, crouched down to make sure Joseph de Menou d'Aulnay's sealskin jerkin was buttoned tight, then fastened the winter cloak their father'd had made for her out of New World sable, and went out into the snow. The sentry at the postern gate saluted as the governor's wife and children passed by. Jeanne wondered how the poor man could stand the cold with a steel helmet and breast- and backplates sucking out what warmth he had in him. But Charles believed an unarmored sentry was no sentry at all. Jeanne had no doubt, and was sure no one at Port Royal had any doubt, that Charles would be the first to march out in armor on the coldest day of the year, if it were necessary.

There was a path already beaten through the new drifts behind the fort. Jeanne let go of Joseph's hand and let him run ahead, bouncing from side to side on his stumpy little legs. If he fell, the worst he would suffer was a faceful of snow.

The millpond was frozen over and a holidaying horde of tenantry and *engagés* were swarming over it, with iron or wooden blades strapped to their shoes. There were twice as many people at Port Royal now than when Jeanne first laid eyes on it. The increase wasn't entirely due to immigration. It crossed Jeanne's mind that the Capuchin missionaries would have a very lazy life if their parishioners paid as much heed to all the rest of the good God's commands as the one to be fruitful and multiply. Perhaps it was something in the Acadian air.

If so—Jeanne giggled to herself—it was something that highborn governors and their wives obviously weren't immune to. Unless the winter had slowed the flow of tides inside her, she had started her third child in four years.

A few *sauvages* stood watching the civilized people cavorting on the pond. As Jeanne shifted Nicole's weight from her numbed right arm to her left, she wondered if the women *sauvages* weren't wiser than a certain chatelaine of Port Royal. They appeared to carry their infant children around with no effort at all, in cradleboards suspended on the mother's back by a band passed around her forehead. It couldn't be all that comfortable for the babies, though. Their legs were propped apart by an open birchbark gutter, so that whatever happened to spill out from between their legs simply dribbled straight down to the ground. It seemed admirably practical in some ways, but it did leave the tenderest parts of their bodies exposed to the air in all weathers. On days like today Jeanne wondered that said parts didn't freeze solid and fall off. But then—she giggled to herself again—that obviously didn't happen very often, given the numbers of new little *sauvages* appearing year after year.

Joseph tugged on her cloak and said: "Want!"

"What is it that you want, *mon cher*?"

"Foot knifes!" He pointed at the skaters. "For Joseph!"

"Not yet, *mon cher*. Your little legs are not yet long enough. Perhaps next year."

Watching *les sauvages* watch the skaters—black eyes and brown faces breaking into laughter as innocent as Joseph's whenever a pantalooned posterior hit the ice—Jeanne blushed to remember that she'd once allowed herself to be thrown into a panic by a kitchen wench's rumors of murderous wildmen. It seemed to her now that only someone very flighty-brained and ignorant indeed could believe that even a renegade like La Tour could rouse those gentle-voiced, shy people to butcher their neighbors.

Nicole began to make it plain that the crisp air had given her

an appetite. Jeanne said to Joseph: "I think we have had
enough outside for one day."

"No! Want more!"

"Come along, now. I will have the cook make you a cup of
hot milk."

"With may sugar?"

"Yes, with maple sugar if you like."

As a footman opened the château door for her, Jeanne heard
the clashing of sword blades from behind him. She looked
through the dining-hall doorway. The great, long table had
been moved against one wall and Jeanne's husband and
brother-in-law were fencing with blunt foils. She guessed they
must've been at it since not long after she'd taken the children
outside, because the hair around both men's foreheads was
ringleted with sweat and there were stains soaking out through
their quilted fencing waistcoats.

Nicole went dozy with the sudden change from wintery air
to warm, so Jeanne was allowed to pause by the dining-hall
doorway to watch. The movements of the men and blades
were so fast she found it hard to tell who was doing exactly
what to whom. But it was enough just to see Charles so perfectly concentrated, with his sword movements varying from
swift little flicks, which could break a man's wrist, to sweeping
arcs and lunges. Watching the focused power in her husband
made her feel safe, and at the same time a bit giddy—like flirt-
ing with a precipice.

He'd only once turned even a fraction of that power against
her, that time when she'd said he should have asked her
whether she preferred to stay behind while he sailed to France.
Since then, she'd learned to understand that the reason he'd
turned on her had to do with the burden he carried, and she'd
used that knowledge to anticipate and divert any possible repe-
tition of the experience. She suspected that only someone as
insipid as she could've failed to see it at first glance. By being
born Charles de Menou, Sieur d'Aulnay et de Charnisay, he
was supposed to be in command of himself and everyone
around him. If at any time he wasn't, then what was he?

There was a sudden flurry of foils even faster than the ones that had come before, then Nicolas Le Creux stepped back and gasped: "A touch."

Charles said: "I believe that makes five."

Joseph crowed: "Uncle *never* touch Papa!"

"Not *quite* never," Nikki panted. "On occasion. When he tries a new trick he hasn't quite perfected yet."

Charles said gravely: "You should not let your uncle Nicolas give you the wrong impression, Joseph. He wields a sword like the soldier he is, and in the maelstrom of battle there is little room for duelists' tricks."

Both men sank into the nearest chairs and called for wine. Nicole was sleeping soundly enough that Jeanne managed to uncloak herself without waking her, while Charles helped Joseph out of his sealskin so Joseph wouldn't catch a chill from overheating after the outside air.

Charles said: "I have a new piece of news from my informant at Jemseg. Well, I suppose it is *old* news by now, but my informant dares not be too brazen about sending information across the bay, unless it be of vitally immediate import. It seems that Charles La Tour has asked for the hand of a 'lady' in France: a worn-out Parisian actress."

Jeanne gawked. "An actress?" and Nikki and Charles slapped their chair arms and laughed.

Nicolas Le Creux launched into a credible falsetto imitation of a Parisian actress addressing an audience of codfish and *sauvages*, which brought Anne downstairs to see what all the laughter was about. All that was needed to complete the jovial family circle of Château Port Royal was Hélène, who had gone back to France to join a convent. But then, Hélène had never been much for joviality.

In the midst of the hilarity about La Tour and his actress, Jeanne felt a sudden chill. She wondered how long Port Royal could expect the devil across the bay to remain nothing more than the butt of jokes or the subject of harmless rumors. But then Nicole woke up and Jeanne carried her up into the nursery to nurse her and forgot about La Tour.

CHAPTER 4

Françoise stood at the stern rail of the *Amitié de La Rochelle*, with Lorette's arm twined in hers, watching the towers of La Rochelle sink out of view. Lorette said: "The good God knows what we are going to."

Françoise replied: "No doubt. But *I* know what we are going from." As far back as Françoise could remember, barely a year had passed without armies of Frenchmen killing other Frenchmen, and any French women and children who happened to get in the way. If it wasn't Catholics and Protestants killing each other, it was the queen regent's supporters fighting to keep her son from ascending the throne, or peasants revolting against the nobility, or the nobility revolting against the crown. No matter how warlike *les sauvages* might be, they couldn't pose more of a threat to her and Lorette than their own people.

Charles La Tour's stepbrother, Godard de Rainville, and Desjardins du Val were onboard as well. Françoise found it reassuring that a comfort-loving businessman like du Val should consider Acadia a reasonable place to set up shop, even if only for a summer.

Off the Azores the sea and sky conspired to destroy the *Amitié*. Françoise and Lorette were thrown from side to side in their cabin as they struggled to secure every article they'd foolishly left loose. A bottle fell and smashed, leaving the floor awash in wine and broken glass. Lorette climbed up into her bed, wrapped herself in blankets, closed the shutters, and began to pray.

Françoise sat down on her own bed, clutching the edges of

the frame. The wall against her back seemed to be pointed sometimes toward the sky, sometimes toward the bottom of the sea. Finally she snatched up her cloak and struggled to the door.

The little corridor outside her cabin was as black as the inside of a tomb, as the captain had ordered all flames extinguished. Françoise felt her way toward the stairwell, reaching ahead to anchor herself to handholds before every step. When she unlatched the dwarf-sized door at the top of the stairs, it flew wide open, letting in a wind-driven wall of rain that almost knocked her off her feet. She fought her way out into the night, forced the door shut again, and felt her way along the rail to the steps up to the quarterdeck.

The wood beneath her feet and in her hands was greased slick with rain. Her hands were too stubby to grip around the railings on either side of the steps, so she hooked them under the rails and climbed with her weight leaned back.

Up on the half deck, three sailors were fighting to keep the long steering arm in line with the bowsprit. The captain saw Françoise down on the quarterdeck and bellowed over the howl of the storm: "Get below!"

"No!"

"Mademoiselle, I am ordering you below!"

"Go to hell! If I am to die, I mean to see it!"

She found a place on the quarterdeck rail that seemed out of the way, crouched down, and wrapped her arms around a post. She had to squint against the rain to see anything.

It was a black-and-white world: black sky and black sea, with flaring white veins of wave crests or lightning. White-shirted sailors were stringing black ropes along the deck. The only color was the yellow flame of the binnacle light, the glass-and-brass encased candle in the compass housing, and the captain's yellowed nose and cheeks when he peered at the compass. Until a burst of lightning showed Françoise another patch of yellow right beside her: a painted watchdog carved into the base of the rails, with his chin on his forepaws and his wet nose sniffing unconcernedly at her knee.

Her cloak and dress had become as much water as wool,

and it was starting to soak in through her shift. She was shivering with cold and fear and the lunatic thrill of riding the wooden horse up each mountain of water and plunging down the other side. The *Amitié* was running before the wind with full sail, its crew hoping the storm would give out before her masts and canvas did.

There was a crack like a pistol shot overhead. Françoise looked up. High above the mainsail, a smaller patch of white was streaming out in the wind like the *Amitié*'s token of surrender.

The captain bellowed down at several sailors lashing down a deck box, ordering the nearest one aloft. The sailor felt his way along the deck ropes to a toolchest, stuck a hammer in his belt and a few nails in his mouth, made a grab for the ratlines, and began to climb. A wave heeled the ship over so far that it appeared to Françoise he was climbing more sideways than upward. But he kept on, with his bare feet clinging to the rope rungs, and his canvas shirt and pantaloons clinging to his body like wet gauze.

By the time he'd reached the crosstree above the mainsail, the ship was upright again and he was only an indistinct patch of white among the much larger ones billowing and flapping in the sky. As Françoise watched that tiny patch of white move across the top of the huge one, she could see in her mind's eye his legs wrapped around the wet spar and his hands edging him forward. She thought she could hear a metallic tapping sound through the roar of the storm, but perhaps she was only imagining it. And then the white flag was a sail again and the sailor was on his way back down. There was no cheering or congratulations when he reached the deck. He put his hammer back where it belonged, replaced the nails he hadn't used, and became merely another of the blurry white figures engaged in some task near the bow.

The wind and rain began to ease and the mountain range of waves shrank to foothills. Françoise went back to her cabin, changed into dry clothes, and helped Lorette clean up the floor. In the following days she tried to pick out which one of the anonymous rope splicers, deck scrubbers, and hornpipe dancers was the one who'd climbed the mast that night, but she could never quite be sure.

They came to a place of fogs, where the captain stopped to fill every space in the hold with fish. From there they sailed southwest along the seacoast of Acadia. One evening at the captain's table, the captain said: "We shall put in at Cape Sable tomorrow and deliver the supplies for Port La Tour."

Françoise said: "I thought his fort was called Jemseg . . . ?"

"Jemseg is his headquarters." Desjardins du Val nodded, scratching the stubble on his throat. He'd been growing steadily less fussy about his appearance the farther they got from France. "Port La Tour is only an old outpost. No doubt you would prefer, mademoiselle, that we sail straight on for Jemseg. But the delay will be no more than a day or two. And stopping at Cape Sable will give you an opportunity to meet your soon-to-be father-in-law."

"Ah!" Françoise turned to Godard de Rainville. "And to meet your mother."

Rainville shook his silky head. "My mother has been dead for many years."

"Oh, forgive me, I—"

"There is nothing to forgive, mademoiselle," although something in his voice suggested that someone had done one or two things in the past he hadn't forgiven. "Relations within my stepfather's families can be easily confusing. You see, Claude Turgis—or Claude de La Tour, as he rechristened himself—is a marrying kind of man. You might say he had a calling for it. His first wife was a noblewoman with a small property styled La Tour. When she died, he encountered my mother—a young widow with two sons and a certain estate. His third and present wife was once a waiting woman to the Queen of England and Scotland. I would say his third and *last* wife, except that he is still barely a year or two past seventy."

In the morning, Françoise considered dressing for the occasion, and then decided that her shipboard costume of uncorseted, wool day dress would do to meet a seventy-year-old father-in-law-to-be. The *Amitié* tacked into an inlet with a sheltered harbor where another ship was already riding at anchor.

Ships were hardly Françoise's métier, but even she could see that this one was longer and lower and sleeker that the *Amitié* and carried more guns.

Rainville remarked: "That is Charlot's hunter."

"Hunter?"

"Dutch-built. They call them *jachts*, or *jaegers*. Hunters. Charlot christened his the *Renard Noir*. He loves her dearly."

Du Val grunted: "He should, for what she cost us."

Françoise squawked: "Then he is *here*?"

"Perhaps. Or perhaps he merely sent her captain here to—"

Françoise was already running for her cabin, shouting: "Lorette, come help me!"

Fortunately, Françoise had had a good deal of experience at dressing quickly, and the *Amitié* was still a ways out from the anchorage. While in Paris over New Year's, she'd had two gowns made, and a new corset. None of which she expected to wear very often, especially the corset. But the corset did create the desired effect of an armored sausage skin with flesh squeezing out at either end. The morning was gray and cloudy, so she opted for the royal-blue velvet instead of the silver silk.

She heard the anchor splash and the ship's boat being winched up off the deck. She still had a little time before they got the boat in the water. With the addition of a string of pearls in her hair, a gold necklace, and a touch of rouge and powder here and there, the looking glass wasn't too merciless.

When she came out on deck, the captain was just starting down the Jacob's ladder. She called out: "Captain! I would like to be among the first to go ashore."

"Looking as you do, mademoiselle, you may go wherever the fancy takes you."

As the boat approached the shore she craned to see over the shoulders of the rowers in front of her. There wasn't much to see. There was a crude landing stage and, just visible among the trees, the front of what some might charitably call a fort—merely a low wall of pointed log pickets. A few men trickled out of the fort toward the wharf and a few black-haired, next-to-naked people of both sexes appeared on the shore.

A ragged line of men came out of the woods, some carrying

axes. Among them was a long, lean, grizzle-haired, brown-skinned tatterdemalion in rawhide pantaloons and a greasy-looking shirt. He suddenly stopped stock-still, oblivious of the other men in the line bumping up against his back. Then he shouted: "Françoise?" and began to run toward the dock, elbowing the men in front of him aside.

He thrust his ax into a passing wharf post without breaking stride, reached the end of the wharf, and kept on running. The last droplets of his splash were still coming down when he resurfaced like a breaching whale—sputtering "Françoise?"—and thrashed toward the boat. Just before the bow ran over his head, he reached up to grab the gunwale and passed himself along the larboard side hand over hand, ducking under the oar shafts.

The captain of the *Amitié* shouted: "Sheer off, you'll swamp us!" But by then the sodden lunatic was already heaving himself up and in, tilting the boat so far to larboard that it was only the oarsmen leaning frantically to starboard that kept them from capsizing.

Charles de Saint Étienne de La Tour flopped into the boat like a landed cod, sprang up beside her, bellowed "Françoise!" across the handbreadth gap between their noses, and pressed his dripping lips and body to hers. They overbalanced and toppled backward. If his arm hadn't come up, Françoise would've cracked her head on the rowing bench behind her. She could already feel the cold harbor water soaking through her splendid garments from his ratty ones. But she was laughing too hard to care.

The men who reached down from the wharf to take the boat lines were laughing, too—but not so hard as if they were particularly surprised to see their governor run off the end of a dock. Said governor bounced up onto said dock, reached down his hand to help her out of the boat, then started briskly down the wharf without relinquishing her hand. She saw a passing blur of raffish-looking, sun-browned men and a few women—the women all with black hair and Oriental eyes—and then a pair of rugged-looking priests. Charles La Tour stopped in front of the priests and said: "This is Mademoiselle Françoise Marie Jacquelin. Come to the chapel and marry us."

Françoise's first impulse was to jerk her hand free of his and shout: "You have yet to ask me!" But the fact was he had, if only by proxy. And the fact that she was there made it obvious she'd accepted.

One of the priests sputtered: "But ... we must post the banns, and—"

"My fiancée already posted the banns in her parish in France—didn't you, Françoise?"

The thought had never crossed her mind. "Yes, but of course."

The priests looked as though they were still dubious but unable to quite get their hands on a good reason not to do what La Tour wanted them to do. Françoise was very quickly getting the impression that the same would be said of anyone who came within talking distance of Charles La Tour.

Something beyond the priest's shoulders caught Charles La Tour's eye. "Ah. Françoise—this is my father, Claude de La Tour."

The priests stepped aside for a silvery-haired man who might once have been as tall as his son, wrapped in a cloak that seemed somewhat heavy for a summer day. Claude de La Tour put his hands on her shoulders, and his watery blue eyes stared down into hers. In a wheezing breath thick with garlic and tobacco and a tinge of something rotting, he said: "Whatever could have possessed such a likely-looking lady to marry such a rogue?" Then he kissed her on both cheeks, leaving an impression of wet lips and dry mustachios.

His son said archly: "If anyone should know the answer to that, *mon père* ..."

There was barely time to bring Lorette ashore before Françoise found herself kneeling in front of a priest in a log-walled chapel. She snuck her eyes sideways to try to paint colors into her memory sketch of the man kneeling beside her. There was a motley of colors to paint in. His hair, now that it had started to dry, was intermingled silver and copper and sun-hennaed brown: rather like a wolf-fur cape she'd once owned, whose color kept shifting. His bright blue eyes might eventually go as pale and watery as his father's, if he lived that long.

The priest's singsong benediction was punctuated throughout by the dripping of seawater from the groom's sleeves and shirt-tails. Françoise had tactfully suggested he change into dry clothing, but he'd replied: "It do seem foolish to put on fresh clothes just to take them off soon."

She wondered what her Protestant Huguenot ancestors might say about her being married under Romish rites. But then, she'd done a lot of things they'd probably have more than a few things to say about. And she hadn't prospered as well as she had in the land of His Most Christian Majesty without learning how to pass herself off as a Catholic from time to time. The priest did look at her askance when she fumbled some of the responses, but perhaps he could pass it off as bridal nerves.

She emerged from the chapel to find that a banquet of sorts had been set out on trestle tables in the courtyard of the fort. Her new husband said: "When we get to Jemseg we can have a true wedding feast, but this will have to do for now."

Through the ensuing bacchanal, Françoise registered a stream of isolated facts: a family of *sauvages* squatting on the ground eating boiled cabbage with their fingers, the just-passable taste of the wine, Rainville and du Val sitting on either side of Lorette so Françoise wouldn't have to spend her wedding night worrying about her, the darkly exotic taste of some of the meats set before her, the shadows of Frenchmen and women *sauvages* dancing around a bonfire that seemed to be the only human light in a world of stars and forest.... But mostly she was aware of the warmth transmitted through her skirts from Charles La Tour's hand resting on her thigh.

His hand moved up to take hold of hers and raise her to her feet as he rose. He whistled with his fingers in his mouth. "Mesdames et messieurs! And the rest of you! My lady and I shall retire. You have one more hour to drink freely and run riot. Then begone with you."

He escorted her to a low, clapboarded building set into one

corner of the palisade, and into a room with little in it but a bed. Draped across the bed was what looked like a gargantuan ermine skin, minus the black tail.

Charles de La Tour herded her toward the bed with his hands on her buttocks and his mouth nuzzling the back of her neck. Just before her knees hit the bed frame she turned to face him and fell backward. He flung himself on top of her, fumbling for the fastenings on her gown. She tried to slow him down, mindful of the fact that he was clearly overanxious and had drunk a lot of wine. She needn't have worried.

She awoke still wearing her necklace and one stocking, and nothing else except the white bearskin. La Tour was standing unabashedly naked by the washstand, scooping water over his face. He said over his shoulder: "My father and his Catherine would be honored did we breakfast with them."

Fortunately she'd had the foresight to have Lorette bring her a day dress off the *Amitié*, one cut to fit her without a corset. La Tour led her out of the fort and into the woods, to a cottage that looked much the same as the one she'd sold in France, except that this one was whitewashed wood instead of stone and its thatch was of reeds.

Claude de La Tour was puttering in the garden. The peas he was hoeing were staked higher than any Françoise had ever seen. When she stooped to feel how fat the pods were, her new father-in-law said with bashful pride: "You know something of gardening, then?"

"Enough to know that these are miraculous."

"It has more to do with the soil of Acadia than my hand in the garden. I came to it late. There was a Recollet priest kept a garden a few leagues up river and showed me some of his secrets." He suddenly wheezed out a laugh. "Nicolas Denys came visiting once and—but no, I should not make myself tedious with tales of people whose names mean nothing to you."

"I am acquainted with Monsieur Denys. He brought me your son's proposal of marriage."

"Ah. Then perhaps"—the old man chortled—"you know something of Monsieur Denys's luck. Someday he will have nothing but his beard to call his own. The Recollet offered to show Denys his garden and they went by canoe. Denys knows more of ships than canoes. He made a sudden movement to gawk at something on the riverbank and over they go—priest, paddles, picnic basket, and all. Fortunately, they were close in to shore, but nonetheless . . . Who else but Nicolas Denys . . . ?

"Well, you must come in and meet my Catherine."

Catherine de La Tour looked to be at least twenty years younger than her husband. She pressed Françoise to her ample bosom and said: "Sit down and eat, before the bread goes cold."

They sat down at a rough-hewn table laid out with a cold salmon, steaming bread, green onions, a decent white wine, and a dish of an oddly delicious white butter that Françoise was informed was made by *les sauvages* from the marrow of the moosedeer. Françoise said to her stepmother-in-law: "I have to say you speak French remarkably—as though you were born to it."

"I was. I was born in Lyons."

"But . . . I was told you and Claude met in England."

"So we did. I was lady-in-waiting to Princess Henrietta Maria, who married the prince who became King of England and Scotland. When Claude was a prisoner in England he found it necessary to come to the royal court often, to petition his freedom. *Very* often." Catherine de La Tour's pudge-rimmed eyes twinkled and she popped in another mouthful of fresh bread slathered with moose butter.

"I'd had the misfortune"—Claude de la Tour shrugged—"to be captured by English privateers." He gummed another pinch of bread and a tiny flicker of wickedness appeared in the watery blue eyes, as though he were debating whether to go on.

"You see," he went on, "the English had declared Acadia to be Nova Scotia and were creating baronets of New Scotland to colonize the country once the French were chased out. I was still captive in England when the day came when the only French commander not surrendered yet is my son here at Port La Tour. So, I go to the English king and swear: 'If my son and I are made baronets of New Scotland, we will be content to live as loyal subjects in an English Acadia.'

"So, I return to Acadia with two English warships filled with soldiers and colonists, and with my new bride by my side. But when I come into Port La Tour under a white flag, and tell my son of the arrangement I have made for us, he replies: 'I would never consent to such baseness as to betray my king.' Is that not what you said?"

His son said dryly: "It must be, for so Monsieur Champlain wrote I said."

"I try for a long time to reason with my son. For a *very* long time. The English allow us to confer in private so I can say the things to him that only a father can say to a son. But he will not be swayed.

"So—what am I to do? I go back to the English and admit that though I'd promised he would surrender, he will not surrender. Although he is my own son, we must take his fort by force. For two days and a night we try, but we accomplish nothing."

"Not quite 'nothing,' " La Tour *fils* drawled blandly. "We killed a few Englishmen."

La Tour *père* shrugged. "A few Englishmen were killed. So—what can I and the English do but sail on to Port Royal? The war goes on another year, but *my son* still holds out against ten times as many Englishmen, and burns their forts all up and down the coast.

"Then of a sudden the English king signs a treaty giving Acadia back to France—to encourage the French king to finally pay the dowry of Queen Henrietta Maria. Well, kings will do that. In forty years the Kings of France and England have traded Acadia back and forth four times.

"So—what am I to do? If I am in slightly bad odor with the English, I stink to the French. But—the missionaries here at Port Royal convince my son to forgive me. He builds a little house for Catherine and me—outside the walls of his fort, of course, since no loyal Frenchman can trust me again. So here we are and here we stay."

Françoise said: "And what if—" then had to pause to chew the backs of her cheeks before going on straight-facedly.

"What would you have done if the treaty had given Acadia to England?"

"I suppose . . ." Claude de La Tour thoughtfully picked his remaining teeth with a salmon bone, then sighed. "I suppose . . . Yes, I would have found it in my heart to forgive my son."

"And you would both be baronets of New Scotland. Oh, pardon me, you still *are*, if it ever comes to that." Her laughter refused to be held in any longer. The more La Tour *père et fils* stared blankly at her and at each other—as though they couldn't fathom what might've struck her as amusing—the harder she laughed.

The last leg of Françoise's journey was to be accomplished on the *Renard Noir*. Lorette, Desjardins du Val, and Godard de Rainville were brought onboard as well, leaving the *Amitié de La Rochelle* to lumber along in her own time.

As the sails of the *Renard Noir* puffed into life, Françoise stood on the afterdeck of her husband's ship, with her husband's long arm around her, watching his father and stepmother walking arm in arm up the path from the wharf to their cottage in the woods. He said: "It was bleak for them the winter they were stuck at Port Royal with the English—after he failed in his promise to deliver them Port La Tour. He told her, since she hadn't expected things to turn this way when she married him, she was free to go back to England and be a lady of the court again. She refused to leave him."

Just as Françoise was beginning to wax sentimental over such a selfless romance, he added: "She is cousin to the Scottish lord who appointed baronets of New Scotland. He usually wanted a lot of money in exchange."

Sailing on the *Renard Noir* was a very different sensation from the *Amitié*—riding the waves instead of ramming them. La Tour left it to Captain Jamin to sail the ship and stayed beside her at the rail getting better acquainted. They passed between rocky islets where silvery-brown seals sunned themselves while seabirds rose in raucous clouds. La Tour said: "It do seem likely we can round Cape Sable in time to catch the tide, and then you will see the *Renard Noir* lift her tail."

"I thought Port La Tour *was* Cape Sable?" Every time she thought she'd understood some detail about the world she was going to inhabit, it shifted.

"We say it so. Twenty or thirty leagues is close enough for Acadia. The Jemseg River is leagues upstream from the mouth of La Rivière St. Jean, but still we call our place Jemseg."

They left the land behind and the *Renard Noir* took on more sail and more speed, to the point where Françoise wrapped her arm in the nearest ratlines for security. La Tour said: "Although you see no land, we are in the bay now. The Baye Françoise is long and deep and wide."

"You seem able to fill it nonetheless."

"You, madame, have the tongue and morals of an alley cat. I knew we would get along."

The sun was setting when the *Renard Noir* trimmed her sails and nosed into a passage between a prickly-looking little island and the mainland. At the end of the passage was an inlet guarded by a stockade of pickets even cruder than the one at Port La Tour. Françoise said: "*That* is your fort?"

La Tour laughed. "That is a Malaseet village. *That* is our fort."

She followed his finger with her eyes. The inlet opened up into a broad harbor within a bowl of brooding hills, with a sandy point of land at its head. On the point was a green castle of grassy earthworks and crenellated stone, with a wide, sloping bastion facing out to sea. A cannon fired from the bastion. The *Renard Noir*'s bow gun replied.

A handful of men wandered out of the fort and down to the landing stage as the *Renard Noir*'s boat approached. One of them pointed at Françoise and began to shout, and then they all did. By the time the boat docked, the slope up to the fort was a melee of people pouring out to gawk.

Françoise's progress from wharf to fort was the same giddy parade as at Port La Tour, only much more so. La Tour escorted her between a pair of iron-bound gates made of beams thicker than her hips, through a stone-walled tunnel that echoed the baying of the mob at their heels, and into a flag-stoned courtyard with a pedestaled cross in the center. He boosted her onto the pedestal, climbed up beside her, and whistled with his fingers until he could make himself heard. "Mesdames et messieurs, and the rest of you . . . I introduce to you, Madame Françoise Marie de La—"

"Jacquelin!"

"Madame Françoise Marie Jacquelin." She hardly heard what else he said—something about a feast tomorrow night—she was too busy looking around at her new home. In front of her were two squared stone buildings flanking the gatehouse and joined to the front palisade and bastion. The courtyard was a cruciform of flagstoned paths joining at the pedestal she was standing on. Everything in front of her was stone and earthworks, everything behind her wood: wooden buildings within palisades of logs. The two stone buildings were each the size of a manor house and had glass in their windows. All in all, it wasn't exactly a cottage in the village of Médard, but it would do.

She realized that La Tour was no longer on the pedestal and was raising his hands to her waist to boost her down. He led her to a door in the larger of the two stone buildings and into a dining hall with a stone fireplace in which she and he could have laid together end to end. He snatched a candle off the table and carried on through another doorway, into a much smaller room with a much smaller fireplace and furniture that hadn't been made by any colonial carpenter. He said: "This is our private sitting room," and gestured her toward an enclosed staircase in one corner.

He followed her up the tunneled stairs with his candle. At the top of the stairwell was a bedchamber with its own hearth. La Tour set his candle down on a chest of drawers, slid open a drawer, and said: "This is for you." He drew out a gold necklace several times the thickness of the one she'd worn to their wedding. "I bought it in hopes I might make it your marriage gift someday." He raised his hands—not that he had to raise them far to get the necklace above her head—and settled it around her neck. It was cold and heavy, but the weight of it on her breasts and shoulders wasn't all that burdensome, and gold warmed up quickly.

Once again she awoke wearing nothing but a gold necklace and a fur robe. But this time the necklace was more an anchor chain than a strand, and instead of a white bearskin the robe was made of many dark, silky pelts sewn together. He said he'd had it made in hopes that she might lie under it someday. He'd called the pelts "marten," but she'd known them in France as North American sable.

The other difference in her second morning of married life was that her husband was nowhere in evidence. She washed and dressed herself and went downstairs. Lorette was sitting in the sitting room. A leather-faced woman of *les sauvages* was trying to cope with both a pot bubbling on the hearth and a waist-high, black-haired girl tugging on her skirt. Françoise said: "Good morning, Lorette."

"Hmm. Good morning."

The woman *sauvage* grunted over her shoulder: "La Tou in woods. Back of fort. New gun. I cook his morning food."

"Oh. Do you always cook his food for him?"

"All ways."

"Oh. Is it a long time you have cooked for him?"

"*Long* time. Cook and more."

"More? You are his housekeeper . . . ? The keeper of his house?"

"I keep his house. And my house. And house of our children."

"Pardon me?"

"Housekeeper, shit—I his wife."

CHAPTER 5

Charles de Saint Étienne de La Tour pulled the trigger of his new musket and once again hit dead center on the big elm at the edge of the woods behind his fort. The only articles he'd insisted be transferred from the *Amitié* to the *Renard Noir* were his new gun and his new wife, and he was delighted with both of them. What particularly delighted him about the musket was the firing mechanism: a Dutch innovation of a flint striker sparking against a steel wing. They called it a snapchance or flintlock. After only an hour of getting acquainted with it, he couldn't understand how a man who'd once held such a gun in his hands could ever go back to nursing the slow-burning rope that fired a matchlock, or fussing with the diabolical complexities of a wheel lock. Excepting his old wheel-lock pistol, of course, which he knew so well that—

"La Tour!"

It was a woman's voice. A very loud one. Coming from behind him. He turned and saw his bride marching across the meadow on a straight heading from the postern gate at the back of the fort. Her gait and expression weren't exactly what might be expected of a woman on her honeymoon.

As she bore down on him he gestured apologetically at the musket and said: "Forgive me for slipping away on you, but you seemed to be sleeping sound, and in this part of the world a new gun is not a plaything to shelve until you feel like getting used to it. I don't guess you have much acquaintance with firearms, but this new lock, you see, is—"

She cut him off with what seemed unnecessary sharpness. "I carried a snapchance pistol all the years I was a traveling player. Some men assume that anything can be imposed upon a woman who earns her living on the stage."

"Oh. Well, then you can appreciate that this—"

"That woman claims to be your wife!"

"Which woman?"

"*Which* woman? How many 'wives' do you have? The old woman who cooks your meals!"

"Oh. You mean Tqope'j. That's Micmac for 'One of Twins,' but few Frenchmen can pronounce it, so we call her Minou."

"I don't give a fig if you call her the Queen of Sheba! *She* calls herself your wife!"

"Oh. Well . . . well, I suppose she *was*, in a way. . . ."

"You *suppose*?"

"We never were formally married. Except Micmac fashion. And only a sketch of that." That seemed safe enough. The priest who'd blessed their union after the fact—in order to satisfy Minou's wish to have the children baptized—was no longer around to confuse Françoise with tales of insignificant formalities of long ago.

"I did not come all the way across the ocean to make a ménage, or enlist in your harem!"

"Minou and I have not lived as man and wife since years ago," barring the occasional winter's night of wine-soaked nostalgia, which it seemed unnecessary to bring into the present conversation. There also seemed no point in muddying the waters by mentioning the other half of One of Twins. "The little brown girl you see clinging to Minou's skirt is my daughter. But she and her brother and sisters are the only trace remaining that their mother was ever more to me than a friend and helpmeet—back in the days when the people of the country were the only friends poor Biencourt and me had. I could cast them out to go live in the bark huts across the harbor, if that would make you feel more at ease in our house."

The pinched-in bud of a mouth uncompressed just enough to let out "No," then appended: "But she stays outside our private quarters."

"Of course, of course. I knew you would understand. Well, it do seem past time you had a look around Jemseg. If you but take my arm, madame, I would be delighted to introduce you to your new domain."

The pudgy little forearm that nestled into the crook of his elbow did it grudgingly. So as he walked her across the meadow he chattered brightly about the wildflowers that didn't grow in France and anything else that might catch her eye. At one point he leaned-aside to blow his nose with his fingers. She said: "I brought a store of handkerchiefs. You may have a dozen, if you find them big enough."

"The people of the country think handkerchiefs disgusting—like carrying your shit around in your pocket."

"I am not one of the people of the country."

They came to one of the slapdash cabbage patches that made up Jemseg's farming colony. Françoise stopped to pull a knee-high weed and said: "They do not appear very assiduous gardeners."

"They have no need to be. The climate here is harder than Cape Sable or Port Royal, but still they need only put seeds in the ground and let the soil of Acadia do the rest. The Hundred Associates would be distressed to know that any pleasant-weathered day will find half our 'farmers' off fishing or hunting. There is no need for people to know things that would only distress them.

"D'Aulnay across the bay takes the colonizing much more to heart. So much as to import a wife from France to serve as broodmare for his noble lineage."

"Is that why you imported me?"

"My lineage is not so noble." That elicited not a *soupçon* of amusement.

He took her down the woods path to the falls, where La Rivière St. Jean came cascading down to horseshoe around the tongue of rock between the river and the harbor. Unfortunately, the tide was coming in, so there were no falls for her to see. But she could see the river running backward, and the great, swirling hollow called the Pot. And the manitou of the whirlpool had kindly chosen today to make a reappearance.

La Tour cautiously put one hand on his wife's bare shoulder, half expecting her to twitch it off, and pointed with his musket.

"Do you see that hogshead on the other side, bobbing up and down?"

"It looks all stuck over like a pincushion."

"So it is. The pins are arrows, or the stubs of them. The hogshead is the top of a tree, or the bottom; the roots and branches are all wore away from years of battering the walls of the Pot. Sometimes it disappears for eight or fifteen days and then bobs up again—sometimes on one side, sometimes the other.

"The Micmacs and Maliseets, whenever they start a journey from hereabouts, shoot an arrow into it, with a beaver pelt or some other gift tied to the end, so as the manitou will protect their traveling. Some people will tell you I put the tree there so I could steal the beaver pelts and such. I *did* once try to tow it out. With three boats with ten rowers each, and the current on our side, we still could not persuade the manitou to leave his home."

He could see she thought he was exaggerating. "Well, perhaps it was two boats with eight rowers each, I disremember." He pointed upstream with his musket. "Upriver is where our coal and limestone grow. They're easy enough to quarry, but not so easy to ship downstream. When the tide is out, no ship can pass the falls. At high tide there is a reversed falls just as dangerous. But there is a gap of moments at half tide when a pilot that knows his business can pass safely—provided he had the sense to bribe the manitou."

She still didn't emanate anything but grudging acquiescence. He wondered if he'd made an irrevocable mistake by not banishing Minou before Françoise arrived. But then, he hadn't known Françoise was going to arrive until she did. That wouldn't be much consolation if Françoise chose to return to France.

When they got back to the fort, the *Amitié de La Rochelle* was in the harbor and boats were ferrying crates and barrels to the landing stage. La Tour sighed. "I meant to show you through the fort, but it do seem best I try to make some order out of this. But when the tide goes out, I will take you to see our fish garden."

"Our which?"

"There"—he pointed across the harbor—"under the water is a fence of poles and branches. When the tide goes out it leaves a salt marsh that will be dotted with flopping fishes of all varieties. We simply amble about the marsh at low tide, harvesting fish like cabbages. Some springtimes the run of salmon or *gaspereau* is so heavy I have to break open the weir or we would have a marsh waist-deep in rotting fish."

La Tour looked down hopefully at his bride and saw a gleam dawning in those oversized eyes peering at that distant swath of water hiding the fish weir. It seemed just possible that she was seeing what he'd spent the morning trying to get her to see: that Acadia held her hand out full of bounties and beauties and legends to anyone who learned the rhythms of her tides and seasons. The left side of Françoise's mouth gradually crooked up in that beguiling smile that showed her crooked tooth. At some point in the past he must've bribed some manitou very well indeed. He made himself a reminder to tell the cook that Madame had a weakness for fresh fish.

But La Tour was only given three days to delight in her delight in her new home. Then three Micmac fishermen came paddling in off the bay to inform him that d'Aulnay's supply ship had hove into Port Royal. He went to Françoise and said: "D'Aulnay couldn't've timed it much more inconvenient—which I'm sure would make him happy. Part of that royal decree that was supposed to solve all our problems was that he and I are to share equally in all fur-trade profits from Jemseg and Port Royal, and so have the right to inventory each other's outgoing cargoes. Neither of us have ever used that right. From what I know of Port Royal—and I traded there a damn sight longer than d'Aulnay has—his annual returns mean he ain't been declaring about ten or fifteen percent, which is about what I forget to declare every year.

"But last year's ledgered returns from Port Royal were down by half. Either d'Aulnay's so busy colonizing he's letting monopoly breakers steal his trade, or he is starting to steal more than decent business partners expect in the natural way of things.

"I have no choice but to get to Port Royal before his ship sails, to make sure we ain't robbed blind. Why not come with me? You can get a look at Port Royal. . . ."

"Will you introduce me to the broodmare?"

"Someone would needs introduce her and me first."

The next ebb tide carried the *Renard Noir* rushing out of Jemseg harbor. As soon as they were safely out of the passage north of Partridge Island, La Tour left Captain Jamin to his business and walked to the bow where Françoise was standing, with her red-highlighted ringlets lifting in the wind and her shift-puffed breasts lifted by her peasant-style corselet. Approaching her from behind, he noticed she had a wide rib cage for her height. Odd how with some women such details of anatomy didn't make them any more or less attractive, just happened to be part of who they were.

They anchored for the night on the east coast of the bay, a little ways above the inlet to Port Royal. The shipwright who'd built the *Renard Noir* had thoughtfully added a narrow, gilded balcony outside the casements of the owner's cabin, a balcony just large enough for two people to sit on a blanket drinking wine and watching the stars—provided one of them had short legs and didn't mind close quarters. After the second empty bottle broke the stars on the waves, he tried unhooking her corselet, but she pulled his hand away, to lead him back inside. He reflected that the crewmen on nightwatch must be deeply disappointed, but he didn't reflect for long.

He woke up somewhat creaky in the morning. For all his bragging that Acadian life kept him as active as any Parisian half his age, Françoise had a knack for drawing more activity out of his forty-eight-year-old bones than most twenty-four-year-olds could absorb easily. He wouldn't have believed that that tiny mouth could stretch like that.

While he was engaged in the delicate process of shaving on a moving ship, Françoise drawled lazily from the bed: "For a man who appears to care little for the elegance of his wardrobe, you go to a surprising amount of trouble to keep yourself clean-shaven."

"Elegance? Shapeless pantaloons and old hunting shirts ain't

elegant?" He cocked his razor toward his throat and paused as
the *Renard Noir* lurched with a wave. "The people of the
country find few things more grotesque than hair on a man's
face."

"Are you still so concerned whether the girls of *les
sauvages* find you grotesque?"

"I haven't the strength left. But what's more valuable than
all the other riches of Acadia—even if that popinjay d'Aulnay
don't see it—is the good opinion of the people of the country.
If the Micmacs and Maliseets see us as unpleasant creatures to
be polite to for the sake of trade, we can get by tolerable well
in good weather. But if they see us as friends and brothers,
they'll see us through the worst of winters."

"They obviously see you as their brother-*in-law*, at the
least." He decided to concentrate intently on his shaving.

When they came out on deck, the tide was coming in and
Captain Jamin had taken the tiller in his own hands to guide
the *Renard Noir* stern foremost through the inlet. As the inlet
opened up and the ship swung around again, Françoise asked:
"Is this Port Royal basin?"

He was surprised she knew enough about Acadia to ask the
question. "It is." He pointed at a swatch of forest where no
tree was more than twenty-seven years old. "That was where
stood the first Port Royal, before the damned Jesuits betrayed
it to the Virginians for spite, and me and Biencourt had to take
to the hills and timber."

She threw her arms up and sang:

> "Great Neptune grant us this day,
> Against thy storm's assurance,
> That all of us yet may
> Set eyes once more on France."

The words threw him back to being a boy in a jury-rigged
merman costume, paddling a canoe in a flotilla coming out
from Port Royal to welcome Biencourt's father home. He said:
"Where the devil did you hear that?"

"I never heard it. I read it in Marc Lescarbot's book. The

first theatrical presentation in the New World—with Lescarbot playing Neptune."

"Huh. He said *that* in his book as well?"

"Not in so many words, but I assumed he wrote the best part for himself."

As the new Port Royal came in sight all the guns of its front bastions fired in unison. It was too much for a salute—more like a warning demonstration of the mass and precision of d'Aulnay's artillery. La Tour ordered a return salute from the *Renard Noir*'s bow chaser. It sounded like a child trying to imitate a clap of thunder by slapping his hands together.

As the *Renard Noir*'s anchor plunged into La Rivière au Dauphin, the gates of Port Royal fort swung open and a troop of sun-mirroring men-at-arms marched out toward the wharf. In front of them strode a figure in green and black decked with snowy lace—plumed hat, matching half cape, and all. The rangier and less resplendent figure marching beside d'Aulnay would be his brother-in-law, Nicolas Le Creux.

As the boatswain lined the *Renard Noir*'s towed longboat around to the side, La Tour went toward the gate in the rail where the Jacob's ladder was clattering down. His hands were tingling so much that he had to keep flexing them. Françoise followed him. He stopped at the gate and said to her: "Wait here. Once I explain our business to the Sieur d'Aulnay, I will send the boat back to fetch you."

"Why should I not just come with you?"

"Because I mislike the look of this."

"You think he means to attack us?"

"No. Not even the Sieur d'Aulnay could be fool enough to think the Hundred Associates would stand for that." There seemed no useful point in mentioning that the blank salvo from Port Royal had been fired when the gunners would still have time to swab out their barrels and load before the *Renard Noir* came in close.

"Then I fail to see why you should send the boat back and forth twice, when there is plenty of room for—"

"Will you *please* for once just listen to someone who's been living by his wits here since you were in your cradle? I'll find it much easier on that wharf if I only have to worry about myself."

Her oversized eyes flared up at him and her undersized mouth tautened smaller. Then she looked away and nodded stiffly.

D'Aulnay and his men-at-arms had taken up a position about halfway along the wharf, leaving barely enough open space for the longboat to dock. No one stepped forward to take the bow-and-stern lines, so two of the boat crew scrambled up onto the dock and one of them reached down to give La Tour a hand up.

D'Aulnay barked: "What do you want here, La Tour?"

"And a grand good morning to you as well, Monsieur d'Aulnay." It took an effort to be even ironically polite to that strutting pup. Everything from his cultured accent to his carefully cultivated mustache told the world that the mere fact of being born Charles de Menou, Sieur d'Aulnay et de Charnisay, gave him a better right to rule Acadia than anyone who'd merely lived with her for thirty years.

"I am waiting, La Tour."

"What brings me here, my brother governor, is my right to inventory all the furs you have warehoused at Port Royal before you ship them off to France."

"You forfeited that right when you refused to surrender Jemseg to me, as the king so ordered."

"I will surrender Jemseg the day you surrender Port Royal, as the king so ordered."

"Remove yourself from here immediately."

"I will *not*. I have a right to protect myself from thievery."

"You call *me* thief, you lout?"

"Well, if you ain't a thief you needn't fear an inventory."

"I will not have you poking and prodding about Port Royal."

"I knew Port Royal in and out before your father started poking and prodding your mother."

Their voices rose higher, to the point where La Tour was no longer aware of what d'Aulnay was shouting at him, he was too intent on shouting at d'Aulnay. He *was* aware that d'Aulnay had crowded in so close that the sweeping brim of the plumed hat kept butting against the tip of his nose. And he was acutely aware that several Micmacs were watching from the shore. The delegation of Micmacs and Maliseets he'd brought with him on his last trip to France had brought back the news that Frenchmen were beneath contempt, after seeing men in France yelling insults into each other's faces without it ever coming to blows or knives.

The brim of d'Aulnay's chapeau flapped across La Tour's nose once too often. La Tour swept his hand up and knocked the hat out of his face, incidentally knocking it off the Sieur d'Aulnay's noble head. Funny how his hands seemed to tingle a little less after striking the hat.

D'Aulnay stepped back, with spots of white appearing through the flush in his cheeks. La Tour smiled at him and opened his mouth to continue the conversation without the butting-in of headgear. But before anything could come out of La Tour's mouth, d'Aulnay tugged off his gloves and slapped them across it.

While his head was jerking sideways from the sting, La Tour heard his own voice without his mouth moving: "If you think me fool enough to play gentlemen's stickpins with you . . ." At the same time his right fist was coming up in an arc that joyously smacked d'Aulnay's cheek and spun him backward. Now his hands didn't tingle at all.

Nicolas Le Creux grabbed his brother-in-law from behind before d'Aulnay'd quite got his sword clear of his scabbard. There were hands on La Tour as well, dragging him back toward the boat. D'Aulnay bellowed: "Coward: You fear to face me in—"

"Anytime! With *knives!*"

"Like the brawling peasant you are!"

"I have the choice of weapons! Ain't that how you dancing masters play the rules?"

By that time the boat crew from the *Renard Noir* had dragged La Tour off the wharf and were about to push off. Before they could, he stood up in the boat—making them grab the dock piles to keep from capsizing—and shouted: "From now on, d'Aulnay, you stay on your side of the bay and I stay on mine!"

"I am the Governor of Acadia! I go where I please!"

"You can call yourself the Queen of Sheba—stay on your side of the bay!"

CHAPTER 6

Jeanne was watching from the parapet when the fist hit her husband, and she felt it with him. It wasn't physical pain, it was the shock of insult—as though some dinner guest had suddenly thrust his hand down her bodice. It was only fortunate the children weren't with her to see it. Excepting Marie in her arms, whose infant eyes and understanding couldn't absorb that flicker of movement on the wharf.

Marie obviously did understand, though, that something nameless had alarmed her mother, which more than alarmed Marie. Jeanne quietened her by jogging her up and down, waggling her fingers across the soft bud of a nose, and chirping nonsense at her in a voice much calmer than she felt. As soon as Marie ceased shrieking, Jeanne hurried down to the courtyard, where the troop that had marched out to the wharf was marching in again.

Jeanne was heading straight for her husband—as directly as she would toward one of her children who'd fallen downstairs—but when she saw his face she realized that husbands couldn't be comforted in public like children. It astounded her that he could line up his troops and dismiss them with the same authoritative composure as always, when she knew that every muscle in his body was knotted to the bursting point. Not that she didn't understand why he was doing it: bad enough that they had seen their commander manhandled, without them seeing it perturbed him. But it was one thing to understand the reason for exercising such self-control, and another thing to be able to do it.

She carried Marie into the château and hurried upstairs to put her to bed so she could hurry back downstairs to Charles. As she settled Marie into her cradle she could see that the baby was getting that thoughtful look that signified she was beginning to identify the odd feeling inside her as hunger. Marie would simply have to wait. Jeanne ducked her head into the nursery for just long enough to make sure that the nurse was keeping Joseph and Nicole happily occupied, then scampered downstairs.

She heard male voices coming from the card room. The voices stopped when she opened the door. Charles and Nikki were sitting drinking wine, with no servant in attendance. There was a coin-sized bruise under Charles's left cheekbone, but something told her not to say a word about it. She closed the door behind her and sat down.

The men still didn't say anything. She offered up: "What can anyone do with a fist-swinging brute like that?"

The chestnut eyes snapped toward her. "Who told you of that?"

"No one. I was watching from the parapet above the gate."

He flushed red, then croaked: "And the children . . . ?"

"Joseph and Nicole were in the nursery."

That seemed to relieve his embarrassment a little, but not much. Nikki eyed his rigid-necked brother-in-law and said: "I'm sure we could all think of more than a few things to do with a fist-swinging brute like that. But he is too cowardly to give Charles the opportunity."

Jeanne could see what Nicolas was trying to do, and she contributed brightly: "No doubt the servants have spread the story of how many times my sister would have been widowed if my husband didn't use blunted foils for practice."

She and Nikki conspired together to try to jolly him out of it obliquely. She didn't want to be making clumsy attempts at banter; she wanted to take one of those quick, strong hands in both of hers and tell him that no one need be ashamed of indignities suffered at the hands of a lunatic. But that would only have made him feel more small. So she kept on chirping jokes about La Tour, even contorting her face into the baboon imitation that Joseph found so amusing. Eventually Charles began to smile and lean back in his chair, and even made a few jokes of his own.

But in the night, after she'd blown out the bedside candle, he gritted out apologetically: "I should not have lost my temper with that lout."

"Who *could* not? It's only fortunate you didn't kill him."

"Fortunate . . . ? Yes, I suppose it would've been difficult to explain. . . ."

"What do you intend to do?"

"There's little I *can* do. Were he a gentleman, we could resolve the matter quickly. But you saw how much he cares for affairs of honor. I shall of course report the matter to La Compagnie de la Nouvelle France. But La Tour is no doubt already composing a sheaf of lies to make the Hundred Associates uncertain what took place."

"But . . . What I meant was: Do you intend to stay on our side of the bay if he stays on his?"

He laughed. "I have no intention of paying the least attention to threatening noises from an old blowhard like La Tour. And neither should you."

She lay awake for a long time, wondering whether a "blowhard" could have survived long enough to become "old" in Acadia. But then Marie started squawking for her midnight meal and Jeanne jumped up to stuff her mouth with her breast before she woke up Charles.

CHAPTER 7

Françoise sat at the captain's table on the *Renard Noir*, joining in the laughter at the boatswain's description of the struggle to drag Governor La Tour off Governor d'Aulnay's wharf. The ship's surgeon extended the hilarity by comparing the scene to an incident wherein an *engagé* lost two fingers trying to separate his mastiff from a Micmac dog.

Françoise felt a sudden shiver, as though someone had stepped on her grave. She looked out the cabin window at the white wake on the blue waves and wondered why. She saw again the scuffle on the dock at Port Royal, and knew. Even from a distance the Sieur d'Aulnay's bearing and costume had marked him unmistakably as a member of an ancient, noble family. In France, a man could have his living entrails cut out and burned in front of his eyes for simply speaking disrespectfully to such a man. And La Tour had struck him with his fist. But then, this wasn't France, and neither La Tour nor any of the officers of the *Renard Noir* seemed to think the event signified anything but another example of "Charlot's" wild and wicked ways.

"Madame?" Françoise turned toward the voice. It was Captain Jamin, and the laughter around the table seemed to have played itself out for the nonce. "I must not forbear to thank you, madame, for simplifying my life."

"How so?"

"My own wife, you see, has not been entirely happy at Jemseg—"

La Tour interjected: "Whose fault is that, pray tell?"

Captain Jamin paid no heed—except to wave his hand by

66

his ear, like brushing away a fly—and continued to Françoise: "Although there are many sides of living in Acadia that please my wife, sometimes she fears our children are growing up wild, and says we must return to France. But now that there is a *lady* living at Jemseg, she can hardly—"

A knock at the door prevented Captain Jamin from specifying what his wife could hardly do now, and prevented Françoise from betraying surprise at being called a lady. The captain called, *"Entrez."*

A crewman slid open the door. "Begging the captain's pardon, but there is a sail approaching."

They all went out on deck. The sail turned out to be a triangular one, on a longboat like the ones used by the European fishermen who set up camps on the Acadian shore each summer. But as it drew closer Françoise saw that the sail had the silhouette of some large-antlered animal painted on it, and that the three men on board were all black-haired and next to naked. She said to La Tour: "I thought their boats were bark canoes?"

"They are. But when it comes to the open sea or the Baye Françoise, a wooden boat is safer. So if they stumble across a fishing longboat cached for the winter, they gladly take it for their own. If someday they meet up with a fisherman who claims it was his, they shrug and give it back and go on their way."

"Are they Micmacs or Maliseets?"

"Hard to know until they speak. Their languages are different, but over the years they've grown more like each other than like other tribes that speak the same as them."

As the skiff swerved in close the *Renard Noir*'s boatswain tossed the end of a long rope off the stern. The Micmac or Maliseet in the bow caught and held it. The one who'd been manning the sail climbed it, leaving his two companions and their boat in tow beside the *Renard Noir*'s longboat. As a violet-daubed brown face appeared over the stern rail, La Tour called out joyfully: *"Bonjour,* Keeshetech!"

"Bonjou, La Tou." Keeshetech's bare feet slapped down on the deck and he stuck his hand out to shake La Tour's. Françoise found it impossible to even make a guess at his age.

The lines underneath the violet eye rays looked too deeply etched for the suppleness of his body, but then the same could be said of her husband.

La Tour gestured toward her. "My wife."

Keeshetech ran his eyes up and down her with undisguised appraisal, then slapped his chest and nodded. "Micmac!" he exclaimed, although it sounded a bit more like "knick-knack." Either way, she found it more than a little eerie: as though he'd been able to hear her conversation with La Tour over a hundred paces of open water and the song the wind and waves played on the *Renard Noir*'s hull and rigging.

La Tour said: "Say it back to him."

She dutifully repeated: "Micmac," and nodded back at Keeshetech—although why he needed her to assure him which tribe he belonged to was beyond her.

La Tour called the galley boy to fetch three cups of brandy. While they were waiting Keeshetech said to her: "I know you, madame. By Paris."

Françoise exclaimed: "You killed the deer!" Keeshetech just nodded and grunted.

When she'd first met La Tour in Paris, he'd had two of the wild men of the New World in tow, who'd been a more than nine days' wonder. The ladies and gentlemen of Paris had clamored for a demonstration of how *les sauvages* went about the business of living in the wilds. So a corner of a park had been roped off as a stage, and a deer herded in. The *sauvage* selected for the performance killed the deer with a bow and arrow, skinned it, started a fire with a wooden drill, roasted a piece of venison, ate it, contentedly smoked his pipe and belched awhile, and then walked over to a corner near some fashionable ladies, unhinged his breechclout, squatted down, and carried the process through to its logical conclusion. The ladies and gentlemen of Paris had taken it as a perfect and disgusting example of uncivilized humanity, but Françoise had wondered at the time whether said untutored brute might not have known precisely what he was doing.

That Keeshetech was the one who'd killed the deer would also make him the one who'd amused her greatly in a Paris tavern, by saying through La Tour: "If the French men call us savages for painting our faces, they must think French women very savage indeed."

The brandy arrived. Keeshetech hoisted his cup with: "To Madame," and downed it all in one swallow. His complexion turned more violet, tears started from the corners of his eyes, and he let out a long, slow sigh, with his mouth belled open like a trumpet. Once he got his breath back, he said: "I hear, La Tou, you, d'Aulnay—" and then shifted into his own language.

Once Keeshetech had said whatever it was he said, La Tour nodded at him and said to her: "He speaks of my little contretemps at Port Royal this morning."

"How could he know of it already?"

"No point asking how news travels among the people of the country; just take on faith it do."

Keeshetech said: "So, La Tou—*now* we do?"

La Tour said: "Do what?" and they switched back into Micmac—with Keeshetech punctuating his words with gestures of grabbing something in his fist and tossing it over his shoulder. It appeared to Françoise that La Tour was finding it difficult to keep from laughing when he finally shook his head at Keeshetech and said: "No."

Keeshetech repeated sadly: "No?"

"I thank you, my brother, but no."

Keeshetech looked disappointed, but he just shrugged and handed back his empty cup and called down something in Micmac to his boat. The Micmac holding the tow rope let it go and Keeshetech unceremoniously vaulted over the *Renard Noir*'s stern rail to plummet into the sea.

As they stood at the rail watching Keeshetech swim through the *Renard Noir*'s wake toward his boat, Françoise said: "What did he want you to do?"

"*He* wanted to do *me* a small favor. Keeshetech, you see, is a *sagamo*, as the Micmacs call their chiefs—although the title don't mean exactly what we might think. Some years ago, when His Majesty d'Aulnay was first beginning to irritate, Keeshetech offered to call his brother *sagamos* together and turn Port Royal into a bonfire they could dance around with d'Aulnay's head. I said no then, but he thought this morning might've changed my mind.

"It don't disturb my digestion in the least when old friends like Keeshetech bully their brothers into bringing furs to me that should by rights go to d'Aulnay, but unleashing an army of savages on fellow Frenchmen is another matter. Besides, Port Royal's too well defended."

She told him of how eerie it seemed that Keeshetech had made a point of identifying himself as Micmac. La Tour laughed and pounded his fist on the rail. "Micmac ain't their name for themselves. *Micmac*, or *nichemac*, means 'friend'—friend and more, friend and blood kin. From the time we and they first started trading together, a Micmac meeting a Frenchman would raise his hand and say 'Nichemac,' and most Frenchman made the same mistake as you just did. They've got used to us calling them Micmacs, and are too polite to rub our noses in our mistake."

"Would that could be said of all Frenchmen."

"Hmm, yes, well ... The night wind's coming up cool; maybe we best retire to our cabin and let Captain Jamin pilot us home. ..."

As Françoise became settled in at Jemseg the hills around the harbor became a slashed doublet, with long swaths of brilliant orange or red or gold flaring between the overlay of evergreens. Fresh facets of her new life would bring themselves to her attention and then be assimilated into the widening picture labeled "home."

A facet she noticed early on was La Tour's chameleon mouth. If he were talking to one of Jemseg's lackadaisical farmers, he would say: "Them cabbages do come along good"; if to one of the Recollet missionaries, it would be: "those cabbages look to be ripening nicely." If he were speaking to her or Rainville or some other intimate, he would slide from idiom to idiom as the fancy took him.

The one thing he never changed was that he never said *"les sauvages."* To him, they were always either Micmac or Maliseet or "the people of the country."

Françoise wondered whether she was changing outwardly as much as those who'd crossed the ocean with her. Desjardins du Val now sported an earring, permanently stubbled cheeks, and a suit of clothes that fit him like an old hound's hide. Rainville was now as likely to appear at supper in smoky buckskins as in brocade and lace, and his porcelain-doll features had grown darker as the sun bleached his cornsilk hair even lighter.

As for Lorette, she was at an age when everything was changing rapidly regardless. She seemed happy enough in her new surroundings, but Françoise detected signs that Minou and her daughters were riding roughshod over Lorette when she wasn't around. An opportunity to do something about it presented itself one morning when Françoise was indulging herself in a cup of coffee in the officers' dining hall.

Most of the cooking done for the officers—and for the *engagés'* mirror-image dining hall next door—was done in the cookhouse across the courtyard. But today Minou was going to fill both dining halls with the savor of half a caribou roasting in each of the cavernous fireplaces. At the far end of the table from Françoise, Minou's daughters and Lorette were rubbing herbs into the halved carcass. The two little Micmac dogs who would soon be shut into tread wheels to turn the spits were slavering around their legs.

Minou crouched down to stir last night's coals alive, fumbling with her free hand in the kindling box while her eyes stayed on the coals. When her fumbling hand found nothing, she grumbled: "Stupid girl. Lorette! Go get wood."

Françoise set down her coffee cup and said sweetly: "If you want wood, Minou, fetch it yourself. Or send one of your girls."

Minou hissed something in Micmac that made one of her daughters gasp and another giggle. Whatever it was, it definitely wasn't a request for them to go fetch wood.

Françoise's heart spurred into that gait that always came on when she was about to step onto a stage—or perhaps it was just the coffee. She said: "Minou, Lorette is not a kitchen slave, she is a cook of great talent and invention. I know that you can teach her much about the meats and fishes and herbs of Acadia. But if circumstances make it that she needs must explore with no guide, she will still find her way. If La Tour and I are forced to a choice between only your cooking or only Lorette's, the choice is already made."

Minou said: "You not speak for La Tou."

"Minou, you can have a smooth road ahead of you or a very, very rough one, whichever you prefer. Jeanne." Françoise turned to Minou's eldest daughter. "Your mother needs kindling."

When La Tour came to bed that night, he said jauntily: "Were I you, my dumpling, I would see to it Lorette does *all* your cooking for the next few days. A few days should be enough to let Minou stew down, and for it to sink into her that there's other people can just as easy sneak surprises into someone else's favorite dish."

"Surprises?"

"The nightshade plant grows in Acadia. And other plants the people of the country know. No need for alarm—Minou has enough wit to know I'd gut her and spit her without trifling about proof. But Minou's wits don't come into play until her spleen cools. Just see you walk wary for the next few days. Particularly since I'll not be here."

"Where will you be?"

"Keeshetech and some Maliseet *sagamos* are making a rendezvous upriver before they all scatter through the woods for the winter. That's the only real power the *sagamos* have: deciding which family gets which part of the forest to hunt in— but it do make their people think twice about crossing them in other matters. I promised to come give them a feast at their rendezvous."

"I'll come with you."

He shook his head. "It's late in the year for traveling in an open canoe and sleeping without a roof."

"The weather's been glorious! Red leaves or not."

"It can turn any day. And I'll be ten days at the least going back and forth."

"The weather that falls on me will be no worse than what falls on you."

He sighed. "If it was all by canoe, you might think of coming along. But the last leg is a long tramp through the forest."

"I can walk."

"Not far in French shoes on a woods path. And your feet are too soft for moccasins."

"They'll harden up."

"If your feet were as hard as your head, we could walk to Quebec."

"Oh please, Papa, I want to come to the feast!"

He sighed even deeper. "What is a man to do with you?"

"You seemed to know that well enough last night. Have you forgotten so soon? No—*parts* of you seem to remember. . . ."

When the Micmacs and Maliseets who were supposed to escort "La Tou" upriver didn't appear on the appointed day, or the day after, La Tour didn't appear in the least perturbed or surprised. The delay did give time for the Maliseet wife of one of Jemseg's "farmers" to measure Françoise's feet and cobble up several pairs of smoked moose-hide moccasins, apologizing profusely that there was only enough time to put a few sketchy flashes of quillwork on the toepieces.

Françoise kissed Lorette good-bye at the postern gate. She'd given Lorette the choice of coming along, instead of being left alone with Minou and her daughters. But Lorette was wise enough to know she couldn't hide behind "La Tou's" wife's skirts forever. Or perhaps, Françoise wondered, Lorette was wise enough to know that La Tour hadn't been exaggerating about how rough the traveling would be.

A half-dozen canoes and a couple of dozen people of the country were waiting just above the falls. The Micmac and Maliseet canoes had an upsweep in the middle, where both sides of the hull rose up as high as the prow and stern. When Françoise had first laid eyes on one, the design had struck her as a lot of trouble for a canoewright to go to for the sake of aesthetic effect. Fortunately, before she'd opened her mouth to express that opinion to La Tour, she'd guessed the purpose was to provide some protection against ocean waves. She didn't at all mind La Tour occasionally correcting her ignorance about Acadia, but there was no point making it too easy for him.

La Tour settled her into the lead canoe and climbed in in front of her, settling his back against the midthwart. The paddlers pushed off from shore to ride the tail of the incoming tide upstream. As Jemseg dropped behind them it suddenly sank into Françoise that it was the westernmost Acadian outpost of what she thought of as civilization, and she was on her way west from there.

It didn't take long for her to see that La Rivière St. Jean was unlike any river she'd known in Europe: wider and wilder, with a current the paddlers had to fight hard against, and craggy shores that made the line of canoes seem like floating flyspecks. La Tour said over his shoulder: "Rivière au Dauphin is well enough if you want pleasant watering for sheep and cattle, but this is a *river*."

After exulting in that for a moment, he added: "It's also more or less the boundary between Micmac country and Maliseet—more or less. North and east of La Rivière St. Jean—all the way around the peninsula to Cape Sable—is Micmac; south and west is Maliseet. But they're a sight more easygoing about the border between them than other tribes."

They traveled upriver for three days, sleeping under the stars. There were a few short squalls of rain, but not enough to soak through Françoise's cloak. She found it remarkable how aware she became of the slightest hint of change in the weather, as soon as she no longer had an indoors to retire to.

On the third day, they stopped before sunset. The paddlers drew all the canoes up into the woods and began to cover them with brush. La Tour smiled at her. "Tomorrow we begin to walk."

In the morning La Tour pointed out one of the paddlers to her and said: "He's our guide. We follow him and the rest follow us." She fell in beside La Tour and behind the guide, but the path soon narrowed to one person wide. Françoise naturally moved to step in front of her husband, but he put his arm in front of her and shook his head. "Not in this part of the world."

So she dutifully walked behind him, hearing the voices of Parisian friends commiserating with her for his lack of gallantry. She glanced back at the line of Micmac and Maliseet men and women. The women carried all the camp gear and the cargo of presents and provisions La Tour was providing for the feast; the men carried nothing but their weapons. But the fact that the paint-daubed matchlocks all had their fuses lit and smoldering, and the bows all had arrows nocked, made Françoise consider that the women might be glad the men had no burdens to free their hands of if a bear came down the path, or a party of the Mohawks that La Tour said came sometimes raiding from the west.

The path they were following through the hills had been worn into a trough by countless generations of moccasins. But that didn't mean it wasn't dotted with stones and tree roots and fallen branches, and Françoise's feet felt every one of them. The difference between moccasins and bare feet seemed nominal, but she didn't say it aloud. She could already hear La Tour's jaunty reply: "So it's meant to be. If you was wearing stiff-soled shoes, you'd not feel the twig under your foot until you and the moosedeer you was stalking heard it snap."

No one in the column said anything aloud. There was none of the grunting and stamping sounds a line of French porters would produce. And there were certainly no raucous marching songs. Without human noises to push it away, the forest took over Françoise's senses: the clacking of treetop branches that seemed above the clouds, the smells of leaf mold and pine, the sweet piccolo of a distant songbird, the ear-splitting shock of a trespassed squirrel. . . .

But what increasingly occupied her attention was La Tour's back in front of her: lean, loose, and limber, with the barrel of his cradled musket poking out beyond his left elbow, swinging his long legs ahead as carelessly as though moccasins protected the feet as much as seaboots. If she'd been carrying a musket of her own, she would've been hard-pressed not to put a bullet in his back.

By the time La Tour called a halt for the morning meal, the soles of Françoise's feet were already painfully tender, and her ankles were tingling from twisting in a different direction with every step. But she refused to give him the satisfaction of hearing her say so. Instead she said: "Is it a custom of the country to pretend we need a guide? This path is as easy to see as most streets in La Rochelle."

He got that same gravely thoughtful look on his face as his father had when she'd asked old Claude what he would've done if Acadia had stayed New Scotland. "Now that you point it out, Françoise, it *do* seem a waste to be paying a guide. What say you take the lead this time? I will be right behind you with my shiny new flintlock musket, should anything unpleasant spring out of the woods."

It was much pleasanter walking with nothing in front of her but the empty path and the forest. For one thing, she caught glimpses of birds or little, furred creatures scurrying deeper into the woods at the approach of human beings. For another, she got to set the pace, one better suited to her less-than-stiltlike legs.

They came out into a meadow, with a few die-hard wildflowers dusting pink among the blown-out goldenrod and thistles and waist-high grass—waist-high for her at least. In the middle of the meadow, the path came to an abrupt end.

Françoise stopped and looked around. Behind her was the rutted path of tramped-low, matted grass; in front of her and on both sides was nothing but the unbroken, waving surface of the meadow, surrounded by the seamless wall of the forest.

La Tour said: "Lost something, my dear?"

"The path! It ends here."

"Hmm. Don't seem like much of a destination, do it? Perhaps there is a trapdoor. . . ."

"*Try* not to be an idiot."

"Well, there may be *some*thing on the ground. . . ." He started pushing aside the meadow growth and peering between. "Here's something."

She looked down. To the left of the end of the path were three hand-sized stones side by side. La Tour mused: "It do seem strange that three stones should happen to come up in a line like that. Perhaps they point at something."

Françoise drew a line with her eyes along the angle at which the stones pointed. The line encountered nothing of any significance all the way across the meadow, and the point where it met the trees seemed no different than any other point along the forest wall.

La Tour said: "What say we go see?" The file of Micmacs and Maliseets followed along. Except that the file wasn't a file anymore; they had fanned out so that none would trample in another's footsteps.

When La Tour reached the edge of the woods, he plunged in through the tangled undergrowth. Françoise followed him, with thorns clutching at her skirt and twigs clawing at her eyes. La Tour stopped a few steps in, at the beginning of a path as obvious and well beaten as most streets in La Rochelle.

The Micmacs and Maliseets laughed long and hard, and so did La Tour. Françoise didn't exactly join in, but neither was she as annoyed or embarrassed as she might've expected. There was something in the laughter that said they weren't laughing at her, just laughing at a good joke and in delight at the ingenuity of their ancestors. And there was something in their laughter that suggested that anything they could find to laugh about was a good thing.

As Françoise fell in behind La Tour and the guide, she noticed a very odd tree beside the point where the path had started up again. Its trunk grew straight up to the height of her knees and then went off at a right angle before growing upward again. The arm of the angle was on the same line as the three stones in the meadow. So much for the accepted wisdom that noble savages didn't plan beyond tomorrow's breakfast.

They didn't walk much farther before stopping to camp. La Tour told her they were stopping early because it grew dark so much quicker in the forest, but it seemed to her they still had plenty of light left. If he was lying to keep her feet from getting punished too much on the first day, she wasn't going to press him to recant.

She was sitting with her back against a tree and her burning feet propped up on a deadfall when one of the Micmac or Maliseet women came to her with a birchbark bowl of some concoction that smelled like raw turpentine. Using a bit of moss as a sponge, the woman daubed the soles of Françoise's feet with

several coatings. It made them burn worse at first, and then it
actually seemed to help. Or perhaps it was just that the cure
made the existing pain seem mild by comparison.

The next day her feet actually seemed to have hardened a
little. They only had to walk through the morning. At midday
the path came out onto a little blue lake, like a sapphire set
into faceted granite. Along the shore were huts made of birchbark sheets and rough-cut poles. Some were shaped like bee-
hives, some like fat cones with the tops lopped off, some were
oval.

Keeshetech was waiting at the edge of the village, but a different Keeshetech from the one Françoise had watched jump
off the stern of the *Renard Noir*. This one's violet eye rays had
been augmented with swirls of red and blue that extended
down across his chest, and his hair had been woven into
strings collared with copper tubes and ivorylike cylinders. He
wore a headband sporting two pairs of blue-jay wings, and a
painted fur cape fastened under one arm like the paintings of
Hercules wearing his lionskin.

Keeshetech shook La Tour's hand and bowed to kiss
Françoise's, then escorted them to his wigwam, where they
were to be housed. Its interior was roomier than Françoise
would've imagined, and the spruce-bough carpet and layered
bark walls felt surprisingly cozy—although she had her doubts
about the overhead smoke hole in a heavy rain. There were
several women and children bustling about inside who seemed
not particularly concerned about states of dress and undress.

La Tour rummaged out a clean shirt and breeches from one
of the packs the porters had stacked outside and said: "I am
afraid I needs must leave you alone awhile."

"Why?"

"You can come see where I go, if you like. But you cannot
follow me there."

" 'Tis not the custom of the country?"

"Decidedly 'taint."

There was a low, rounded hut set apart from the others. La
Tour pointed her toward a nearby knoll. "If you're curious, sit
and wait there. When you get tired of waiting, one of

Keeshetech's wives has enough French to give tolerable good gossip."

She went and sat on the knoll, kicking off her moccasins to press the soles of her feet against the cool, damp moss. La Tour dropped his clean clothes beside the hut's rounded doorway, stripped off his trail-soiled clothes, and scuttled inside. A cloud of smoke or steam puffed out to mask the twin, sky-pointed arrowheads of his buttocks until the door flap dropped behind them.

A chanting and clacking came from inside the hut and kept up. Keeshetech and other men came and stripped and stooped inside. Women came bearing rocks on smoking slabs of wood and passed them through the doorway.

After a while of waiting for something else to happen around the steam hut, Françoise let her attention drift to the life going on outside it. Children and square-shouldered little dogs chased each other around the birchbark village. Women busied themselves with pieces of meat and an open fire. Two men were in a canoe out on the lake, one paddling and the other standing in the prow with a prong-headed spear. Several squatted men were shaving the rims of wooden frameworks and handing them to women weaving thongs through them like tennis rackets.

Françoise couldn't help but wonder whether the life of a Micmac or Maliseet was any more precarious or less interesting than a Parisian's. But then, of course, they had to live without the benefits of true religion. She wondered how the missionaries explained to *les sauvages* why two Christians would kill each other because one believed that consecrated bread and wine *were* the body and blood of Christ and the other believed that consecrated bread and wine were a *symbol* of the body and blood of Christ.

The door flap of the steam hut suddenly sprang open. La Tour and Keeshetech shot out, ran to the lake, and leaped in. They splashed and laughed and ducked each other's heads, then walked lazily back to where they'd left their clothes, giving Françoise the opportunity to observe that the good God hadn't shaped the heathens of the New World all that differently from Christian Frenchmen.

La Tour came up the knoll with his clean clothes clinging to his dripping skin, looking like a layer of callus had been steamed off his face. He collapsed bonelessly beside her and drawled: "Well, it cost me some convincing, but you can come to the feast."

"I should *hope* so—after flaying the soles off my feet to get here."

"By custom, the formal feasts, like the sweatlodge, are only for the men. Excepting the groom's mother at a wedding feast. That 'excepting' gave me a wedge. Well, that and the keg of gunpowder one of our paddlers' women broke her back freighting from La Rivière St. Jean. Keeshet still don't like it, but Keeshet can swallow it or miss the feast."

"Keeshet?"

"Keeshetech's older brother. 'Keeshetech' means 'little Keeshet.' They have a habit of naming a boy child after his father or older brother. If Keeshet dies before he do, Keeshetech will take a different name so as not to make everyone sad by reminding them of Keeshet."

"And what, pray tell, had you planned to do if I'd dragged myself all the way here to find they wouldn't let me in their feast?"

"Oh, I knew they could be convinced. Everybody can be convinced, if you got something to convince 'em with."

The feast was held in the longest and tallest of the oval huts. Relays of women came to the door flap bearing platters of meat and fish and what appeared to be everyone's favorite delicacy: ship's biscuit. An old man at the head of the feast circle stood up and launched into a speech. La Tour leaned over to translate it to Françoise, which didn't make her feel any more singled out, since the Micmacs who knew Maliseet were translating for the ones who didn't—or perhaps it was Maliseets translating Micmac.

La Tour murmured: "He is following the custom of praising the man who provided the feast—telling of what a great hunter I am, like my father before me, and his father before him—

who was also a famous warrior—and my father's father's father, the great seafarer and killer of whalefishes. . . ."

"Your great-grandfather hunted whales?"

"Who's to say? The people of the country like to know each other's lineage back to the tenth generation and more. So I gave them one."

Françoise didn't have to understand the language to appreciate that the old man had a resonance to his voice and a range of tone and gesture that would've sent most French grand tragedians scuttling back to their apprenticeships. And it wasn't all in a venerable style; sometimes he punched a phrase that would make one or two men start laughing and the rest join in, until they'd all exhausted the humor of it and were ready to hear more.

But one lesson the old man could've learned from French actors was when to stop. When he finally sat down, the man next to him stood up to orate, and then the next man. Françoise began to fear it was going to go all around the circle one by one. Small wonder the women allowed themselves to be excluded.

La Tour muttered to her: "The bone you just chewed the meat off is beaver; throw it in the fire. If the dogs are allowed to gnaw on beaver bones, the beaver people will be so insulted they will go away and not come back."

A man who was neither young nor old thrust a platter of meat at her, grinning and smacking his lips. She took a taste. It was somewhat like pork, but sweeter. She smiled at him and nodded and took another taste. His grin turned evil and he rubbed his stomach and barked like a dog. She held her gorge down and said in her mind: What a pleasure to make your acquaintance, Keeshet.

It came La Tour's turn to stand and speak. Although Françoise couldn't understand his words, she could hear that it was another demonstration of his chameleon mouth, sliding into the tones and inflections of the previous orators. Whatever it was he said, it called forth several spates of communal laughter and several chants of *"Hau, hau, hau!"*—which appeared to be their version of "bravo."

When La Tour sat down again, Keeshet leaned toward him and said something through his smarmy grin. La Tour glowered and shook his head, but Keeshet insisted. La Tour muttered to Françoise: "He says if you can eat among the men, you must be able to speak among the men."

She looked around the smoke-wreathed ring of faces. Some of the faces looked abashed, some as malevolent as Keeshet's, some might as well have been carved in wood. She put her hand on La Tour's shoulder and levered herself to her feet.

She could easily call up several dozen speeches she'd given to several thousand audiences, but this seemed definitely the wrong circumstances for one of Columbine's coy flirtations or Pierrette's fey poesies—although Keeshet would no doubt be delighted to see her simper and twitter in front of the *sagamos*. But she'd played opposite enough Scaramouches in her time to know how to throw herself into an imitation that could leave the rest of the greenroom helpless with laughter.

She gave them the scene wherein Scaramouche tells Columbine how he was solely responsible for the victory at Wallenstein, unaware that Pantalone is listening from a window. It wasn't quite the same without a slapstick and Pantalone's asides, but she had enough bombast and mimed sword flourishes at her command to compensate—half-improvised and half-pirated from previous performances, in the grand old style of the commedia.

The *hau, haus* at the end near took the roof off. She gave Keeshet a pretty little curtsy and sat back down. La Tour was biting his mouth shut, with his cheeks and eyes bugged out like a blowfish. She whispered to him: "Does the older brother of our friend speak French?" He shook his head. She smiled sweetly at Keeshet and said: "You should know better than throw pebbles at an old cannoneer, child."

When the signal gun of Jemseg fort saluted the governor and his lady, walking arm in arm out of the woods, Lorette came running and said, goggled-eyed: "*Françoise*—what's happened to you?"

"To me?"

"You look like you've been dragged behind a horse and come out ten years younger!"

"I suppose I have."

But the feeling only lasted until the next day. She and Lorette were taking the air along the palisade when a canoe came scudding into the harbor, the wind off the bay belling out its sail, and a Micmac or Maliseet came running from the wharf calling for "La Tou." A moment later La Tour was bellowing in the courtyard and men whom Françoise had never seen move at more than a saunter were pouring out of doors, buckling on sword baldrics and shouldering pikes.

Françoise scuttled down to her husband and shouted over the din: "What has happened?"

"D'Aulnay is sailing up our coast with two warships! Ah, Jamin—is the *Renard Noir* fitted out to sail *now*?"

Captain Jamin replied dubiously: "The wind is against us—"

"Fuck the wind, the tide can carry us out! *Is* she fit for action?"

"If needs be. But I'm not so sure it's wise to—"

"Do you think it *wise* to leave her riding at anchor until d'Aulnay starts bombarding us? Get aboard."

Françoise said: "Perhaps Captain Jamin *is* being wise. You said d'Aulnay has an outpost in the south; perhaps he's just skirting up our shore on his way back from there to Port Royal."

"If so, he'll make no fuss about sheering off from our waters when he's told. Nothing to fear, my dear. One way or t'other, I'll be back for supper—once our friend has been showed we don't just draw lines in the sand."

Françoise and Lorette and Madame Jamin stood on the gatehouse palisade watching the *Renard Noir* ride the ebb out of the harbor. Godard de Rainville stood a little ways apart, looking miffed at being left behind to guard the women.

Madame Jamin said: "I pray the good God our husbands know what they're about."

Françoise said: "I'm sure they do," but she wasn't at all.

Chapter 8

Charles de Menou, Sieur d'Aulnay et de Charnisay, stood on the rolling deck of the ketch *St. Jacques*, trying not to think about money. Every element of Port Royal cost him money, from the bell in the church steeple to the *St. Jacques* and her sister ketch. But a church had to have a bell, and the *St. Jacques* and *St. Eustace* were necessary for coastal expeditions, such as the supply trip to the southern outpost they were on their way home from.

He tried to think of whether the *St. Jacques* was carrying enough sail for this wind, of whether the clouds coming in from the west looked like a squall, of anything but money. Every attempt to make Port Royal cost less tomorrow cost him more today. He saved money by importing raw iron bars instead of finished trade hatchets, but the cost of building a forge at Port Royal and importing a smith put him further into debt. The indentured laborers he imported would eventually make Port Royal self-sufficient, as more and more of them chose to stay on after their term and become tenant farmers; but in the meanwhile he had to carry the debt for their wages and passage money. Every sheep or cow that died on the voyage from France cost him just as much as one that lived to fatten on the marsh grass along La Rivière au Dauphin.

D'Aulnay knew there was no point in thinking about money, because there was nothing he could do about it. All he could do was keep shoring up Port Royal with his own money and hope that his tenants grew well enough established to start paying him rents before his scaffolding of new-debts-to-pay-old-debts collapsed beneath him. But once his mind had stumbled through that door where he kept the subject of money locked away, it was difficult to extract himself—even though he knew it was only a downward spiral of possible disasters that would put him in a state of inward panic and outward sharp temper.

There were times—such as now—when he cursed himself for not having been content to stay in France and live on the income from the *seigneurie* he'd inherited from his mother; the income that now annually disappeared into the sinkhole of Port Royal. But once he'd made the choice, there was no going back from the fact that Port Royal was his responsibility. If Port Royal prospered, he would be responsible; if it withered and died like the earlier Port Royals, he would be responsible. He didn't know why the good God had cursed him with ambition, but there was nothing he could do about that, either.

"A sail! Off the larboard bow!"

Well, that was certainly something to take his mind off it: English and Dutch privateers had been known to cruise the Baye Françoise. He said to the captain of the *St. Jacques*: "Have your men stand to their guns, and the quartermaster issue arms," then lifted the speaking trumpet and hailed the *St. Eustace*: "Stand to arms!"

The captain of the *St. Jacques* was training his telescope ahead and to the left, scanning the bay. He stopped in midsweep, focused on a point in the distance, then lowered his telescope. "It is La Tour, monsieur. Or his ship, at least." The captain proffered his telescope to d'Aulnay, but d'Aulnay declined; if the captain said it was La Tour's ship, it was La Tour's ship. "Shall I have the men stand down, monsieur?"

D'Aulnay considered it, then shook his head. "Not yet." When he'd made the decision to set a homeward course up the west side of the Baye Françoise, instead of crossing to the Port Royal coast at the bay mouth, he'd wondered what La Tour might do, if anything. It appeared he was about to find out.

The *Renard Noir* came within view of the naked eye. With half the bay in bright sunlight, and half under a light drizzle of rain, she seemed to shimmer on the waves. D'Aulnay couldn't help but admit that for all La Tour's oafishness, the oaf knew the difference between a lump of planks and a ship. About a quarter league off, there was a puff of smoke from her bow, then a muffled boom. A geyser went up not twenty paces from the *St. Jacques*'s bowsprit, as though a whalefish had chosen that instant to surface and blow.

D'Aulnay found himself smiling. All the cobwebs of debts and creditors and future worry had been swept clean by that one culverin shot. It seemed beyond miraculous that La Tour could be wise enough to avoid crossing swords with him and yet fool enough to come out after him on the open sea. The *St. Jacques* and the *St. Eustace*, with their total complement of sixteen light guns and some fifty men, were hardly the warships d'Aulnay had commanded for His Most Christian Majesty, but the principles of naval warfare remained the same.

The captain of the *St. Jacques* said: "Shall we sheer off from the warning shot, monsieur?"

"Who's to say it was a warning? He may have aimed for us and missed." D'Aulnay could hear the upsurge of blood in his own voice, and moved to correct it. Not only was it unbecoming for a gentleman to betray too much emotion, it was unsettling for men in battle to think their orders might be tinged by anything but strategic and tactical considerations. "I will take command now, Captain."

D'Aulnay didn't expect the captain to reply—it was a statement of fact. While making it, d'Aulnay was already taking up the speaking trumpet to hail the *St. Eustace* again: "Follow, and engage his larboard quarter!"

The captain of the *St. Jacques* said dubiously: "Even with two of us, monsieur, he still has us outgunned."

"Outgunned is one thing, Captain, outgunning is another." D'Aulnay could feel his voice turning jaunty, but a little jauntiness in a commander never did troops any harm. "Master Gunner!"

"*Oui*, monsieur?"

"Aim your starboard guns for her rigging and adjust your elevations as we approach. Stand to until I give the order."

"*Oui*, monsieur."

There was no time for d'Aulnay to call for his cuirass and helmet, and he was just as glad. He had a horror of drowning, and a man in armor went into the water like a stone. His hardest task of self-discipline during his naval career was to go into battle wearing armor, when he would've much preferred the risk of getting picked off by an enemy sniper than that of going over the side strapped into a back- and breastplate.

As the two ketches bore down on her the *Renard Noir* swung into the wind to bring her starboard guns to bear on the *St. Eustace*. It left the *Renard Noir*'s stern beam on to the *St. Jacques*, but the sterncastle of the *Renard Noir* was too narrow a target at anything but a stone's throw. If that's what La Tour was gambling on, he knew more about sea fights than d'Aulnay had expected.

D'Aulnay called out: "Full sail! Helmsman, quarter to larboard, take the wind!"

The helmsman's "*Oui*, monsieur," and the captain bellowing his sailors aloft, were eclipsed by a broadside from the *Renard Noir*. A tearing and rending sound came across the waves as the *St. Eustace*'s mainmast came down. D'Aulnay noted in a side compartment of his mind that La Tour must be using chainshot—his gunners couldn't possibly be good enough or lucky enough to hit a mast with roundshot.

But what entirely occupied the forefront of d'Aulnay's mind was the stern of the *Renard Noir* growing steadily larger in front of the *St. Jacques*'s plunging bowsprit. Under ordinary circumstances, the *St. Jacques* could never have made headway against the *Renard Noir*. But La Tour had trimmed sail to give his gunners time to sight on the *St. Eustace*, and the *St. Jacques* was running before the wind with every inch of canvas she could muster. The question was how close in the *St. Jacques* could get before the *Renard Noir* lifted her heels.

It was the same as every naval battle d'Aulnay had known: an agonizingly slow dance with the enemy and the wind, waiting for an instant's flurry of cannon fire. But experiencing it several dozen times didn't make it any easier to remain calm. Nor did it help that La Tour had been a constant source of insult and inconvenience for ten years, and it could all be wiped away in an instant, if only the stern of the *Renard Noir* kept growing wider for a few moments longer. And were La Tour to expire in an unprovoked attack upon his brother governor, all future income from Jemseg would naturally flow to Port Royal.

The *Renard Noir*'s yardarms angled to catch the wind again and she began to surge away, but d'Aulnay still had reason to hope. The belled-out sails of the *Renard Noir* suddenly went slack and flapped flabbily. The *St. Jacques*—as d'Aulnay had gambled—had stolen her wind.

The crew of the *St. Jacques* sent up a cheer. D'Aulnay roared: "Silence!" The last thing he needed now was for his orders to be drowned out by celebrations of a victory that was yet to be consummated. "Master Gunner, aim your starboard guns for her sterncastle."

"But, monsieur, she is not to starboard of—"

"*Imagine* she is! Aim for her sterncastle!"

"*Oui*, monsieur."

"Helmsman, hard to larboard."

The *St. Jacques* heeled over with the turn. D'Aulnay gave his master gunner a moment to adjust for the angle. It did seem odd that the flag drooping from the stern in front of the *St. Jacques*'s guns should be the same fleur-de-lis she flew. "Fire!"

The deck beneath d'Aulnay's boots shuddered as the starboard guns bucked and roared in unison. Powder smoke filled the air, stinging his eyes. As the smoke began to dissipate he saw the *Renard Noir*'s sterncastle in tatters and the fleur-de-lis floating in the sea among broken spars. Someone on her deck was waving a bit of sailcloth tied to a pikestaff, or perhaps a longboat oar.

D'Aulnay said: "Helmsman, bring us alongside. Boatswain, I need a boarding party. *Armed*."

The captain said: "They show a white flag, monsieur."

"I see it. I will trust it once we've boarded her and have La Tour in hand. *Then* we will serve out a measure of wine." But first, there was another matter to attend to while the boarding party was being assembled. "Master Gunner . . ."

"*Oui*, monsieur?"

"You questioned an order."

"I did, monsieur. It was a fool thing. It might well be *us* blown to flinders instead of them—because I questioned. It shall not happen again."

"It *shall* not because I *will* not have a man in a position of responsibility I cannot trust. For the sake of my own skin, and that of everyone else at Port Royal and upon our ships, it would only seem prudent that anyone who questions orders should carry no more responsibility than a powder monkey's or barrel swabber's. But a man who has mastered the art of gunnery as well as you was clearly born with an ability to learn a lesson once and keep it. So when you tell me it shall not happen again, I must perforce believe you."

"Thank you, monsieur."

The crew of the *St. Jacques* had fixed grappling hooks to the *Renard Noir* and were gradually lining the two hulls side by side. D'Aulnay drew his sword, handed his hat to the captain, said: "The ship is yours again," and went to lead the boarding party.

Most of the *Renard Noir*'s crew were backed onto her fore-deck, showing their empty hands. D'Aulnay said: "Boatswain, detail three men with muskets to guard the prisoners. The rest of you, follow me," and headed for the shattered sterncastle.

La Tour was slumped against a remnant of the stern rail, covered in blood. Unfortunately, little or none of it appeared to be his. In his arms was Pierre Jamin, the captain of the *Renard Noir*. The portion of Captain Jamin's face that didn't look like pounded beefsteak looked like an apprentice sculptor's first attempt in paraffin.

D'Aulnay said: "You and your crew, monsieur, are my prisoners."

"My crew are not responsible for any of this."

"That may be so. I shall decide at Port Royal. But *you*, monsieur, are going back to France in chains." Now that d'Aulnay'd had a moment to think about it, it wasn't at all unfortunate that the blood was Jamin's and not La Tour's. Far better he should live to face the consequences.

CHAPTER 9

Jeanne was almost finished feeding Marie when the signal gun fired. She called the nurse to take Marie, dabbed her breast dry, shrugged her shift back onto her shoulder, and buttoned her blouse as she hurried out the door. Outside, the courtyard was clattering with men-at-arms bustling to their posts. On the far side of the parade square, little Joseph was trying to help Nicole up the steps to the palisade—among all those steel-shod boots and swinging weapons.

Jeanne bawled: "Joseph!" and started to run, shouting whatever words came to her tongue along the way. Before she got there, one of the men-at-arms leaned his pike against the wall, scooped the children up one in each arm, and carried them safely up to the catwalk above the gates.

But when Jeanne got up above the gates, Joseph and Nicole weren't there. She found them in the northwest bastion. Their uncle Nicolas had set them ahorse on a cannon barrel and was keeping one arm propped around them while he peered out at the basin.

A ragged flotilla was making its way into La Rivière au Dauphin: the *St. Jacques*, followed by Charles La Tour's ship towing the *St. Eustace*. The *St. Eustace* had no mast and La Tour's ship had a ragged-looking stern, with a spar rigged in place of the steering arm.

Trying not to let the children hear her fear for their father, Jeanne said: "Do you think they were set upon by privateers?"

Nikki looked at her sideways and, oddly, said: "I would like to think so, but I fear not."

She would've pressed him to explain, but at the moment she

90

was too consumed with worrying about Charles. The three ships anchored in the river and let down their boats. Out of the first boat to touch the landing stage sprang a plume-hatted figure in black and scarlet, whose bouncing stride belied even a minor wound.

Joseph crowed: "I see Papa!"

"Yes," Jeanne exhaled, squeezing her son with both arms, "I see Papa, too. Come along, dears, we must hurry down and welcome him home."

As the gatehouse guards presented arms to their governor, he swept his hat off and bowed to kiss her hand, saying: "Madame, your chevalier begs to report that we were attacked on our way home by a brigand named La Tour and—though outgunned and taken by surprise—utterly vanquished him. Sergeant of the Guard."

"*Oui*, monsieur?"

"There will be some thirty prisoners brought ashore. See that they are placed in the cells and guarded day and night."

"Thirty, monsieur? It will be cramped quarters."

"They'll not be there long. Not most of them, at least. La Tour himself is to be manacled, but the rest should be secure enough simply under lock and key.

"Well, my dear"—he rubbed his hands together—"I've not had a bite of food since dawn."

She left Charles and the children in the dining hall for a moment while she went to tell the steward to serve up the cold half *tortierre* left over from last night's supper. Then she sat down with Anne and Nicolas and Joseph and Nicole to hear Charles tell the story of the battle—in between devastating every plate of food set before him and washing it down with deep quaffs of wine. He certainly had an appetite.

The tale appeared to exorcise whatever it was that had made Nicolas say that odd thing on the ramparts. He now said enthusiastically: "When word of this gets back to France, there should be no more doubts about La Tour."

Charles leaned back in his chair, unbuttoning his jerkin, and beamed. "I expect you may be right."

Nicolas raised his goblet. "Here's to the governor of all Acadia."

Charles blushed and waved his hand diffidently, but Jeanne could see he was delighted with the world and all things in it. For her part, she felt a bit giddy, and it wasn't from a few small sips of wine.

She remained buoyant throughout the day, despite having to attend the funeral for two sailors from the *St. Eustace* and Captain Jamin and two of his crew. Supper at the governor's table that night was boisterious with ships' officers and brandy. For once, Charles didn't seem to mind in the least if some of the verses for "Vive La Compagnie" got a bit vulgar, or the occasional candlestick found its way to the floor. But it wasn't far into the evening when he stood up and bowed. "I believe my lady and I shall retire."

As the bedroom door closed behind her Jeanne naturally started toward her undressing screen. But Charles took hold of her from behind, bending his head over her shoulder to kiss the hollow beside her neck, while his left arm clasped the front of her waist and his right hand unhooked the back of her blouse. She reached her arms back to bury her fingers in his hair, then lowered them again to let the stiff-fronted blouse fall away. He walked her toward the bed, pressing his body to her back while his hands pushed her breasts up free of her corset and pulled the neck of her shift down below them. When her knees hit the bed frame, he turned her around and came down on top of her, with the feather-cloud mattress giving out a soft whoosh as they landed.

He leaned back for a moment and she seized the opportunity to jig the facings of her corset together, to pop the hooks free of their eyes before she suffocated. It was lucky she'd snatched the instant, because he'd only leaned back to unfasten his breeches and pull up her skirt, didn't even take his boots off. He certainly did have an appetite.

In five years of married life, she'd never had cause to complain of a lack of amorous attentions. But this was like being ridden by a tiger. Small wonder cats purred.

When they were finally settled under the bedclothes in their nightclothes like respectable married people, and Jeanne had stopped blushing—at least enough to feel that it might not burn Charles's shoulder to lean her cheek against it—they murmured of deliciously mundane matters. She told him of the man-at-arms who'd scooped up Joseph and Nicole before they'd gotten themselves trampled or beheaded. Charles said: "Do you know the man's name?"

"Lemay, Nikki said. Or perhaps it was Lemaire?"

"Lemay. I shall have him disciplined for setting aside his weapon during a stand-to-arms."

She reared up to protest, then realized he was joking.

In the morning all the prisoners except La Tour were brought out under guard and assembled at one end of the dining hall. Charles sat at the other end in his high-backed chair. Jeanne looked on through the crossed halberds of the guards in the doorway.

It appeared to Jeanne that the crew of the *Renard Noir* would have made a raggedy-looking lot even without the occasional bandage or arm sling here and there, and the downcast look of prisoners. Apparently Charles La Tour didn't care whether the men under his command wore canvas pantaloons frayed halfway up the thigh or velvet doublets or bones through their noses.

Charles began by saying: "I could have you all hanged for piracy, and not a magistrate in France would dispute me.

"But I realize you were but following your duty to obey your captain and ship's owner. Having seen your ship asail, and the condition she's been kept in, leaves me no doubt that you are good sailors all, and not ashamed to work with your hands and put your backs in it. There is always a place for such men at Port Royal.

"Any man of you who chooses to enter my service shall be paid a just wage, fed and housed well, and presented with a new suit of clothing immediately and every year thereafter. Any who choose not to accept my offer are free to take the *Renard Noir* and return to Jemseg—although she would be my lawful prize, were I to exercise the right."

The prisoners murmured among themselves. Out of the

murmurings, Jeanne distinctly heard several times: "Charlot."
She was more than a little surprised that Charles would allow
common sailors to name him so flippantly, then realized they
were referring to Charles La Tour.

The murmurs died down and a keg-bodied ruffian with an
earring showing through his greasy hair stepped forward as
spokesman. When she heard his voice, Jeanne was shocked to
recognize her father's sometime business associate, Desjardins
du Val. "Monsieur de Menou d'Aulnay, you make us a very
noble and generous offer. But we all of us prefer to return to
Jemseg with Monsieur de La Tour."

"You misunderstand me." Charles's voice had grown crisper.
"*Monsieur* La Tour stays here."

After another huddle of murmurings and "Charlots,"
Desjardins du Val turned to face Charles again. "We still all
prefer, Monsieur de Menou d'Aulnay, to accept your magnani-
mous gesture of allowing us to return to Jemseg."

The crispness in Charles's voice had sharpened to crystalline
hardness. "If you so prefer. Sergeant at Arms, escort these men
to the wharf."

"Monsieur," Desjardins du Val interjected, "might we not
first bid our adieus to Monsieur de La Tour?"

"He will be informed of your departure. Depart."

After the prisoners and their guards were gone, Jeanne went
to her husband, sitting rigidly in his chair, and said: "That was
very charitable of you, to set them free."

"Was it? It was either that or hang them. We will find it difficult enough to feed our own people through the winter, much
less thirty useless prisoners."

"What do you mean to do with La Tour?"

"Keep him safely caged in our dungeon until he can be sent
back to France on our next year's supply ship."

She felt a twist of apprehension. "Charles, in the years I've
been at Port Royal, you've never kept a man locked up down
there all through the winter. I've been told you tried once,
years ago, and the man died before the spring. What if La Tour
should die in your custody?"

"Then the Associates in France will be spared deciding what

to do with him. Now, if you will excuse me, I should have inspected the warehouse yesterday to see if the traders have prepared it for the trapping season, as they swore they would do in my absence. Various little matters have kept me from my duties."

Jeanne had duties of her own, what with three children and the château to manage. Today she performed them by rote, as though only part of her were present while the rest of her was engaged with another matter entirely.

The more she thought about it, the more she became convinced that Charles was underestimating the reaction if La Tour should die while in his hands. She was sure there had to be some alternative to keeping La Tour imprisoned all winter, but she was also sure that Charles would never be the one to initiate any further negotiations with the man.

When she came back up from the wine cellar after making tonight's selection from the governor's private stock, Charles still wasn't back from the warehouse. His absence and the trip down into the cellar combined to make a decision.

There were two sets of cellar stairs in the château. The one on the west side led down into the earth-and-timber-walled wine cellar and root cellar. The one on the east side led down into the stone-walled dungeon.

At the head of the stone steps was an alcove that passed for a guardroom. The guard jumped to his feet when Jeanne entered. She said: "I wish to have a few words with the prisoner La Tour."

The guard didn't look entirely comfortable with the idea, but he said: "*Oui*, madame," and picked up a wheel-lock pistol and a glass-encased candle. He held the lantern high to light her way as he followed her down the steps. The stones were damp with seepage and with condensation that was already forming patches of frost.

At the cell door the guard said: "If you please, madame," and handed her the lantern while he tugged a spanner out of his belt pouch and wound the wheel on his pistol. Holding the pistol in firing position, he unbolted the door and swung it open, saying: "Prisoner La Tour, you have a visitor."

There was no reply. The guard took the lantern back from her and thrust it through the doorway, still pointing his pistol in front of him.

In the light of the lantern, Jeanne could just make out three stone walls, with a sunlit slit high in one corner and a straw-covered floor. Directly opposite the door, the straw had been mounded up against the wall. Sitting on his haunches against that improvised backrest was Charles La Tour, with his manacled wrists propped across his upthrust, bony knees. His ankles were manacled as well. He had large hands, which, even dangling slackly from his knees, looked gnarled and dangerous. There was grizzled stubble on his cheeks and chin and he looked dirty and disreputable. But then, Jeanne suspected he always did, once one got close enough.

"Monsieur La Tour, I am Madame d'Aulnay."

"Ah, the broodm—that is, I am charmed to make your acquaintance, madame. I would rise and kiss your hand, but I have an inkling your friend would shoot me if I came too close."

"Are you warm enough, and being fed properly?"

"Well, the Bordeaux with last night's duckling *à l'orange* was but an indifferent vintage. And the chambermaid neglected to slip in a warming pan when she turned down the bedclothes. I thought perhaps she meant to slip in herself to make up for it, but no.

"All in all, though, this inn do seem about as comfortable as anyone could expect in this part of the country. Does that ease your conscience?"

"I would not speak of other people's consciences had I attacked my neighbor's ships and tried to sink them."

"Ah, it do seem clear-cut when it's told that way, don't it? Madame d'Aulnay, I do not need to be told that it's all due to my folly that my captain and two of my sailors are dead and my ship maimed. If you came down here to make certain I knew that, you have put yourself to needless trouble."

It was maddening, the way he could twist everything she said and make her feel almost obliged to explain herself. She reminded herself that she'd come down there for a reason, and to stick to that. "Do you know that my husband intends to keep you here throughout the winter, until you can be transported to France?"

"I guessed something of that sort, since he ain't hung me yet."

"Perhaps if you were to offer him your parole to surrender yourself when our supply ship is ready to return to France, he would let you go free till then."

"I doubt he'd trust my parole. I doubt I'd blame him."

"I'm sure you must own something valuable enough that if you gave it to him as a bond, he would trust you to keep your word."

"Ah, but then I would have to trust *him* to give it back when I kept my word."

"I'm sure if you suggested to him you would be willing to give him a surety of some sort, I'm sure the two of you could barter it out to something you could both agree on. I would suggest it to him myself, but—"

"But he don't much listen to what you suggest, do he?"

She flushed and opened her mouth again to tell him that wasn't at all what she'd been going to say. But he went on, in a tone of voice that suggested he saw something humorous in what he was saying: " 'Tis very kind and generous of you, Madame d'Aulnay, to so concern yourself with the health of your husband's enemy—just for the sake of Christian charity. I will propose this notion of a ransom to him next time I see him." Then the blue eyes within the tangled fringe of mottled hair glimmered up at her. "Though it'd almost be worth fading away to my grave in his custody, just to ruin him."

On the way back up into the sunlight, Jeanne considered how much simpler life would be if justly enchained knaves weren't dejected with self-blame but still able to make jokes about their knavery. She also considered the fact that wise rabbits didn't look into the eyes of snakes.

The supper guests that evening were two Capuchin missionaries who were taking a respite from nomading from one Micmac camp to another. When Charles rose from the table to bid his good nights, one of the Capuchins said: "Might we prevail upon you, Governor d'Aulnay, to tarry a moment longer? There is a matter we would like to speak with you of."

"Certainly, Father." Charles sat back down and so did Jeanne.

"My son . . . it would bring tears to the eyes of a saint to see two representatives of His Most Christian Majesty waging war on one another."

"We *know*," the second Capuchin injected, "that this was none of your doing. You merely defended yourself and your ships."

"But," the senior Capuchin continued, "now that your brother who raised his hand against you has been humbled, and languishes in chains, would it not be a Christian act to set him free, and leave it to the king and his ministers to pass judgment upon him?"

Jeanne could see that Charles's features and posture were settling into that bland calm that meant his blood was congealing into ice. The younger Capuchin said: "We spoke with Monsieur La Tour this afternoon—"

"A number of people"—Charles smiled—"seem to have spoken with Monsieur La Tour this afternoon. I shall have to furnish him with an appointment book."

"He is willing to swear to us on his hope of salvation that he will keep the peace, and deliver himself up to any judgment rendered by the lawful authorities in France."

"Perhaps you are not aware," Charles replied coolly, "that Monsieur La Tour pins his hope of salvation whichever way the wind is blowing. When he is dealing with Huguenot merchants or *les Bostonais*, he is a devout Protestant. When it is more convenient for him to be a faithful son of Holy Mother Church, he will kiss any crucifix within arm's reach."

The two Capuchins glanced at each other, as though debating whether to broach something further. The senior Capuchin coughed delicately, trellised his fingers, and looked back in Charles's general direction. "My son, I suppose it is no secret that Cardinal Richelieu's generous gift to our humble order is proving too much for us. When His Eminence granted us a section of Acadia to finance our missionary work, we did not realize how difficult it would be to administer.

"Our superiors in France wonder whether we would not be wiser to place our Acadian territories in the hands of a lay person who knows Acadia, and who already has in place all the mechanisms necessary to manage the fur trade and the fisheries, so that we can go back to attending only to the work of God. In experienced hands, the income to our order would no doubt increase, even subtracting a just percentage paid to the administrator.

"All our order has been praying that we might find a man who possesses such wordly attributes and resources, yet also shows himself to be possessed of a true Christian soul."

Charles looked from one to the other of the Capuchins, then said: "I will most certainly take all you've said to heart. Now, if you will excuse us . . ."

As Jeanne and Charles were on their way toward their bed from their separate dressing corners, Jeanne said: "Perhaps the holy fathers give you good advice that—"

"Does *every*one know my business better than I do? Two of *my* sailors are dead and one crippled for life because of La Tour!"

She let it go. He wouldn't have snapped like that if he weren't seriously debating whether he oughtn't to change his mind.

The next afternoon the alarm gun banged again. This time Jeanne made sure she had Joseph and Nicole safely in hand before starting for the ramparts. It was La Tour's ship again, this time flying a white flag. The sailors who climbed down into her longboat reached back up to assist a woman in a dun-colored dress.

Charles said: "I suspect we are about to meet 'Madame la Poseuse.' Might I prevail upon you, my dear, to receive her with me? Women are much less inclined to play high drama when there is another woman present."

They waited in the sitting room. Nikki opened the door just wide enough to poke his head in. "Madame La Tour asks for an interview, if you are not too busy."

Charles said: "Madame La Tour? You don't say. Hmm. Well, yes, I suppose you might just as well show her in."

She was shorter than Jeanne would've imagined, and she appeared to have two different faces—a size larger from the nostrils up. She was wearing a simple, rough wool skirt and a peasant-style corselet that somehow managed to be revealing and demure at the same time. Her only adornment was a string of pearls barely long enough to encircle her throat, with a small, silver cross dangling from it. There was no paint on her face that Jeanne could discern, but the red highlights in her hair seemed just a bit too burnished to be true.

Madame La Tour made a hesitant little curtsy and said: "Monsieur d'Aulnay . . . ?"

"Yes. And this is Madame d'Aulnay."

"It is an honor to meet you, Madame d'Aulnay."

Jeanne couldn't think of how best to reply to that shy, soft voice; obviously chastened, but still holding on to its self-respect. Charles said: "Do sit down, madame. Might I offer you a glass of wine?"

"Just a little, if you please." The pudgy little fingers twined together in the lap of the dun-colored skirt. "Monsieur d'Aulnay, you know why I have come here. My husband has been a fool. In the short time I have had with him, I've learned that he does have a good heart under all the rough corners, but he will fly off into the most mad acts and regret the consequences too late. I had hoped that, in time, I might—" She got a catch in her voice and blinked her eyes; then squared her shoulders, as though forcing herself to face what must be faced.

"None of that, of course, Governor d'Aulnay, is of concern to you. My husband has done what he has done. I am prepared to pay for the repairs to your ship my husband dismasted, and compensation to the families of the poor, innocent sailors killed—"

"We have at Port Royal the finest mast trees in the world, free for the cutting. As for compensation: I take care of my own people."

"Yes . . . Yes, of course . . ." The oversized eyes sighed

downward and the plumped-up breasts fluttered in their shift. Jeanne had never seen breasts actually flutter before. "I had merely thought . . . that I might offer . . ."

The eyes came up again; glistening with moisture, but not without their pride. "Governor d'Aulnay, I know you have reason to misdoubt that setting my husband free would not be putting more of your own people in jeopardy. But if you release him to me, I will give you any bond you wish, and pledge to do all I can to see he keeps his parole. We have not been married long, but I believe I have some influence over him.

"I have not lived the properest life in the world, monsieur. I came to Acadia hoping to find some peace. I believe my husband is old enough to want the same. If there is any more assurance you desire, tell me, and if I can furnish it—"

Madame La Tour didn't choke herself off this time, but instead popped out an achingly rueful laugh and threw her hands up hopelessly. "But what am I and mine to you, monsieur? I could beg and promise and froth about upon my knees, and what would that mean? Let my husband go, and should he ever be tempted to overreach himself again, I will do my fish-wife best to make his life more miserable than any judgment that may come down on him from France."

Charles said: "Go back to your ship. I will have an answer for you tomorrow."

"Might I see my husband before I—"

"No. As you intimated yourself, madame, there is no telling what your husband may concoct if given the least ingredients. I shall send a boat out when I have decided."

After Madame La Tour was gone, Jeanne said: "She is quite the little actress, isn't she?"

"Hmm? Oh, yes, I suppose so."

"What do you intend to do?"

"Intend? What, *I* . . . intend? I intend to wait a decent enough interval to give the impression *I've* made a decision, and then pull out my hook and toss the bastard back. Until the next time. And when the next time comes, I trust that neither you nor any holy fathers nor anyone else will pluck at me to give him mercy. If there are any of us left to consider the question."

CHAPTER 10

La Tour spent another sleepless night, with nothing but mounded straw to keep him warm and nothing in his belly but the coarse bread and vinegary wine they gave him twice a day. He tried to remind himself that he'd eaten worse before. After the Virginians burned the first Port Royal, he and Biencourt had lived for a time on boiled rock tripe, the stone-like flakes of moss that caribou nibbled off the rocks.

But he'd been young then, and not spoiled by twenty years of eating and drinking the best that extravagant fur-trade profits could buy. Perhaps he might still be able to find an appetite for the kind of fodder d'Aulnay fed his prisoners—after a day spent jogging along a forest path or paddling against the current. But not in this cage.

The slit at the top of the wall hadn't been showing sunlight for very long when he heard boots coming down the stairs. No doubt the morning watch bringing his delectable breakfast.

La Tour considered the possibility of getting his jailers accustomed to having to wake him out of a mound of straw for his morning and evening meals. One night the mound would be there as usual—perhaps with a boot sticking out of it—but the prisoner would be flattened against the wall beside the door, with his wrist chain poised to take the guard around the throat.

But then he would still be faced with the problem of getting out of the fort, and the chain between his ankles meant he wouldn't be doing much climbing or running. But if the guard carried the manacle key on him . . .

The door clanged open. The guard wasn't bearing breakfast after all, just the lantern and the wheel-lock pistol that seemed to go from guard to guard promiscuously. The guard stood back from the doorway and gestured with the pistol. "Stand up and come out."

La Tour did as he was told, pausing only to shake out as many as possible of the straws that had found their way between his skin and clothes, and to finger-comb out a few of the ones entangled in his hair. When he stepped outside the cell the guard gestured toward the stairs and followed after him.

The chain hobbling his ankles was just barely long enough to let him raise a foot from one stair to the next. The guard didn't offer to remove it or lend him a hand. As he struggled up the steps, scuffing his shoulder along the wall for balance, he asked the guard: "Where are you taking me?"

"You'll find out soon enough. Keep moving."

In the alcove at the top of the stairs, the guard set down the lantern and pointed at the outside door. La Tour obediently worked the latch and stepped out into a crisp, bright, autumn morning. The sun blinded him. He was bringing his hands up to shield his eyes when the guard prodded him hard with the pistol. He stumbled down off the doorstep. The guard said: "Turn to your right," then shoved him forward with the pistol barrel. "Move!"

La Tour regained his balance and moved along with short, shuffling steps. It occurred to him with a jolt that d'Aulnay had decided to hang him after all.

He was still half-blinded by the sun flares. What he saw on the backs of his eyelids seemed just as substantial as what he glimpsed between blinks: a sunrise over Jemseg harbor, the black-and-white facing of Château Port Royal, the wide eyes and hips of Françoise Marie Jacquelin, the camomile between the flagstones beneath his feet. . . .

He could see himself whirling around to slam the pistol out of the guard's hand. Perhaps he'd be able to get his hands on the pistol, or perhaps the guard would shoot him—which was bound to be better than the kind of inexpert hangman likely to be found around Port Royal.

The guard yanked the back of his shirt and barked: "Stand!" The last of the sun-flares faded away. He was standing in front of the raised portico at the main entrance of the Château Port Royal. D'Aulnay was standing above him, along with a few of his officers, including Nicolas Le Creux. The broodmare was there as well, with a couple of little d'Aulnays peeking out from behind her skirt.

D'Aulnay handed a key to Le Creux, who came down the steps and crouched at La Tour's feet to unlock the leg irons. D'Aulnay said: "The Capuchin fathers have persuaded me to be merciful and release you. They assured me you would give your oath on all the books of the saints to keep your parole. I assured them your oath was worthless.

"But do not delude yourself you have escaped retribution. The matter shall be reported in France, and the justice you deserve shall be decided upon by our superiors. Your ship waits in the harbor. Go."

By that time the wrist manacles were off as well. La Tour massaged his wrists and said to D'Aulnay: "I thank you for the hospitality of Port Royal. Maybe someday we can extend the same to you at Jemseg."

He turned and started across the parade square. Men-at-arms and tenant farmers and fort servants stopped to watch him pass by, calling out such pleasantries as, *"Au revoir, Monsieur La Tour, come visit us again soon."* A few Micmacs in front of the trading house stood watching silently.

The gatekeeper unbolted a door set into one of the massive front gates and slammed it to after La Tour stepped through. La Tour walked down the path to the landing stage without looking to the left or right. At the end of the long wharf two crewmen from the *Renard Noir* stood holding the boat lines. Between them stood a short woman in a silver silk gown glistening with jewelry, and pearls in her hair.

He wanted nothing better than to feel those pudgy little arms around his back, and those puffed-pigeon breasts pressed to his chest. But not while d'Aulnay's retainers were watching from the palisades and riverbank. Françoise appeared to be of like mind, so for once he restrained himself, and merely bowed to kiss her hand.

When they reached the ship, he held the bottom of the Jacob's ladder to keep it from swaying as she climbed up, and to get a good look up her skirts. Once he had his boots on deck, he wrapped his arms around her and lifted her off her feet, trying to devour her mouth with his. The crew laughed and some of them shouted: "Charlot!"

The broken steering arm had been replaced by the one that poor Jamin had insisted be always kept on hand at Jemseg. The stern railing had been crudely patched with raw lumber. There would be plenty of time over the winter for the carpenters to match the old rail with good Jemseg oak.

There was barely enough of a breeze to make much headway, and in an hour or so the tide would be running out, but La Tour didn't much feel like looking at Port Royal any longer than he had to. As the *Renard Noir* began to inch down La Rivière au Dauphin, the guns of Port Royal discharged a sarcastic salute.

La Tour said to his wife: "How did you know to be here when he set me free?"

"I didn't know he meant to release you until this morning. I came here yesterday to try to convince him."

"You *spoke* to him?"

"To him and to his wife."

"Huh. She wanted him to set me loose, too."

"Oh, did she, now?"

"She was worried I might die in his dungeon and put a splotch on his escutcheon. *He* told me it was the Capuchins persuaded him."

"You seem to have friends in a good many places."

"I have one in the best place of all."

Once the tide had carried them out into the bay, La Tour stood on the afterdeck of his ship with his arm around his wife, the salt wind scudding them across the waves, and porpoises gamboling alongside. Perhaps it was high time he started learning not to press his luck.

Françoise said: "The waves have no pattern, do they? At least none the human eye can understand. They ripple and disappear at will—as hypnotic as a campfire. If you ever again cause me to grovel to that prissy bastard, I will cut your fucking throat."

They made good time across the bay and anchored in Jemseg harbor at sunset. The fort guns roared a welcome home and the populace of Jemseg came straggling and streaming down to the landing stage; ruffians and scalawags and daughters of the forest who'd disgraced themselves with white men, men-at-arms gone *couriers de bois*, Basque fishermen who'd jumped ship to find a hiding place in La Tour's employ, half-breed children growing up wilder than their heathen mothers, sandaled priests who were as liable to drink their communion wine as serve it, farmers who rarely saw their gardens between planting and harvest. . . . They were a grand crew.

La Tour was making his way through a noisy gauntlet—shoulder punches, queries about the fleas in d'Aulnay's dungeon, rude suggestions as to why Madame had been so intent on getting her husband back soon—when the crowd suddenly quieted and parted in front of him. Down the opened aisle came Captain Jamin's widow.

Madame Jamin's eyes were red and blurry, but she held herself straight and walked with a purpose. She stopped in front of him. Before he could think of something to say to her, she spat in his face, just missing his left eye.

He had a second or two to wonder at the fact that spittle could scald, and then she was hammering at his chest and face with her fists, shrieking curses and kicking at his legs. He stood there and let her. But when she clawed her hands at his eyes, Rainville's hands took hold of her from behind and Desjardins du Val helped drag her away.

Françoise reached up her handkerchief to wipe the spittle off his cheek, saying softly: "She'll not be here much longer. Desjardins du Val made arrangements that the last of the inshore fishery ships to leave this year would come to take him back to France, and Madame Jamin has asked that she and her children go with him."

"Good. That's good du Val will be in France before
d'Aulnay can guess. While d'Aulnay is spending the winter
composing his version of what happened, du Val will already
be telling them in La Rochelle and Paris that we only sailed
out to warn d'Aulnay to stay on his side of the bay and
d'Aulnay replied with the broadside that killed Captain Jamin."

CHAPTER 11

Charles d'Aulnay knew himself to be no more nor less
susceptible to vices than most men, but there was one
he had a particular weakness for: he liked to surprise people. So
he was quite pleased to be given a double opportunity to indulge
himself. It came on the evening when the first heavy snowfall
officially commenced the season of homemade entertainments
and music and indoor games, when everybody at Port Royal
would tax their inventiveness to stave off ennui and short-
temperedness while they were walled in for the winter.

D'Aulnay waited until the last supper course had been
cleared away and the *digestifs* poured out, then pinged his sig-
net ring against his pewter cup and said: "Mesdames et messieurs, I would beg to announce . . ." He waited until the room
was hushed and all the heads along the table were turned toward him. At the far end of the table his wife was doing her
best to pretend she had no more idea of what he was about to
announce than anyone else, but her best wasn't really all that
convincing. But then, it hadn't come as a terrible disappointment to him that deceitfulness wasn't his wife's strong suit.

"I have been informed, by the best of authorities, that
the spring shall see a fourth little de Menou d'Aulnay to get
underfoot at Port Royal." He paused just long enough for the

congratulations to begin and then cut over them with: "And he or she shall be born—God willing—in France!"

His wife's eyes gratifyingly popped out of her head and she squawked: "In *France*?"

There was laughter and astonishment and celebratory toasts all jumbled together. D'Aulnay couldn't have enjoyed it more. When it died down enough that he could make himself heard without raising his voice, he said: "Yes, my dear, in France. The more time passes since the sea fight with La Tour, the more I believe I should report the truth of the matter in France as soon as possible, before La Tour can fog the air with lies. If I wait until spring to sail, you will be in too delicate a condition to come with me. You have not seen civilization for five years, and our children's grandparents have never set eyes on them. So, I have given orders that the *Vierge* be put in readiness for an ocean voyage."

Nicolas Le Creux said: "At this time of year?"

"I have sailed the Atlantic in winter before."

"Sailing her in winter is one thing, crossing her's another. Summer storms in midocean are dangerous enough, and they don't coat the sails and rigging with ice."

"You should not speak so much to your own disadvantage, Monsieur Le Creux. You see, my decision to cross the ocean in the winter will make you Governor of Acadia until next summer, or perhaps longer."

Le Creux raised his goblet in salute and nodded his gratitude, but then added: "Well, Governor of Port Royal, at least." Le Creux did exhibit an odd turn of indecipherable irony at times.

Le Creux was proved right about the storms. Barely a week out, the *Vierge* lost two sailors trying to climb ice-coated rigging to free ice-fouled tackle. The only way to make any eastward headway was to allow the storm winds to drive the *Vierge* steadily northward—how far north, d'Aulnay couldn't say. When the gales subsided, it was still impossible to get a true fix on the ship's position under a gray sky with no sun or stars.

It required an increasing effort for d'Aulnay to put a calm

face on when he went down into the cabin where his wife and children were suffering their *mal de mer.* When Joseph asked him where the ship was now, d'Aulnay would spin out a phantasmagoria of degrees and minutes of longitude and latitude that no four-year-old could comprehend. It appeared to shore up Joseph's deluded belief that his father had matters safely in hand.

D'Aulnay was pleasantly surprised by how well Jeanne bore up under the endless tossing and turning. She even made jokes about how she might just as well have *mal de mer* when she'd be suffering morning sickness anyway, and that the universal queasiness was making Marie's weaning much easier than Joseph's and Nicole's had been.

But there were times when d'Aulnay found himself losing patience at his wife's absorption in cabin discomforts while up on deck he and his crew were fighting like demons in the wan hope that anyone on the *Vierge* might live to see the coast of France. It was all he could do sometimes not to tell her.

At last the sky cleared enough to see the sun. D'Aulnay hung his astrolabe to take a sighting. The reading didn't make sense, so he checked it with his cross staff—again and again, until his arm was too tired to hold the cross staff steady. The *Vierge* was closer to the latitudes of Iceland than of France. As for longitudes, until someone invented a chronometer that kept more than approximate time, a navigator might just as well pin a map to the wall and toss a dart. Blindfolded.

He set a course southeast and put the crew on half rations. There was no point in disrupting Jeanne and the children by telling them of the *Vierge's* situation.

When the *Vierge* finally hobbled into sight of La Rochelle, she could go no farther than Chef de Baye, outside the harbor mouth. Parts of the harbor channel were so shallow that ships could only pass in or out at the high tides of the full or new moon. The *Vierge* and her crew would have to wait there for a week, but her owner and his family could be rowed ashore immediately.

When all the baggage had been loaded into the longboat and the oarsmen sitting ready, Jeanne was still combing and brushing the children's hair and clothes. D'Aulnay subtly tapped his walking stick against his shoe heel. His wife clucked. "They will think we have such sickly children. . . ."

"After a day or so of getting back their land legs and their appetites, your mother will only *wish* they were sickly children. Come along now, or we will have to be rowed in by torchlight."

As the longboat entered the harbor Joseph and Nicole gawked and shrilled: at the towers of La Rochelle, the stonework quays, the ranks of ships, but mostly at the *people*. The dockworkers alone composed several times the population of Port Royal. It was definitely high time the children were made aware that there was a larger world outside Acadia.

Unfortunately, that wasn't the only thought the sight of La Rochelle harbor brought to mind. D'Aulnay could feel his cheeks beginning to burn with a memory he'd just as soon forget, of the first time he'd brought a ship from Acadia to La Rochelle. He trailed his hand in the water to cool his blood and keep the blush from showing.

It had happened in the days when Governor Razilly was still alive. Governor Razilly had entrusted d'Aulnay with the annual shipload of furs. Upon arriving in La Rochelle, d'Aulnay had gone directly to a certain petty official and ordered him to authorize the unloading of his cargo, to take an inventory and to assume responsibility for any items lost or damaged in the unloading process. The petty official had replied rudely that the duties of his office did not include running errands for La Compagnie de la Nouvelle France, at least not without a written request from the Hundred Associates. When d'Aulnay reminded the official that he'd had no qualms about performing those duties for the previous year's fur ship, the response was: "That was only because the captain was Charlot La Tour. Now kindly vacate my office and come back when you have something signed by your superiors."

As the *Vierge*'s longboat kissed the quay the boatswain leaped out and scurried off to hire a carriage. Jeanne wanted to send a messenger ahead to give her family some warning, but d'Aulnay wasn't about to let a surprise like this slip through his fingers.

The house of Louis Motin de Corcelles was a new-built, stone-and-brick affair with its nose pressed to the street. D'Aulnay tapped the head of his walking stick against the door and then stepped side. A footman stuck his head out with a supercilious expression that dissolved into: "Mademoiselle *Jeanne* . . . ?" And then there was a bedlam of echoing shrieks, clatterings down the hallway, Jeanne's father padding along in his carpet slippers, Joseph and Nicole gaping dumbly at these aged strangers picking them up and covering them with kisses. . . . D'Aulnay couldn't have enjoyed it more.

Eventually the whirlwind set the de Menou d'Aulnays and the Motins down in a sitting room looking out onto the neatly ordered gardens behind the house. D'Aulnay sat turning a cup of wine in his hand, silently surveying his surroundings while everyone else chattered.

He'd forgotten how *new* everything was at *chez Motin*. The chair he was sitting in, and all the other sumptuous pieces of furniture, had been made during Louis Motin's lifetime. The rose bed beyond the window had the too-pristine look of green growth. At Château Charnisay, or any of the other de Menou residences, there wasn't a room without at least one chair or painting that had been old before there was a New World, and the climbing vines in the rose arbors were as thick and gnarled and dark as a Nubian blacksmith's arm.

He found it difficult not to feel at least slightly offended that the newly rich could be so newly rich. But then, he reminded himself, this particular son of Château Charnisay wouldn't have much of a life at Port Royal if it weren't for a certain family of nouveaux riches bourgeois.

His father-in-law broke in on his musings with, "I still find it hard to believe you crossed the ocean in midwinter." D'Aulnay shrugged as though someone had evinced surprise that he'd walked safely to the end of the garden and back. "It is a stroke of fortune for us all that you did, though, or there might've been no supplies to Port Royal next year."

"Excuse me . . . ?"

"The widow Jamin, through Desjardins du Val, has accused La Compagnie de la Nouvelle France of her husband's death. La Compagnie's supply ship has been impounded until the suit is settled."

It was d'Aulnay's turn to be surprised, and he didn't enjoy it in the least.

CHAPTER 12

Françoise sat gazing out her frosted windowpane at the snow-and-flagstone cobweb of the courtyard and the outbuildings caught like insects in the web, feeling gloomy. She knew that her gloominess wasn't because Jemseg had been hip-deep in snow for three months. She preferred the pristine Acadian snow to the slush and muck that made up so much of the winter in France. And the snow meant La Tour was constantly bundling her and Lorette up in furs to teach them how to snowshoe or careen down the hills on a toboggan. As long as Jemseg was choked with snow there was also a feast at least once a week, with the twin dining halls filled with firelight and music and the intermingled smells of several dozen different kinds of dishes steaming on both tables.

She suspected that a part of her gloom came from the gloominess of the sky. It had been unbroken gray for more than two weeks. Without a bit of sunlight from time to time, living things were bound to start wasting away.

But she knew that was only a small part of it. She knew what was at the heart of it, but she didn't want to dwell on it, because there was nothing she could do to change it. She had woken up that morning to discover she was having her *règles*—that her body was once again obeying the law of cycles ruling women. She was a few days late, and during those few days she had allowed herself to hope.

She couldn't shake herself out of that ever-narrowing spiral leading down to those two occasions long ago in that hag's kitchen. The good God knew what other damage those knitting needles had done inside her. It seemed a harsh judgment of the good God that she and La Tour should pay now for mistakes she'd made when she was so very, very young. But the Huguenot God she'd grown up with was not only good, He was just. She wondered just when it was, somewhere back along the road of her life, that she'd stopped wishing there was some justice in this world and started wishing that there wasn't.

Loud voices broke in on her from the sitting room below. It sounded like Lorette shouting, "Out! Out!" and a deep, male voice grumbling something unintelligible. Françoise wiped her eyes and went to look, grateful to find something outside of herself to draw her attention.

There was no man in the sitting room. Lorette was sweeping the floor and Jeanne La Tour, Minou's eldest daughter, was standing oddly transfixed, with a feather duster poised over a side table and her eyes on Lorette. Françoise said: "Who was being murdered down here?"

Lorette's reply was metronomed by the swish of broom straws. "I was trying to sweep the floor and a Micmac came in the back door looking for 'La Tou.' I told him La Tour was over at the trading shed, and Jeanne translated it to him, but he still would not leave. He squatted down on the floor to wait. I swept around him as long as I could, and then swept him out the door."

The picture of Lorette brooming an armed savage out the door was so perfectly Lorette that Françoise couldn't help but giggle. Her giggles were interrupted by the bang of the door from the sitting room to the courtyard. Jeanne La Tour was gone.

Françoise and Lorette looked from the door to each other and shrugged in unison. Françoise said: "If you've done with your sweeping, perhaps you will sit down and take a cup of tea with me and tell me what I've decided we should have for supper."

But they'd barely gotten the kettle on the fire when the outside door was flung open again. La Tour stood in the doorway with snowflakes drifting in over the shoulders of his bearskin coat. One mittened hand held his coiled dog whip. He said: "Neither of you cross this threshold till I've found the trail," and slammed the door.

Françoise looked at Lorette, who appeared to be at least as mystified as she. Françoise went to the door and opened it. La Tour was kneeling in the snow, trying to tie on his snowshoes and whistle with his fingers at the same time. She started toward him, saying: "Whatever is—"

"Don't," he barked, "cross that threshold till I've gone." He whistled out a piercing blast and all his dogs came running, along with every other dog that happened to be loitering about the fort. He whipped them back, all except the ridiculous-looking one with the shaggy fur of a Micmac dog combined with the floppy ears and saddle-patch markings of a French hunting hound.

He pointed the dog's nose to a trail of biggish-looking footprints that was quickly getting feathered over with new snowflakes. The dog got down to business. It started following the trail with a stiff-legged gait, its nose plowing a furrow in the snow, then raised its head and began to run. La Tour loped after the baying hound and disappeared into the tunnel through the gatehouse.

Françoise stepped back inside and closed the door. Lorette looked to her for an explanation. Françoise could only shrug and sit down to drink tea with Lorette and wait for an explanation to present itself.

They waited a long time. Françoise had just about decided to go back upstairs and try once more to coax that devilishly complicated tune out of her flageolet, when she heard voices approaching the outside door. La Tour, looking flushed and glistening from a run in the fresh snow, held the door open and said: "Lorette, come outside. And bring your broom."

"Why?"

"Because I tell you to. Come along now."

Lorette put on her shawl, picked up her broom, and went outside. Françoise trailed after her. There was a shambling-looking Micmac or Maliseet standing in the snow. He had a very painful-looking, raw, red welt under his jaw. Other people around the courtyard had stopped what they'd been doing to see what was going on.

La Tour said to Lorette: "Kiss his hand."

"What? I will *not*!"

"Do it. Or the next ship that leaves here for France will have you on it."

Françoise started to say: "*I* decide where Lorette does or does not go!" but the look she got from La Tour cut off her words like a knife across her throat. In the time they'd had together, she'd seen La Tour in many moods, but this was the first time she'd seen a La Tour who made her believe the whispered stories weren't exaggerated, the stories of the La Tour whose enemies died by the sword, or gun, or poison, or inexplicable accident, but invariably died before they crossed him twice.

La Tour spoke in Micmac to the shambling-looking man, who squinted at him and then dubiously extended his right hand. La Tour gestured fiercely at Lorette, who stooped with her face burning and took hold of the hand. The Micmac started to jerk his hand free, then goggled in amazement as she kissed it. When she let go his hand, he raised it up to stare at it and then at Lorette, tentatively rubbing the fingertips of his left hand over the back of his right.

La Tour said: "Now hand him your broom." Lorette held the broom out. The Micmac looked at La Tour, who nodded. The Micmac took it from her uncertainly, then got a glint in his eye and swept some snow up against Lorette's skirt; just a few brushed flecks at first, then enthusiastic scoops. He swung the broom up over her head with a murderous howl, then laughed and just shook it, so that the snow clinging to the straws filtered down on her head. Still laughing, he proffered the broom back to Lorette. She snatched it and ran back inside, with her hand over her mouth and her eyes fountaining.

There was general laughter all around the courtyard, but not from Françoise. She said to La Tour: "I would speak with you," and followed Lorette through the door.

Lorette was nowhere to be seen, although Françoise could hear her footsteps pounding up the staircase. Françoise took up a position beside the hearth and restrained herself until La Tour had come in and closed the door, stomping snow off his high-topped winter moccasins. Then she let fly with, "What kind of swine-hearted excuse for a man amuses himself by humiliating a girl like—"

"Humiliating? *Humiliated*, is she? So, in her humiliation she will hide herself away and cry her eyes out and sulk for a day or two? I found *him* hanging from the limb of a tree!"

"What?"

"People *saw* him being chased out the door by a girl slapping at him with a broomstick! Even if no one else had seen him, he saw himself. He was too polite to take the broom away and break it over her head, or stick his knife in her belly. But he was shamed. So he found himself an oak tree with a convenient knoll beside it, knotted one end of his tumpline around his neck and the other around a stout branch, and jumped off the knoll.

"If he had had some better schooling in the hangman's art, if his tumpline hadn't stretched a little, if Hound didn't have such a good nose, Birdwhistle's family would now be gutting him and encasing him in birchbark until the weather clears well enough for a trip to the burial island."

"Just because of . . . of *that*?"

"It might seem ridiculous to us, but it would seem ridiculous to them that you or I might feel guilt for bludgeoning the other to death while we was drunk. As things are, Lorette might just as well've stuck a pistol in his eye and pulled the trigger."

"How was Lorette to know that?"

"Well, that don't change what—"   ,

"And she *still* does not know."

"Then I guess I'd best tell her, hadn't I?"

"If she will listen, after that."

She found Lorette sniffling in her room, hugging her knees on her bed with the quilt pulled up over her head. "Lorette . . . ? If you come downstairs, La Tour has something to say to you."

"*More?*"

"Come along now, dear. He wants to explain. Dry your eyes and hold your chin up. Never let them see you weep unless it's useful."

When Lorette had been sat down grudgingly beside the sitting-room hearth, La Tour pulled his chair up close and leaned forward to tell her why he'd done what he'd done to her. As it sank in, both her hands flew up to cover her mouth again, and her eyes swelled wider. She squeaked through the latticework of fingers: "I didn't know!"

"But of course you didn't," La Tour soothed. "How could you? After thirty years and more here *I* am still befuddled. Just last spring, when they all go out to the nesting islands for seabird eggs, I went along with them and I happened to do something or other that broke some taboo or other—I still ain't sure which. As things was, it seems the only way to wipe away the insult was for me to stay where I was while they all came up one by one and cracked an egg atopst my head."

"*You?*"

"Decidedly me. The worst part was the children. I had to crouch, you see, so's the little ones could reach the top of my head, and by that time I was so blinded with egg drippings I could hardly keep my balance. It went on for hours: *crack*, dribble, dribble; *crack*, dribble, dribble. . . . And I couldn't have picked an island of dainty little plovers—not me—it had to be an island of big, fat gannet eggs and goose eggs and . . ."

By the time he'd done spinning out the story, Lorette's tears of humiliation had become tears of laughter, and Françoise had begun to wonder just which member of the family had spent half a lifetime on the stage.

When Françoise and La Tour were cosseted in under their impossibly extravagant bedcovering of interwoven marten pelts, he started to nuzzle her neck and grope her belly in a decidedly unslumberous manner. She pushed at his hands and murmured: "La Tour . . . La Tour?"

"Hmm?"

"It's . . . um . . . It's my full moon."

"Your which?"

"I am bleeding like a stuck pig, you dolt!"

"Oh. Then you do wrong to go anywhere near the cook-house. Or near me, for that matter."

"Excuse me?"

"The people of the country believe that if a woman in her fully-stuck-pig moon touches her hand to any food her man may eat, or any tool or weapon he may use, he will grow weak and lose his breath on the trail. Why do you think Minou disappears for a few days from time to time?"

"I took it as a blessing and left it at that."

"You still have much to learn. For my part, I believe in doing as the Romans do—when the Romans can see me. When in dark corners, I does what I likes, regardless what customs rule in Rome or Acadia."

"Then, were I to touch my hand now to some tool or weapon you may have in mind to use . . . ?"

"A dolt like me would likely go ahead and use it anyways."

CHAPTER 13

Jeanne Motin de Menou d'Aulnay sat in a closed carriage rolling along a slushy road outside Loudon, feeling uncomfortable. Her torso was rigidly encased in a stiff-bodiced gown and a corset laced as tight as her advancing pregnancy would allow. But that wasn't why she was feeling uncomfortable.

They were traveling to one of her husband's family's country residences to spend a few days with her father-in-law, René de Menou—the "d'Aulnay" hadn't become part of the family name until Charles inherited the *seigneurie* of Aulnay from his mother.

Jeanne had met René de Menou only once before, and briefly, when he'd passed through La Rochelle to have a look at the girl his son appeared to have an interest in. She remembered a white-wigged man in white silk, who was neither warm nor cold. He was a councillor of state and adviser to the king. He was accustomed to drinking his chocolate with the queen, or with his cousin Cardinal Richelieu. No matter how many times Jeanne tried to assure herself that she was a member of the family now, she couldn't stop feeling that her hair was on crooked, and that the finest manners she could master would seem fit for a barnyard in the eyes of René de Menou.

The carriage slowed and turned to the right, careening for a moment as one of the wheels mired. Charles fingered up the slotted shutter beside him and said: "See, Joseph, we are approaching the gates of your grandfather's house. Those crooked black lines in the snow over there are your grandfather's vineyards. These trees flanking the drive were no taller than you when they were planted by your grandfather's great-grandfather, and now the ends of their branches meet high above us. Riding down this road in summer is like entering a green cave."

Jeanne lifted the shutter on her side of the carriage, wrapping her cloak around herself and around Nicole in her lap. Before turning her gaze out the window, she glanced at the seat opposite, to make sure the nurse was doing the same with her own cloak and Marie.

Beyond the gnarled trunks of the avenue of trees, Jeanne could see a stand of garden trellises showing silvery with age against the muddy snow, and a statue who looked very cold with nothing to cover her but a coating of ice. And then she saw the house.

It was a Renaissance castle, with turrets and towers and crenellated palisades. The carriage passed through the gates into a courtyard that the entire fort at Port Royal could have been set down into. The coachman eased to a halt in front of a broad, marble stairway guarded by two stone warriors who weren't all that much better robed against the weather than the poor nymph in the garden.

Footmen came running to swivel down the carriage steps and offer their arms as banisters. When Jeanne and her family reached the top of the grand entrance stairs, the great door swung open magically and an aged man in livery bowed them in with, "Welcome home, monsieur."

Charles said: "Thank you, Gilbert. It is good to see you are still spry enough to remain on active duty."

"We can but try, monsieur."

They were in a long, high-ceilinged hallway lined with full-length portraits of people wearing court dress or pieces of armor. Through a doorway at the distant end of the hall came a man in black silk and white lace and a curled white wig that looked like spun glass.

Charles pushed Joseph forward. Joseph cast a look of terror back over his shoulder. Jeanne nodded and smiled, to assure him he'd be safe, and motioned him ahead. Joseph turned his head to face the oncoming apparition and manfully steeled himself to take a few steps toward it. Then he swept off his little hat, just managed to maintain his balance through an attempt at making a leg, and said: *"Bonjour, Monsieur mon grandpère."*

René de Menou responded effortlessly with a courtier's making-of-a-leg that any ballet master would envy, simultaneously fluttering his hand down in a beautiful series of arabesques. "Monsieur Joseph de Menou d'Aulnay et de Charnisay, I presume," he said.

Charles and his father kissed each other on both cheeks and then the councillor of state turned to Jeanne. He wasn't as tall as she'd remembered, and his sharply handsome features had begun to blur with age. "And my dear daughter-in-law." His lips touched both her cheeks like a breeze barely lifting a lock of hair.

Jeanne said: "This is your granddaughter Nicole."

"What a pretty, delicate child." He made no reference to the fact that Nicole had been Charles's mother's name.

"And this is little Marie."

"What a pretty, delicate child." He turned back to Charles. "I had expected you to arrive at an earlier hour."

"So had I, *mon père,* but the roads are mud and ice."

"I suppose no man is master of the weather," although it seemed to Jeanne his tone implied that men of sufficient substance could negotiate with it. "But this does mean—as desolated as I am to confess it—that dinner shall be served within less than half an hour of your arrival. Which puts you at a great inconvenience to have so little time to make yourselves at ease in the rooms prepared for you and to exchange your traveling garments for dinner attire. The fault is most entirely due to my ill planning. . . ."

"Not at all, *mon père.* The half of an hour is more than time enough for us to prepare ourselves. It is *my* regret that our rudely late arrival has robbed you and us of the opportunity to sit down together and reacquaint ourselves in a leisurely fashion before dinner, as we all would wish."

"It is more than generous of you, Charles, to so take the fault upon yourself when it is not deserved. There will be time enough at dinner, and into the evening, and throughout the remainder of your stay, for all of us to say and hear all those things which circumstances and distance have made us perforce leave unsaid for so long. Gilbert will show you to your quarters. The footmen will have brought your baggage up the service stairs by now."

The children were to eat in the nursery where their father spent much of his childhood, so there were four at dinner. The fourth was a priest who looked more to Jeanne like a bishop-in-waiting than a household chaplain. The glare off the candlelit rows of silverware emblazoned with the de Menou arms was next to blinding. In the shadows beyond, liveried servants lurked poised to whisk away each course at a snap of the steward's fingers.

René de Menou ate elegantly, taking only a few bites from each course, as though the point of sitting down at table were to demonstrate one's artfulness at manipulating various sizes and shapes of glittering utensils. The priest and Charles both followed suit in maintaining the impression that their bodies weren't subject to such coarseness as requiring food. So Jeanne did her best to restrain herself from gorging for two. The corset helped.

Over the second fish course Charles told his father of the sea fight on La Baye Françoise, and of the La Rochelle law courts impounding the company's supply ship. His father said: "It is unfortunate you happened to kill this Captain Jamin."

"It could not be helped."

"I suppose not—not once you made the decision to attack the sterncastle, where the officers stood, rather than any other part of the ship, where the deaths of a few common sailors would not come back to haunt you and La Compagnie de la Nouvelle France.

"But, fortunately, I still have some little influence at court. In the face of a decree bearing the king's seal, any order from the petty courts of La Rochelle would melt away like an April snowfall. Would you like me to see to it that the matter is represented to the Conseil du Roi?"

"I would be very grateful, Father."

"It is but a trifle. What father would hesitate to do the same for his son—were he fortunate enough to be in a position to do so."

The father-and-son conversation about Charles's life in the wilds of Acadia carried on throughout the meal. But it seemed to Jeanne that it was just the same pattern repeating itself over every fresh course: anything Charles had done that could be construed as a mistake was pointed up; every success was taken as a matter of course.

After the last palate-freshening sorbet had been cleared away, René de Menou said: "Who would have thought there might ever come a time when a son of the de Menous would find himself enmeshed with shopkeepers, and vitally concerned with their affairs? For that is all La Compagnie de la Nouvelle France and all their brethren are. A well-fed shopkeeper is still a shopkeeper.

"It is hardly to be laid against your account, Charles. It is the same in every corner of France in these bright new days. People who could hardly tell you the names of their own grandfathers are sailing about the streets of Paris in sedan chairs; building pink marble châteaus on the profits of tradesmen's usury; granted audiences with the king; buying marriage alliances with families who impoverished themselves in the service of France while these *people* stayed safely away from the battlefields, toting up their profits from the sale of swords—people we would not have had for *servants* in the old days."

Jeanne screwed her jaw tight and fixed her eyes on the fragments of a standing suit of armor that were catching the candlelight, back in the shadows where the servants lurked, saying to herself: I *will* not let him see a tear. It took all the restraint she had in her not to shout: The de Menous were quick enough to take my dowry of shares in a trading company! But that would have been exactly the kind of outburst René de Menou expected from a shopkeeper's daughter.

Once she and Charles had retired to his dead mother's bedroom, though, Jeanne could restrain herself no longer. "How *could* you sit and nod and smile and not say a word while he said those things of us? Or do you agree with him?"

"Of us? Which things?"

"Us! You and me and our children! 'Tradespeople we would not have had for servants . . .' "

"He was not speaking of us."

"Of *who*, then? Who else? Is my father not a *tradesman*, even if a fat one?"

"Shh—I can hear you well enough, my dear, without the whole house having to hear as well. I am sure my father would be desolated to think that his beloved daughter-in law—"

"Beloved?"

"Yes. In his way. You must keep it in mind that my father has spent his life at court, and carrying the de Menou name through intrigues and wars and insurrections. . . . He does not so easily reveal himself, like . . . like . . ."

"Like some tradesman?"

He sighed and pushed his fingers through his hair. "The world that he and all the de Menous before him lived in is changing, and he is too old to change with it. He was merely expressing his confusion. It is a very rare event for my father to admit to anything of the kind, and I think you should feel privileged that he so regards you as part of the family that he did so in your presence."

"*Privileged?*"

"Jeanne—my father is my father, and your father is your father, and we cannot exchange them for other fathers. Now, you may be perfectly content to wear your corset all night long, but I intend to rid myself of this tight-waisted jerkin immediately."

CHAPTER 14

In the spring Françoise was late again. After the last time she refused to be tempted by hope. It was difficult, though—with the berry bushes in clouds of blossom and the trees growing greener every day—not to be seduced by the conceit that the same thing was happening inside her.

To keep her mind off it, she decided to plant a garden of her own behind the fort. One of Jemseg's "farmers" had gone completely *courier de bois* and let his cleared field go wild again. It was a simple enough matter to pace off a not-too-ambitious plot and hire one of the "farmer's" less-feral brothers to burn off the brush and plow it anew.

She discovered, though, that putting little onion seeds and peas into the earth wasn't the best thing for keeping her mind off what she wanted to keep it off. But working in the garden did leave her too tired at the end of the day for her mind to race in many circles, and she could distract her evenings by making lists of seeds and hardy roses to send back with this year's supply ship to a nursery gardener she knew in La Rochelle. She'd decided that the building housing her and La

Tour's quarters needed climbing roses to make it look less like a barracks.

As La Tour was massaging her aching back one night, he grumbled: "I fancies myself able to sympathize with most quirks of humankind, but one I won't ever understand is some people's habit of working when they don't need to. We already get all the green food we can eat from our farmers' gardens, and from the people of the country bringing in wild roots and such."

"And how long do you think we will get all we need from the 'farms' of Jemseg, as they grow more slovenly every year? Besides, I have an ambition to show your father even bigger cabbages than he grows at Cape Sable."

"How many cabbages can a man eat?"

"If you ate more cabbages and less meat, you might not keep me awake with groaning over your swollen belly."

"If I ate more cabbages you'd not sleep at all, at least not downwind. Well, break your back like a peasant if it amuses you, but at least don't go paying out good money for plowmen and such. I already pay them beyond their worth."

She had to laugh. What else could she do with a man who balked at two or three sous extra paid out to some of his *engagés*, and then would spend a thousand *livres* over the winter feasting those same *engagés*?

The moon passed through all its phases and her garden sprouted higher, with still no sign that there wasn't life sprouting inside her as well. She resolved to wait another week at least, perhaps two, before allowing herself to believe it.

But the day after she'd made that resolution, Keeshetech came to Jemseg with the bottom half of his face painted black. "La Tou. You father, Monsieur Claude, seen his last sun. Two, three days ago."

La Tour put his hand over his eyes and slumped into the nearest chair. Françoise moved behind his chair and put her hands on his shoulders. Without lowering his hand, he rasped out a question in Micmac. Françoise had assimilated enough of the language by now to understand from Keeshetech's reply that Claude de La Tour had died in his sleep beside his Catherine.

The ropy shoulders under Françoise's hands leveled out as La Tour straightened his back. He rubbed his hand across his eyes and lowered it to the arm of his chair, sighing in a long breath through his nose. Then he said flatly: "Well, there's no one can say he didn't live himself a life."

Keeshetech wrinkled his eyebrows, raised his eyes to meet Françoise's, and then lowered them again to La Tour. She interpreted it as Keeshetech's version of looking astounded. La Tour thanked him for bringing the news and Keeshetech departed, glancing back over his shoulder with the perplexed vee still creasing his forehead.

La Tour said: "Keeshetech had braced himself, you see, to see me fly into a weeping fit and tear at my clothes. Then all the surviving family members would gather and weep together and make speeches about the dead man for three or four days without taking a bite of food. Different customs. As for me, I think I will drink a bottle of brandy."

He called one of the house servants to fetch a bottle from the cellar, and called another to fetch the new captain of the *Renard Noir*. Before opening the bottle, he instructed the captain to sail for Cape Sable with the next tide and bring Catherine to Jemseg if she so desired, along with whatever she wished to keep from Port La Tour.

Then the cork came out of the bottle and went into the fire. Françoise helped him drink the brandy, although if she'd matched him cup for cup she wouldn't have stayed upright for long. It went to his head quickly. He began to tell long, misty-eyed stories of his father, some of which made him laugh so hard he was in danger of falling out of his chair. Perhaps customs weren't so different after all.

Old Père Montagne came running from the chapel to express his condolences and to assure the bereaved that God's mercy was infinite, or nearly so. La Tour said gravely, although it seemed to Françoise he was suppressing something just the opposite of grave: "I suppose you'd best say several Masses for his soul."

"If you would have it so, my son."

"Three at least, I'd guess. My father did do a bit of sinning in his time."

"If you wish it, my son."

The instant Père Montagne was out the door, La Tour exploded in guffaws that threatened to choke him. Françoise slapped his back and indulged him by asking what was so amusing. He took another drink, gasped, wiped his eyes, and said: "Dead Masses are Père Montagne's prime stock-in-trade. When Keeshetech's father died, Père Montagne told him his father's soul was in purgatory, and painted a very grim picture of the place. He told Keeshetech the only way to get his father out of purgatory was for Masses to be said for him. But Masses don't get said for free. So they struck a deal that Keeshetech would do some bits of work around the chapel while Père Montagne was saying the Masses, and would pay Père Montagne a half a dozen prime beaver pelts as well.

"So for three days Keeshetech chops firewood and suchlike and then comes with his string of beavers and says to Père Montagne: 'My father out of that bad place now?' And Père Montagne says: 'Yes,' and reaches for the furs.

"But Keeshetech holds the furs back and says: 'You certain sure my father out of that bad place now?' And Père Montagne says: 'I am certain your father is no longer in purgatory,' and reaches for the furs again. And Keeshetech—"

La Tour sputtered and had to take another drink before going on. "Keeshetech says: 'Then he be some damn fool to go back there,' slings his furs over his shoulder, and walks back into the woods."

The people of Jemseg began to trickle in. They would come in twos and threes, have a small drink with their governor, perhaps reminisce about his father if they were old enough hands, and then exit to make room for the next little group. Another bottle came up from the cellar, and then another.

At a moment when Françoise and La Tour were alone, and he was mumbling for the hundredth time that there was nothing to be sad about—because the old man had danced with the

devil for seventy years and always come out smiling—
Françoise said: "It *is* sad he did not live to see his grandchild."

He squinted at her, blinking confusedly. Then he had to
blink faster, to keep the tears from running down and melting
the bumpkin grin.

Rainville and La Tour's master gunner had to help him up
to bed—Rainville having the easier time of it, because he
didn't have to stoop to get his shoulder under his stepbrother's
arm. They eased him down onto the marten-fur blanket, patting
his hand and muttering: "Sleep good, Charlot."

The *Renard Noir* returned with Catherine de La Tour. She
informed her stepson that his father had been laid to rest beside
his garden, and that she wouldn't be staying at Jemseg very
long. "There is a war in England. The Puritan Parliament has
rebelled against the king. The queen has fled to Holland for
safety. When your supply ship comes, I will go back with it to
rejoin my queen."

When Françoise told her her own news, Catherine waggled
a finger at her. "I *thought* that was not rouge on your cheeks.
I know it is frightening to think of giving birth out here in the
back of nowhere, but some of the women *sauvages* are as
good midwives as any in France, and we are all the same
under our skirts. What do you intend to call him or her? Or
have you thought?"

"Claude."

"Yes, so you would."

The next ship to sail into Jemseg harbor found Françoise beginning to show a little. She'd ceased wearing even the abbre-
viated, peasantish corselets, for fear of constricting her
blossoming miracle. She wasn't certain how much of her per-
petual, Madonna-golden haze was natural and how much was
her playing up the part, and she didn't care.

She stood with La Tour on the battlements above the gatehouse, watching the unknown ship negotiate the passage past
Partridge Island. La Tour squinted hard, then said: "Ah, she's
the *Jonas*. Some years du Val sends the *Amitié de La Rochelle*,
sometimes the *Jonas*. What say we go down and welcome
her?"

Standing on the landing stage watching the *Jonas* find an anchorage beside the *Renard Noir*, Françoise was amazed to realize what the *Jonas* signified about the life she'd relegated herself to. Once a year, if that, there would be news and goods from France. The annual supply ships and the occasional visit from a fishing ship were the only vestige of an umbilical cord between the mother continent and the limpets clinging to the new one. The amazing part was that it didn't bother Françoise in the least, except for the practical consequences if the cord should be severed.

When the *Jonas*'s boat was about halfway between the mother ship and the landing stage, Françoise made out a black-haired man wearing several shades of black, hunkered like a boulder in the boat's bow. La Tour suddenly began to hop up and down like a birthday child and shout: "Gargot . . . ? Gargot?"

The man in black stood up to wave his arm over his head, much to the consternation of the oarsman. La Tour's hopping and shouting grew even more frantic. Françoise clamped her hands around his arm and said: "Don't *dare!*"

"Don't dare what? Oh. No fear, I would only do that for *you*, my dear." But she kept a tight hold on his arm just in case. "Gargot helped me with the building of our fort. Truth to tell, he was the one made all the decisions about guns and bastions and such. The last I heard, he was back soldiering for the king and got hisself captured by the Spaniards."

As the boat drew closer Françoise could see that the black-haired man's black clothes were closer to gray in places: layers of salt-rimmed, battered leather and wool and patched sea-boots. His face was so deeply pockmarked she had to look carefully to discern that he was probably about ten years younger than she.

Once the boat was alongside the landing stage, Françoise decided it would be safe to let go La Tour's arm. He practically tore the black-bearded man out of the boat. They slapped each other's backs and then La Tour turned to her. "Madame Françoise Marie Jacquelin, Monsieur Nicolas Gargot de La Rochette."

"*Enchantez,* madame." His voice was like a keg of nails rolled down a gangplank.

La Tour said: "I thought you were rotting in a Spanish dungeon?"

"There was an exchange of prisoners."

"How many Spaniards did they get for you?"

"Not so many as they could if they knew the king meant me to oversee the defenses of the coast of Brittany. But that grew so dull I was glad when Desjardins du Val said Jemseg fort was more than due getting put in order by a man as knows his business."

"And *I* do not?"

"You may be a fine man for rallying the troops, La Tour, but not for seeing to it that their gun barrels ain't rusted through since last used."

La Tour called to Rainville to launch the shore boats to help off-load the *Jonas*'s cargo. Gargot muttered: "There may not be near so much cargo as you expect."

La Tour said: "How so?"

"The Sieur d'Aulnay launched a countersuit to the widow Jamin's. We had to slip out of La Rochelle before we got impounded, with half our cargo still sitting on the quai.

"*But*"—the cratered face turned to Françoise—"Desjardins du Val made a particular point that our cargo included the article requested for madame—a lady's maid who is also a seamstress, complete with many bolts of cloth for manufacturing Milady's gowns."

In point of fact, any gowns manufactured at Jemseg in the near future would be for Lorette, who was filling out like Claude de La Tour's pea pods. Françoise intended to wear nothing but shapeless smocks for the next five or six months. But she curtsied graciously. "*Merci*, Monsieur de La Rochette."

"Make it 'Gargot,' madame, if you please."

"If you will make it 'Françoise,' monsieur."

Over supper Gargot said: "Tomorrow morning, La Tour—if you can rouse yourself from your bed—I can start inspecting your ordnance to see how badly it's decayed since I put it in place. I might even give you a lesson or two on the best fields of fire to defend your harbor."

La Tour said: "While you are still snoring in your bed I will be roused and waiting impatient."

Françoise said: "And so will I."

Gargot furled his forehead at her. La Tour shrugged. "Madame do like to acquaint herself with all matters pertaining to her garden, including how to defend it from corsair woodchucks."

So for the next three days Françoise followed La Tour and Gargot and Jemseg's master gunner around the palisades, learning the difference between culverins, demi-culverins, sakers, cannons. . . . She also learned that Jemseg's only real artillery was all in the stone bastion facing the harbor mouth; the log-walled redans at the other three corners of the fort held only stubby little, short-ranged guns.

Another thing she learned was that whatever Gargot said about his craft was gospel, and she didn't learn that from Gargot. Jemseg's master gunner was old enough to be Gargot's father, but he ducked his head apologetically when Gargot clucked at the residue on his finger after wiping a touchhole, and he beamed when Gargot cocked his head and nodded appreciatively at the line a cannon was permanently sighted on.

Gargot loaded one of the long-barreled sakers in the stone bastion and said: "You see here, La Tour? Any enemy who don't want to get his ship mired on the way in must come through that narrow channel between the sand spit and the island. Look along the line I sighted her and you'll see you have him. Watch. . . ."

The master gunner handed Gargot a smoldering match. Gargot blew on the end of it and reached it toward the saker's touchhole, but La Tour blocked him with his arm. "Gargot . . . the fish weir is close beside the channel, and the Maliseet village just beyond. I would rather you did not—"

"Then I *will* not. But perhaps Madame would be so kind. . . ." and Gargot handed Françoise the ruby-headed rope.

She blew on the end of it, arched an eyebrow at La Tour, and thrust the match into the powder in the touchhole. The blast and buck of the gun made her jump and drop the match. Out in the channel between the sand spit and the island, a fountain rose out of the water.

Gargot stooped to pick up the match, saying: "Forgive me, I should have known you would be startled."

"Can we do that again?"

After supper every night Françoise got the distinct impression that Gargot wanted to say something in particular to La Tour, but was waiting for her to leave them to themselves. So she made a point of sitting up until one or both of them went to bed.

One night Gargot finally gave in to the fact that whatever he wished to say to La Tour would have to be said in her presence. He clunked his goblet down decisively and said: "Things are going ill for you in France."

La Tour said: "Things?"

"Desjardins du Val is doing what he can, but the de Menous have so many friends at court. . . . Du Val can't swear the furs you send back on the *Jonas* won't get impounded. He don't know if he can send you any supplies at all next year."

La Tour very carefully lined up a crumb on the table and flicked it off, then said: "He had best find a way. We have barely enough powder and shot for this winter's trade, much less to defend ourselves."

"Ain't much even a clever snake like du Val can do until the suits and countersuits get settled. Could take years, once the lawyers get their teeth into it."

"How the Christ am I supposed to live? How does du Val expect to live?"

Gargot just shrugged helplessly.

Françoise looked at the two case-hardened warriors staring at the tabletop. She clunked down her own cup and said: "Take your furs south to Boston."

Both men looked at her like she'd gone witless.

"Have you not told me that the English in Boston have more resources than many towns in Europe? *Les Bostonais* trade in furs, do they not? They have powder and shot and whatever else we need to live, do they not? You have traded with them before, have you not?"

La Tour said: "Only a little. By the backstairs. Not so much that their assembly would have to take notice of and approve."

"Why would they not approve?"

Gargot tugged his lip thoughtfully. "It would not be as though they'd be trading with the pope. A good Protestant like La Tour . . ."

La Tour shook his head. "Even if the Boston Assembly approved, word would get to France. And His Most Christian Majesty would *not* approve."

Françoise said: "We are already being strangled in France! And it would only be until du Val can resolve the suits and—"

"No," La Tour cut her off. "You may even be right, but it don't make any difference, because I can't go to Boston. I can't leave Jemseg."

"Why not?"

"I suppose, Gargot, you'd best tell her why Desjardins du Val thought it was time you came and polished up our defenses. I didn't need to be told."

Gargot seemed reluctant, but nonetheless said: "No one can say whether du Val's wits or d'Aulnay's bloodline will win out in France. But either way would make no difference, if Jemseg was already in d'Aulnay's hands, or the hands of his man Le Creux. The courts in France could wash their hands of the matter and d'Aulnay would be Governor of Acadia."

Françoise said stupidly: "You think he means to attack us?" It seemed madness to picture a French ship sailing in to bombard a French fort. She reminded herself of all the French armies who'd fought French armies in her lifetime, and that English armies were even now fighting English armies. But she'd thought that the New World was supposed to be an escape from that.

La Tour stated flatly: "It would be a fool thing for him to try, as long as I'm here."

Gargot shrugged. "La Tour may not know a demi-culverin from a siege mortar, but I wouldn't fancy coming after him on his home ground."

"Who knows," La Tour continued, "what orders d'Aulnay left with Le Creux? So far, Le Creux's stuck to his own side of the bay while his master is away. But if he knew that I was gone to Boston . . ."

"Then stay here and let Gargot go to Boston in your stead. Gargot knows what supplies we need, and you can send one of our fur traders along to do the dickering for him." Both men leaned back in their chairs, raised their eyebrows, and scratched their chins. "And while you are in Boston, Gargot, you should be able to find at least one gardener who grows climbing roses. . . ."

CHAPTER 15

As springtime in France steadily fattened into summer, d'Aulnay grew steadily more anxious to be back in Acadia. His wife had presented him with a healthy new son, and both mother and child were now perfectly fit to travel. But the *Vierge* remained riding at anchor in La Rochelle harbor. There was a myriad of reasons, but they all came down to the same two things: money and La Tour.

Those two pernicious elements had become so intertwined that d'Aulnay could hardly see a skin between them, and they infected every facet of his life: the Capuchins were reluctant to let him manage their money until he was absolved of the sea fight with La Tour; the contretemps with La Tour had so discomforted Governor Razilly's heir that he was willing to sell out all his Acadian rights to d'Aulnay, but that required money.

So while Jeanne and the children whiled away the summer in her father's house, d'Aulnay was traveling to Paris and Loudon and Lyons and various estates along the way, working

at being charming to his father's friends on the Conseil du Roi
and his father-in-law's friends in banking and trading houses.
He felt like he was trying to assemble an intricate machine
while circumstances pressed a pistol against one ear and a ticking clock against the other, and the pieces kept coming apart in
his hands.

What time he did manage to spend with his family wasn't
necessarily a respite. After a day of actually clapping eyes on
his own children, he was padding barefoot toward a bed he'd
actually seen before, with his actual wife in it, when she said:
"How long will you be here this time?"

"Three days. Perhaps four."

"And then?"

"Then it is back in that bedeviled carriage to Paris and another interview with Claude de Launnay-Razilly."

"You spent less of your time pursuing La Tour in Acadia
than you do in France."

A rocket went off behind his eyes. He stood stock-still,
breathing very slowly, to restrain himself from throttling her
while screaming: I am trying to keep us from *drowning*, bitch!
He reminded himself that she could hardly be expected to
know that his peregrinations had as much to do with money as
La Tour, since he hadn't told her.

He considered telling her now. But just the thought of putting his burdens onto her, like a boy whining to his mother,
made him blush with shame. So he just said: "I do not do
these things for pleasure." He climbed into bed and took her,
but there wasn't much pleasure in it.

The roses in Louis Motin's garden bloomed and died and
the supply ship came back from Port Royal. D'Aulnay and La
Compagnie de la Nouvelle France had managed to free her
from the lawsuits brought by La Tour's agents, but only by
posting a substantial bond of money.

Along with her cargo of Acadian furs and hides and Micmac
gimcracks, the ship carried a long letter from Nicolas Le
Creux. D'Aulnay sat down in the rose garden to read it without
interruption. But before he reached the bottom of the first

page, there was a sentence that made him spring up and go looking to tell his wife.

He found her in their bedroom, feeding baby René. D'Aulnay had grown accustomed to the sight over the years, but it still seemed a bit distasteful that she should do it herself instead of hiring a wet nurse. But then, there weren't many wet nurses available in Acadia, and he intended the family to be back there before René was weaned.

D'Aulnay flourished the letter and announced: "I have been reading this, from Le Creux—"

"Oh! Are Anne and the children well?"

"Oh. He mentioned that everyone is in good health. No doubt he contributes further domestic detail farther down. But *first* he informs us that . . ." He had to pause to restrain himself from crowing it. "La Tour sent his henchman Gargot to Boston, and has entered into a formal agreement with *les Bostonais* for trade and mutual defense!"

She merely regarded him quizzically with those distended, nursing-bovine eyes. Sometimes she could be exasperatingly obtuse. He gave her a hint. "Boston is an English colony."

"I know that."

"La Tour has allied himself with a foreign power. It is *treason*."

"Oh."

He could see she still hadn't grasped it, but she would when its effects unfolded. In the meanwhile nothing could restrain the little imp at the back of his head from capering and singing: *La Tour is money, money is La Tour. . . .*

The effects took their time unfolding. Winter came down on France without the Conseil du Roi bringing down a judgment on matters in Acadia. At times d'Aulnay found himself harboring the treasonous thought that his father's influence at court wasn't what it once had been.

While he waited for the mill wheels of court to grind along in their stately fashion, d'Aulnay settled on a merchant named Emmanuel Le Borgne as the likeliest cure for his financial ills. Jeanne's father warned that once Le Borgne got his hooks in they were difficult to extract, but d'Aulnay was willing to do a deal with the devil at this point.

D'Aulnay sat sipping chocolate in Emmanuel Le Borgne's office while the merchant peered at lists of annual returns from Port Royal. Le Borgne looked the perfect type of a La Rochelle Huguenot: a rodent of a man dressed as though a hairsbreadth too much lace on his collar would bring the wrath of God down on his head.

Le Borgne set down his rolls of paper and said: "If Acadia is such a mine of gold, why do you not do your father-in-law the favor of allowing him to invest?"

"He has already invested heavily. Although he is far from a pauper, he is not the richest man in France."

"Louis Motin does well enough for himself. And what he has he did not get by putting his money into sinkholes." It would be such a pleasure to apply the pommel of a sword to those rodent teeth. "You said that you and Claude de Launnay-Razilly had settled on a figure . . . ?"

"Yes. He has agreed to sell to me all his interests in Acadia for fourteen thousand *livres*, payable at two thousand *livres* a year over seven years."

"At what interest?"

"Interest? He is a gentleman. The figure is more than reasonable. His share in Port Royal alone is worth"—d'Aulnay couldn't resist a smug smile—"some sixty thousand *livres*."

"Strange, then, he would sell out for so little."

D'Aulnay cursed himself for so smugly misstepping. On the deck of a warship, or with a rapier in his hand, he knew within a hairsbreadth not to overreach himself, but this mincing about with bankers' ledgers was another matter. He tried to repair the damage with, "Monsieur de Launnay-Razilly has lost his stomach for the stakes, just at the moment when he was about to recoup—thereby leaving it open for another man to reap the profit from his investment. I doubt the profit will come this year, or even the year after, but it will come. I am told, Monsieur Le Borgne, that a lack of tenacity is not one of your failings."

"I like to think not."

Oh well, a lack of any sense of irony wasn't crippling in a financier. "Monsieur de Launnay-Razilly has also agreed to advance me four thousand *livres* against the expenses I will incur by assuming his responsibilities."

"On what security?"

"I have an older brother who is sickly and childless."

"That is a stroke of luck. Monsieur, if I am to be your agent in France, I must have a free hand. I will see to fitting out your ships, to marketing all your exports from Acadia. . . . In short, a marriage of commerce. Polygamy is an abomination."

"A marriage requires a dowry."

"How much?"

"In order to establish me—*us*—in secure mastery of all Acadia, I would require an advance of, say . . . twenty thousand *livres*."

"That would strain my capital to the bursting point. Say fifteen thousand *livres*."

"I am not adept, Monsieur Le Borgne, at market haggling. Say eighteen or have done with it."

"Eighteen, then. I will have the papers drawn up within the week."

D'Aulnay went back out to his snowcapped carriage unsure of whether he'd settled for less of an advance than he might've, or whether he had indeed become adept at market haggling. Either way, he didn't feel particularly proud of himself. He was only glad his father hadn't been there to see it.

In the spring the *Vierge* sailed out of La Rochelle at the head of a convoy of three chartered ships and one new-bought, all four loaded down with trade goods and colonists and armaments and men-at-arms. In the strongbox in the owner's cabin was a deed from the Holy Order of Capuchins, entrusting all their lands in Acadia to Charles de Menou, Sieur d'Aulnay et de Charnisay. Snugged in beside the deed was a declaration from Governor Razilly's heir, assigning all his inherited rights to govern Acadia to the Sieur d'Aulnay et de Charnisay.

But the prize document in the strongbox was a decree bearing the seal of His Most Christian Majesty, ordering Charles de Saint Étienne de La Tour to surrender all his Acadian strongholds into trustworthy hands—namely those of the Sieur d'Aulnay et de Charnisay—and return immediately to France to answer charges of treason.

As the towers of La Rochelle dropped into the distance, d'Aulnay stood on the sterncastle of his ship with his nostrils drinking in the clean air of the ocean opened up in front of him, his seaboots braced wide against the plunging of the waves, and his wife and children beside him. He put his arm around his wife and said to his family: "I hope you can find it in your hearts to forgive me for neglecting you this past year. I shall never need to do the like again."

CHAPTER 16

La Tour lay in the sun on the hill above his fort, with his head pillowed in his wife's lap, watching the wet nurse feed his son. He was of two minds whether Claude oughtn't to be weaned as soon as possible. He knew Françoise would be much happier when she didn't have to be reminded several times a day that her own breasts gave hardly enough milk to feed a mouse. No one could suddenly embark on motherhood at the age of forty and expect all the machinery to function perfectly. But he knew there was nothing he could say to persuade Françoise she wasn't failing to be a whole mother to Claude. Women were funny that way.

Fortunately, Keeshetech had come up with a Micmac girl who'd just had a baby of her own and had breasts more than adequate for two. Besides being more than adequate, they were damned decorative, which was why La Tour was of two minds.

At the moment said taut, ripe, copper-tinged globes were

dappled with soft green light filtered through the willow leaves nodding above. Claude was selfishly obstructing his father's view of the right one, but the left was interesting enough on its own: with a willow-leaf pattern of light and shade molded around it, caressing the brown areolae as the wind tickled the leaves. . . . Watching Claude's fingers knead the right one, La Tour could feel the ermine-smooth skin and buoyant texture through his own fingertips. If he weren't an old married man . . .

The girl settled Claude into the crook of her arm and, sad to say, lifted the shoulder thongs of her dress back into place. She rose gracefully to her feet, saying in French: "She fed good." The Micmac language had no gender differences. Consequently, depending on which of the French pronouns a given Micmac happened to learn first, everything and everyone was "she" to one or "he" to another. La Tour had gotten used to it, but if Claude didn't get weaned before he started absorbing words, it might cause him permanent confusion.

Françoise pushed his head out of her lap so she could reach up and take Claude to burp him. The Micmac girl took her daughter's cradleboard down from the bough she'd hung it on and wandered away. La Tour leaned his elbow on a handy pad of moss and plucked a grass stalk to work between his teeth, listening to the sounds of Françoise's voice crooning chirpy nonsense, the soft slapping of her hand on naked baby flesh, and Claude's gurgling and hiccuping.

Out of the gurgling erupted a belch that sounded like a cannon going off. La Tour looked up to see whether Claude had blown himself to flinders, then down at the fort. A puff of smoke was dissipating over the seaward bastion. It *had* been a cannon going off.

He stood up—a somewhat creakier operation than it once had been—and squinted at the harbor. There was a shallop coming in. He muttered: "That's odd."

Françoise said: "What's odd?"

"A boat coming in, not one of ours. It do seem unlikely any *Bostonais* would come all this way in a shallop. . . . Maybe Le Creux across the bay has trouble."

"Or maybe his master is back."

"Not without some Micmac or Maliseet bringing me word of it first. Unless he sent the shallop off the instant he made port . . ."

"If he *is* back, I hope he learns from Le Creux that it *is* possible for Jemseg and Port Royal to get from one year to the next without shooting at each other."

"Well, I suppose I could stand here scratching my chin all day. . . . Do you want to come along and see, or . . . ?" She held up her hand for him to help her to her feet. Claude started to wail against being jerked awake just when he'd dozed off with a belly full of warm Micmac milk, then promptly dozed off again with the swaying motion of his mother's progress down the hill.

Gargot and Rainville were sitting in the dining hall with three sea-weary-looking gentlemen. Gargot said: "I was about to send a search party. These gentlemen bear a dispatch from the Sieur d'Aulnay et de Charnisay. I haven't broke the seal."

The glob of red sealing wax bore the de Menou arms. La Tour took delight in cracking them apart. The paper appeared to turn red as his eyes absorbed d'Aulnay's words: His Most Christian Majesty Louis XIII ordered Charles La Tour to surrender all his Acadian establishments and present himself in France to explain why he should not be hanged as a traitor.

Before La Tour's eyes got as far as the elegant signature, his hands clapped together, crumpling the paper between them. He mashed it into a ball, threw it into a corner, and said: "Lock these men up."

One of the three gentlemen sputtered: "But, monsieur . . . !" Another sprang out of his chair and started to draw his sword. Without leaving his own chair, Gargot kicked him behind the knee and he sat back down abruptly on the floor. Rainville had his own sword out and had placed himself between the gentlemen and Françoise.

La Tour whistled through his fingers and a half-dozen good-for-nothing layabouts came running, armed with everything from an harquebus to a beam auger. La Tour detailed Rainville to escort the three gentlemen to Jemseg's dungeon: a log shed with a bolt on the door. As the prisoners were being herded out La Tour shouted after Rainville: "And their crew as well! And impound their boat!" Rainville cocked a flaxen eyebrow over his shoulder, but he knew better than to ask why he'd been asked to do something until after he'd done it.

Françoise said: "What the devil did it say?"

La Tour retrieved the ball of paper and uncrumpled it for her. She read it aloud for Gargot's benefit. Gargot chewed on a mouthful of wine for a moment, swallowed, and shook his head, growling: "This don't look good, Charlot."

"Good? It's enough to make a man lose his dinner— d'Aulnay flouncing off to France and coming back with *this*!"

Françoise said: "Imprisoning the messengers will not change it."

"No, but it *will* let him know I ain't one of his peasants he can send lackeys around to bring to heel. Do you see the king's seal anywhere on that paper? For all I know, what the actual decree says—if there even *is* a decree—don't resemble in the least what that paper says it says."

Françoise said: "Were it not the truth, he would have to be the fool of the world to inveigle you back to France with that letter in your possession. Not even his noble family could save him then."

"He knows I dare not go to France. The instant I sail out the Baye Françoise, he comes and takes Jemseg. That's what all of this has always been about. He wants Jemseg."

Françoise looked skeptical, so he explained. "His fattest year for furs at Port Royal ain't a third of a lean year here— even ignoring those Micmacs on his side of the bay who bring their furs here for old time's sake. Rivière au Dauphin is only one little river on a tongue of land. On La Rivière St. Jean, and the ones within a short carry of her, canoes can come here from as far as Quebec or the Gaspé or halfway to Boston. Even when he and I still kept up the rule to share our profits, he was salivating for it all."

Gargot said dourly: "You may be right, Charlot, that he wants Jemseg. But methinks he'll not be satisfied until he has your head."

"He'll not have it."

Françoise said: "Gargot can keep d'Aulnay out of Jemseg while you're gone to France."

Gargot shook his head. "I must go back to France on this year's supply ship—if du Val manages to send one. If he don't, I must get myself across to the seacoast before the fishing ships sail home. A year away from the duties the king pays me for is bad enough. Two years would ruin me.

"But even could I stay here, I couldn't stand in La Tour's stead. Commanding disciplined soldiers is one thing, but I misdoubt anyone but your husband could rouse Jemseg to face down a siege. And if you think that a compliment, it takes a motley to lead a motley crew."

The big eyes in the small face turned to La Tour. "So what will you do?"

"Would that I knew."

"You cannot ignore an order from the king."

"Who's to enforce it? I can hold this place against any force d'Aulnay can muster."

Gargot grunted: "No doubt. And the next year, or the year after, two or three of the king's warships will sail in here and pound this place to dust if the outlaw don't surrender himself."

La Tour was beginning to find them both increasingly annoying. Particularly since they both kept sounding right. He said: "I will give him Port La Tour, to show obeyance to the order. He could take it with a toy cannon anyways. And when you go back to France, Gargot, you can carry a letter to Desjardins du Val. Du Val can explain to the king's ministers that I fear to leave Acadia until they can arrange some assurance that I will still have something to come back to after I prove to them I am no traitor."

That seemed to satisfy both of them for the nonce. But Françoise wasn't at all satisfied with the reply he penned to d'Aulnay. She said: "I will sit down and write it for you, and you can sign it."

"I know I ain't near so elegant as your Parisian poets, but—"

"Elegant? Was it necessary to suggest that the earliest de

Menou founded the line upon a consort who was half-baboon and half–truffle rooter?"

"Well . . . my father always taught me to tell the truth, when necessary."

A week after La Tour had given a Maliseet a row of fish-hooks to carry the rewritten reply across the bay, the *Vierge* appeared off Partridge Island and dropped her anchor out of range of Jemseg's guns. Her boat rowed in under a white flag, delivered a sealed piece of paper to the first *engagé* to reach down from the landing stage, and scuttled back to the *Vierge*.

La Tour cracked apart the de Menou arms once more. The Sieur d'Aulnay et de Charnisay would have it known that he had already taken possession of Port La Tour and all the goods and chattels therein, for which he had not required permission from the traitor La Tour. And that from this day forward, until such time as the rebel La Tour complied with every article in the royal decree, the mouth of La Rivière St. Jean was under blockade.

La Tour laughed. "I'll sink the bastard! His ship's a sitting duck out there."

Gargot said: "Sink her with *what*? I misrecall stumbling over any siege mortars hidden away around here."

"We can take the sakers from the bastion and build a shore battery on—"

"And while you are dragging your sakers through the bush, he will sail in past you and merrily blaze away at a fort stripped of its guns."

"Then what we will do is sail the *Renard Noir* out and—"

"La Tour, I first went soldiering when I was thirteen years old, and I'm still in the trade. But if you mean to sail out your *jacht* to take on a ship with two gun decks, commanded by a man who kicked your teeth out when he had nothing but a few squib guns on a ketch, you do it without me."

"Well . . . then it do look as though the only choice we have is wait him out."

It turned out to be the other way around. La Tour was expecting a ship from Boston, bearing trade goods, provisions, and arms to barter for Jemseg furs and coal. The Boston ship appeared right enough, and turned tail at the first shot across her bow from the *Vierge*, clapping on full sail for home.

A Micmac brought the news that there was another ship coming up the bay, a bigger ship than *les Bostonais'*. La Tour had himself rowed across the harbor and climbed the hill to take a look. When the mysterious ship came into view, he blessed that sly contriver Desjardins du Val. She was the *Amitié de La Rochelle*.

The *Vierge* moved to intercept her and the *Amitié* sheered off. As night came down they anchored within sight of each other but not within gun range. D'Aulnay was subtle enough to know the fine line between blockading and piracy.

Given the *Vierge*'s position in the ship channel, La Tour gauged it wasn't possible to sneak even a rowboat past her in the night. But it was possible to sneak a dozen canoes through the woods to a launching place opposite the *Amitié*. A totable canoe couldn't carry as much cargo as a longboat, but they would have all night to relay back and forth.

The birchbark flotilla was halfway to the *Amitié* when the moon came out. La Tour looked to the *Vierge*. The moon was only a sliver, but that was enough for the *Vierge* to weigh anchor and drift toward the dark shapes on the water with her bow guns blazing.

The canoes raced back to shore. In the morning the *Amitié* was gone.

La Tour sat in his firelit dining hall sucking a pipe of Maliseet tobacco to death and drinking the last of last year's shipment of brandy. Françoise, Rainville, and Gargot sat trying not to look glum. Gargot said: "Keeshetech says he can take me across the bay tomorrow or the next day, and set some of his people there to taking me across the peninsula before the fishing ships set sail for France."

"Then I best get busy on the letter for you to carry to du Val."

"No use now," Gargot pronounced grimly. "That strategy was for du Val to mount a delaying action. Delay is your worst enemy now."

La Tour considered asking Gargot to represent him to the

Conseil du Roi. But Gargot had already compromised his military commission enough without irrevocably binding his name to that of an accused traitor. Desjardins du Val was too obviously mercenary an advocate, and was doing all he could as it was. Rainville would undoubtedly take it on if asked, but seductively charming colorations of testimony were hardly Rainville's strongpoint. And, in the end, any representative who might be construed as an errand boy would be an insult to the Conseil du Roi.

La Tour turned his pipe around to stare at the bear's face carved into the stone bowl and asked it: "What the Mother of Christ am I supposed to do? I must go to France and I must stay here."

Françoise Marie Jacquelin stretched her stubby little hands wide on the tabletop and said to them: "I have been wondering what they're wearing in Paris this year."

PART II

ALWAYS EXPOSED

"It is indeed quite certain that one can live there with as much satisfaction as in France itself, provided that the envy of the French, one against another, does not ruin the best-intentioned plans. . . . Otherwise nobody will ever work with zeal to make this land habitable, and it will continue always exposed to the encroachments of the strongest, or of those who will have the greatest influence."

—Nicolas Denys, *The Description and Natural History of The Coasts of North America (Acadia)*, 1672

CHAPTER 17

Nicolas Denys sat on the quai at La Rochelle, furling his fingers through his beard and looking out across the harbor at the ruins of his dream. It wasn't much to look at, actually: just the tip of a mast poking out of the water where the seawall met the chain tower.

He had finally managed to scrape together the twelve thousand *livres* to hire a ship and fill her hold with empty barrels and salt and trade goods. Although it was late in the season, there was still time to get to the Grand Banks before the cod migrated to warmer waters, then do a bit of trading along the Micmac coast and be back in France before the worst of the winter storms. With the profits from the voyage, he would be able to equip a ship for the inshore fishery next year. After a few successful seasons at the inshore fishery he would have enough capital to persuade La Compagnie de la Nouvelle France to grant him a concession to build a fortified trading post and fishing base in northern Acadia, and eventually a sawmill. By the time Denys's new daughter grew old enough to take communion, there would be a permanent establishment there, with an army of *engagés* working the fishery in the summer and taking lumber out of the forest through the winter. All that from the seed of his scrimped and borrowed twelve thousand *livres*.

Last night had been a new moon, so Denys had been due to sail that morning. His chartered ship's captain—a man with a reputation for watchfulness at sea—had left her riding by one anchor only, manned only by half a dozen indifferent sailors on the night watch. A southeast gale had come up in the night and

149

snapped her cable and drove her toward the seawall and the chain tower, dashing her against them till her hull cracked and she sank in the harbor.

Denys was vaguely aware that a boat with two females onboard was docking at the end of the quai. But his attention remained concentrated on that forlorn mast tip fingering out of the waves, to see if it showed any signs of angling out of the perpendicular. If the ship beneath it managed to stay upright until low tide, there was still a chance he might be able to pump her out and caulk her and float her free. But if she heeled over and turned turtle with the motion of the tides, he'd be lucky to salvage a few brass fittings and a sack or two of trade beads.

"Monsieur Denys . . . ?"

It was a female voice, coming from behind him. He turned to look, then jumped to his feet and tugged his hat off. "Ma-demoiselle Jacquelin! That is—Madame La Tour!"

She favored him with that impish smile that showed her crooked tooth. " 'Madame Jacquelin.' I was too old to change. You remember Lorette . . . ?"

"But of course. And Gargot! I thought you were in a Span-ish prison?"

"Not recently."

"And this"—Madame Jacquelin lifted the bit of white cloth sheltering the head of the infant in her arms—"is Monsieur Claude de La Tour."

"Ah, and so the world turns. Claude de La Tour is mourned and Claude de La Tour is born. And where is Monsieur Charles de La Tour?"

"Still in Acadia. I suppose it is no secret that the Sieur d'Aulnay inveigled the Conseil du Roi into bringing charges against him?"

"I did hear me some rumor."

"But my husband hesitates to leave Jemseg unprotected while the Sieur d'Aulnay is in Acadia."

"Your husband is a wise man."

"So I am come to France to plead his case for him. And

you, Monsieur Denys? Do you still have a wish to return to Acadia someday?"

"I *will*. It is but a matter of time. The good God sends us tribulations, but if we persevere, like Job ... Where will you be staying in La Rochelle, madame? You must come and sup with my family some evening."

"Most probably at the sign of the White Shell, but only for tonight. Tomorrow morning we must start for Paris to set about arranging an audience with Cardinal Richelieu."

"You cannot speak with Cardinal Richelieu."

The large eyes sparked impishly and the small mouth twitched into dimples. "Oh, I may not have the advantage of an illustrious family name, but I still have some influence at court. Cardinal Richelieu is a devoted *amateur* of the theater. I once acted in a play he wrote—though it was hardly my métier. He may not be fond of Huguenots, but he knows that without us there would be no theater, since the pope has forbidden Catholics from the stage."

"Be that as it may, madame, you still cannot speak with Cardinal Richelieu. No one has spoke to him these past two months, excepting his doctors and the king. The king comes to his bedside every morning, to feed His Eminence a coddled egg with his own hand. All of France expects to go into mourning any day."

A flicker of lost child passed over her face. But she firmed up her features and said: "Then I suppose I shall have to find another avenue."

"Just so, madame. May the good God show you the way. If there is any assistance I can lend you in my poor way, I can always be found through La Compagnie de la Nouvelle France."

"Thank you, Monsieur Denys. *Au revoir.*"

"*Au revoir*, madame. *Au revoir*, Gargot."

Instead of *au revoir*, Gargot replied: "Shoulder to the wheel, Denys," with an odd tang distorting his face into something resembling a wink. But then, Gargot had always been subject to inexplicable twitches of the humors.

Denys sat back down to trellis his fingers in his beard and

go back to peering at that scratch line of a masthead against the seawall. It appeared to have moved. The tide was going out. Perhaps it was only the lowering of the waterline that made the mast appear to move.

Almost deniably at first, and then with gathering speed, the tip of the mast dipped toward him until it disappeared under the waves. The water bubbled with a trapped pocket of air escaping from the hold. An empty barrel bobbed up to mark the grave until the tide carried it away.

CHAPTER 18

Françoise sat in the inner sanctum of the La Rochelle offices of Desjardins du Val Associates, sipping Rhenish wine and waiting for Desjardins du Val to say what he was thinking of saying. He was affecting to study the inventory she had brought with her, itemizing how low Jemseg's stores had sunk since the blockade set in. But she was quite sure he'd absorbed it at a glance. He kept pursing his mouth and chewing on his mustache, or flicking his eyes up toward her and then dropping them back to the inventory, or clearing his throat and opening his mouth and then abruptly sealing it shut again.

Since she'd last seen du Val, he'd gone the reverse way through the metamorphosis she'd seen on their way to Acadia. His earring was gone, his cheeks were unstubbled, his lank hair no longer looked like water would run off it, and his keglike torso was encased in immaculate, stiff-starched wool and linen. She had a feeling he imagined he would rather be living as rough-edged a life as La Tour or Rainville. No doubt he truly would have during the summer just past, which he'd spent as a guest in one of His Most Christian Majesty's prisons, for attempting to smuggle aid to the rebel La Tour.

Du Val finally leaned back from the inventory, tapping his fingers on the arms of his chair. He directed his gaze at a spot just beyond her right shoulder and said: "The Grand Prior of France, Cardinal Richelieu's nephew, is now also the Vice Admiral of France. He has final authority—next the king—over all marine matters. He could, if he chose, inform the Conseil du Roi that Charlot must be allowed to remain in Acadia to defend the Baye Françoise from privateers. He could even furnish you with a warship to carry our supplies past d'Aulnay's blockade.

"But, people wait months for an audience with the grand prior. And, once you had waited those months, there is still no certainty he would listen to *you* over a decree from the Conseil du Roi.

"However . . . there is a certain admiral he *does* listen to, on all matters. This admiral could arrange an immediate audience, if he so desired. And he could advise the grand prior that it would be for the good of France to assist you. If he so desired.

"The admiral, you see, is . . . an old man." Du Val's eyes shifted to meet hers for the first time since she'd sat down in his office. "But not *that* old." The keg-head shoulders gave a twitch—as though his natural inclination was to add a shrug, but wasn't certain it would be appropriate.

Françoise went back to the inn and dug out the gown she'd brought along in case she had to tell her tale to other men than Cardinal Richelieu. Her seamstress-maid back at Jemseg had made it for her for the New Year's feast, when Françoise had decided it wouldn't hurt to remind La Tour that birthing one child hadn't made her into a shapeless matron.

She stripped to her shift and sat down to attend to her face and hair. It wasn't easy without a proper dressing table, but Lorette held the hand mirror for her and saw to the back of her coiffure. With a bit of powder and rouge and kohl, and a judicious beauty spot here and there, she was quite clearly a woman still in her prime. And quite clearly a woman who—though respectably married—was still known to be occasionally flattered by gallant attentions. But only occasionally, and only very gallant ones.

She had Lorette lace the corset somewhat tighter than her rib cage had become accustomed. But being able to breathe in only short, fluttery gasps would have its advantages. The deep burgundy velvet of the gown brought out the henna highlights in her hair. What with the corset and the stiff brocade bodice panel, her breasts were so squeezed together it was a struggle to insert a delicate cambric handkerchief down between them. But that would also have its advantages.

She completed the effect with a heart-shaped locket on a short gold chain, to draw attention to the hollow of her throat and next-to-bare shoulders, then debated whether to add on a crucifix. She'd grown so out of practice she hadn't thought to ask du Val which religion the admiral practiced. She decided that even in La Rochelle, an adviser to the Grand Prior of France must be Catholic.

Lorette stepped back and cocked her head. "You look beautiful, Françoise." But there was something stiff about the line of Lorette's mouth.

The officer who threaded his way toward Françoise through the mob in the admiral's waiting hall smirked. "You are Madame du Jour?"

"La Tour."

"That, too. You wish to see the admiral . . . ?"

"Yes. I do not expect his time will admit for seeing me today, but if an appointment could be arranged for—"

"Oh, I expect he will see you today. Almost immediately, in fact, if you will come along with me."

He escorted her up a staircase and along a broad corridor where men wearing swords stood berating each other, men not wearing swords scurried back and forth with stacks of paper, and women with mops and rags attended to the floor and windows. There was an anteroom with several secretaries standing scribbling at high desks, and beyond it a cavernous room with several richly dressed men gathered around a chart table. They raised their eyes off the map when she was ushered in.

The officer escorting her said: "Monsieur? This is Madame de La Tour."

"Ah." The oldest of the map readers smiled. "Madame de La Tour." He had a nose like a scimitar and teeth the color of strong tea. "We will continue this later, messieurs."

The other gentlemen bowed and made their exits, the last to go closing the door behind him. Françoise said to the admiral: "It is in fact 'Madame Jacquelin,' monsieur. I had lived a full life before I married, so I kept my own name."

"Ah, Madame Jacquelin."

There was a settee set against one wall, the kind modeled after a Roman dining couch: a sloping arm at one end and the other end open. The admiral gestured her toward it, saying: "I have not been privileged to meet your husband, madame, but I have certainly heard much of him. You say he has been unjustly accused?"

"Most certainly, monsieur." She perched at the head of the couch, with her corset holding her torso rigid. The admiral lounged back at the foot of the couch. "My husband can be impetuous at times, as all men can, but he is no traitor. Whatever violence he has done has been only to protect himself, and me."

"Tell me how it has come to pass that two officers of France should be attacking each other's ships and blockading each other's harbors?"

She told him, at some length. He seemed genuinely appalled that Acadia had degenerated into civil war, and genuinely intrigued when she pincered her thumb and forefinger deep down her décolleté for her handkerchief to dab at her eyes. Not that she wept outright: any actress worth her salt learned early that it's trying *not* to weep that does the trick.

By the time she'd finished, the admiral was holding her hand and patting it soothingly. He said: "Your tale has deeply affected me, my dear. I should like to learn more of what life is like in the wilds of Acadia. Would you be so good as to sup with me tonight?"

"Oh, monsieur, that is a gracious invitation, but—" She got that little catch in her voice that always sounded so natural if she didn't use it more than three or four times per performance. "So long as this sword hangs over my husband's head, I am so distraught that I can think and speak of nothing else, and am no fit company."

"I understand. I shall look into the matter further, and report it to the grand prior. If all is as you say—which I am sure it is—I believe he will decide it would be in the best interest of France that Monsieur de La Tour remain in Acadia until peace is restored there."

"Oh, monsieur, that is *very* kind of you. But I fear it will do no good."

"No good? If the Grand Prior and Vice Admiral of France decides your husband must protect the Baye Françoise from privateers, not even the Conseil du Roi can dispute him!"

"I do not doubt that for a moment, monsieur. But even if it is decided my husband may remain in Acadia, how can he without provisions and trade goods and ammunition? Our supply ships are not strong enough to win past the Sieur d'Aulnay's blockade.

"It is not only my husband and myself I think of, but of France. The Sieur d'Aulnay has not lived long enough in Acadia to inspire the same loyalty in *les sauvages* as they feel for my husband. If their old friend were gone from La Rivière St. Jean, *les sauvages* would have no reason not to take their furs to *les Bostonais*. Half the trade of Acadia might be forever lost."

"You give me much to ponder on, madame. And I rarely ponder long before I act. I shall speak to the grand prior about granting you an audience. Go back to your lodgings now and rest, and know that you have a friend who is doing whatever is in his power."

"Oh, monsieur! Already my mind is more at ease."

Not many days passed before a message came to the inn informing her of an audience with the Vice Admiral and Grand Prior of France. She dressed somewhat more discreetly than she had for the admiral—although one never knew with clerics. She took along the letter from the Recollet missionaries headquartered at Jemseg, attesting to the fact that La Tour was too ill to travel to France. Well, he *had* been cripplingly hungover the morning she left.

The audience was brief. She was as persuasive as she could be in so short a time, making a point of reiterating the threat of privateers and of France losing Acadia's trade, in case the admiral had forgotten to mention them. She left feeling that the matter had already been decided, but the grand prior had inherited enough of his uncle Richelieu's manner that it was impossible to guess which decision he had made.

A messenger came to her inn bearing a communiqué from the admiral. *Madame, I believe I have accomplished your desire. If you come to me tomorrow afternoon at two of the clock, I shall have something to place in your soft little hands.*

She arrived at the appointed time wearing the exact same costume he'd appeared to find so appealing the first time, except for the addition of a string of pearls in her hair and a bit of slack in her corset. The chart table had no map on it this time. Instead there was a dusty bottle of wine, two silver goblets, two official-looking pieces of paper, a lit candlestick, a stick of sealing wax, and a cylindrical, silver seal.

As the door closed behind her the admiral showed her his brown teeth and proffered one of the goblets, saying: "I presumed you might find this an occasion for celebration."

"I can but hope so, monsieur."

He gestured her toward the settee and remained standing by the chart table. He held up one of the documents. "This, madame, informs the Conseil du Roi that the Vice Admiral and Grand Prior of France has decided that it is for the good of France that Charles de Saint Étienne de La Tour remain in Acadia until the Baye Françoise is safe from privateers."

"Oh, *monsieur!*"

"And this"—he held up the other piece of paper—"is a decree that the agents of Charles de Saint Étienne de La Tour may have the use of one of His Most Christian Majesty's warships, and a retinue of marine soldiers, to safely deliver the supplies required by Monsieur de La Tour to maintain his presence in Acadia."

"*Oh*, monsieur!"

"And *this*"—he picked up the silver cylinder—"is the seal of the Grand Prior of France." He rolled it between his fingers and mused: "Who would think to look at it that so much power resided in so simple-looking an object?"

He put the seal back down on the table, picked up both documents again, and approached her, saying: "No doubt, madame, you would enjoy to see them for yourself before I affix the seals." He sat down beside her and laid the papers in her lap. As she put her hands on them he whispered intently: "Your husband is a very fortunate man, my dear." It wasn't her eyes he was staring into. "Dumplings . . . such delectable dumplings . . . so ripe for the kissing . . ."

As he nibbled on her breasts he butted forward with his head to nudge her down against the arm of the settee. Looking over the top of his head, she could read just enough of both documents to see that they said what he'd said. He lifted her skirts while lifting her legs up onto the couch, fishing in his breeches with his free hand. She'd had the foresight to dab on a bit of lard before donning her gown, to facilitate matters.

She focused her eyes on a corner of the ceiling where the plaster had crumbled away, exposing the ribs beneath, and recited: "Oh, monsieur, oh . . . ! The power in your loins! Oh!" Whatever it was he was grunting out he'd probably pronounced several hundred times before. She clutched onto the pieces of paper in her hand, and onto the fact that La Tour would never know.

When she got back to her lodgings, bearing her two wax-weighted documents, she wasn't in the least surprised that Lorette had arranged to have the requested hip bath set in front of the hearth and had filled it with hot water. Françoise poured in half a bottle of eau de cologne before climbing in. She held Claude up in the air while Lorette poured in another boiling kettle between her legs, then settled her naked son back between her breasts and into the cloud of perfumed steam rising to the ceiling.

Lorette dutifully attended to the fire and bath and kettle, but no words escaped her pursed mouth. Lorette's lips stayed vised

together even when Claude giggled and splashed at the bubbles
that resulted from adding in his own perfume.

Françoise considered informing Lorette that there were
things that had to be done in life which didn't fit into the
Chanson de Roland. But then, there were things she didn't
want Lorette to have to learn. So, in the end, all she said to
Lorette was: "It seems the Baye Françoise is still not safe from
privateers."

CHAPTER 19

Jeanne put one or two drops of perfume into her bath
before climbing in, but only one or two—Charles
didn't like too thick a smell of perfume. She hadn't seen her
husband for more than two weeks out of the winter, only when
Nicolas Le Creux went across the bay to relieve him for a few
days as commander of the *Vierge.* Nikki had left Port Royal in
a pinnace yesterday morning, so Charles should be home
sometime today.

She leaned back in the bath—tentatively, until her skin adjusted to the heat—and began to soap her belly and thighs.
Even after four children, the soap-slick flesh her hands glided
over didn't feel loose or saggy in the least. As that thought
passed through her hands up to her mind, she wondered if she
hadn't just committed a sin of pride. But she was quite sure
she could truthfully say she'd been thinking more of her husband than of herself. It was bound to give him a certain
amount of satisfaction to come home to a wife whom he could
trust to manage his household but was still as taut and smooth
as any other twenty-six-year-old.

It occurred to her that trust cut both ways. She might not

like it that the blockade kept him away so much, but she had to trust his decision that it was necessary. With four children under the age of seven, and the château to keep in order, there wasn't much of her left for analyzing the outside world. For his part, he had enough to cope with without learning how to maintain the domestic domain. Thinking of how much they had to trust each other warmed her insides as much as the bathwater warmed her skin. Although the water wasn't nearly as warm as when she'd climbed in ...

"Madame?" the maid's voice came from the other side of the screen.

"A moment." Jeanne reached down to the bedsheet furled on the floor and pulled it across to cover the bath and herself. *"Entrez."*

The maid came around the screen carrying a steaming kettle, set it down next to the emptied one beside the bath, opened the spigot at the base of the bath to let a little of the cooled water drain into the empty kettle, then carried the cold kettle out to the hearth on the other side of the screen. Jeanne pushed the sheet aside and hefted the hot kettle to pour it carefully between her knees. It would've been much easier for the maid to do it. But then Jeanne would've had to find some way of covering herself while uncovering the bath. She'd heard of grand ladies in France who'd solved the problem by bathing in their shifts, but that seemed to be defeating the purpose.

The house suddenly shook, as the fort's big guns all fired in unison. There was an answering salute from an approaching ship.

Jeanne squawked and tried to pull herself out of the bath, falling back with a splash when her hands slipped off the rim. She managed to extricate herself, ran a towel up and down her body, flung her shift on, and ran out from behind the screen with her wet feet slapping and her shift sticking to damp patches of skin.

There was a flurry of skirts and stockings and corset hooks. Fortunately, her hair was only steam wet, and Port Royal was having a warm snap.

She ran for the bedroom door with her shoes in one hand

and her maid still fastening the back of her blouse. Flinging open the door, Jeanne hollered for the nurse and hopped along the hallway, trying to cover distance and put her shoes on at the same time. The children emerged from the nursery all combed and primped and dressed in their best clothes, excepting swaddled René, who was squalling in his nurse's arms.

Jeanne snatched René from the nurse and herded his older brother and sisters down the stairs. Outside on the parade square, men-at-arms were scrambling into polished ranks. The gates were already swinging open. She just managed to get to the gates and line the children up in formation before their father appeared at the crest of the riverbank, pivoting his walking stick along the slushy path like an elegant pendulum.

The men-at-arms fired a volley from their matchlocks. Charles stopped in front of her, flourished his hat off, and bowed to kiss her hand. Then he kissed each of the children in turn and extended her his arm for the procession to the château. She was more than glad he didn't pause to inspect the troops. Warm spell or no, she could feel the droplets in her hair beginning to crystallize. On the way across the courtyard, he sidled his eyes at her and one corner of his mustache twitched up. "Been sporting with the harbor seals, my dear?"

She'd had more foresight about the kitchen than about her bath. The meal she'd instructed to be prepared for him was one that didn't need to be fitted to an exact arrival time: cold capon, onions, cheese, and buttered bread. The only item on the menu not grown and manufactured in Port Royal was a white Bordeaux from a vintner whose table wines were perfectly comparable with his competitors', despite the competitors' more elegant labels and much more elegant prices. The steward had had a tendency to buy by label until Jeanne took him in hand.

Jeanne sat down at Charles's right hand and Anne at his left. Before he began to eat, he called in the master of his fleet and instructed him that two of the pinnaces and the fregate he'd bought in France were to be fitted out for two months at sea. Then Charles turned to his left and said to Anne: "I am afraid you will have to do without your husband for the next two months."

Although Jeanne felt sorry for her sister, she couldn't help but also feel a thrill that Nikki commanding the blockade would mean that Charles would be home. But then Charles turned to his right and said: "And so will you, my dear. But you were already expecting to see little of me until matters are resolved."

"What has happened?"

"Nothing. Which is precisely what disturbs. For four months now the *Vierge* has corked the mouth of La Tour's harbor and he has made no attempts to dislodge us or to escape. Methinks Monsieur La Tour is acting suspiciously like a man who is waiting for something."

"For what?"

"I have no more idea than you, my dear. But whatever it may be, I do not intend for it to take me by surprise. With the fregate and two pinnaces, we can patrol the mouth of the Baye Françoise so that not even a canoe may enter unbeknownst to us. Le Creux will maintain the *Vierge* at the mouth of La Rivière St. Jean while I guard his back at the mouth of the bay. I would it were not necessary, but when a man like La Tour does nothing, it is time to be vigilant."

In the night Jeanne lay awake long after him, pushing sleep away so as not to be robbed of this feeling of contentment. The moon was full and the pale light streaming through the window shone on the head on the pillow beside hers. His hair was growing thin in front and a little roll of fat had grown under his chin. The flesh under his eyes was growing saggy, weighted down with a spiderweb of lines of care that were still there while he slept. The evidence of the burdens he carried for so many people made him even more beautiful than the *beau chevalier* who'd swarmed up the rope of the *St. Jehan*.

She didn't gaze at him for long, though. Sleeping with one's head steeped in moonlight was known to disorient the mind and bring on strange fancies. She sat up and drew the bedcurtains, moving carefully so as not to wake him. When she lay back down he stirred in his sleep, rolling over and draping one arm across her.

She managed to keep herself awake a little longer by trying to count all her blessings. The only winds that troubled the smooth surface of her life as chatelaine of Port Royal—outside of the inevitable heartaches that came with loving anything or anyone—all blew from the same quarter: the devil across the bay. Her husband's occasional spates of fragile humor were largely due to his frustration with La Tour. His enforced absences from Port Royal were entirely due to La Tour's refusing to obey the king's decree. She prayed that justice might come soon to Charles La Tour, then closed her eyes and let sleep take her.

Chapter 20

La Tour sat listening to his quartermaster read out his litany of woe. The early thaw meant they'd officially made it through the winter, but that wasn't much to celebrate. Jemseg had run out of flour a month ago, and now the last crumbs of ship's biscuit had been eaten. All that was left from last year's runs of salmon and bony *gaspereaux* were two barrels of dried fish. There wouldn't be any more, as long as the fish weir was in range of the *Vierge*'s guns.

Under ordinary circumstances, Jemseg's half-*courier de bois* farmers and *engagés* could be relied upon to augment the larder with the fruits of their hunting and fishing. But they couldn't range far from the fort in case the *Vierge* launched an attack. The people of the country were starting to trickle back out of the woods to harvest shellfish and seabird eggs, but they could hardly be expected to feed all of Jemseg when they had their own families to provide for.

As the quartermaster droned out the doleful inventory of what he didn't have, La Tour considered the possibility of taking the *Vierge*. He could sneak out a fleet of small boats under cover of darkness and hope to board her before her gunners could roll out of their hammocks. But he highly doubted the commander of the *Vierge* wasn't alert to such a possibility, even after she'd been sitting out there unmolested for five months. A month ago his lookouts watching the *Vierge* had seen Nicolas Le Creux arrive and d'Aulnay leave and not come back. But Le Creux was no more likely than d'Aulnay to let his crew get into the habit of nodding off on night watch.

"La Tou." It was Keeshetech in the doorway. "Some thing funny."

The quartermaster looked not at all inclined to interrupt weighty matters to indulge a Micmac's sense of humor. La Tour waved the quartermaster's mouth shut and said in Micmac: "What is the funny thing, my brother?"

"My younger son, the one who carries the burn scar on his arm from the night the wigwam caught on fire on Yellow Island . . . ?"

"I remember him well."

"He was sitting on a rock looking at your fish weir with his chin in his hands, looking for washups from the big storm last night. A crow came flying from the north. Crow came down next to my son and cawed and cawed. It did seem strange to my son that Crow was not interested in a rotting fish nearby. Then Crow began to clean his feathers with his beak, combing and combing his wings, as though they were all thick with grease. And it seemed to my son that Crow was shining even more than any other gleaming black crow would shine in any sunlight—as though his feathers were slicked with bear fat for a festival.

"When Crow saw my son was watching him, Crow flew up again and back toward the north, cawing over his shoulder. Is that not a funny thing, La Tou?"

La Tour rubbed his hand back and forth across his mouth, then said: "To the north?"

"To the north, along the shore."

La Tour said in French to the quartermaster: "You can entertain me with the rest of the dirge later. Find Rainville and tell him he is in command till I get back." Then he switched back to Micmac. "Shall we take a walk, Keeshetech?"

"To the north?"

"As the crow flies . . ."

La Tour paused at the door to reach down his sword baldric from the wall peg, crossed his other shoulder with his bandolier of powder charges, shoved his wheel-lock pistol in his belt, and took up his musket and shot pouch. Keeshetech raised his eyebrow at the arsenal. La Tour shrugged. Keeshetech patted the sheath knife hanging from a thong around his neck and shrugged back.

Beyond the last of the half-thawed garden plots radiating out from the fort, there was a path heading north through the woods—though hardly as the crow flies. Keeshetech let La Tour take the lead. They walked long enough for La Tour to begin to forget what lay behind him and begin to notice the first buds on the willows, the smell of rising spruce sap, the sound of a returned songsparrow. . . . He had definitely been penned up in that damned fort too long.

The path swerved closer to the shore after crossing the base of the headland to the south of which lay the *Vierge*. An odd sound up ahead disturbed the lull of lapping waves and rustling boughs: a raucous squalling of crows and gulls and yipping foxes.

La Tour turned off the path to break his way through to the shore. The sound grew louder and the forest smells grew overpowered by a reek of blood and rotting seaweed and sunmelted fat.

Across the gray shore rocks and pink tidal flats stretched a glistening ridge of black streaked with red and white, half-hidden in a cloud of crows and seabirds; as though one of the granite nesting islands had hove in off the bay. It was a beached whale.

Keeshetech said: "Our brother the crow is never stingy. When there is food, he comes and tells us *sauvages* to come and help him eat it."

"Just as *les sauvages* do with their French brothers."

Keeshetech shrugged. "Those French who are *sauvage* enough to be brothers."

CHAPTER 21

As soon as April heralded the end of winter storms, Françoise set sail on His Most Christian Majesty's warship *St. Clément*. She knew that naval matters weren't her métier, but it seemed to her the *St. Clément* wasn't exactly the terror of the seas. In fact, the difference between warships and merchant ships seemed to consist mainly of whether the name on the ownership papers was that of some ordinary mortal or that of the king.

The *St. Clément* did carry a few more guns than the average merchantman, and a complement of twenty soldiers. On this voyage she also carried forty-five new *engagés* in the service of Charles de Saint Étienne de La Tour. There were carpenters, stonemasons, domestic servants, a tailor, a surgeon, a pharmacist. . . . But many of them had no trade at all, except war. Among that faction were a half-dozen Swiss mercenaries Françoise didn't like the look of. But maybe that was a good recommendation.

The man Desjardins du Val had nominated to captain the voyage was, by pure coincidence, his brother-in-law. Whether there was some truth to du Val's shining recommendations or whether his brother-in-law was just lucky with winds, the captain brought the *St. Clément* from La Rochelle to the mouth of the Baye Françoise in less than three weeks.

As the tide carried them into the bay Françoise went out on deck, leaving Claude sleeping in the box the ship's carpenter had fitted beside her bunk. The swaying of the ship would rock him better than any cradle.

The sight of Menane Island looming beyond the bowsprit brought a pang of memory. The first time she'd seen it was from the deck of the *Renard Noir*, the day after her wedding. Desjardins du Val had pronounced authoritatively: "That is Menane Island. We steer for it to avoid the shore shoals and then skirt around."

La Tour had snorted: "*Menane* is Maliseet for 'island.' So when a Frenchman says 'Menane Island' he is saying '*Island Island.*' "

Françoise had said: "What do *you* call it, then?" and La Tour had shrugged.

"Island Island."

As Island Island grew steadily larger Françoise debated whether to present La Tour with the surprise as soon as they'd done kissing each other hello, or wait until the cargo was unloaded. Among the other articles in her traveling trunk was a pink, ceramic half cylinder. In the hold were several cratefuls of the same; roof tiles, to replace the rough shingles topping their quarters. La Tour could laugh at her all he liked, but he was going to live in a rose-vined, shining-roofed house if it killed him. And next year she would start doing something about the furniture.

"A sail!" drifted down from the lookout on the foremast. "Larboard of the island!"

The captain peered through his telescope and muttered: "She's built low, like an English ship. . . ."

Françoise said: "The *Renard Noir*?"

The captain shook his head. "A full-scale fregate, more like."

"I seem to recall La Tour saying d'Aulnay bought an English ship last year."

"Another sail! Starboard of the island!"

The captain peered through his glass again, chewed his cheek, and muttered: "A pinnace . . ." The crack of a distant cannon raised a cloud of seabirds from an islet up ahead. "Helmsman, hard to larboard! Trim the mizzen to bring her head around."

The helmsman said: "We'll not make much headway running against the tide, monsieur."

"Neither will *they*. Hard to larboard!"

"*Oui*, monsieur."

As the triangular sail above the quarterdeck swung to take the wind at an angle that would help the rudder turn the ship, Françoise said tautly to the captain: "I thought the purpose of this voyage was to win past d'Aulnay's ship."

"Just so, madame; *ship*, not *ships*. And now, madame, I will have silence on my quarterdeck. As it is, we'll have a close run of it to reverse our heading and get some wind in our sails before we're in range of their guns."

"A third sail! Off the starboard beam and coming on fast!"

Françoise found a place out of the way and watched the sailors, scrambling overhead like monkeys or hauling fiercely on the intricate spiderwebs of ropes fixed to the deck rails. It seemed agonizingly slowly that the *St. Clément* lumbered her way through a wide half circle. Françoise could make out the tall sails of the fregate now, and of the third ship; another pinnace, running before the wind. If the *St. Clement* couldn't get away, Françoise wondered whether she'd rather the captain fight a three-to-one sea battle while Claude and Lorette were on board, or surrender immediately and make her whole last eight months gone for nothing.

The captain ordered a blank broadside fired from both larboard gundecks, to make the pinnace coming in fast from the east think twice about closing with the *St. Clément* before the fregate and the other pinnace came up. At last the *St. Clément* began to take the wind again, tacking southwest, then southeast, then southwest again, following a zigzag course back out of the bay.

The captain stood gripping the stern rail, eyes fixed on the pursuing sails, barking orders over his shoulder to change tacks with no apparent rhyme or reason or rhythm—at least none Françoise could discern. She assumed it had to do with wind and currents and other sea knowledge beyond her. But after watching him for a while, she began to feel what he was doing, and it wasn't at all beyond her. He was guessing what the captains of the other three ships were guessing about what tack he was going to shift to or stick to. If he could keep them off balance they would find themselves constantly adjusting to his maneuvers, with a lag time for each adjustment, rather than anticipating and cutting him off. Captaining a warship was apparently not at all that different from being a woman living by her wits.

The sails of the three pursuers didn't drop away behind the *St. Clément*, but neither did they grow noticeably larger. They were still in sight when nightfall found the *St. Clément* rounding Cape Sable on a course that would carry her back to France.

But when full dark came down, the captain turned her head around back to the west and ordered that no lamps be lit and the fire in the cooking grate be doused. Françoise couldn't sleep, so she stayed on the quarterdeck. It was like riding on a ghost ship, with no sound but the slapping of the waves against the hull, the creaking of the halyards, and the ghostlike whispering among the officers on deck. Even the binnacle light was out, the captain steering by a star.

Two of the officers began paying out the log, which was at least one bit of nautical arcana Françoise understood: tossing over the stern a log float on a long, knot-studded rope and counting how many knots passed through the linesman's hand as a ten second sandglass ran out. The captain came over to her and whispered: "If they are close enough to us to hear the splashes of the log, they will think it only a fish or a seal. I hope. We have no choice; if we do not know how many knots we are traveling, we might well run up against the coast before dawn."

An unearthly shrieking split the night and didn't stop. Claude. Françoise kicked off her shoes and scurried down the gangway, then felt her way along the dark corridor for the door of her cabin. Now that she was closer, she could tell that Claude was merely doing his usual midnight fussing; it was only the silence all around that made it sound like he was being dismembered. But on such a still night she was sure he could be heard for leagues across the sea.

As Françoise slid open the door Lorette wailed: "I cannot make him stop!"

"Here." She took Claude from Lorette and jogged him up and down and sang softly in his ear. He began to quieten. She lay down on her bed and rocked him on her breast until they both fell asleep.

When she went out on deck in the morning there was a wooded coastline ahead and no other ship within the circle of the horizon. The captain said: "If you will permit me, madame . . ." and knelt at her feet with her shoes in his hand. She put her hand on his shoulder to balance herself while she raised first her right foot, then her left. "You have such tiny, delicate feet, madame, like a child's."

"Glass would still be very impractical."

"I suppose. But it is a pretty conceit, is it not?"

They anchored in a sheltered cove. Françoise asked the captain if his plan was to slip up the Baye Françoise when night came down again.

"No, madame. This coast is far too dangerous to sail at night. And if we go out into open water, I expect we'd find the Sieur d'Aulnay's flotilla quartering the bay. All I can think of to do is send a few men in the ship's boat to try to bring word to your husband we are here. Methinks a longboat hugging the shoreline could slip past the fregate and the pinnaces—though how to slip past the *Vierge*, if she still blocks the harbor entrance, is another question."

"They needn't. If they go ashore as soon as they pass Island Island—Menane Island—it's easy enough to walk to Jemseg. Even easier if they have the good fortune to stumble across some of the people of the country. Any Micmac or Maliseet, even those without a word of French, will understand 'La Tour.' We have some paint on board . . . ?"

"The deck trim would be in sorry shape if we did not."

"If you will allow me to spoil your longboat's sail, methinks I can arrange that if one of d'Aulnay's lookouts does catch sight of it, they will think it only a boat of *les sauvages*."

While the boat was being winched off its resting place on the hold hatch and lowered into the water, Françoise spread its sail out on the foredeck and painted a big red fish across it. She doubted it bore much resemblance to any fish found in the waters of Acadia, but it only had to fool white men.

Seven men set off in the longboat. Four days later they came back, with a message from La Tour: the *St. Clément* was to stay anchored where she was and wait for him.

The longboat also brought back news of recent events that convinced Françoise the captain had been wise not to try to bluff his way past d'Aulnay's flotilla. A week before the *St. Clément* tried to enter the Baye Françoise, d'Aulnay's fregate had blown the foremast off a Boston ship trying to carry supplies to La Tour. That taste of gunpowder had so enthused d'Aulnay that he'd sailed his patrol ships to La Rivière St. Jean and landed men-at-arms and cannons to pry the rebel out of his fort. The guns Gargot had sighted and refurbished drove them back onto their ships and back out onto the bay.

"There is also a personal message for you, madame. Perhaps some manner of code?"

"What did he say?"

"Monsieur La Tour says to tell you to trim for action."

Two nights passed. The third night was a new moon. Françoise was jerked out of sleep by a bellow from above. "Who goes there?"

A voice hissed back from the water, a voice Françoise had heard only in her mind's ear for the past eight months. "Shout a trifle louder so they can hear you in Port Royal."

Françoise threw on her peignoir and scampered barefoot up the stairs. In the light from the binnacle, a tall, mottle-haired man in a black cloak was just emerging from the top of the boat stairs hinged to the side of the quarterdeck. She ran toward him and leaped. As her breasts hit his chest his arms came up to clutch her and he spun around to prevent her momentum from carrying them both over the side. He lowered her, gasping like an old man in a footrace. As her body slid down his she said: "Have I grown so much heavier in a few short months?"

"May've seemed short to *you* . . . Captain, forgive me for keeping you riding at anchor so long. I needed a dark night and an outgoing tide."

There were other men coming up the boat stairs—Rainville and several *engagés* and two of Jemseg's Recollet missionaries. Below them Françoise could just make out the gunwales of a shallop.

The captain of the *St. Clément* said: "You rode the tide down this coast at *night*?"

"Thirty-five years sailing the same waters do teach a thing or two. The testy part was sneaking past the *Vierge*."

"We'll never sneak the *St. Clément* past the fregate and pinnaces."

"I've done with sneaking. Tomorrow dawn we set a course for Boston, even if I'm still abed. As for tonight—or what's left of it—Milady and I shall retire."

Lorette had also been awakened by the noises on deck, which made it easier to shift her to another cabin. The *St. Clément*'s bunks were short for La Tour, and narrow for two, but they managed.

CHAPTER 22

La Tour stood on the afterdeck of the *St. Clément* watching the green islands of Massachusetts Bay glide by. Rainville, who'd been to Boston with Gargot, was guiding the helmsman through the ship channel, using the captain's telescope to refresh his memory.

La Tour couldn't think of what more he could do to prepare himself for *les Bostonais*. Françoise had trimmed the shaggier ends of his hair and made adjustments to his blue suit of clothes: lopping the ribbons off the breeches cuffs and sewing shut the slashing meant to show off the fine linen of his shirtsleeves. His English wasn't of the best, but Françoise had traveled to London more than once to perform in pastorals and she could help with translation. No doubt they would both get plenty of opportunity to practice as they worked their way up the ladder of functionaries to the governor. That is, if the governor didn't prove so reluctant to get enmeshed in French affairs that he refused to see them at all.

If so, La Tour wouldn't get a chance to play the only card he had: his inheritance. His father had often said that all he could expect to inherit was more valuable than any estate—the fact that if either of them could just be sat down face-to-face with any man or woman, they could persuade their way out of or into anything.

La Tour had never shared his father's belief that it had anything to do with inborn powers of persuasion. It was simply that if you proposed the most sensible course of action under the ruling circumstances, people were bound to agree with you eventually.

"Madame Gibbons!" It was Rainville's voice. La Tour looked over to see Rainville lowering the telescope and raising his hand to wave, then blushing to the roots of his silky blond hair as he realized that whoever he'd seen through the glass couldn't see him.

La Tour said: "Who?"

"Madame Gibbons—on the boat out there," pointing ahead to a small sailboat crossing the bay. "She is wife to Major Gibbons. They entertained us in their home one evening when I was here with Gargot."

La Tour mused: "*Major* Gibbons . . ." then turned to Françoise, who was looking quite respectable in a high-necked dress, with her hair bound up simply and no jewelry to speak of. "It do seem only polite, my dear, we should pay our respects to Madame Gibbons. Captain—find an anchorage out of the channel and wait for us, if you would."

They set off in the shallop—Rainville at the tiller, La Tour and Françoise on the midbench, and six sailors rowing. As soon as the sailboat saw them coming out to intercept her, she sheared off and made for the nearest island. Rainville shouted: "Madame Gibbons!" but the sailboat kept making away from them.

La Tour told the oarsmen to double the stroke, to bring them within hailing range. If they paused to set their own sail, they'd never catch up. He found it quite odd sitting there among sailors rowing furiously to get close enough to tell the boat they were pursuing there was nothing to fear, given that the harder they rowed, the more fear they no doubt engendered.

As they drew closer to the island La Tour saw there was a landing stage there, with a large white house beyond it surrounded by orchards and a vineyard. The sailboat docked and the people in it scrambled out: two rough-dressed men, a woman, and several children. There were people hurrying down from the house: a tall man in black and several retainers carrying muskets.

La Tour bellowed: "Madame Gibbons!" The woman stopped and turned. The men raising their muskets half lowered them confusedly.

As the shallop touched the wharf La Tour levered himself out with the help of a handy sailor's shoulder, stooped to offer his hand to Françoise, and beckoned Rainville with the other. When they'd got halfway down the wharf, Rainville removed his hat and said in English: "Mrs. Gibbons, it is just I, Rainville."

"Oh!" Mrs. Gibbons's hand flew up to her mouth. "What a goose I am."

"We see you from the ship," Rainville continued. "And Governor La Tour say we must come to pay our respect."

"Oh dear." Mrs. Gibbons blushed. "And I thought . . . So we ran for the nearest island, which is"—fluttering her hand at the tall, gray man in black and white—"Governor Winthrop's."

La Tour said in his mind to the shade of his father: Out of all the gifts a man might be born with, none's a patch on blind idiot luck. He swept off his hat and made a little half bow. "*Enchantez,* Governor Winthrop."

Governor Winthrop bowed back. "How do you do, Governor La Tour." He had a long nose and a long face made longer by a gray spade blade of a beard. His eyebrows appeared to be permanently arched. But there was some encouragement in the fact that his clothing wasn't nearly as severe as the general run of Puritans. And he gestured graciously with one long hand up the path from the wharf. "You must come up and meet my family. We had only this morning come out to spend a few quiet days away from town."

In between La Tour's halting memory of traders' English, and Françoise and Rainville helping each other to translate, they managed something resembling communication. They were introduced to the Winthrop family and then settled into chairs set out under a generous oak tree. A servant brought a tray of tiny glasses filled with the latest vintage from the Winthrop vineyard. It tasted like horse piss with sugar in it. La Tour congratulated his brother governor on proving it was possible to grow sweet wine grapes north of Virginia.

"From what Goodwife Gibbons has said, Governor La Tour, am I to understand that you sailed a ship flying the fleur-de-lis straight up the ship channel into Boston harbor, and no one challenged you?"

"Just so."

Governor Winthrop looked perturbed, but offered up hopefully: "Perhaps because it was only a harmless-looking merchantman?"

"She is a warship on loan from the King of France, with two gun decks and some hundred and forty men on board."

The long face grew even longer. "This won't do. You could have taken me prisoner and plundered half the town by the time an alarm was raised."

"I might yet."

The arched eyebrows arched even higher, threatening to pop out the eyes. La Tour shrugged and winked and the Puritan governor actually laughed. "By heaven, Governor La Tour—they told me you had a bit of the imp in you, and now I believe it. You must stay and sup with us."

Over supper La Tour explained through his translators why he had come to Boston: to procure enough ships and men to break d'Aulnay's blockade. He had no doubt that Winthrop already had a pretty fair notion of how matters stood in Acadia, but there were certain details that needed to be pointed out to him. Details such as that the reason Jemseg was being persecuted was because La Tour and Françoise were Protestant Huguenots and practiced religious tolerance.

"It's true we do have popish priests at Jemseg. Two even came with us on the *St. Clément*. But our Jemseg missionaries are Recollets, who follow the teachings of Francis of Assisi—which do seem fitting for the wildernesses of North America. They are so unlike the gilded priests of Rome that it took some convincing before they'd change their sandals for moccasins in winter.

"From the very first days of Acadia, we've had no tradition of strict papistry—until Monsieur d'Aulnay. I've heard it said that in that first gruesome winter Frenchmen spent in Acadia—when so many died of the *mal de terre*—they buried the priest and the Protestant chaplain in the same grave, to see if they could get along any better in the next life than they did in this."

Françoise swiveled her eyes from side to side, to show she wasn't about to translate that last sentence. Perhaps it was better not to explore the limits of Governor Winthrop's sense of humor.

By the end of supper La Tour was quite certain Governor Winthrop had seen that helping his beleaguered northern neighbor would be the Christian thing to do. And that an Acadia ruled by an Inquisition-minded aristocrat would not bode well for the scattered New England settlements. Not to mention that Jemseg's coal and limestone and furs could ease the way of pilgrim saints struggling through their stay in this world of tribulations.

Winthrop cautioned: "But you must understand I do not rule

by decree here. The other magistrates must debate and vote on the matter. Democracy is a godless institution. Not *one* of the states mentioned in the Bible employed democracy. I suppose democracy may have its godly uses, but I fear too much of it will be the ruin of us."

Françoise said: "Too much of anything will ruin any man," which appeared to arouse Governor Winthrop's approbation.

They set off toward the town in the *St. Clément*'s shallop: La Tour, Françoise, Rainville, and Winthrop. Halfway across the harbor, three boatfuls of armed oarsmen came charging out to rescue their governor. Winthrop managed to calm their fears, and the rescuers became a ceremonial escort.

The town of Boston had been built on a swelling at the end of a narrow neck of land. La Tour couldn't help but admire the founders' taking advantage of topography in defense against any possible land attack. He might not have Gargot's military schooling, but he had a deep appreciation for enlisting the lay of the land.

In the last embers of daylight he could see lines of brick and wooden houses climbing the peninsula's three hills, a windmill and several water mills, a fleet of ships of all varieties moored around the wharves and shipyard of the inner harbor, and a swarm of people massing in the square in front of the landing stage. La Tour had been living in Acadia for a quarter of a century before the first Englishman set up housekeeping on Massachusetts Bay, and now this town alone had several times the population of all New France.

He supposed some might see it as sad proof of the superiority of English colonizing mechanisms. But he had not the least desire to see Acadia become a suburb of Paris or La Rochelle. Let *les Bostonais* build factories and turn their forest paths into cobblestone streets. He and Françoise would take their ease in their château in the wildwood and trade clean furs and raw coal for the made goods that would cover the Boston hills in soot.

The crowd of gogglers in the square parted to let their governor and his guests pass by. The gawkers were more brightly dressed than La Tour would have guessed. Perhaps Puritans

weren't all as dowdy as he'd been led to expect. Or perhaps
John Winthrop's City of God hadn't turned out exactly the way
he'd expected.

They went up a short street leading off the square and came
to the house of Major Gibbons, who had offered his hospitality
to Governor La Tour and his lady during their stay in Boston.
Rainville was dispatched back to the *St. Clément* to tell the
captain he was free to sail her into the inner harbor and find
an anchorage.

As they settled into their English bed Françoise said: "It was
very generous of them to invite us into their home."

"Generous and clever. As it do seem clever of *us* to accept.
So long as we are in their hands, *les Bostonais* have no fear of
the French warship anchored in their inner harbor."

"Has anyone in your life ever done anything for you without
some sly reason?"

"Once or twice. But only fools go through life never thinking of their own advantage. Have you reread your marriage
contract lately?"

The next morning the Boston magistrates and deputies convened in the meeting hall. The balconies ringing the hall were
stuffed with spectators eager to see the Frenchmen and to hear
what had brought them to Boston.

After six hours of explanation, translation, cajoling, charming, and virtual capering in cap and bells, La Tour sat back and
waited through the magistrates' deliberations. Their eventual
verdict was that the recent agreement for mutual defense
signed with Plymouth, New Haven, and Connecticut meant
that the Commonwealth of Massachusetts could not involve itself in military adventures without the other colonies'
approval—which was not likely to be forthcoming. However,
any private citizen of Massachusetts who chose to enlist himself in Governor La Tour's expedition was free to do so.

That was all La Tour needed. Major Gibbons was easily persuaded to take a mortgage on Jemseg in exchange for enough
money to hire several ships crewed with temporary mercenaries.

Working out the details, hiring ships, and enlisting recruits took some time. In the process, La Tour grew better acquainted with just which tails wagged which dogs on Massachusetts Bay. The self-anointed saints turned out to be only a portion of the population, but the saints ruled.

When the Sabbath came along, Françoise suggested that it wouldn't be a bad idea if two such staunch Protestants as themselves were to ask their brothers in Christ if they could join them in divine services. La Tour explained to the Recollets that it was only a matter of politics.

An honor guard of Boston pikemen escorted Governor and Mrs. La Tour to the meeting hall, which functioned as the church as well as legislature and courthouse. And "functioned" was the word: stained-glass windows and such might have distracted the worshipers from the business at hand.

The minister turned over an hourglass before beginning the sermon. La Tour watched the sand drain out as the minister droned on like a hammer trying to drive a very dull spike through very dull heads. Buttocks stiffening on wooden benches got the occasional respite: standing to pray for long enough that stiffening legs yearned to sit again. Finally, the sand ran out. The minister turned the hourglass over and got his second wind.

La Tour decided it was fortunate that Françoise had been relegated to the women's side of the congregation. If she'd been sitting beside him, he would've pressed his luck by whispering: "Jemseg ain't worth this."

But once the price had been paid, the prize was snatched away. Winthrop came to the Gibbons house and apologetically explained that fevered complaints had been pouring in from places with names like Salem and Ipswich: the Boston magistrates had allied Massachusetts with an idolatrous Frenchman, "Monsieur Donny" was bound to take revenge on all New England, any Massachusetts man who joined the blockade-breaking expedition would surely end up sliding into hell for shedding human blood. . . .

There was another meeting in the meeting hall, with the Boston Assembly augmented by magistrates from outlying towns. At least for this particular meeting-hall ordeal, La Tour was allowed to have Françoise beside him as translation assistance. Among other advantages, it meant he could be reassured by the sidling of her eyes that he wasn't the only one wondering if he'd landed in a madhouse. Steel-eyed men in starched collars were debating a matter of warships and gunpowder by comparing the case of Solomon and Sheba with that of Judith and Holofernes. Bibles were flourished and thumpingly quoted in passages La Tour barely understood a word of, except for names like Ahab or Jehoshaphat or Sodom.

Blessed Major Gibbons finally saved the day and his mortgage on Jemseg by declaring that Frenchmen and Englishmen could be equated to Jews and Samaritans, and that the parable told by Our Lord clearly taught that true Christians should help their brothers regardless of their differences.

La Tour sailed from Boston on the *St. Clément*, leading four rented ships carrying thirty-eight cannon, fifty-four sailors, and sixty-four militia volunteers. He reflected that it was only by a hair that the words he'd spoken the night he'd first set foot on the *St. Clément* hadn't turned out to be a lie. He'd done with sneaking.

CHAPTER 23

D'Aulnay sat at his ease while his valet de chambre shaved him, perfectly confident that the servant had become expert at adjusting his razor strokes to the gentle rocking of the *Vierge* at anchor. His chair had been arranged to face the cabin windows with a pleasant view of the Maliseet village at the mouth of Jemseg harbor, La Tour's fort at the head of the harbor, and the *Renard Noir* floating at the anchorage where she'd lain trapped ever since the *Vierge* took up her vigil over La Rivière St. Jean. The casements had been opened to let in the clean, late-summer air, scented with pine and kelp. It was all very pleasant.

The most pleasant part of all was that La Tour might very well be standing on his palisade at this very moment, looking out at the *Vierge* and gnashing his teeth. It was only a question of time now, and not very much time at that. When winter approached, La Tour would have to give in to the fact that the ship he was waiting for had been chased back to France. The only choices left to him were surrender or starve.

As the razor scraped delicately across his throat d'Aulnay indulged himself by projecting the difference that the income from Jemseg was going to make to his finances. Even if La Tour and Desjardins du Val hadn't been stealing more than ten percent in their annual reports to La Compagnie de la Nouvelle France, the furs that came down La Rivière St. Jean in a single year would pay off Emmanuel Le Borgne and half the debt to Claude de Launnay-Razilly.

D'Aulnay had already decided what he would do with La Tour's establishment once La Tour had been removed. Jemseg's farmers would be transplanted to the more verdant clime of Port Royal, as would most of the fort's *engagés* and tradesmen. The fort itself would be replaced by a small, seasonally occupied trading post. It made no sense to have the meager population of Acadia scattered helter-skelter in isolated pockets, instead of concentrated in one substantial settlement. Which was why he'd burned the fort at Cape Sable, and the houses and gardens and Capuchin monastery. The people were far more secure, and happier, at Port Royal.

"A sail!"

If the casement hadn't been open, d'Aulnay wouldn't have heard the lookout calling down from the crosstrees. No matter, it was probably just another of the fishing boats stolen by *les sauvages*—which was a habit he would put a stop to once Acadia had been purged of La Tour's *laissez-faire*.

"Two sails! Three—no, more!"

D'Aulnay pushed the valet's hand away and said: "A towel."

"But, monsieur, only a few strokes more and—"

"A *towel*!"

"*Oui*, monsieur."

The valet handed him first a damp towel to sponge off the lather, then a dry one. D'Aulnay wiped his face and said: "Did I get it all?"

"*Oui*, monsieur."

He thrust the towels back at the valet and proceeded out on deck, slinging his sword baldric over his shoulder. The captain said: "Monsieur, the lookout sees—"

"I heard." He called up at the mainmast crosstrees: "Who are they?"

"I do not know, monsieur. Four ships and a smaller boat, coming up the bay. The lead ship flies the fleur-de-lis; the others, no flags that I can see."

D'Aulnay cursed himself for abandoning the patrol of the bay mouth after the relief ship had been chased away. But then, what could one fregate and two pinnaces have done against a fleet five strong? "Captain, weigh anchor and take us out onto the bay."

"To meet them, monsieur?"

"*No.* Take her out north of Partridge Island." If the five ships' destination was Jemseg, they would come up the ship channel southwest of the island.

Fortunately, he hadn't allowed the *Vierge*'s crew to grow sluggardly during the months of blockading. Nonetheless, it took an agonizing time for the capstan to raise the anchor and the sails to unfurl. The wind was from the northwest, which meant he'd have to sail a bit to windward to get past the island, but he couldn't ask for much better if it came to making a run for Port Royal.

As the *Vierge* began to round the island d'Aulnay just caught a glimpse of the other sails coming up the ship channel. They were holding their course, instead of turning east to intercept him. But then, they couldn't intercept him now without running into Partridge Island.

Once safely through the passage between the island on the starboard side and the rocky cape to larboard, d'Aulnay told the captain to clap on all sail and keep her running straight before the wind, then stood gripping the stern rail, waiting for those five ships to reveal their intent.

They did soon enough, by emerging one by one through the passage between the cape and Partridge Island's hidden shoal to pursue him. Whoever was in command of the lead ship knew these waters.

Although it was impossible to be certain at that distance, the lead ship did appear to bear more than a passing resemblance to the three-master he'd chased out of the bay two months ago. Her bow guns fired. It was no salute; two fountains spouted out of the waves about fifty paces behind the *Vierge*. At this range they could only lob long shots when the waves lifted the bow, and hope for blind luck. Either the man in command was more of an idiot than his navigation around Partridge Island would suggest, or they had more powder and shot than they knew what to do with.

The captain of the *Vierge* said: "Who are they, monsieur?"

"Whoever they are, they are clearly not our friends. Are we carrying every inch of sail?"

"I could lace the bonnets on the mainsail, and set the spritsail, but with this much wind—"

"Do it. And turn her a hair into the wind, to point her nose for Port Royal."

"*Oui*, monsieur."

It was a long race. The pursuing fleet fanned out in a line, with the ship flying the cross-and-lilies in the middle. The line grew ragged as that ship and one other began to gain on the *Vierge*. D'Aulnay ordered the stern guns loaded and the gunners to stand to their guns, but to keep the gun ports battened until further orders.

The hills of the eastern shore appeared as hazy black waves beyond the gray ones plunging under the bowsprit, then ripened to green as they grew larger. The two faster pursuit ships were almost within reasonable gun range now, but the inlet to Port Royal was just ahead.

The captain ordered his crew aloft to furl the sails, and called down to the helmsman to turn her head into the wind.

"No!" D'Aulnay overrode him. "Brail up the sails, but keep her bow on for the passage."

"But, monsieur, the tide is running in. If we do not go in stern foremost—"

"If we *do*, they will blow us to pieces as we crawl through the passage. Furl the sails so I can see!" Then he threw open the hatch to the helm and scrambled down the ladder.

The *Vierge*'s rudder was manipulated by a whipstaff under the half deck. The helmsman had only a narrow window to see out of. D'Aulnay barked at the helmsman: "Stand aside," and took the whipstaff in his own hands.

At first there was nothing he could see but the white banks of sails rimmed by the green shore rushing forward. The sprit-sails furled just in time for him to see that the *Vierge* was being carried in on an angle that would drive her aground on the larboard side of the inlet, or at the very least snag her bowsprit in the trees. He heaved the whipstaff hard to larboard—too hard. As her beak swung around toward the starboard shore of the passage, he corrected and brought her straight, fighting to hold the whipstaff steady against the force of the tide on the rudder.

The channel ahead of him looked like open water under the rising tide, but he knew there was a rock ahead to starboard and then a silt shoal on the larboard side. He brought her dangerously close to the larboard shore to pass the rock, then swung her hard to starboard again—as hard as he dared without chancing the tide getting a grip on her flank and turning her beam on. Her hull ground against the tip of the shoal and caught for a moment, then scraped clear, leaving only a few barnacles behind.

The *Vierge* spat out of the passage doing a few more knots than the old girl was accustomed to, even under full sail running before a gale. She settled down to a slightly less dizzying speed as the surge of the tide spread itself out across the basin.

D'Aulnay handed the whipstaff over to the helmsman again and climbed back up the ladder, trying to breathe slowly through his nose instead of gasping. His arms and lungs were no longer those of a twenty-year-old sailor.

The captain said: "Lucky for us their aim is not so lucky, eh, monsieur?"

"Aim?"

"They were firing at us with their bow guns as we came through the passage. They cut a few holes in the forest."

"Ah. I hadn't noticed."

Outside of a few fishing boats, the only craft currently anchored in Port Royal basin was one of the pinnaces. The fregate had gone up to the Grand Banks and the rest of d'Aulnay's fleet were ferrying supplies and men to trading outposts for the winter. So a naval battle on the basin was out of the question.

As the tide carried the *Vierge* up the basin into La Rivière au Dauphin, d'Aulnay stood at the stern rail watching to see if any of the pursuers came inching through the inlet after him. By the time Goat Island blocked his view, none had yet appeared. Perhaps they were ferrying a land force ashore, perhaps they were afraid to follow him until the tidal race had slowed, perhaps they were waiting for La Tour to join them with the *Renard Noir*. Any of those possibilities would just give Port Royal that much more time to prepare a proper welcome.

As Port Royal came in sight d'Aulnay ordered the ship's boat lowered and instructed the captain to proceed upriver past the fort and anchor within gun range of the landing stage. It was a delicate procedure climbing down into the boat splashing alongside the *Vierge*. On the way down the bouncing Jacob's ladder, d'Aulnay had to struggle against being paralyzed by the image of his boots missing the boat, and the crew of the *Vierge* watching helplessly as the tide carried them away from their drowning governor. When he was finally safely ensconced, he lifted one gloved hand airily and the boat crew cast off.

He was pleased to see, as he climbed up the path from the landing stage, that the fort had responded smartly to the sound of gunfire from the bay—although he expected no less from Nicolas Le Creux. The palisades were studded with glistening helmets, and above the bastions rose a just-perceptible tracery of gray threads from smoldering gun matches.

Le Creux was waiting for him just inside the gates, as was Jeanne; with his helmet and cuirass at her feet. Sometimes she showed a foresight that was quite remarkable.

As they helped him buckle his breastplate to his backplate, he said to his wife: "Methinks we may be under bombardment soon. Best you take the children down into the cellars and keep them there."

She said tautly: "Is it La Tour?"

"No. He was still bottled up in his fort when these ships appeared. But he may well be following after them. Have no fear, my dear; whoever they may be, they'll wish they'd never followed me home."

As he and Le Creux climbed the parapet stairs, a lookout in the northwest bastion bellowed: "A sail!"

D'Aulnay moved in that direction, expecting to hear more, but didn't. He said: "Only one sail?"

"*Oui*, monsieur. A three-master, flying the fleur-de-lis. She's passed beyond that gap in the trees there now, but should come back in sight soon."

She didn't. Instead a boat appeared, flying a white flag. D'Aulnay said: "Monsieur Le Creux, the fort is yours till I return. I shall take an escort down to the landing stage to meet them."

On the march down to the wharf d'Aulnay finally convinced his shoulders not to square themselves up against the weight of the cuirass but not to slump under it either. He would definitely have to start making an effort to take more physical exercise.

Out of the boat climbed La Tour's decorative little stepbrother, Godard de Rainville. Rainville said insolently: "*Bonjour*, monsieur. Monsieur Charles de Saint Étienne de La Tour, aboard His Most Christian Majesty's warship *St. Clément*, entrusted me with this message—"

"La Tour?"

"*Oui*, monsieur. The *St. Clément*, the same vessel you unlawfully fired upon and pursued out of the Baye Françoise, was under orders from the Grand Prior and Vice Admiral of France to deliver supplies and reinforcements to Jemseg—"

"If you expect me to believe that you managed to sneak back and forth to France this summer, and arrange an audience with the grand prior—"

"Nothing of the kind. Madame Françoise Marie Jacquelin spent last winter in France, and returned on the warship the grand prior had assigned to her. When it came clear that the *St. Clément* could not alone break your blockade, Monsieur La Tour rendezvoused with her and sailed to Boston to procure further forces there to make good the grand prior and vice admiral's orders. The Boston ships stand waiting for high tide before following us here. But rest assured, monsieur, they *are* coming."

D'Aulnay's stomach had begun to eat itself at the thought of how much time he'd had to launch another attack on Jemseg while La Tour was gone to Boston. But he kept his mouth vised and endeavored to keep the acid burning from rising into his face.

"The message from the Sieur de La Tour is—"

"*Sieur de* La Tour? I am not aware of any *seigneurie* in France bearing the name La Tour."

"He wishes only for reasonable recompense money for the losses he's suffered from your unlawful blockade. Then he will consider the matter closed."

"Unlawful? I have been acting under orders from the Conseil du Roi—which the *Sieur de* La Tour has refused to comply with."

"The decree of the Conseil du Roi is old, and wiped away by the decree of the vice admiral."

"In a pig's eye. Wait until the Vice Admiral of France learns you have descended upon a French colony with English pirates! You tell La Tour he can take his 'recompense' and his vice admiral and his *Bostonais* and go to perdition. Or he can save himself the journey; because if he ventures within gun range of Port Royal, we'll blow him there."

CHAPTER 24

On the deck of the *St. Clément*, the ship's carpenter had set up a grind wheel to put as much of an edge on cutlasses as they would take. La Tour drew his sword, bypassed the waiting line of sailors, and said to the ship's carpenter: "If you will permit me . . ."

The carpenter stepped aside and La Tour took his place, humming as his foot worked the treadle and his fingers passed the blade across the whirling grindstone, sending off showers of sparks. His sword wasn't the elegant beestinger of a duelist but a *sword*; with a cutting edge as well as a point, and weight to it. He knew he would've been a fool to face d'Aulnay with rapiers under dancing master's rules. But if d'Aulnay came out to meet him today, in the flailing confusion of a hand-to-hand melee, it would be another matter.

He flicked his thumb along the blade to test the edge, let the ship's carpenter have his grinding wheel back, and stepped to the rail to see how the day was shaping up. The sky over Port Royal was turning gray, with a hint of a misty drizzle that would make it difficult to keep matchlock fuses from sputtering. Beyond Goat Island the first of the Boston ships was coming into view.

That he'd just sharpened his sword pointed up how odd it was to think of *les Bostonais* as reinforcements. Some of the men on those ships might've even been among the tyro fur traders who'd set up shop too far north ten years ago. When La Tour had arrived to evict them, in the name of His Most Christian Majesty, one of them had been fool enough to demand to see his commission. La Tour had shown the fool his sword and informed him: "This is the only commission I've needed here these twenty years. If ever it fails me, then I'll show you my pieces of paper." Well, he had been known to lose his temper in his younger days.

Françoise was standing on the quarterdeck with Claude in her arms, murmuring with Lorette. La Tour went over to them and said: "It do seem unlikely d'Aulnay will send the *Vierge* back downstream against us. But if she *does* come, the *St. Clément* will take the brunt of her. So, once the Boston ships are anchored behind us, I'll have you rowed over to the last one in line."

Françoise said: "And what shall you be doing while we sit on the Boston ship?"

"What I *would* be doing—if I thought *les Bostonais* had the stomach for it—is moving some of the *St. Clément*'s guns to make a shore battery aimed at the back of the fort, where d'Aulnay has only a log wall and no guns to speak of. Once we knocked a few holes in the wall, the men off our five ships are more than enough to storm in over all the men-at-arms d'Aulnay can muster.

"But, *les Bostonais* only agreed to help break the blockade. I misdoubt many of them'd fight at all, except to defend their ships. So what I *shall* be doing is taking forty men off the *St. Clément*, along with as many of *les Bostonais* as will volunteer for a healthy bounty, and marching around out of range of d'Aulnay's guns, taking whatever we can carry from Port Royal as the recompense he refused to give."

"And taking revenge."

" 'All work and no play . . .' 'Tain't just revenge. If we leave without doing him a bit of damage, he'll think the worst we can ever do to him is chase him back home and then scuttle away from his guns. Next spring would see him anchored in our harbor mouth again."

"If you do him too much damage, the Conseil du Roi *will* outlaw you, without the formality of a hearing."

"You have my sworn word, madame, that we shall plunder judiciously." But his private opinion was that if the Sieur d'Aulnay happened to get himself deceased trying to defend his property, the Conseil du Roi would forgive anything, in exchange for a surviving governor with a proven ability to transubstantiate the wilds of Acadia into French gold.

Françoise turned to Lorette. "You go to the Boston ship. I feel safer among our own people."

Lorette said: "If you do, Françoise, so do I."

La Tour didn't like it, but he couldn't very well have them trussed up and transported in sacks, although the thought was tempting. He said to Françoise: "Well, at least come along and help me with my English—make yourself useful."

She handed Claude to Lorette and followed him down into the shallop waiting to ferry him to each of the Boston ships in turn. The offer he made to *les Bostonais* was perfectly simple: one gold *livre* and a share in the booty to any man who joined the shore party. Françoise presented it magnificently, striking a pose and pointing toward Port Royal as though it were a combination of the City of Gold and an imminent threat to their wives and daughters. But, in the end, only thirty volunteered. It didn't help that their ship captains all mentioned that some people might look upon such a venture as something resembling piracy.

When the shallop got back to the *St. Clément*, La Tour kissed his wife *au revoir* and headed ashore with the first boatload of men. He divided his seventy men into two contingents. Those who happened to possess helmets and cuirasses were put under the ex-sergeant whom Desjardins du Val had sent him, the rest under Rainville. Then he loaded his musket with birdshot instead of a ball, and instructed Rainville's troop to do the same.

The path through the woods came out onto La Petite Rivière about a quarter league from the fort. La Tour led the way toward the ford upstream. They were in plain view of the fort, but La Tour was quite sure they were out of range of the small guns in the rear palisades, and that the big guns in the front bastions would take a devil of a time to move. Unless, of course, d'Aulnay had already moved them . . .

The postern gate at the back of the fort swung open and a troop of men-at-arms marched out. There were no more than fifty of them. As La Tour had gambled, d'Aulnay wasn't about to gamble that the shore party wasn't just a ruse to draw the bulk of the defenders out of the fort so the ships could sail in unopposed. All fifty of them were wearing armor and some of them carried pikes, as though d'Aulnay expected that both sides would form squares and march toward each other with drums beating a stately cadence.

La Tour called to the ex-sergeant: "Range your men in a firing line along the crest of the bank," then turned to Rainville. "Bring yours with me." He slid down the streambank and worked his way forward through the mud and reeds until he had a clear view across La Petite Rivière, then knelt down in the muck and checked the priming on his flintlock. He murmured to Rainville: "Aim for their legs, and no one fire till I do." Rainville passed the order along.

The glistening troop from Port Royal formed up in a line facing across the stream at the ex-sergeant's men, who were blowing fiercely on their sodden matches. La Tour could hear d'Aulnay's voice giving orders and then made him out, strutting at the far end of the line under the fluttering fleur-de-lis.

La Tour's hands itched to aim his musket in that direction, but at that range there wasn't much chance of killing a man in armor with birdshot. So instead he took aim at about midthigh of the man-at-arms directly across the stream and pulled the trigger.

The volley that rose up out of the reeds was hardly in unison, but it did the job. Gaps appeared in the line on the opposite shore, as a dozen or so bright-armored men fell writhing on the ground. The ones still on their feet followed d'Aulnay's order to fire at the ex-sergeant's armored line as the ex-sergeant's line fired at them. Maybe one in three matchlocks actually fired. If any of them did manage to hit a breastplate on the other side of the river, the man wearing it probably suffered nothing worse than getting knocked on his back.

By the time La Tour had reloaded, it was too late to take the legs out from under any more of d'Aulnay's troops, because they were in an orderly retreat back to their fort, dragging their wounded. La Tour waded across La Petite Rivière—not difficult now that the tide was going out—and stood on the eastern bank to see what he could see.

Across the meadow in front of him were farms and orchards sloping down to meet the bend of La Rivière au Dauphin. Off to his right was a substantial-looking wood-and-fieldstone gristmill on La Petite Rivière. That looked like a good place to start.

He waved the men still wading across the stream to follow him in that direction. When he came within about fifty paces of the waterwheel, a musket fired out a loophole in the mill house. He dropped to one knee and fired back. Spouts of sparks and powder smoke cracked out of every window, loophole, and doorway. A swarm of invisible bumblebees buzzed through the air over his head and someone behind him cried out: *"Merde!"*

La Tour took the chance that the men d'Aulnay had been clever enough to post inside the mill had been foolish enough to fire all at once. He threw down his musket and ran for the mill, tugging his pistol out of his belt and counting off how long it would take them to reload.

He reached the mill unscathed and flattened his back against the wall, gasping for breath and thanking whatever saints cared to take the credit. He wound the wheel lock, shifted the pistol into his left hand, and drew his sword. A musket barrel poked out of the loophole next to him. He thrust his sword in over it. There was a shriek as the point drove into flesh and bone. He jerked the sword out, fired his pistol into the loophole, and shouted: "Surrender and you'll not be harmed! Or we burn the mill with you inside it!"

A voice called back: "We surrender!" But it came too late to stop the Port Royal man-at-arms and the Jemseg good-for-nothing thrashing about in the weeds beside the millrace. The young man from Jemseg stood up wiping his knife, with his blue Norman eyes gleaming around his broad Micmac nose.

La Tour called into the loophole: "Shed your weapons and come out one by one with your hands showing!" Seventeen of them came out. There had been twenty to begin with.

There wasn't much in the way of portable plunder inside,

beyond the weapons and a few mill tools and sacks of flour. The miller's hearth had a goodly store of kindling and split wood stacked beside it for the coming winter. La Tour piled some of it in the middle of the floor, dribbled a trail of gunpowder, and struck a spark with his wheel lock. It didn't take long for the flames to start tonguing through the roof.

La Tour turned to look across the fields at the back of Port Royal fort. He could see as clearly as a telescope Charles de Menou, Sieur d'Aulnay et de Charnisay, standing on the palisade eating his tongue as the smoke from his mill billowed up to the sky. That should be enough. No point pressing the luck of the La Tours against the amount of time it would take for d'Aulnay to remount one of the big guns from the front bastions, or to decide that the *St. Clément* and her Boston sisters weren't going to try to ascend La Rivière au Dauphin against the tide.

Just in case, La Tour kept the seventeen prisoners marching along between his shore party and the fort until the path swerved into the forest, then let them go. The return to the boats was slowed a little by the half-dozen sheep who would make a fine victory feast back at Jemseg, and by a litter-borne marine soldier from the *St. Clément*, who made his living by chancing his skin.

La Tour stayed ashore until the last load of the shallop that was shuttling back and forth to the *St. Clément*. When he reached the top of the boat stairs, the assembled company sent up a cheer. His wife came toward him with a chalice of brandy, looking like a butter-fleshed little Venus come to tell Mars her husband was out of the country.

He took a deep quaff, sighed and wiped his mouth, drank again, crooked his elbow onto one of those deliciously bared little shoulders, and told the captain: "Weigh anchor, if you would, monsieur, and let the tide carry us out. In the meanwhile—Milady and I shall retire."

The laughter that followed them down the gangway wasn't entirely from Jemseg throats. Apparently some of the *St. Clément*'s crew had begun to absorb the fact that *politesse* in Acadia wasn't that of the Louvre.

La Tour shot the bolt on the cabin door and turned to Françoise as she was turning to him. He walked her backward to the bed, thrusting his left thigh between her skirts with every second step, while his fingers massacred the hooks at the back of her blouse. They'd just hit the bed when a shout came down from above: "A sail!"

La Tour growled: *"Merde,"* and then *"Merde!"* again as the back of his head hit the bunk frame on his way up. He managed to get to his feet, holding one hand against the back of his head and blinking, and said: "Wait here."

"Perhaps."

When he got out on deck, they were passing Goat Island. The "sail" turned out to be not technically a sail, but a longboat rowing up the basin against the tide. It was loaded down with furs for Port Royal. A quick glance guessed their worth at roughly ten thousand *livres*. The Boston captains' delicate principles against taking part in anything that might be construed as piracy didn't appear to preclude sharing in the booty.

CHAPTER 25

Jeanne carried a pitcher of wine and several tin cups over to the barracks infirmary. As she stepped up to the door she heard a man inside screaming like a scalded child. She swallowed hard and tautened her neck and opened the door.

Candles in shoulder-high stands were burning on either side of a table where the surgeon was working on a soldier wearing only a shirt. There was a man at each corner of the table, holding down their comrade's arms and legs. The portion of leg Jeanne could see was hairy and rivered with blood.

The surgeon turned to drop a bit of metal into a bowl held by an assistant and saw her standing in the doorway. "Madame . . ." He reached back to pull down the hem of his patient's shirt.

"I . . . brought some wine. . . . For the wounded."

"Very kind of you, madame. They are there," gesturing his bloody forceps toward a row of beds. "This one is not ready yet."

She started toward the beds and the surgeon went back to work. But there were no more shrieks from the man on the table, as though he were ashamed to give voice to the pain with a woman in the room. Jeanne didn't know whether that made it better for him or worse.

The man-at-arms in the first bed looked more like a boy, barely taller than a musket. He propped himself up on his elbows and muttered: "Thank you, madame," as she poured him a cup of wine. He seemed more embarrassed than in pain.

The older man in the next bed said: "We'll do better the next time, madame."

"The next time . . . ?"

"E'en though there was a few more of them than us, if they'd fought like men instead of *sauvages* . . . But e'en so, madame, if they'd tried to take the fort—e'en with all their ships—we'd've stopped them, I swear."

"I know you would have."

She stayed with them until her pitcher was empty, asking them which part of France they were from and whether they had wives and children. She went back outside feeling like she'd tried to mend a broken arm by kissing it better. The only light in the parade square came from stars and windows. Only a week ago the sun wouldn't quite be down yet. But there was still a red glow in the southern sky, from the mill.

When she came back into the château, Anne told her: "Charles is in the card room, sitting in the dark."

"I thought he was still fighting the fire . . . ?"

"It was no use. The most they could do was keep the fields from catching."

Jeanne lit a candle and carried it to the card room. When she opened the door, he put his hand over his eyes and said: "No light."

She blew out her candle and closed the door, but he still kept his hand over his eyes. The only light left came from a small fire in the grate. She waited for her eyes to adjust to the flickering shadows, then moved toward him. He murmured: "It seems all day I have been staring into flames. . . ."

She sat down on the footstool of his chair and took hold of the hand dangling off his chair arm. His fingers were gritty with soot and his clothing smelled of smoke. Without dropping his other hand from his eyes, he whispered: "I have been a fool."

"If you'd not marched out to fight them, Charles, they might have done far worse than burn the mill. They might even have attacked the fort."

"They never meant to attack the fort."

"You can't know that for certain."

"I *do*. Now. Although the only reason I can think of is that *les Bostonais* lacked the stomach for it. If La Tour had thrown his whole force against our palisades, he would have taken us—from the landward side. In all my years here it would've been the work of one summer to make the south and east walls as strong as the riverfront bastions. . . ."

"You can now."

"I *will*. Too late. Three men dead and ten wounded . . . And the people of Port Royal have no mill to grind their bread for the winter."

"You can build the mill anew. The fire won't have hurt the millstones."

"Perhaps not. Given enough heat, even stones can crack, but perhaps not. Regardless, by the time we raise a new mill house on the old foundations, and build a new waterwheel, it would be winter. Ice does not turn waterwheels."

"We can build a windmill, instead. And then, next year, we can import another set of millstones and build a new water mill. The way Port Royal keeps growing, we'll need two mills soon anyway."

"Yes, I suppose I could always *buy* another set of mill-stones, and *pay* to freight them here. . . ."

Although the surface of his words was less bleak than what had gone before, there was a new source of bitterness in his voice that Jeanne didn't understand, so couldn't guess how to counter it.

The hand covering his eyes suddenly slapped down on its chair arm—leaving a streak of soot across his nose—and the hand she was holding gave hers a reassuring squeeze that next to splintered her fingers. He said in a firmer voice: "Well, 'tis an ill wind . . . Forgive me, my dear, for indulging in whimpering. The moment has passed.

"The good that comes of this ill wind is that the *Sieur de* La Tour has finished himself. Once the Conseil du Roi learns he attacked Port Royal with an English force . . . But, that does mean sailing to France again to report the matter. *Before* the winter storms, I assure you.

"Odd, though . . ." he added. "The prospect of spending the winter in Paris only brings to mind that we will not be able to be in Port Royal when the apple orchards blossom. Is that not odd?"

"Not so odd."

CHAPTER 26

D'Aulnay stood on the eastern palisade, watching relays of men with wheelbarrows and spades heaping up earth for the new bastion. The logs they were using for the framework had been meant to crib the new dike along La Petite Rivière, but it would just have to wait another year.

He let his gaze drift away from the workmen and up the

gilded hills framing Port Royal. Even though the leaves were
turning, he was quite sure he could linger in Port Royal a few
days longer and still be safely across the ocean before the winter gales set in.

He turned to look out over the farms along La Rivière au
Dauphin. From this distance they looked like toys that he
could scoop up and hold in his hand: cottage, barn, gnat-sized
milk cow and all.

At least one advantage to spending the winter in France was
that he could advertise for more peasant farmers to bring back
with him. It would mean borrowing more money to provide
for them until their first harvests, but he could simply add it on
to the money he'd already have to borrow. The *Vierge* alone
had cost him two thousand *livres* for each month of the blockade, in victuals and wages for men who might have been employed making land, or cutting timber, or laying in furs and
fish and seal oil to sell in France.

But whatever further debt he had to incur for further colonists would be worth it—and not just for the sake of future
rents, or to satisfy the Hundred Associates' commitment to colonize Acadia. There was a satisfaction in knowing that he
could close his eyes and see the wilderness that had been there
the day he'd first sailed up La Rivière au Dauphin, then open
them again and see the peaceful little farms nestled around the
church spire and Capuchin monastery and the school for teaching *les sauvages* the ways of civilization. Gazing out over his
seigneurie, he actually forgot for a moment the shame that had
been riding him since the day Charles La Tour raped Port
Royal and sailed away.

D'Aulnay winced as the source of his moment of peace
turned on him: the first and most sacred duty of any *seigneur*
was to protect the people huddled against his château walls.

"Monsieur le Gouverneur?"

D'Aulnay turned. It was the leather-faced Capuchin missionary who helped with translation with *les sauvages*, having
learned the languages from Biencourt and La Tour. "Yes, Father?"

"There is a difficulty in the trading house. One of the

sagamos—you presented him with a musket last year—says he must have a new one."

"After one year?"

The priest shrugged. "He says if you do not give him a new one, he must go to La Tour for one, and La Tour will not give him one unless he instructs his people to trade at Port Royal no more."

"What became of the perfectly good musket I gave him?"

"The *sagamo*'s son died. You know how they are about their children. The *sagamo* interred the musket with him so the boy would have something to hunt with in the next life."

"This is ridiculous. It's past time, Father, that we put a stop to this manner of nonsense. Come along."

The *sagamo* in question was squatting on the trading-house floor with his arms crossed. He had a yellow triangle painted under one eye, and his headband dangled a fringe of small, white shells. D'Aulnay said to the Capuchin: "Tell him that everything his son needs in the next world will be provided without he need hunt for it. Tell him he can dig the musket up and his son's soul will never miss it."

The priest translated that and then translated the *sagamo*'s reply. "He says that all that may be true of Frenchmen's souls, but his people still must hunt and fish in the next world—otherwise, how would they pass the time?"

"If I prove to him that the gifts buried with the dead do not go with them to the next life, but merely lie wasting in the earth, will he cease this practice and instruct his people to do the same?"

"He says yes he *would* do so, but *will* not—since you cannot prove what is not true."

"We'll see what can be proved. Tell him to take us to the burial island."

When the missionary translated that, the *sagamo* gave out a grunt and sidled his eyes up—*les sauvages*' equivalent response to getting a knife shoved in the guts and twisted. The *sagamo* murmured some words that the Capuchin translated as: "He says he cannot take us there. Were anyone not of his tribe to learn where their dead are buried, they could desecrate the graves."

"Oh, for God's sake—forgive me, Father—anyone wishing to know where their dead are buried has only to follow the keening of a burial canoe. Tell him we will go in a sloop with only a skeleton crew—which seems appropriate—and every man of them will swear to you on his hope of salvation not to give out the secret."

The *sagamo* looked skeptical, but what he said in response sounded a good deal longer than "no." "He says: When you discover you cannot prove what is not true, will you give him a new gun?"

D'Aulnay had to laugh. "Yes! Upon my honor if the gifts buried with their dead have been magically transported up to heaven, I will most certainly give him a new musket. And a barrel of rum to steady his aim."

They took four oarsmen and a boatswain. Once out on the Baye Françoise, d'Aulnay ordered the sail set, and the *sagamo* pointed in the general direction of Cape Sable. Late in the afternoon, with Menane Island hazy in the distance, the *sagamo* pointed them toward a smaller island with a crest of straggly pines.

The surface of the island was pocked with hummocks of earth and piled stones. The place had an eerie undertone of unknown centuries of superstition. D'Aulnay pointed to the nearest hummock and said: "Break it open."

The sailors went to work with mattocks and spades. D'Aulnay raised a scented handkerchief to his nose. Not that he expected a great deal of putrescence, given that the gutted body would have been hung in a tree to sun-dry for a year before interment, but a *soupçon* of putrescence was more than he cared for.

The spades unearthed a birchbark-shrouded corpse and several surrounding objects, among them a beaver pelt that would have fetched ten *livres* in La Rochelle. The corpse was probably female, since one of the gifts buried with it was a copper kettle now grown green with verdigris.

D'Aulnay twitched a gloved fingertip through the crusted

green flakes and said: "This kettle might just as well have been tossed in a latrine, or in the sea. It has *not* gone to the land of the dead with this woman. And the living have had no more use of it than the dead."

The *sagamo* drew his knife from the sheath hung 'round his neck and tapped the blade against the kettle, then spoke to the missionary. The Capuchin cleared his throat a few times before speaking. "He says . . . he says, monsieur, the kettle has no voice; that a copper kettle struck with a knife should make a ringing sound, but this one does not."

"Precisely. It's verdigrised to uselessness."

"That is not, um . . . not *precisely*, Monsieur le Gouverneur . . . not precisely how the *sagamo* puts it. He says that the soul of the kettle has obviously gone with the soul of the dead woman, leaving their bodies behind to rot."

One of the boat crew snickered. D'Aulnay said: "Boatswain, take that man's name."

"And," the priest continued, "the *sagamo* wants to know: Will you give him his new gun now or when we get back to Port Royal? And he remembers you saying something about a barrel of rum. . . ."

D'Aulnay looked down at the black eyes under the bobbing white shells. The eyes and the visage around them expressed nothing, as was those people's wont. But d'Aulnay knew the creature was laughing at him.

CHAPTER 27

Among the new recruits Françoise had brought on the *St. Clément* were two young men who hadn't come as *engagés* but to make their fortunes in the fur trade. They had both grown up in the same town in France, had both been apprentices to the same merchant, and had pooled all their money to buy a few trade goods and pay their passage to Acadia. Another thing they had in common was an eye for Lorette.

Françoise could only hope Lorette had the sense not to take young men too seriously, but there was no denying it was pleasant to watch her blush and blossom as the two young men wooed her in their very different ways. Jean Pierre was by far the more intelligent, quick with his hands and his tongue—perhaps a shade *too* quick. Gaspard had the gawkiness of a boy who still hadn't adjusted to his last spurt of growth, and his efforts to impress Lorette by playing his fiddle were more likely to impress with his doggedness than with his musical soul.

Lorette asked Françoise for the first time in years to tell her again who her parents had been. Françoise had to think for a moment to remember whether she'd said Lorette's mother and father had died in the siege of La Rochelle or in the smallpox epidemic.

The one thing Jean Pierre and Gaspard didn't share the same opinion on was how to find furs: Jean Pierre insisting they should sail a shallop down the coast and Gaspard holding doggedly to the notion of trekking inland along La Rivière St. Jean. La Tour gave them the license to go wherever and do whatever they wished, as long as he was given a percentage of any furs they brought back.

A freak early dusting of snow announced the beginning of the trapping season. It also made the captain of the *St. Clément* apoplectic to get started back to France, but for some reason Françoise couldn't fathom, La Tour cajoled him into waiting a little longer.

The day the two young fortune hunters set off on their first trading expedition—Jean Pierre in a boat rented from La Tour; Gaspard hobbling awkwardly on snowshoes in a finger's breadth of snow—Françoise happened to be outside the fort, introducing Claude to the wonders of falling leaves. A funeral canoe came over the carrying path, was lowered into the harbor, and paddled out past the *St. Clément*.

Françoise had seen enough funeral canoes go by to recognize the difference in keening that signified a child. She had once been in a wigwam where the only sign that the man lying quietly by the fire had a broken leg was a sheen of sweat on his forehead; but if the same man had lost a child, he would have wailed like a whipped dog.

The funeral canoe gave her a chill, reminding her just how fragile anyone's happiness was. She bundled Claude up tightly in his rabbit blanket and carried him back through the gatehouse.

She stood in the courtyard for a moment with her son in her arms, gazing at the striped roof of her house—snow glistening between the ridges of the glistening pink roof tiles—and at the slumbering rose vines twined around the door. In another three or four years they would have climbed high enough to train them into an arch over the lintel.

Gaspard returned just as La Tour had predicted, with nothing to show from two weeks in the woods but frostbite and leg cramps and a few rabbit skins. La Tour generously offered him a contract at the same rate of pay as any other *engagé* who had no trade—except that La Tour wouldn't have to pay Gaspard's passage from France.

Jean Pierre was another matter. Françoise was just sitting down to caribou ragout with the officers of Jemseg when a salt- and ice-rimed apparition toted in a bulging sack and dumped its contents by La Tour's chair.

La Tour bent to rifle through the pelts and said: "God's teeth! Look at this—a sealskin robe! And *this*," thrusting a beaver pelt at Françoise. "I ain't seen the like in years. See? The guard hairs are all worn off, so they won't have to be shorn off. When we first started trading, all the beaver pelts were like this, from the people of the country wearing them against their skin all winter. We laughed at them for taking glass beads and suchlike trash for furs; they laughed at us for buying such trash as worn-out, stinky, old pelts."

He turned from her to Jean Pierre. "Where the devil did you . . . ?"

"There was a hunting party moving along the coast."

"At *this* time of year?"

Jean Pierre just shrugged as though anyone of sufficient intelligence could find a fur-laden hunting party anywhere at any time of year. From the doorway of the *engagés'* dining hall, his friend Gaspard stood staring gloomily at Lorette.

A few days later Françoise and La Tour were busy trying to tickle Claude out of his teething temper when Rainville came dripping snow into the sitting room. "Charlot, Keeshetech is outside, with several other *sagamos*."

La Tour said: "Several? What are they doing on the coast at this time of year?"

Rainville had no reply, but his porcelain-doll features looked drawn taut. Françoise stopped tickling Claude and looked to his father, who made a very poor show of unconcernedly saying: "Well, I'd best ask them, then," and followed Rainville out the door.

A moment later La Tour came back in, picked up his wheel-lock pistol, and bellowed: "Lorette!"

Lorette's voice wafted from the dining hall: *"Oui?"*

"Do you know where Jean Pierre is?"

"He is here with me."

"Jean Pierre!"

Jean Pierre appeared in the doorway, with Lorette hovering behind him. *"Oui*, monsieur?"

La Tour spoke offhandedly without looking at Jean Pierre, as though the focus of the moment was to tamp the powder, wadding and ball into the pistol and wind the wheel lock, a process Françoise guessed he could accomplish in his sleep. "There is some difficulty with some of the people of the country. You and I must speak to them. They are a peaceable people by and large, *but* . . ." He cocked his elbow to prop the pistol against his shoulder and winked at Jean Pierre: "We are well enough insured."

La Tour slung his shot pouch and powder flask over his shoulder and ushered Jean Pierre outside. Françoise slung Claude into the crook of her arm and followed them curiously, with Lorette falling in behind.

A dabble of freezing rain was coming down. Keeshetech

and a half-dozen other *sagamos* stood with their arms crossed under their fur robes. Rainville was coming from the warehouse, carrying one of Jean Pierre's worn-smooth beaver pelts.

La Tour said a few words in Micmac to the *sagamos*, then snatched the beaver pelt from Rainville and brandished it at Jean Pierre. "Where did you get this?"

"I told you, monsieur, there was a hunting party of—"

"Dogshit. Someone rifled the graves on their burial island."

"Monsieur, I—"

"Tell me the truth! Was it you? I can save you if you tell me the truth! Otherwise . . ." La Tour jerked his head to indicate the waiting *sauvages*. "Tell me the *truth*, for the love of God!"

Jean Pierre had turned gasping and pale, "*Oui*, monsieur, but I only—"

Whatever Jean Pierre had "only" done was lost in the roar of Keeshetech and the other *sagamos* springing toward him. Jean Pierre started to back away, but La Tour grabbed his arm, shook his head not to worry, and pointed his pistol at the *sagamos*. The *sagamos* stopped dead and Jean Pierre exhaled his relief. Then La Tour swung around, pushed the mouth of the pistol into Jean Pierre's face, and pulled the trigger.

As the wheel spun and sparked, Jean Pierre ducked his head and squealed. La Tour tracked him with the muzzle for the instant it took for the powder to explode. There was a fountain of blood and brains and bone chips and Jean Pierre flopped on the ground with his feet and hands twitching. The twitches obviously wouldn't last for long.

Françoise had clamped her hand over Claude's eyes when she saw the pistol come up, but he was screaming nonetheless. Lorette fell back against the wall and sank down it, shrieking. Françoise knelt beside her, trying to comfort Lorette and Claude at the same time.

La Tour came toward them, reloading his pistol and rewinding the wheel. He crouched in front of Lorette and shook her shoulder. "Lorette . . . ? *Lorette!* Listen to me. . . . He would've destroyed us all. But, if . . . *if* . . ." His voice had grown thick with emotion and resignation. He pushed the loaded pistol into Lorette's hands, then stood and stepped back, opening his arms to present his torso as a target. "*If* you think I was wrong to . . ."

Lorette raised the pistol in both hands, the barrel gyrating, then suddenly dropped it and leaped up to press her torso against his. He closed his arms around her and kissed the top of her sobbing head. She broke away from him and ran inside.

La Tour turned his back on Françoise to face Keeshetech and the other *sagamos* and made a "W" with his arms. Keeshetech nodded and the *sagamos* turned to go. Françoise shifted Claude onto her left arm, snatched up the pistol with her right hand, and yelled: "La Tour!"

He turned to face her and she pulled the trigger. The pistol bucked in her hand. The burning wad hit him in midchest and fell smoldering between his feet. She said: "I *thought* I saw you palm the ball."

"You *thought* . . . ?"

CHAPTER 28

As the autumn grew older La Tour grew shorter of excuses to keep the captain of the *St. Clément* from embarking. He knew he couldn't hold the captain back forever, but the longer he did so, the longer he could avoid making a decision he didn't want to have to make.

Despite all his rational explanations to Françoise for making the raid on Port Royal, he'd begun to wonder if he wouldn't have been far wiser to have simply broken the blockade and then stayed peaceably at Jemseg. But after all those months of staring at the *Vierge* blocking his harbor, and then the chase across the bay, by the time they'd gotten to Port Royal, his blood had been up. Whenever that happened, second thoughts were a matter for another day.

He knew d'Aulnay was planning to spend the coming winter in France. La Tour was reasonably certain that an adroit advocate could make the Conseil du Roi understand that burning d'Aulnay's mill and employing English mercenaries had been acts of self-defense—given that d'Aulnay had done his best to take Jemseg by storm and then had set himself to starving fellow Frenchmen to death. But he highly doubted that d'Aulnay intended to draw the Conseil's attention to the latter details.

One night, as the company in the officers' dining hall was thinning out, the captain of the *St. Clément* leaned across the table to say: "I *must* sail with tomorrow's tide. It is my duty to the king, and to my crew, to bring the *St. Clément* safely to La Rochelle before the winter storms set in. Already I may have waited too long."

La Tour took a careful sip of wine and sighed resignedly. "Methinks you should have plenty of room for passengers, after leaving off my forty-five *engagés*."

"What passengers?"

"The messengers and shallop crew d'Aulnay sent me last summer grow aweary of my hospitality. And I grow aweary of housing and feeding them. But d'Aulnay already has more than enough troops at Port Royal, so I shall send these thirteen back to France with you. And . . ." La Tour paused to take another sip of wine and a last desperate search for alternatives. There were none. "And I will be going with them."

Françoise's eyes shot toward him, but if she'd intended to say anything she didn't get the chance, because Rainville jumped in with, "You can't!"

"I have no choice. I've been trying my damnedest to think of another. If I don't go to France this year to tell the other side of the story d'Aulnay will tell them, next year the king sends warships to help him take Jemseg."

"If you go to France," Rainville barked, "there will *be* no Jemseg when you get back. 'Tis one thing to keep Port Royal from knowing you've snuck to Boston for a month or two, but six months going back and forth to France—six months at the *least*? When Le Creux learns you are gone, he will come with every man and ship and gun he can lay hands on! How long do you think our men will die for you when you're not here to take your chances with them?"

La Tour shrugged. "I misdoubt Le Creux will come. He ain't near so ambitious as his master."

"But he follows his master's orders. Do you misdoubt d'Aulnay will leave Le Creux orders to take this place if you're not here to defend it?"

La Tour sighed again. "I do not dispute you, Rainville, but 'tis a chance we must take."

"And what *chance* will any of us here have if d'Aulnay's relatives on the Conseil du Roi clap you in the Bastille?"

La Tour rubbed his hand across his mouth and repeated: " 'Tis a chance we must take. I see no other—"

"I have been wondering"—Françoise cut him off without raising her voice—"what they are wearing in Paris this year."

In the night, while he was trying to memorize the body he'd barely had a chance to get reacquainted with, she said: "How long would you have waited for me to volunteer?"

"If you think I *want* you to go, after we only had the summer together—and half of that in *Boston* . . ."

"But you knew you could not go yourself."

"I'd've had to chance it, regardless that Rainville was likely right. But the least I can do is see you don't go traveling unprotected. Last time Gargot happened to be traveling in your same direction. This time I'll send Rainville with you."

"Rainville?" She laughed. "He's pleasant enough company, but when it comes to a watchdog . . . Sending Rainville in Gargot's stead do seem rather like replacing a mastiff with a spaniel."

"You do have a point. If some lout annoyed you, Gargot would simply hit him with a chair. Rainville would kill him."

"Little Rainville?"

"You've never seen 'Little Rainville' with a sword in his hand. If ever you do, pray God I ain't the one at t'other end of it. Rainville, you see, is left-handed."

"I know that."

"Ah, but do you know what that means in a sword fight? A left-handed man has been fighting right-handed men all his life. A right-handed man may have faced a left-handed man once or twice—twice if he's lucky enough to live through the first one. Add to that the fact that a left-handed boy as small and pretty as Rainville was meat and drink to bullies, until he grew old enough to wield a sword. . . . Add to *that* that Rainville adores you beyond reason—or at least any reason as I can see—and you will see why I ask you not to show you've been annoyed or insulted by any man you meet between here and Paris and back. Unless the man deserves what 'Little Rainville' will give him."

"I never would've thought, to look at him . . ."

"Neither would most people. That's another reason why a number of men have ended up with surprised looks on their faces and a length of steel in their guts."

"I will try not to slip his leash unless it's necessary. Can I trust you to keep half an eye on Lorette while I'm gone? I don't expect she'll want to come with me this time, since Gaspard is working so hard to console her for Jean Pierre."

"More than half an eye; she's filling out quite nicel—" Her elbow took him squarely in the ribs. Remarkable that there could be such a sharp-pointed bone in such a roll-fleshed arm. When he regained his breath, he said: "Will you take Claude with you?"

"I couldn't bear to be parted from him as well. And I would hardly trust you to take care of a toddling child. Besides, he is old enough to start playing his part; a lone woman with a child is so much more an object of sympathy." She added in an oddly acid tone: "And I do not know that *all* the Conseil du Roi are old enough to see me as an object of anything else."

"Pardon me?"

"Enough talking. We have only one night."

They said good-bye on the wharf. La Tour stood watching that diminutive, red-cloaked figure growing ever smaller as the boat carried her out toward the *St. Clément*. It did seem odd that the sight of a cherub-sized, big-eyed woman diminishing eastward should make him feel perfectly certain that anything

that might be done for him in France would be done as well
as he could himself, or better. Of all the strokes of idiot luck
he'd ever stumbled into . . .

He sniffled and wiped his eyes. He was definitely getting
old, and incontinent of sentiment. The little red patch disappeared up the boat stairs onto the deck of the *St. Clément*, the
boat turned back, and the ship weighed anchor. La Tour raised
his arm and the guns of Jemseg fort thundered a parting salute
that echoed off the hills cupping the harbor. The stern guns of
the *St. Clément* replied as the ebbing tide carried her out into
the bay.

La Tour turned and made his way back along the wharf and
up the path to the fort. The master gunner said as he passed
by: "Looks like another long, cold winter, Charlot."

CHAPTER 29

When d'Aulnay judged that the *Vierge* was within a
day or so of France, he ordered the ensign raised.
There was no need of it on the open sea, unless they were en-
countering another vessel. The next day passed with still no
sight of land, but at sunset a ketch appeared, also flying the
fleur-de-lis.

The children crowded the rail to peer out at the proof that
there actually was other human life upon the planet Oceania.
Their mother hovered behind them to make sure none of them
poked more than their noses beyond the balustrades. D'Aulnay
took up the speaking trumpet and hailed the ketch. "How far
out from La Rochelle?"

"One hundred leagues!" which was a good deal farther than
d'Aulnay had estimated.

"What news have you of France? We've had none fresher than April!"

"The king is dead! He outlived his cardinal by only half a year! The queen rules for the little dauphin!"

D'Aulnay slammed the speaking trumpet down on the rail, causing the children to jump and the captain to wring his hands in anguish for his instrument. If d'Aulnay had known the king had died, he would've postponed the trip to France until next year, when the factions in the court of Louis XIII had had time to reposition themselves around the future Louis XIV and his mother.

For all d'Aulnay knew, his father and his friends might have been ousted from the Conseil du Roi. For that matter, the Conseil du Roi might be meaningless, now that the king they were supposed to council was barely five years old. But there was nothing d'Aulnay could do about it except order an extra measure of wine served out, to pledge *"Le roi est mort, vive le roi."*

When they made port, d'Aulnay stayed only overnight in La Rochelle, then set off in a carriage for Château Charnisay. He might've said he dreaded the coming interview, except that the very thought was ridiculous; how could a man dread to see his own father? Especially a father as esteemed and venerable as René de Menou.

But d'Aulnay did acknowledge to himself that there was one event he would rather it weren't necessary to relate to his father: the fact that Charles de Menou, Sieur d'Aulnay et de Charnisay, had stood looking on impotently from the palisades while Charles La Tour burned his gristmill and killed or wounded a dozen of his people.

His father merely raised an eyebrow and pursed his mouth—as though he'd just bitten down on something distasteful, but was far too well-bred to embarrass his hostess—then said: "I suppose it will be of use in giving the man La Tour the character of a renegade. Did you bring documents which I might use as proof of the event?"

"I wrote a memoir which communicates quite clearly, I believe, that La Tour has put himself outside the law." It had cost d'Aulnay a good deal to refer in the memoir to the *Sieur de* La Tour, but it had seemed politic to display that he could be tolerant of La Tour's pretensions but not his crimes.

His father responded with a courtly shrug that communicated quite clearly that a memoir from the complainant wasn't likely to stand as proof among the dwellers of the higher altitudes. D'Aulnay hastened to add: "And two sworn statements from Capuchins who witnessed the attack on Port Royal. The holy fathers also related that La Tour attended the Puritan church in Boston, and allowed Puritan clergy to come on board his ship and pray loudly within hearing of the Recollets. The Capuchins have that on good evidence, from a wounded man La Tour left behind to die but did not."

"Those indiscretions on the matter of religion will be useful to us. Although it is still a policy of the state to tolerate Protestants in places such as La Rochelle, the very reason they are not allowed to emigrate to Quebec is the apprehension that they might ally themselves with the Protestant English colonies. The more proof we have that this La Tour has done precisely that in Acadia . . .

"But even so, it will not be easy to bring the matter to a successful conclusion. In these times no one knows who rules France from one day to the next. Or who rules the queen regent, more precisely—although it becomes increasingly clear that that which lies within her crown pays less heed to what arises in the crowns of councillors than doth that which lies within her *skirts* pays heed to what arises in the skirts of Cardinal Mazarin.

"Fortunately, although our kinship to the blessed Cardinal Richelieu was of great use to us during his life, I was not such a fool—as many others were—as to not realize that even he was mortal, and that the queen who loathed him would outlive him. So I never failed to pay her compliments, through all those years when others thought to flatter themselves by displaying that they were grand enough to snub a queen.

"*Un*fortunately, though, there is also the matter of that woman."

"Which woman?"

His father said incredulously—or as near to incredulous as the court of ice allowed: "Do you have no informants in your enemy's camp?"

"There *was* one, years ago . . . but he met with an accident. Since then . . . La Tour does seem to have an ability to discourage disloyalty in those who serve him."

"Some men have that ability."

"I suppose they are all terrified that his friends among *les sauvages* would find them out."

"I suppose. But then, what discourages disloyalty in his friends among *les sauvages* . . . ?" D'Aulnay started to formulate an answer, but it proved to be a rhetorical question. "Regardless, you should have it made known to you now that which should have been made known to you before you set sail from Acadia—that which I most mistakenly assumed was the very reason you set sail from Acadia: the case of your travails with that fellow La Tour is already being represented in France, and in a very different light than you have represented it to me."

"By whom?"

"Whom else? By that woman: Françoise Marie Jacquelin."

CHAPTER 30

In the house that the de Menous kept in Paris, within a short walk of the palace of the Louvre, Jeanne sat with her husband interviewing a woman who would go back to Port Royal with them. A sudden cascade of servants in the foyer signified that René de Menou was home. Charles said: "If you will excuse me for a moment," and left the room.

Jeanne carried on with interviewing Madame de Brice, a

widow whom the Capuchins had persuaded to take on the task of educating Micmac girls. The Capuchins had been educating Micmac boys for some years now, but the girls had had to wait until a female teacher could be found. Madame de Brice might also serve as tutor for the governor's children, if Jeanne decided she was suitable.

"Your own children, Madame de Brice, are all grown?"

"That they are, madame—as much as any mother's children can ever seem grown. Two of my sons are Capuchin fathers. The prefect of missions has very kindly agreed to delegate them both to Port Royal. My third son is clerk to a merchant in the Vendôme. He is a very clever boy—oh dear, 'young man,' I should say. Perhaps someday it might be possible for Governor d'Aulnay to employ him at Port Royal . . . ? And then we could all be together."

"That may well be. The governor will be greatly in your debt if you can teach the Micmac girls to be as little out of place at Port Royal as in the forest."

"Oh, the governor will owe me nothing for that, madame. I will feel blessed that the good God uses me to bring their souls out of the darkness."

"Not only their souls." Madame de Brice looked confused. "You see, Port Royal is growing, but not so quickly as it might. An *engagé* who finishes his term might be inclined to stay and build a farm there, but not so many do, since the only marriageable women there are the few household servants we bring out from France. Your school will change that."

"You cannot mean, madame, that Christian Frenchmen should marry with women of *les sauvages*?"

"But after they have gone through your school they will not be *sauvages*, will they?"

"But they will still be . . ."

"They are still children of God, the same as all of us. Is that not so?"

"I am corrected, madame. You remind me that I go to Acadia to learn, as much as to teach."

"Your teaching will also be helping the governor by preventing desertions. More than once in the past an *engagé* or man-at-arms has lost his heart to a daughter of the forest. But until now there's been no school where she might learn to be at ease at Port Royal. So they slip across the bay to Jemseg and are lost to us."

"Jemseg is where lives this La Tour?"

"Yes. La Tour."

"And he has no scruples against taking in contract breakers and women of the woods?"

"Methinks he hath no scruples whatsoever." A flicker of alarm crossed Madame de Brice's horsey face. "But he can do no harm to us at Port Royal."

"Did he not kill twenty of your people last year, madame, and burn half the town?"

"*Three* of our men-at-arms were killed in driving him off. And all he burned was a gristmill set far apart from the fort and settlement. And now that Charles—the governor, that is—has strengthened our defenses, there is no danger of the like ever happening again. And by the time we sail from France, with a new decree from the Conseil du Roi, the name La Tour will mean nothing to us but an unpleasant memory."

"Do you truly believe so, madame?"

"If I believed he could do any further harm to us at Port Royal, would I be taking my children back there?"

Charles came back into the room and sat stiffly pretending to listen while Jeanne told Madame de Brice which books Joseph was able to read on his own and of Nicole's remarkable aptitude with figures. Finally, Jeanne turned to him and said: "Did you have any more questions you wished to ask Madame de Brice?"

"I think not. If you are done . . . ?" Jeanne nodded and he turned to Madame de Brice. "You will be hearing from us soon. The sedan chair awaits to take you back to your lodgings."

After Madame de Brice had curtsied her way out, Jeanne said: "What did your father say?"

"I have been a fool yet again. That is not what he *said*, but that is the fact. All the while I have been wary only of La Tour, but that slut of a woman is just as dangerous.

"She had an audience with three of the Conseil du Roi this afternoon and beguiled two of them—by holding her brat in her lap the whole time so she could play the pitiable Madonna. My father believes the damage can be repaired, but nothing is certain."

"It *is* certain you are in the right. No amount of beguiling can change that."

"Would that I had your faith."

"You always have my faith. I know you will do whatever needs doing to make things right. And then, when we sail home in the spring, we'll know we never need fear again what lies your enemies may try to spread in France."

He smiled and reached across to pat her hand. But there was something mechanical in the gesture that made her wonder if her faith in him wasn't more of an added burden than a support. She offered up brightly: "I believe we need look no further for a tutor than Madame de Brice."

"If you believe so, then the matter is settled. I must confess, I had my doubts whether we could find another educated woman willing to cast her lot in Acadia, if Madame de Brice had not met with your approval."

"Then the only question left is the matter of her salary."

"Salary? The Capuchins have already secured a gift of fifteen thousand *livres* from the queen to subsidize the girls' school."

"But the school is a separate matter from tutoring our children. You needn't concern yourself with it; leave it to me to find out what tutors' salaries are in Paris and La Rochelle, and come to an arrangement with Madame de Brice. I believe she could be very easily accommodated, if you could find a position for her son at Port Royal."

He said through his teeth: "With another *salary*?"

"He is said to be very able—"

"Mother of Christ!" He slammed his hand down on the delicate little side table. "I am barely able to keep my *own* family from drowning!"

For an instant she couldn't move. Then she rose to her feet, shaking, and turned toward the door. She heard him call after her, but once she'd started moving she couldn't stop. Her feet chose to carry her along the corridor and onto the staircase.

It wasn't the shock of his anger; she'd seen him angry before. It was the sudden revelation that the La Tours might not be the worst of his troubles. Perhaps all the while that she'd been congratulating herself on saving a few sous on a shipment of wine, he'd been gritting his teeth as each new domestic comfort whittled the scaffolding beneath him. She had never thought that the Sieur d'Aulnay et de Charnisay could mine out his resources. She had never thought . . .

There were no more stairs to climb. She would have to turn to the left or right to keep on moving. She turned toward the nursery. When she opened the door, Joseph looked up from the draughts board, giggling. His crowing over his latest triumph over Nicole dissolved into a stricken: "*Maman!* Why do you weep?"

"I do not weep, my dear. Merely a speck of dust got in my eye. You keep on playing now, I have to rest a little while."

She went into her and Charles's room, closed the door, and sat looking out at the gray Paris snow. She hadn't realized up till now how complacent she'd become about playing the role of the governor's lady—mimicking aristocratic speech, wearing her chatelaine's keys—when she could never change the fact that she was middling Jeanne Motin from La Rochelle.

But then, she *was* the wife of the Sieur d'Aulnay, and he her husband, and there was nothing anyone could do to change that. Not that she would want anyone to if they could. She reminded herself of the facts of life, wiped her eyes, and resolved to do better. Instead of spinning out imaginings of what might be tormenting him, she should ask him. But she stayed sitting in the closed and darkened room, looking out at the gray snow.

CHAPTER 31

The relief of venting his frustration only lasted d'Aulnay an instant before it turned on him with a vengeance. By the time Jeanne's back was through the doorway, he realized he'd broken the Eleventh Commandment: Thou shalt *not* show doubt or fear to those dependent upon thee.

He sat there for a long time, berating himself for shattering her serenity for the sake of an instant's self-indulgence. He rehearsed a thousand ways to undo what he'd done.

The thought crept in that perhaps it were better he not undo it. Perhaps it was past time that Jeanne stopped living in a faerie castle, unaware that he was sneaking down into the dungeons at night and frantically shoring up the foundations. But if she did become aware, there would be nothing she could do about it except worry that her castle might collapse. And as soon as La Tour was removed, her husband's finances would be truly as secure as she imagined they were now.

As the supper hour drew nigh, d'Aulnay went up into their room and found her sitting at the dressing table while her maid put the finishing touches to her hair. He said to the maid: "You may leave us for a moment." When they were alone, he put his hand on his wife's lithe, wide, beautifully bared shoulder and said: "Forgive me, my dear. I should not allow that woman Jacquelin to so try my patience as to lose my temper. I was not angry at you."

"I know that, Charles. Charles ... if Port Royal and all the rest you have to carry is putting a strain on money, there are many places in the household expenses where I can spend a little less here, save a little more there—"

"Not at all, my dear." He looked down into her pink-rimmed eyes in the mirror. "You are no doubt aware that this wearisome business with La Tour has meant unlooked-for expenses, as well as inhibiting income. But we are hardly in such straits that the chatelaine of Port Royal need serve *vin ordinaire* to guests, or be niggardly over the salary of a tutor for her children, or hesitate to suggest to her husband that he provide employment for the tutor's son."

"You would tell me, wouldn't you, Charles, if we were in difficulty?"

"Of course I would." He twined one soft, brown lock around his finger. "You need never fear, my dear, that you have married a man who cannot provide for you and your children."

Once a date had been set for the Conseil du Roi to render its decision, d'Aulnay's father grew exceedingly tight-lipped, saying only that as the deliberations drew closer to a conclusion it was no longer proper for a councillor of state to discuss matters of state with a petitioner. All d'Aulnay could do was wait.

He had plenty to occupy himself with while he waited, such as explaining to Emmanuel Le Borgne why he needed more money. "Once the Conseil du Roi has issued the order condemning La Tour, it will still be up to me to execute it. I learned firsthand last year that it will take a greater force of arms than I have presently at my command to pry La Tour out of his fort."

Le Borgne thoughtfully scratched a fingernail up and down his rodent teeth, then said: "Among my other ships, monsieur, is an old warship, the *Grand Cardinal*, carrying sixteen heavy cannons. She is sound, but not in trim. To refit her would not be sound business for me, unless it were for a lease of . . . fifty thousand *livres*."

D'Aulnay blanched, but said matter-of-factly: "Which sum you would of course be willing to advance me."

Le Borgne looked pained. "You must understand, monsieur,

that I have partners, who demand a certain amount of reason behind my decisions. *If* the Conseil du Roi condemns your rival, another fifty thousand *livres* would be a reasonable investment toward making you master of all Acadia. If, however, the Conseil does not decide entirely in your favor . . ."

"They will."

"I am a man of business, monsieur, not a seer. But if you are so certain, then you may rest easy that the *Grand Cardinal* will be put in fighting trim for you—once the Conseil du Roi has handed down its judgment."

The judgment came down on a sleety day in March. Among those assembled in the council hall of the Louvre to hear the edict read were Desjardins du Val, Godard de Rainville, and Françoise Marie Jacquelin, with La Tour's whelp in her arms. D'Aulnay stayed on the far side of the room from them.

Among those not present was René de Menou. D'Aulnay didn't know whether that meant his father was being squeezed out of the Conseil du Roi, or the edict was going to be so onesided against La Tour that his father thought it politic to avoid any appearance of family influence.

D'Aulnay began to worry when the edict granted permission to "the wife of the said La Tour" to send a ship carrying two months' provisions for his establishment at the mouth of La Rivière St. Jean. But then the edict went on to specify that said ship was forbidden to carry military supplies or reinforcements.

Said ship *would* carry the royal command to all French subjects in La Tour's employ that they immediately cease obeying the outlawed rebel's orders and instead place themselves in the service of the Sieur d'Aulnay et de Charnisay. Any who did not do so were guilty of treason, with no appeal or trial. It would be up to whoever captured them whether to carry out the sentence by hanging, drawing and quartering, the bastinado, breaking upon the wheel, or any other prescribed method.

Desjardins du Val was condemned to another unspecified sentence in one of His Most Christian Majesty's prisons, for conspiring to smuggle arms to the outlaw.

But the penultimate clause was one that d'Aulnay wouldn't have dreamed of praying for. The woman Françoise Marie Jacquelin was herewith forbidden to leave France, upon pain of death.

When d'Aulnay strode down the steps of the Louvre to his waiting sedan chair, the sleet was still dribbling down out of a dishwater sky and the streets were deep in muck. All in all, he hadn't seen such a glorious spring day since he was a boy roaming free in the gardens of Château Charnisay.

Chapter 32

La Tour was sitting on the floor of the officers' dining hall, trying to convince three *sagamos* from upriver that he would pay them for their furs as soon as his supply ship came from France, when the sentry bellowed: "A sail!" The practice of firing a signal gun had been discontinued until the few kegs left in the powder magazine grew less lonely.

La Tour excused himself and stepped out into the courtyard, past the climbing roses that Lorette was keeping weeded for Françoise's return. His impulse was to run straight to the wharf, but it might only be a passing fishing ship. Or, for that matter, d'Aulnay was expected back in the bay any day now. So instead he climbed to the parapet on top of the gatehouse and looked out over the harbor.

The ship was a medium-sized merchantman flying the cross-and-lilies. She looked a bit storm-battered, and carried barely enough guns to threaten a canoe. She anchored near the *Renard Noir* and lowered a boat. From one of the first figures climbing down the Jacob's ladder billowed the unmistakable, mustard-colored cloak of Rainville.

La Tour bellowed: "Open the gates!" and clattered back down the steps.

As his boots hit the courtyard Lorette called from the rose border: "Is it her?"

He hollered back: "Yes!" and kept on running. He didn't run far, though. Ever since his fiftieth birthday he'd found he couldn't sprint more than a couple of hundred paces without his lungs and heart threatening to abandon ship. He slowed to a brisk walk and got his breath back in time to grab Rainville's outstretched hand and yank him up onto the landing stage. With his eyes fixed on the ship, he clapped Rainville on the back and shouted: "Does the wench expect me to swim out to her again?"

Rainville stepped back and said: "Charlot, she is not there."

"What?"

"She is forbidden to leave France."

"What?"

"Upon pain of death. She decided it was safest and best for all of us if I sailed on the supply ship—"

"So you *left* her?"

"Charlot"—there were tears in Rainville's eyes—"I can no more sway Françoise than command the tides."

La Tour patted his stepbrother's shoulder. "Of course. Of course you could not. Well . . ." It seemed he hadn't gotten his breath back after all. "Come up to the house and help me drink the bottle of brandy I've been hoarding. It do sound as you have much to tell."

"And I have letters. From Françoise, and from Desjardins du Val."

On the way up to the fort Rainville told him—although La Tour only heard with half an ear: "We were forbidden to carry military supplies to you. But du Val arranged from his prison cell—"

"I thought they let him out . . . ?"

"They put him back in again. But he managed to see to it that our ship carried a tremendous store of powder and shot for her five little guns. If the authorities at La Rochelle ask our captain why almost none of it came back to France, he will tell a harrowing tale of an encounter with Dutch privateers."

Long after the celebration of the end of strict wine rationing had played itself out, La Tour sat alone with one candle in the cavern of the dining hall—alone but for old Père Montagne snoring in his chair. He tried rereading Françoise's letter again, but there was nothing in it he didn't already know by heart. It told him of how many rude new words Claude had added to his vocabulary, of the edict of the Conseil du Roi, and warned him of the *Grand Cardinal* and the new-hired men-at-arms d'Aulnay would be bringing back with him. But it said nothing of what she planned to do.

It ended, though, with: *If you were to make me the same offer your father did his Catherine during their bleak winter at Port Royal, I, too, would say no.*

CHAPTER 33

In a lodging house in the port of Calais, Françoise sat with a hand mirror and shoe polish, streaking a bit of gray into her hair. It had been night when she'd come to the inn and she'd kept her head covered so it was unlikely the innkeeper would notice any suspicious change.

Claude sat watching her with his mouth agape. He said: "Play pretend, *maman?*"

"Yes, Claude. But a very serious pretend. If we are found out, I will be punished very bad. Your part in the game is to pretend you are not as clever a boy as you are; so much less clever that the only words you know are *'maman'* and 'papa' and 'yes' and 'no.' If you need to say anything else, you must whisper it in my ear. Can you do that for me, Claude?"

"Yes, *maman*," but he sounded dubious. He climbed down off the bed and toddled toward her, glancing over his shoulder and beckoning her with his hand. She lowered her head and he whispered against her ear: "Claude can know 'Claude,' too?"

"Yes, dear. But only 'Claude'; you are not 'Claude de La Tour' until the pretend is over, just 'Claude.' So, you have five words. You can count them on your fingers."

He beckoned her to lower her head again and stood on tip-toe to whisper: "How long Claude pretend?"

"All day today, my dear, and perhaps tomorrow as well. I will tell you when we can stop pretending."

Claude nodded gravely and rehearsed, counting off on the fingers of his right hand: "Claude—*maman*—yes—no—papa . . ."

Françoise wet a fingertip and added a tinge of gray hearth ash under her eyes. Fortunately, the winter in France had taken the Acadian sun out of her cheeks, so she could leave her face primly unpowdered and still look appropriately pallid. She put on a nearly threadbare gown and finished off with a large crucifix prominently dangling over her breasts.

The sun was barely up. People opening their shops or dumping last night's slops stared at her as she went by. She was quite sure it was only because they were surprised to see an apparently respectable woman walking the streets with no escort but a three-year-old boy and a porter wheeling a trunk in a barrow. She was quite sure.

The porter knew the berth of the ship due to sail for Dover with the morning tide. As she followed the porter down the wharf Françoise tried not to notice the man-at-arms guarding the gangplank of a warship, or the lounging idler who looked too well fed for a dockworker. She didn't know whether she had reason to be wary or whether she'd turned into a rabbit that imagines a hunter behind every bush.

On and around the Dover ship sailors were scampering in all directions, rolling barrels up the gangway or covering the hatches with tarpaulins and planks. Françoise called up at the man who appeared to be in charge: "Pardon me, monsieur—are you the captain?"

"The captain is below, madame."

"I must speak with him."

Flustered, the man started: "Madame, the tide is—"

"*Please*, monsieur—I realize the captain has much to attend to, but it is a matter of life and death." Which was most certainly true, but not for reasons she had any intention of revealing.

The captain was sent for and appeared at the rail bobbing above her. She called up to him: "I am Marie Saint Juste. My husband, Charles—"

"Papa!" Claude cut in, holding up the baby finger on his right hand.

"Yes, Claude—but hush now."

"Yes"—Claude unfurled his second finger—"*maman*," his forefinger. She'd seen more eccentric stage mannerisms get past an audience.

"My husband, Captain, went to England two years ago, to fight in the cavalry of Prince Rupert of the Rhine against the Puritan rebels. I have had no word of him until two days ago, when I learned he had been wounded and captured and held in London, where he has been condemned to death for refusing to deny his faith. I must go and plead for his life—if . . . if it is not too late. . . ." She blinked against the tears even more assiduously than usual; if even one escaped, the haggard gray tinge under her eyes would turn to streaks of soot.

"It may not be safe for you there, madame. The city of London declared for the rebels at the beginning. They will not welcome a Catholic lady."

"There must be at least some gallantry left in them."

The captain shrugged. "The English and gallantry, madame . . ."

"I must go, regardless. I will pay you for a full cabin passage and still share a cabin, if needs be, or lodge in a corner of the hold—"

"That will not be necessary, madame. A cabin is available." He started down the gangplank to gallantly escort her up.

Françoise knew that if she set one foot on that gangplank she might just as well be climbing a gallows, if she were caught. Although the morning wind was blowing from the North Sea, trickles of sweat tickled down from her armpits. The captain extended his arm and she took it.

She stood at the stern rail with Claude in her arms, smelling the sea salt and pine tar that had become as familiar to her as hearth smoke, watching the coast of France disappear for what might very well be the last time. It surprised her that she didn't feel like she was leaving her homeland behind. A strange thing seemed to have happened over the last four years: she was no longer a *femme de France*, she was *Acadienne*.

On the coach from Dover to London, she surreptitiously slipped off her crucifix. The London inn she took Claude to was no longer the rollicking actors' haven she remembered; one of the first acts of the Puritan city council had been to shut down all the theaters. One of Françoise's first acts upon arriving was to order hot water to scrub the gray out of her hair, and to tell her little ace of trumps that the game was over. Although, for her, that wasn't strictly true. If she couldn't carry off the next "pretend," she and Claude would be stranded in England.

In the morning she put on a newer gown—adding on a scarf to hide her shoulders and décolleté—and tied her hair back with a simple ribbon, then set off with Claude in a hired carriage for the address Desjardins du Val had given her.

The people they passed along the way were all dressed in black or gray or brown. Respectable-looking women walked the streets unescorted. There was a man in the stocks in one public square, which caused Claude great amusement until Françoise asked him how he would like it if it happened to him.

"*Not* happen. Claude is a very good boy."

"People do not always have to be bad for such things to happen to them."

Their destination proved to be a large, unornamented, wooden house on a street of equally stolidly wealthy houses. To the servant who opened the door, Françoise repeated the formula Desjardins du Val had given her: " 'I am a woman of La Rochelle.' "

"Come in, madame. The master is in his study. If you will
but wait in the drawing room . . ."

She and Claude didn't have to wait long before a bald-
headed man in carpet slippers and a discreetly fur-trimmed
robe padded in and breathed: "Madame?"

"I am Françoise Marie Jacquelin. My husband is Charles
de La Tour, Governor of Acadia. Because we are Huguenots,
Cardinal Richelieu appointed a rival governor, the Sieur
d'Aulnay—"

"I have heard something of this situation, madame. Come,
sit. You of us who elected to remain in France even after the
first siege of La Rochelle are the brave ones. To so many of
us, the siege proved that the French crown would allow us our
rights only so long as we were too strong as to give them no
choice. Perhaps if we had stayed, La Rochelle would still be
too strong for them. Tell me how I may help you."

"I came to France last autumn to plead my husband's case
and to purchase supplies. We can hold out in Acadia against
the Catholics' attacks, but not without gunpowder and arms.
The Conseil du Roi has now forbidden anyone to send military
supplies to my husband, or to purchase his furs. I am under
sentence of death now for leaving France. But I could not
abandon my husband."

The gray-lashed eyes blinked mistily as he muttered:
" 'Whither thou goest, I go. . . .' So, madame, you wish to procure arms and a ship in England."

"You read my heart in a glance."

"It will not be easy—even though it is fortunate you come
when you do, before the season is far enough along for the armies of the king and of Parliament to take the field again.
There are some London aldermen who begin to murmur we
were fools to declare for Parliament, when the king's cavaliers
are bound to win out in the end. *But*"—he lined a finger along
his nose—"there is a young man named Cromwell who I believe is about to show the knights of popery a thing or three."

"Pray God."

"Pray God"—he nodded—"and strong sword arms. *But*, you
and your husband can hardly afford to wait until the day of our

victory. And, though your cause touches my heart, and will those of even English businessmen, in this world charity can only go so far. . . ."

"Because of last year's blockade, and this year's edict, my husband's warehouses in Acadia contain two years' harvest of furs. The yield for the last year we were allowed to trade was, in English money, some ten thousand pounds."

The gray tongue licked the gray lips. "I believe, madame, that even English businessmen could be induced to . . . You see, madame, English men of business are not the same as French. In France today a man invests in business only long enough to make sufficient capital to buy himself an *officier* so he can spend the rest of his life lording it about in a sedan chair collecting tithes and taxes. In England, a man who makes a hundred thousand pounds in business uses it to make another hundred thousand pounds in business, instead of aspiring to no higher state than a gilded parasite. That difference will be the ruin of France yet. *But*, methinks it also means that English businessmen will listen when I present them with your situation."

The good ship *Gillyflower* sailed from Brighton with a cargo of gunpowder and other necessities for the Huguenots besieged in Acadia. Her captain was well acquainted with Acadian waters, having captained the Boston ship the *Vierge* had dismasted on the Baye Françoise. On board the *Gillyflower* was the brother of a London alderman who'd invested heavily in the charitable expedition to succor his Protestant brethren. And also the wife and son of Charles de Saint Étienne de La Tour.

CHAPTER 34

When La Tour toted up all the cargo off Rainville's relief ship, he didn't feel all that relieved. The trade goods and provisions the Conseil du Roi had allowed were just enough to keep Jemseg a prospering concern until d'Aulnay arrived at his leisure to take it over. The powder and shot du Val had ingeniously found a way to smuggle only meant that Jemseg would be able to put up a defense for a day or two at most.

He could expect no ships from Boston to come bearing supplies to trade for furs and coal. He'd been cut off from *les Bostonais* once again, but not by a blockade this time—with the *Vierge* in France, Le Creux had no ship large enough to stand against the *Renard Noir*. But Governor Winthrop's "godless democracy" had caught up with him. The way La Tour had heard it, the reason Winthrop had come second in the latest election was that he'd embroiled New England in the messy affairs of New France.

No matter how many times La Tour added up the situation, it always came out to the same unpleasant conclusion: he would have to go to Boston again and convince the new governor that New England could ask for no better neighbor than a Jemseg governed by Charles de Saint Étienne de La Tour. It was damned inconvenient. But what with kings dying and parliaments revolting and the fickleness of electors, it seemed there wasn't a country in the world where a man wouldn't find himself rolling the same boulder up the same hill every time the wind shifted at the summit.

The *Renard Noir* was kept constantly in trim, so it was

merely a matter of loading on a few sacks of dried moose meat to flesh out the ship's biscuit, tightening a few ropes, and filling the hold with furs to remind *les Bostonais* of the righteousness of his cause. He took Rainville with him to help with translation, leaving the master gunner in command of Jemseg's remaining defenders. La Tour could only hope that if d'Aulnay got home while he was gone, he wouldn't move on Jemseg immediately. There were so many things he could only hope for these days, one more made little difference.

Once the *Renard Noir* was skimming down the bay on the outgoing tide, La Tour found his spirits lifting with her sails. D'Aulnay could buy all the *Grand Cardinal*s he wanted; no ship in the world could catch the *Renard Noir* in waters where La Tour knew every shoal and current and hidden cove.

Major Gibbons proved more than happy to offer the hospitality of his home again, and to accept a bale of beaver pelts as interest on his mortgage on Jemseg. Another assembly was called, to debate once more the question of La Tour, although it took some time for the magistrates and deputies to make their way to Boston from their settlements along the coast or in the deep woods.

The new governor was from one of those settlements, Salem. Governor Endecott was a well-padded man with a round red face and a white goatee and the commanding habits of an ex-soldier. But he wasn't a hard man to get along with. La Tour had found over the years that most men weren't, once he'd had a chance to sit down and talk with them awhile. Endecott spoke French, which facilitated matters. Best of all, he'd been among the magistrates at last summer's assemblies, so he'd had a chance to grow a bit softheaded about Françoise.

In a private conversation at the Gibbons house, Endecott confided: "However just be your cause, it is our duty to consider that if we help you and your lady, Monsieur d'Aulnay may take revenge on New England."

"Why the devil need you fear that? You outnumber him a dozen to one!"

"In plain numbers, yes. But we are farming colonies, scattered wide. You French colonize by trade, and settle close to your forts. If Monsieur d'Aulnay were ever to set his sights on one of our outlying settlements, or arm the Indians to come a-raiding . . ."

"So long as I am in Acadia, the people of the country will never enlist themselves with d'Aulnay." Endecott looked very thoughtful on that.

By the time the assembly convened, word had come that d'Aulnay was back and patrolling the Baye Françoise again, but this time in a monstrous warship with three gun decks. La Tour presented the assembly with every argument he could dredge up, from his legal standing as a baronet of New Scotland to the likelihood that an ambitious and intolerant Catholic like d'Aulnay would not be satisfied with taking Jemseg. Then he sat back down and the magistrates began to debate, and debate, and debate. When they'd debated it among themselves for several days, the magistrates and churchmen went back home and began the debate all over again with the citizens of Salem or New Haven or Connecticut. La Tour found it increasingly an effort to remain charming to men who dithered and dithered while he hung twisting in the wind.

He was sitting down to breakfast with Major Gibbons's family when the sound of a mob came up the street and hove to in front of the Gibbons house. A man with a constable's staff was ushered in, escorting a rumpled Rainville. Rainville muttered: "Good morning, Charlot."

La Tour's latest mouthful of coddled egg had coagulated into lead in his throat, but he said cheerily: "Good morning to you, Rainville. Been raping the local dairy cows again?"

Rainville didn't smile, just muttered on dolefully: "Last night there was a man . . . an English sailor from the Portuguese salt ship in the harbor. . . . He drank more than was good for him. . . . When his riot ran out, his shipmates carried him back to his lodgings and put him to bed. But the constable on watch last night is a very godly man. So he roused the man out again and put him in the stocks.

"I was making my way back to my own lodgings and saw the man in the stocks. He looked so uncomfortable. . . . And a man should not be set in a trap like a beast. . . . So I set him free.

"Immediately, a mob of *les Bostonais* come at me, howling I know not what. So I draw my sword to defend myself. I am ashamed to say, they knock it from my hand before I can deliver so much as a pinprick. Then they . . ." Rainville blushed. "They put *me* in the stocks. After a while they think maybe that is not legally right, so they take me out again and throw me in their jail. After a while they think maybe that is not legal either, but they know not what to do with me instead, so they bring me to you. And so here I am."

La Tour wiped his hand across his mouth, trying not to think of what the crew of the *Renard Noir* might be moved to do if *les Bostonais* held Rainville in their jail. Or of what the Boston magistrates might be moved *not* to do if Governor La Tour showed he had no respect for their laws. He said: "I will go his bail."

The constable set his mind to thinking, which appeared to be not unlike a bull climbing a tree. Eventually, he pronounced: "I cannot accept bail from a man what lives in a foreign country."

The Boston magistrates were hastily convened. La Tour endeavored to explain to them that being set in the stocks was an indignity no French gentleman could abide. Two of Rainville's fellow officers volunteered to stand bond for his good behavior in future. The magistrates deliberated and decided that if it weren't legal to let Governor La Tour stand bail, they obviously couldn't accept sureties from anyone else not resident in their jurisdiction. And then two blessed, venerable Boston churchmen stood up and announced that they would stand bail for "Mr. Gutteredy-Reignvee."

As the meeting hall emptied out, La Tour allowed his head to loll back and began to breathe again. Rainville appeared in front of him. "I am sorry, Charlot, to be the cause of so much trouble. But it is not right to set men in traps, and the poor man did look so uncomfortable. . . ."

La Tour started to laugh. Rainville gratefully dropped his penitent air and joined in, but La Tour could see he had no idea what the real joke was: neither Rainville nor any English sailor off a Portuguese salt ship had the least notion what it was to feel uncomfortable or trapped.

CHAPTER 35

Twice a day, unless a gale was blowing, Françoise would take Claude on a walk around the deck. It wasn't much of a walk, given that the *Gillyflower* was only forty of her paces long by twenty wide, but there was always a sailor whittling chess pieces or splicing rope or scampering among the ratlines for Claude to gawk at. When a gale was blowing, Captain Bailly merely furled all sails and battened the hatches, and Françoise and Claude were left to amuse themselves in their cabin while the *Gillyflower* pitched and yawed and stood on its head.

Captain Bailly's habit of drifting in any storm didn't seem to help his navigation. Françoise would often see him crouched beside the binnacle, squinting from his log book to his traverse board—a pegboard fixed into the compass stand, with a centipede cat's cradle of colored threads.

They were three months out from Brighton when they came to a place of fogs where many other ships were drifting with the current. Françoise wasn't at all perturbed when the *Gillyflower* let down a drift anchor and the fishing lines came out. But it soon became apparent that the intention wasn't merely to spend a day or two taking on a few fresh fish. Crewmen were lashing empty barrels to the deck rails and unfurling long-aproned oilskins. Another work party was winching the ship's boat up off its berth on top of the hold hatches.

Françoise went to Captain Bailly and said: "What is the meaning of this?"

"Of what?"

"Of all these preparations?"

"We are preparing to fish, madame. In a month or so we'll have a fine cargo of salt cod."

"A *month*? You already *have* a cargo—of supplies for Jemseg!"

"That alone won't make this voyage profitable. I have a duty to the owners."

"*I* am the owner until the charter is fulfilled."

"Do not think to tell me my business, madame. Do you think the sole purpose of this voyage was to satisfy you?"

He started toward the gangway, but she stepped in front of him. "If you must take on a cargo of fish, do it on the return voyage. There will be more room in your hold after—"

"By then the cod will have left the banks." He moved to pass around her, but she stepped in front of him again. He pushed her out of his way. She tripped on her skirt and fell back against the rail, hitting the back of her head on a belaying pin. A cloud swept forward to her eyes and out again. The only thought that passed through with it was that at least Claude was down below, having his afternoon sleep.

The alderman's brother, who was supposedly one of her partners in the charter, gallantly helped her up. But all he said to Captain Bailly was, "Thou shouldst not manhandle women, Brother Bailly."

Françoise wanted to yell after Captain Bailly's receding back that he would regret this when he arrived at Jemseg. But squalling threats would only make her seem more helpless. And if Captain Bailly pondered too much on his eventual introduction to La Tour, he might think of a way to avoid it.

For five weeks the *Gillyflower* became a drifting magnetic island to a blizzard of screeching seabirds, her decks slippery with fish guts and bird droppings, her atmosphere a reek of cod liver and packing salt. From dawn till dusk, sailors took their turns at standing in the lashed-down barrels that kept them secure against the pitching of the ship while leaving their hands free for their work.

Claude took great glee in seeing the crew turn into comic

nuns, with their hooded aprons and belled-out, barrel-and-oilskin skirts. And he loved to watch the flashing knives of the headers and splitters, and their card-dealer tossing of fillets down the hatchway to the packers in the hold. But Françoise was aware that Claude knew something had changed in the equation of his mother and the ship. She continued to perform the part of the great lady charter holder, but he'd seen too many of her performances to be completely taken in.

When the *Gillyflower* finally proceeded down the Acadian coast, it was by fits and starts. Whenever a shore camp of Micmacs sent a boat out to hail her, Captain Bailly would drop anchor to spend a day or two fleecing the natives.

The Micmacs who came on board would invariably begin by putting across in halting French and hand signs that it had been a lean year and they had nothing much to trade. But after being thoroughly plied with brandy, they would suddenly remember an old woman with a few tobacco pouches, who might be willing to part with them if a bit of brandy were brought back to her. Once the tobacco pouches had been ferried from shore, and traded for a greater quantity of birdshot and beads than if tobacco pouches had been in copious supply, the *sagamo* would suddenly remember that his younger brother had a marten pelt. Once the brother had been brought on board, plied with another share of brandy, and had traded his marten pelt for twice what he would've got for one if he'd brought three, he would suddenly remember that his cousin back on the beach had another one.

Françoise got some gratification out of watching the innocents of the forest fleece the fleecers, but it was small consolation for the days melting away. It was September by the time the *Gillyflower* rounded Cape Sable.

Françoise stood in the bow, with one arm holding Claude and the other twined in a rope, enjoying the rush of air as the tide swept the *Gillyflower* into the Baye Françoise. The red mudflats and pine-studded crags looked like home to her. She suspected she was growing vindictive in her old age, because she wasn't looking forward to feeling her husband's arms around her near as much as to seeing his hands on Captain Bailly.

The lookout bawled: "A sail! Off the larboard beam!"

Françoise set Claude down and bustled back with him to the better vantage point of the sterncastle. Captain Bailly bellowed up at the lookout: "What sail?"

"A four-master! Bearing down on us fast! She looks like a French warship!"

Captain Bailly muttered: "D'Aulnay . . ."

Françoise said: "The *St. Clément* outran him and then snuck past him in the night."

"This tub is hardly the *St. Clément*. If he wants to board us, I'll have to let him."

"I did not come all this way to end up in the dungeons of Port Royal!"

"*I* did not come all this way to have my ship blown to bits. You didn't see what he did to my ship when he had only the guns of the *Vierge*! Take your brat down into the hold and hide yourselves."

A sailor lighted their way with a lantern, through the suffocating lower deck, where thirty sailors had been hammocked head to toe for five months, and down into the worse reek of the hold; a compendium of bilgewater and aging cod and rotting salt pork. Françoise and Claude squeezed between two barrels into a niche where the hull curved away from the cargo. The sailor left them there and took his lantern with him.

As soon as the light was gone, the rats began to scurry. Claude began to whimper. The waves thudded against the hull and Françoise's back pressed against it. She whispered: "Do you remember when you were little, Claude, you used to say you saw white horses on the waves . . . ? Can you hear the horses kicking their hooves against the ship?"

"Will they break in?"

"I think if they have not yet, they will not." She settled his head against her breast and softly sang him "Au Clair de la Lune" and any other song she could think of that wouldn't encourage him to shout the chorus. She heard and felt the two hulls thump together and, a while later, heard the sounds of boot heels on the planks above her head, accompanied by a sharp tapping. She put her hand over Claude's mouth and stopped singing.

Two pairs of seaboots came down the steps into the hold. Light and voices approached. Captain Bailly held a lantern. The Sieur d'Aulnay held his walking stick in one hand; the other held a perfumed handkerchief up to his nose.

Françoise could see them clearly through the gap between the barrels, but she'd learned enough of light and shadow on the stage to be quite sure they wouldn't be able to see her and Claude unless the lantern was held directly above their hiding place. If it were, she was also quite sure she wouldn't have to languish in the dungeons of Port Royal for long, only until she could be transported to France to be executed. She doubted that that would disturb Captain Bailly in the least, except that the Conseil du Roi had decreed that any shipmaster found with her on board would be considered an accomplice.

D'Aulnay paused occasionally in his progress along the hold to thrust his walking stick between barrels or bales or crates. He remarked to Captain Bailly: "For a merchant ship, you carry quite a store of arms and gunpowder."

"*Oui*, monsieur. My owners expect to fetch quite a profit for them from *les Bostonais*. Which is why we are on our way to finish up our voyage in Boston, before turning home."

"So you say. It does seem somewhat odd to enter the Baye Françoise en route to Boston."

"As I said, monsieur, I misread the tides. I meant to cross the mouth of the bay and then follow the coast south to Boston. But the tide was going in, not coming out—fool that I am, ha-ha—so I could only hope to drag against the current as much as possible and wait for the ebb to carry us back out."

"So that you could proceed to Boston."

"*Oui*, monsieur. Boston is where we are bound."

D'Aulnay smiled. "Boston being your next and last port of call."

"*Oui*, monsieur. Boston."

D'Aulnay thrust his walking stick between the two barrels next to the hiding place. Françoise saw the gleaming silver tip butt up against the hull not an arm's length from her shoulder. She hugged Claude tighter and he whimpered in protest as her hand over his mouth blocked his nostrils as well.

Captain Bailly spoke, flustered. "The rats, monsieur. Fool that I am—ha-ha—I forgot to recruit a ship's cat to replace the one what fell overboard last voyage."

D'Aulnay said: "I have written a letter to the Governor of Boston. Since Boston is where you are bound, would you be so good as to deliver it for me?"

"But of course, monsieur. I am honored you would entrust me with so important a commission."

"What I trust in you, Captain Bailly, is your ability to count as high as the number of guns on the *Grand Cardinal*. I have seen all I need to see here. Whatever you have illegally traded with *les sauvages* on your way down my coast is obviously of such little consequence as to be easily hidden."

"Monsieur, I would *never* . . . !"

"What you will never do is make your fortune by trespassing on my monopoly for such minuscule profit. But better you not make your fortune, I suppose, than make yourself an ornament upon my yardarm. You may light the way back up now."

The darkness came back and with it the rats, although they now seemed like relatively reassuring company. Françoise waited for a sailor with a lantern to come and tell her it was safe. After waiting until both her legs were asleep, she boosted Claude out and felt her way through the dark, stumbling on tingling legs and fumbling her hand along barrel rims.

There was a crack of light from the hatch up to the lower deck. She eased the hatch up a handsbreadth and hissed in English: "Is he gone yet?"

The hatch was thrown open by a sailor, who said: "If you mean yon silken devil, ma'am, he be gone long past—and taken with him what spine the captain had."

When she came out on deck the sun was setting, the tide was ebbing, and the *Gillyflower* was beating southward with all sails set. Captain Bailly glanced at her and said: "Oh, there you are."

"Where are you taking us?"

"Boston."

"The charter says Jemseg!"

"You can roll up your bloody charter and use it for a man. I mean to put you off in Boston and be well rid of you."

The course he set stayed in sight of land. In the morning Françoise was taking Claude for his walk around the deck when the lookout called: "A sail! Off the starboard bow!"

Captain Bailly shouted up: "What sail?"

"A three-master! Swift! She's—she's . . ."

"She's *what*, man?"

"She's . . . vanished."

"Vanished? Three-masted ships don't bloody vanish!"

"Maybe a cove, sir, or . . . She vanished. . . ."

"Coxswain! Send another man up there as lookout. And clap that one in irons for drunk-on-watch."

The *Gillyflower* was three days longer reaching Massachusetts Bay. As the anchor splashed down in Boston harbor and the ship's boat was warped forward by the towrope it had been leashed on since the Grand Banks, Françoise led Claude toward the gateway to the Jacob's ladder. Captain Bailly stepped in front of her and said: "You'll go ashore when I say. The captain takes the first boat."

She jammed the heel of her shoe down on the instep of his seaboot and twisted, while pushing against his belly with both hands. He hopped backward, holding his foot in one hand and raising the other in a fist. But the alderman's brother shouted: "Brother Bailly!"

It wasn't easy getting down the Jacob's ladder with Claude clinging to her neck, but she managed. Once settled into the boat, she told the boatswain: "Cast off and take me ashore."

The boatswain looked uncertain, but Captain Bailly bellowed from above: "Cast off and good riddance to her!"

A smattering of curious *Bostonais* had gathered on the wharf. Among them were Major and Mrs. Gibbons, both of whom gaped dumbstruck as Françoise climbed out of the boat. Françoise said: "Forgive me my brusqueness, Major, but you are a magistrate and I wish to lay suit against the captain of that ship for breaking his charter contract and assaulting me. I must have his ship impounded *immédiatement*, before he can sail away."

"Certainly, Mrs. La Tour, but—where is *Mister* La Tour?"

"*Pardonnez-moi?*"

"Did you not meet him? He sailed from here not eight days ago, with a shipful of supplies for Jemseg."

Chapter 36

D'Aulnay sat by his sitting-room hearth, horseying his two youngest children on his knees. His two oldest children were upstairs taking their afternoon lessons. On the other side of the hearth his wife was attending to her needle-work frame, bending around the unmistakable evidence of an impending fifth child. After a month spent crisscrossing the Baye Françoise on the *Grand Cardinal*, it was good to be reminded what it was all for.

"Monsieur le Gouverneur?" came from the doorway. It was the Capuchin father François Marie de Paris.

"Ah, Father, good of you to come so promptly. My dears, you must dismount for now. Papa has business and your horses needs must rest." He went into his office with Father François and called a servant to bring wine. "I am going to ask you, Father, to undertake a delicate mission for me. For me and for all Port Royal. For the sake of all New France, for that matter.

"Perhaps you have been wondering, Father, why I have not moved directly against La Rivière St. Jean, though I returned from France with an edict and sufficient strength to enforce it . . . ?"

"We have all been hoping, monsieur, that it is because you still hope the matter might yet be resolved peacefully."

"But of course we *all* hope, Father, that La Tour will surrender himself peacefully. But his past character suggests that unlikely. It *is*, though, in the interest of peace that I have held back—peace with *les Bostonais*.

"So long as *les Bostonais* remain entangled with La Tour, and so long as they believe his lies that this is a contretemps between two rival governors—instead of the truth, that I am acting for the Conseil du Roi against an outlaw—there is no predicting what *les Bostonais* may do when I move to drag La Tour out of his lair. They may send him reinforcements—which would not change the outcome, but would entail a greater amount of bloodshed in the doing of it. They might even attack Port Royal in revenge. It could be the start of a war between New France and New England."

"God forbid."

"God may forbid, Father, but man will do, regardless. The letters I have exchanged with the New England confederacy are promising, but words on paper can only do so much. I am told that your English is better than most Englishmen's, and I know you to be a wise and careful advocate. . . ."

"But, monsieur, does it not seem unlikely that Puritans would be willing to listen to anything from a priest?"

"They might be willing, if he appeared in a plain suit of clothing instead of vestments. And if instead of representing himself as Father François Marie de Paris he were simply, say . . . 'Monsieur Marie.' The letters I have received from *les Bostonais* suggest they are willing to go some distance toward accommodating us, if we go a little ways toward accommodating them."

"But, monsieur, is that not one of the crimes Monsieur La Tour is called to account for: accommodating himself to the heretic?"

"That is entirely different, Father. La Tour would grovel at the altar of Baal to gain advancement; you would merely be humbling yourself a little for the sake of peace and His Most Christian Majesty. And what could be more Christian than to persuade the deluded allies of an outlaw and rebel that they should instead be enlisting their guns and ships and men in the cause of the law?"

"But . . . does it not seem unseemly to you, my son, that a servant of the Prince of Peace should make himself active in affairs of guns and warships and men-at-arms?"

Father François Marie de Paris suddenly seemed very small and far away, with front teeth made for gnawing. D'Aulnay endeavored to make himself understood across the distance. "Other servants of the Prince of Peace—such as Cardinal Mazarin and the late Cardinal Richelieu and His Holiness himself—have not been above soiling their hands with such affairs. I should think you hardly need be made aware that the Capuchin order has a monastery in Port Royal to base its missionary work, and that the monastery lives on the income from the order's Acadian territories administered by the Governor of Port Royal. If Port Royal does not prosper, neither does the Capuchin order and its holy work. I realize that your vows of humility make you reluctant to shoulder such an important commission, but I have faith in you."

"I will have to ask permission of my superiors."

"I have no doubt they will grant it. And I have no doubt, Father François Marie de Paris, that once you have put your hand to the plow you will not look back."

Once "Monsieur Marie" had embarked for Boston on the *Vierge*, it was time for d'Aulnay to climb aboard the *Grand Cardinal* for one last quartering of the Baye Françoise before the advance of winter made it virtually impossible that any ship would come smuggling help to La Tour from France. On the third day out the *Grand Cardinal* encountered a ketch off Menane Island. D'Aulnay put a shot across her bow and boarded her. Through Nicolas Le Creux as interpreter, d'Aulnay discovered that she was on her way home to Boston with a load of salt fish after delivering supplies to La Tour. D'Aulnay told her captain: "Perhaps you are not aware that any ship carrying cargo to or from La Tour shall be impounded."

"That be French law. It has naught to do with English subjects."

"When in the Baye Françoise, Captain, do as the Frenchmen do. Which, in this instance, means you will forthwith lower your boat and ferry yourself and your crew to my ship."

The ketch's crew were imprisoned in the hold of the *Grand Cardinal* and replaced by a prize crew. D'Aulnay had several reasons to feel jaunty about stumbling across the Boston ketch. For one thing, the fact that her cargo consisted entirely of salt fish meant La Tour had no great store of furs to tempt blockade runners. For another, having the Boston captain and his crew as hostages gave d'Aulnay an opportunity to do something he'd been waiting to do since returning from France.

He set a course for La Rivière St. Jean and summoned Le Creux and the Boston captain to his cabin. He proffered Le Creux a copy of the Conseil du Roi's decree and said: "I would like you to deliver this to La Tour. When you present it to him, make certain that any of his officers and *engagés* who happen to be present know what it is—so he cannot keep it secret. We need not fear that you will suffer the same fate as the last gentlemen I was fool enough to send as heralds to La Tour, because *you*"—turning to the Boston captain—"will sit down now and pen a message to your friend La Tour, informing him that you and your crew are my prisoners, and that if he harms or detains my envoys, he will be treated to the spectacle of all of you being hoisted one by one to my yardarm, by the neck."

The Boston captain scrawled a few lines and offered them up for inspection. D'Aulnay waved him off. "There is no need to peruse them. I believe that you believe that I do not use descriptive phrases for empty effect."

Le Creux was rowed ashore in a boat displaying a white flag. D'Aulnay watched him disappear through the gates of La Tour's fort and then retired to his cabin to read a bit of Madaleine de Scudéry's *Ibrahim* to pass the time. He read until his eyes began to blur, then went back out on deck. The hem of the sun was almost touching the treetops cresting the hills behind the fort, but the gates were still closed and the crew of the *Grand Cardinal*'s boat were still lounging on the landing stage.

D'Aulnay stood scratching his fingernails across the deck rail, wondering if he'd miscalculated. He was certain La Tour knew his threat hadn't been idle. It was difficult to believe that even La Tour would force the execution of fourteen innocent men.

One miscalculation d'Aulnay was certain of was that he should've set a deadline for Le Creux's safe return. "Deadline" seemed particularly appropriate under the circumstances. As things stood now, he had no idea whether Le Creux was being detained by making arrangements for the transportation of La Tour's retainers, or by La Tour's attempts to quell a mutiny, or by manacles and a dungeon door.

The treetops started poking up the sun's skirt. D'Aulnay could see that if he waited much longer to start carrying out his threat, he'd have to wait till morning. There wasn't much point in doing it after sunset, when no one in the fort would be able to see.

The gates swung open and Nicolas Le Creux came out. D'Aulnay realized that all the crewmen on the decks of the *Grand Cardinal* and the ketch could see their commander waiting anxiously at the deck rail. He went back into his cabin to look at his novel until his lieutenant presented himself.

After he'd read the same page a dozen times without it registering, there was a knock at the door. *"Entrez."* Le Creux's weather-browned face wasn't wearing the expression one might expect of a man who'd just successfully accomplished a dangerous mission. D'Aulnay called for wine. Le Creux began to apologize for the delay, but d'Aulnay waved it off with: "I have no doubt it could not be helped. Did he read the edict?"

"Yes."

"Were you able to give his officers and *engagés* some hint of what was in it?"

"More than a hint. La Tour assembled all his company in the courtyard and insisted I read it aloud to them."

"And?"

"They . . . well, they . . . laughed. I had to wait between sentences for them to laugh themselves out. When I read out the clause commanding all followers of La Tour to cease obeying his orders and obey you instead, Godard de Rainville laughed so hard La Tour had to hold him up."

"They were putting on a show for fear of La Tour."

Le Creux said reluctantly: "I think not."

"Then they did not believe it was truly an edict from the Conseil du Roi."

"I think they did."

"They cannot *all* be mad!"

D'Aulnay stayed anchored in the harbor mouth overnight, to give Jemseg's deserters the opportunity to escape to the *Grand Cardinal* under cover of darkness. None came.

When morning came, there was nothing for it but to sail back to Port Royal, where he bought the ketch's cargo for a generous price and paid her captain compensation for the days he and his ketch had lost. It was money d'Aulnay could ill afford—as though there were any other kind—but the captain could spread the news in Boston that there was more than one openhanded Frenchman in Acadia.

CHAPTER 37

Jeanne sat with a pillow propped against the small of her back, resting her hand on the child forming inside her and watching Charles and Joseph playing draughts. She found it as warming as the hearthfire to watch Joseph concentrated so seriously on the board, his elation when his father let him win, and Charles's passable imitation of a man outmaneuvered by a clever opponent. She luxuriated in the fact that Charles had finished patrolling the Baye Françoise for this year, and that even if "Monsieur Marie" settled matters with *les Bostonais*, Charles had no intention of moving against La Tour before the spring. She and the children would have almost half a year to get to know him again.

A servant brought in a cup of tea for her and tripped on his master's walking stick propped against his chair. The cup fell on the draughts board, scattering pieces and spattering Charles. The servant sputtered: "Forgive me, monsieur, I—"

Charles stood up slowly, his face as placid as a priest at prayer, and slapped the servant with a force that snapped the man's head around. The servant hunched into himself, holding his hands up limply in front of him. Charles picked up his walking stick and whipped it down twice across the fellow's back. The servant fell to his knees, whimpering. The cane whistled down one last time, ending with a crack and a shriek, like a bough and a spirit breaking. Charles nudged him with the tip of the walking stick and said: "Fetch a rag and clean up your mess."

"*Oui*, monsieur."

As the servant scuttled away, Charles said: "You see, Joseph, servants, like dogs, must be beaten at times to remind them of how much they wish to please their masters. It is not pleasant, but it is necessary."

Jeanne said: "Is it necessary to do it with so much force?"

He turned to her with a betrayed look in his chestnut eyes. "Is it necessary to question me in front of the children?"

She could feel Joseph's eyes on her as well. Neither he nor his brothers and sisters had ever seen their parents argue, and she didn't intend to change that now. So she sat silently until the servant had cleaned off the draughts board and Joseph and Charles were back at their game. Then she stood up and left the room.

Once out in the courtyard, she looked to left and right and started toward the postern gate at the back of the fort. She was no more than five months pregnant, so walking wasn't yet a chore.

She knew that many people beat recalcitrant servants. She'd seen her father do it more than once. But she wasn't sure it

was a habit she wanted her children to learn. Especially with
the efficient viciousness their father had just demonstrated.

She said nothing to the guard at the postern gate, just gestured him to unbar it and let her out. She walked across the
meadow behind the fort and through the orchard of weighted-
down boughs. Walking usually helped her digestion, but she
still couldn't quite seem to swallow the fact that the man who
was the father of her children and the man who'd so coldly
whipped that servant into the floor were the same.

She found herself at the border: the wall of brush and vines
and towering trees where Port Royal ended and the domain of
bears and wolves and *sauvages* began. She pushed her way
through.

Once she was past the sunlit border where the undergrowth
could thrive, the spaces between the trees opened up into a carpet of moss and pine needles and parti-colored leaves. Her
shoe heels sank into the moss and she grew tired of heaving
her swollen ankles over deadfalls, so she sat down with her
back against a tree trunk twice as broad as her shoulders. Once
she was sat down quietly, the squirrels began to go on about
their business, and the songbirds who hadn't yet flown south.
The presence of other life was soothing and frightening at the
same time, making her wonder whether anything larger than a
squirrel might come nosing around.

But although her senses were occupied with the smells of
leaf mold, the sighing of pine boughs, and the flitting of a tiny,
blue-backed bird, her mind was still back in the place where
her husband had shown her son how to grind his heel in a
helpless face. After nine years of marriage she would certainly
have seen that in Charles before if it were truly part of him.

The explanation she found was—as it so often was—La
Tour. Charles had done everything necessary to make La Tour
surrender peacefully, from cutting off his supplies to making
sure La Tour's *engagés* knew of the edict, but still found himself facing the ultimate necessity of unleashing the guns of the
Grand Cardinal on La Tour's men.

Her brother-in-law had told her what had happened when he
read out the decree at Jemseg. It now seemed so obvious that

that was bound to gnaw at her husband's heart, and it was almost enough to make her think that the good God could be unfair. Charles had worked so hard to make certain the people of Port Royal had good reason to respect their governor and expect to prosper in his service. And he had succeeded, insofar as that they obeyed his orders without question and trusted that he would keep them fed and housed and clothed and pay the wages that he promised. But across the bay a criminal like La Tour was *given* loyalty beyond reason.

Now that she'd thought it through, she could see that once La Tour was removed, Charles would be himself again. In the meanwhile she would have to find a way to explain to Joseph that servants were human beings without sounding like she was criticizing his father. She was imagining ways to do that when a male voice broke in from the edge of the forest: "Jeanne?"

"I'm here, Nikki!" She pressed her palms against the fissures of bark behind her to crabwalk her way back up to her feet, then moved toward the sound of Nicolas Le Creux thrashing through the undergrowth. He was carrying a musket and looking anxious.

He said: "The postern guard said you came this way. Charles would have come himself, but a ship came in from Boston. . . ."

"I merely wanted a walk in the woods. I've had it now." She took his arm and they emerged from the menacing wildwood, but she was quite sure it wouldn't be for the last time.

The orchard was filled with people now. Barefoot men in shirtsleeves perched nimbly on makeshift ladders or in the crotches of trees, stretching the limits of their balance points to add a further apple to the Micmac baskets on their shoulders. Women sat in a circle, sorting from filled baskets into one pile of bruised or wormy apples and another of those fit to barrel for the winter. Children chased away wandering hogs looking for one more windfall before sausage-making time.

On her way past, Jeanne called the overseer over and said: "The way some of your people are tossing and jouncing about, seven eighths of the crop will be good for nothing but cider—or perhaps that's what they have in mind."

"*Oui*, madame. You there! Those ain't rocks in that basket. . . ."

The footman who opened the château door for her said: "Monsieur le Gouverneur is in his library, madame. There are gentlemen from Boston in the dining hall."

When she opened the library door, Charles was sitting at his desk perusing several layers of creased paper. He looked up and exhaled: "There you are. Wherever did you—"

"I just wanted a walk in the woods."

"You must not—well, of course you may go walking in the forest anytime the fancy takes you. But take Le Creux with you, or a musketeer. There are bears and wolves and *sauvages* and rocky streambanks you might tumble down and no one find you. What would the children and I do without you?"

She had an intoxicating revelation that she did actually wield some power over him, in that he truly feared the threat of living without her. Except that there was only one way open to her to ever leave him.

He said: "We have visitors in the dining hall."

"So I hear."

"It seems the captain of the ketch I captured spread the tale of my liberality with such enthusiasm that another captain of *les Bostonais* immediately loaded up his ship with trade goods and came looking for a windfall. I fear that this other captain and his associates are about to learn to their regret that in matters of business I am not such a fool as to not realize they have no choice now but to sell at my price or take their cargo back home."

"They could take it across the bay to La Tour."

"I think not. Not with the *Grand Cardinal* to escort them out of the bay."

"Is trading with *les Bostonais* not one of the crimes La Tour is condemned for com—"

"Would *you* snipe at me, too?"

"Of course not, Charles. I merely worry he may use it against you."

"You need have no fear of that. Forgive me, my dear, I should know you think only of me." He snapped his finger against the pages in his hand. "*Les Bostonais* also brought a letter from 'Monsieur Marie'—or a novel, more like. I excused myself to peruse it before proceeding to business."

"Should I go keep them company in the meanwhile?"

"I am sure they would be honored."

She started out, then paused to straighten a book that had fallen sideways on its shelf. Behind her, her husband's voice spat out: "Bitch!"

She turned around slowly. His red brown eyes were blazing at the papers in his hands. She said carefully: "Pardon me, Charles?"

"What?"

"What was it you said?"

"Did I speak?"

"Yes. I believe you said . . . 'bitch.' "

"Oh. Not surprising. Fortunately, the children are—I must learn to keep better control of myself—though how any man could, under . . ." He paused to push in the corners of his mouth with his thumb and forefinger, then continued in a more detached tone. "Father François Marie de Paris is explaining, you see, why he is having some difficulty accomplishing a treaty with *les Bostonais*. It seems that he arrived in Boston to discover that the whore had somehow contrived to make her way there before him."

"The whore?"

"Is there another? François . . . Marie . . . Jacquelin."

CHAPTER 38

Françoise sat in the window seat of the bedroom in the Gibbons house that had been her and Claude's home for five weeks now, looking out at Claude and the Gibbons children jumping in a pile of red-and-yellow leaves, wondering what she was going to do. She had won her suit against Captain Bailly and the alderman's brother within four days of landing in Boston. The court had awarded her the *Gillyflower*'s cargo and compensation to a total of "twenty hundred pounds sterling." But as soon as the suit had been decided, Captain Bailly and the alderman's brother had launched an appeal. Among other grounds, they claimed that the charter agreement had never been intended to be anything more than a blind, in case the parliamentarian-owned *Gillyflower* encountered a royalist warship.

While the appeals and counterappeals were sawing back and forth, "Monsieur Marie" had arrived to launch negotiations. He came up with a clever way to keep her from arguing against him: pleading poor English, he spoke in Latin to the learned theologians who made up the Boston Assembly. The Boston Assembly and "Monsieur Marie" were quite delighted with each other, the magistrates purring whenever Father François expressed his surprise at how cordially he was being treated in a city of Protestant dissenters.

Françoise didn't need Latin to understand what "Monsieur Marie" had been sent to accomplish. And he'd miraculously found a foothold in English for just long enough to inform the court that Françoise Marie Jacquelin "is known to have been the cause for her husband's contempt and rebellion. Therefore you would be working against peace if you allow her to go to him. Any Boston ship found carrying her will be taken as a prize of war."

Over the last five weeks Françoise had learned that the Boston magistrates and churchmen, for all their certainty about the next world, were afraid of a great many uncertainties in this one. They were afraid that if they aided their Puritan brothers fighting the king in England, the king might punish New England if he won the war. They were afraid that if they impounded the property of London shipowners, whoever governed in London after the war might take away their right to govern in Boston. They were afraid that if they didn't get themselves extricated from the civil war in Acadia, it might spill over into New England—and afraid that if they extricated themselves completely, they might lose all that lovely trade. All those fears and more were leaving her tossed about like the manitou in the whirlpool of La Rivière St. Jean.

Françoise was quite sure, though, that all the arguments put forth by her and by Captain Bailly and the alderman's brother and "Monsieur Marie," and the missives sent to the assembly from La Tour and from d'Aulnay, had finally succeeded in uniting all the magistrates and deputies and churchmen in one heartfelt opinion: "How did we get ourselves into this mess?"

Claude and the Gibbons children came running toward the house as Mrs. Gibbons called: "Dinner!" out the back door. Françoise refastened the choking collar button on her Boston-style dress and went downstairs, with still no better idea of what she was going to do than when she'd sat down on the window seat to think of what to do.

There was another guest for dinner besides herself and Claude: the Reverend Dr. Orland. After he had said a long, grim grace, and the boiled beef and potatoes began to be passed around, Françoise said: "You know, Reverend Orland, that I was raised in the Huguenot faith?"

"That I do, Mrs. La Tour. And no doubt many members of your family were blessed martyrs for that faith."

"Yes, but before I was born—except for distant relatives in

La Rochelle. I say I was *raised* a Huguenot, but, you see, I had to make my own way in the world. . . ."

"I had heard something of that sort."

"And though I did not *abandon* my religion, it became to me one of the memories of my childhood, like the spring perfume of the mulberry tree that grew beside the window of the room where my sisters and I slept. But now . . . You know that my son and I have been attending the Sabbath meetings with our kind hosts?"

"That I do, as does everyone else in Boston."

"A strange thing has happened. It is like the scent of mulberry blossoms. I feel transported to my childhood. And yet, all is not familiar. There seem to be differences between my memories and the meetings here."

"There *are* differences between the Huguenot faith and the Reformed Church of England."

"But the strangest thing is that that which is unfamiliar to my memory seems the most familiar—as though the echoes from my childhood were only the echo of an echo, and now I hear the voice itself. I suppose it is only a foolish fancy. . . ."

"Mrs. La Tour, it seems to me to be the furthest thing from a foolish fancy."

"Does it so? Reverend Orland, could you . . . ? I know this is too much to ask, but would you . . . would you teach me?"

"I would be humbled by the honor, Sister La Tour." All of the adult faces around the table wore transfixed smiles. Mrs. Gibbons had to put down her fork to dab her napkin at her eyes.

Claude said: *"Maman, est-ce que* cock *est la même chose que pénis?"*

From that day forward Françoise spent an hour out of every twenty-four with the Reverend Dr. Orland or one of his colleagues. She found herself actually seeing the devil's snares set all around her, in everything from a deck of cards to a child's curiosity. She couldn't say for certain if it wasn't just that to play any part convincingly one had to believe it. But it also seemed to her—although she kept it to herself—that if human souls were born irrevocably predestined as either saved or damned, they might just as well do whatever they felt like.

As her lessons progressed she did become certain of two things. One was that the Bible bearing the name of the current embattled English king's father put most poets of the theater to shame. The other was that the Boston magistrates, who'd never been less than polite to her, had become positively solicitous.

Solicitousness didn't prevent them from dragging their heels on the suits between her and Captain Bailly and the alderman's brother until December. But the original decision was upheld. The cargo, now whittled down to a value of eleven hundred pounds, was hers. Captain Bailly and his partner were ordered to make up the nine-hundred-pound difference.

That still left Françoise with the problem of how to get her cargo and herself to Jemseg. No Boston shipmaster would trifle with "Monsieur Marie's" threat that any ship found carrying her would be taken as a prize of war, and no ship in Boston could face down the *Grand Cardinal*.

But there was a captain from Barbados with three ships in Boston harbor, on the last leg of his annual trading triangle from the West Indies to England to Boston and home again. He was staying at an inn run by a certain Sister Temperance Sweete, whose name the good ladies of Boston affected not to know.

As she crossed the threshold of Sister Temperance Sweete's inn, Françoise undid the strangling collar button and a few others besides. The captain from Barbados was in the public room, demonstrating that Jamaica rum could be a lucrative import. There was a small side room where she and he sat down to do business. They agreed finally on a sum of five hundred pounds for the captain to carry her and three holdfuls of supplies to Jemseg. He said: "What bank shall I be drawing on, marm?"

"Whichever London bank a certain London alderman keeps accounts with. Captain Bailly and his partner are required to sign a surety to me for nine hundred pounds before they sail from Boston. I will sign a surety to you for five hundred pounds, which you can redeem when next you are in England." The captain looked doubtful. "I assure you, Captain, English law makes that paper as good as gold."

The captain thought about it a moment, then said: "*Six* hundred pound."

"I thought you were a merchant, Captain, not a pirate."

"Ye're asking me to run a pirate's gauntlet, marm. Rest easy, if Monsewer Donny puts a shot across *my* bows he'll wish he'd stayed home darning stockings. That should be worth six hundred pound starling."

"It is."

"Give me your hand on it, then."

"I have already given it to my husband."

"Was I him, I'd not've let it stray out of my sight."

When Major Gibbons went out on his next morning's constitutional, he came running back before Françoise and Mrs. Gibbons had finished fixing breakfast. He panted out: "She's gone!"

Mrs. Gibbons said: "Who's gone?"

"The *Gillyflower*!"

Françoise said: "Gone?"

"Captain Bailly and his partner said they had to fetch some documents from their ship before they could sign the surety to you. The instant they were on board, they weighed anchor. They're out at the mouth of the bay now, taking on passengers and provisions."

"Well *stop* them!"

"We cannot. The bay mouth's beyond the harbormaster's jurisdiction. By the time we convene an assembly to make a ruling ... They must've been planning this for weeks."

Françoise put her hands over her eyes. Then she exhaled, lowered her hands, and went upstairs to her traveling trunk. Under the layers of clothing was a power of attorney La Tour had signed to her before she sailed to France. She tucked it in her waistband, threw her cloak on, and wandered down the winding streets of Boston to the inn where goodwives didn't go.

The captain from Barbados and a tableful of cronies choked off paroxysms of laughter when she came through the door.

Perhaps one of them had just told a story he would rather not repeat in mixed company, or perhaps Captain Bailly's clever trick on her was the day's delight.

In the side room she presented the Barbados captain with the power of attorney and said: "As you can see, my signature upon a contract is as binding upon my husband as his own. The warehouses of Jemseg are filled with two years' harvest of furs. If I sign an agreement that you will be paid in furs to the value of the charter fee, it is as good as gold."

The captain rasped his fingernails across the stubble on his chin. "*Seven* hundred pound starling."

Once the agreement was signed, the ships still had to be readied to sail, and Françoise still had to persuade Major Gibbons and his business partners to augment the cargo off the *Gillyflower* with more gunpowder and shot and muskets. While all that was being accomplished "Monsieur Marie" became suddenly anxious to return to Port Royal with anything even remotely resembling a treaty. Three days before her chartered convoy sailed, he embarked on the *Vierge*, bearing nothing more substantial than a tentative agreement that the people of New England and Acadia would not interfere in each other's internal affairs. But Françoise knew that arranging a treaty was no longer the point of Father François's mission. The point now was to inform his master that she was on her way.

When she straightened up again from handing Claude down to the boatmen bobbing beside the Boston dock, Major Gibbons said: "Our prayers go with thee, Sister Frances."

"Fortunately, so doth several hundredweight of thy gunpowder." Both Gibbonses actually laughed. The Reformed Church of England did allow humor, as long as it was the gallows variety.

The captain from Barbados earned his "seven hundred pound starling." All the way up the Baye Françoise, the only sign of d'Aulnay was that a lookout spotted a sail off Island Island, but it sheered off.

As Françoise's flotilla came out of the ship channel past Partridge Island, she stood in the bow of the lead ship with Claude in her arms. "There is Papa's fish weir, Claude—do you remember? And Papa's ship, the *Renard Noir*. And the big tree with the chestnuts that look tempting but you mustn't eat . . . And . . . and . . ."

And a horde of curious riffraff drifting down out of the fort gates, among them a mottle-haired scarecrow in a leather shirt, elbowing his way to the front. Claude said: "And Papa."

Once the ship's boat was secured to the wharf, Françoise stood up with Claude in her arms, intending to set him on the dock and then climb out. But before she could do either, La Tour was crouched in front of her and his long arms were around her and Claude, and all three of them were weeping like onion skinners.

When the parade had made its way to the officers' dining hall, Françoise said: "I must go upstairs and change into a gown fit for a homecoming feast."

La Tour said brightly: "I will help you."

"No. You will sit down and satisfy the captain."

"I would rather satisfy you."

"Business before pleasure, La Tour. And I look forward to the pleasure, Lorette, of the first feast worthy of the name in eighteen months. La Tour—the captain has a contract to show you."

"Oui, mon admiral."

The bedroom looked the same as she remembered. The marten-pelt coverlet was still on the bed, and someone had even kept the furniture dusted. There was an odd scent of bear grease and smoked leather that she didn't remember, but perhaps she'd ceased to notice it when she'd been home.

Out of the clothespress she took her blue velvet gown, and out of the jewelry box the thick gold chain La Tour had given her for a wedding bribe. When she came downstairs dressed like the Queen of Acadia, La Tour didn't appear to notice. He and the captain from Barbados were sitting on either side of the dining table, staring sourly at the contract lying between them. The captain looked up and said: "You lied to me, marm."

La Tour drawled: "Say that again, monsieur, and I'll show

you what happened to the last man that spoke hard to my wife in my house."

Françoise said: "What ever is the matter?"

The captain said: "Your husband has no furs."

La Tour said: "Have I not just finished telling you I do?"

"Beaver pelts to the value of one hundred twenty pound ain't seven hundred pound starling."

"What the Christ do you expect at the beginning of the season? In another month or so I'll have—"

"I'll not languish about here for another month or so."

"Then come by on your next year's trip to Boston. I'll have it then."

"I have my own creditors. One hundred twenty pound won't satisfy—"

"Would," Françoise cut in, "one hundred fifty?"

The captain scratched his chin. "It might. . . . I'd still be hard-pressed, but it might hold me till next year—given interest on the balance. . . ."

Françoise lifted the gold chain off. "This necklace is worth thirty pounds at least—more likely forty. Good as gold."

La Tour corkscrewed his arms around his chest and mumbled: "Only if you'll allow as it can be redeemed."

"They say we all can be redeemed."

PART III

AND TAKEN THE LADY

"We understand for certain afterwards that [the] fort was taken by assault and scalado . . . and that he had put to death all the men . . . and had taken the lady. . . ."
—John Winthrop's Journal, 1645

CHAPTER 39

Nicolas Denys made his way into the Baye Françoise by dragging a longboat across the ten leagues of snow between the head of the bay and the Gulf of St. Lawrence. If it had been summer, he could easily have gotten where he wanted to go by canoeing the Micmacs' river routes. If he'd had an abundance of time, he easily could have sailed his ship down the coast and around Cape Sable. But it wasn't summer and he had no time.

Last spring he'd finally accumulated enough money and credit to convince the Hundred Associates to grant him a concession on the beautiful island of Miscou in the north of Acadia. He'd managed to get a snug fort built before the leaves turned, and the autumn supply ship he'd been counting on had arrived safely. But when the cargo was being ferried ashore, a sea cow chose to surface under the boat carrying all the gunpowder.

Denys had calculated hopefully that he still had enough powder left to hunt fresh meat through the winter. By the time his calculations turned out wrong, the sail route to Quebec was a jungle of ice. Port Royal was bound to have plentiful stores, but Denys had a strong suspicion that d'Aulnay wasn't about to help anyone winter over in *his* Acadia, unless they gave him an ironclad guarantee that they'd be gone come spring. That left La Tour.

By the time Denys's boat crew finished dragging the longboat across the isthmus, they were growing almost competent on snowshoes. They launched into the bay with the first outrunning tide and caught a north wind—skimming through the gray waves spraying salt ice over the oarlocks. Denys calculated that if they capsized, the ones who could swim would live maybe five minutes longer than the ones who drowned immediately.

Through the grace of God and a lot of bailing, they hove into the harbor of La Rivière St. Jean with their gunwales still above water. No signal gun fired from the fort, but a number of men trooped out the gates and down to the floating dock. In the lead was La Tour, with a bearskin robe across his shoulders, a glazed-clay flagon in one hand, and a wheel-lock pistol in the other.

La Tour squinted down into the boat and said: "Damn me, is that you, Denys? You look like a pickled cod. Come up to the house—we're celebrating Saint Philion's Day."

"Saint who?"

"Saint Philion. We always celebrate Saint Philion's Day—unless we're too exhausted from celebrating Saint Melina's Day or Saint Pudenda's."

Godard de Rainville and one of La Tour's raffish retainers kindly took hold of Denys's elbows to help his frozen knees negotiate the slope up to the fort. As they walked him through the gatehouse he began to hear the sound of music.

The common dining hall was empty. Servants and tenants and officers were all crammed nose to elbow into the gentlemen's dining hall. The room was ablaze with smoky light: from a conflagration in the great hearth and from myriad smaller flames that Denys at first assumed were candles. On second glance, though, and first whiff, they were the fish-oil lamps that *les sauvages* concocted out of hollowed stones and floating wicks. A rapscallion with a fiddle and another with Breton bagpipes were trying to make themselves heard over the general shouting and laughter and tankard-banging singing.

La Tour sat Denys down by the hearth and handed him a flagon from a passing servant's tray. "We're reduced to spruce beer, I regret, but it do get almost drinkable after the first four or six cups."

Denys had just thawed out enough to attempt conversing when La Tour stood up and bellowed for silence. "Mesdames et messieurs—and the rest of us—I give you: the Queen of the Spice Islands."

Françoise Marie Jacquelin emerged from the private sitting room in a costume Denys wouldn't have allowed his wife to appear in, especially with the backlight of the lamps. She struck a pose and sang a song, accompanied on the flute by a busty young woman whom Denys eventually recognized as the little slip of a girl he'd met at Mademoiselle Jacquelin's cottage and on the quai at La Rochelle. When the song was done, Madame Jacquelin delivered a speech about her tropic queendom in the Indies and a dusky young lover kidnapped by a rival king and a great deal of other nonsense, which somehow transported Denys onto a sun-seared beach with turquoise waves lapping and palm trees waving overhead, although he wouldn't have recognized a palm tree if it fell on him.

She finished with a pretty little curtsy and the denizens of Jemseg vied to see who could applaud the loudest, stamping on the tables they'd climbed up on for a better view. Denys stood up as she approached the empty chair beside La Tour's. She said: "Welcome to Jemseg, Monsieur Denys."

"Thank you, madame. And thank you for the delightful recitation."

"Thank *you*, monsieur. You are too kind." She favored him with that odd, unsettling smile that showed her oversized canine tooth. Someone brought her a rabbit-fur wrap. Whether it made her more comfortable or not, it certainly did Denys, by covering up at least some portions of the gauzy confection she was dressed in.

She and her husband both appeared to have absorbed the custom of the people of the country, wherein even the most unexpected of visitors was unceremoniously sat down by the fire and made at home before anyone thought to ask his business. Denys didn't mind. It gave him an opportunity to observe these two people he knew separately but had never seen together.

They couldn't seem to keep their hands off each other. But then, they'd only recently been forced to spend a year and more apart, so it wasn't that unnatural.

Françoise Marie Jacquelin certainly hadn't gotten any physically younger in the five years since Denys first laid eyes on her—although there still wasn't a trace of gray in her hair. But she did seem younger in a way. Back in her cottage in France she'd appeared to be a self-protective woman harboring her remaining, cloistered years. Here, she was loose and wild, leaning back in her chair to shout a bawdy insult at someone across the room, or leaning forward to tug on Godard de Rainville's hair when she made mock of him plying his soup spoon with his left hand. The Queen of the Spice Islands might be only the product of some poet's imagination, but Françoise Marie Jacquelin was definitely the Queen of Jemseg. She was also obviously the Queen of La Tour's heart, which would have come as a surprise to those who said he hadn't got one.

Eventually La Tour said: "So what brings you scudding down the bay at this time of year, Denys?" When Denys had told him, La Tour rubbed his hand across the back of his neck and squinted. "A sea cow?"

"Yes. Capsized the boat and sent every keg of powder into the water. It was only by good fortune we got another boat launched in time to save the crew."

"But . . . didn't the kegs float?"

"Yes. But the powder was sodden, you see."

"But . . . couldn't you dry it out?"

"Well . . . my gunner did spread it out on the beach to dry in the sun. . . ."

"And?"

"And then . . ." Denys knotted his arms together and fixed his eyes on the floor. "And then, you see, my gunner sat down on the beach to smoke a pipe of tobacco while he waited for the powder to dry. . . ."

La Tour flung back in his chair and laughed like the tide roaring up the falls of La Rivière St. Jean. Denys muttered miserably: "By good fortune we managed to save the fort, but the rest of the island of Miscou is a bed of ashes."

"Oh, Denys," La Tour wheezed, wiping his eyes. "Forgive me, but . . . oh dear . . . was there ever a man for good fortune like you? That story is worth at least several hundredweight of gunpowder. I'm afraid, though, that we ain't exactly drowned in supplies here."

"I feared that might be so."

"We'd have more than enough gunpowder to get us through the winter, if all we needed it for was hunting and trading. But these days one never knows when other needs might arise. But if you think one keg would see you through . . . ?"

Denys exhaled: "Most certainly."

"I couldn't even spare that much, except that I'll have to be bringing in fresh supplies soon regardless."

"In the winter? How do you propose to do that?"

La Tour's lips sharpened. "Meaning no offense to your discretion, Denys, but there are some things it's best not too many people know about until they're done."

"I take no offense. One thing the good God forgot to do was connect the hinges of men's tongues to their brains."

"Why, Monsieur Denys!" Madame Jacquelin put in. "You made a joke!" There was definitely something odd about that woman.

"It do seem chancing your luck," La Tour said, "to try going the length of the bay twice in a longboat at this time of year. You are perfectly welcome to stay here until the rivers open up, and then my friends among the people of the country will volunteer to see you safely home."

"Thank you, but I must get back quickly to my family and *engagés*." Which was true, but Denys would have dredged up an excuse even if it weren't. There was an air of desperation in the gaiety at Jemseg. A desperate Charles de La Tour was not a landscape feature Denys fancied lingering by. La Tour had a generous disposition, but when he got that cornered-wolf glint in his eyes, what he was about to give was something someone else would not enjoy receiving.

CHAPTER 40

Françoise went with La Tour down to the landing stage to see off Nicolas Denys. Fat, gentle snowflakes were wafting down so thickly that the longboat disappeared before its oars carried it out of the harbor. The last thing Françoise saw of it was Nicolas Denys hunched in the stern with the tiller under one arm and his hands muffed in his beard.

La Tour said: "The man's mad, of course."

"I seem to recall he said much the same of you, when he brought me your proposal of marriage."

"That don't say much for the levelness of your own head." He scooped up Claude in one arm, offered her the other, and they climbed up the path to the fort, slipping in the fresh layer of snow.

When she came down into the sitting room from reading Claude to sleep, La Tour was squatting on the floor smoking tobacco with two Maliseets. It seemed those two had decided to spend part of their winter hunting the shoreline for a cached fishing boat, instead of hunting moose in the deep woods. She lingered long enough to politely express her delight that they'd gotten lucky and had spent the last few days scudding back and forth across the bay. Then she hunted up Lorette and they crunched across the courtyard to the cabinetmaker's workshop.

The cabinetmaker was going to help her make a costume. In one of the books she'd brought back from Paris was a play with a speech for Athène. No one in France would ever have cast her as Athène, but in Jemseg she had a captive audience. But one couldn't very well portray Athène without a breastplate. If the cabinetmaker could fashion a frame, she and Lorette could finish it off with plaster of paris and the gilt paint kept on hand for the *Renard Noir*'s trim.

The cabinetmaker seemed excessively shy about measuring her torso. But he gallantly begged to differ when she said: "At my age, you might just as well fit it to a barrel."

When she got back to the sitting room, the Maliseets were gone, but La Tour was still squatting in front of the hearth, smoking alone. He took his pipe out of his mouth, looked at the bear carved on the bowl, and said flatly: "D'Aulnay will come in the spring."

A cold hand clutched her bowels. "Are you sure?"

"As sure as anyone can be of anything. The Maliseets told me the white men across the bay seem to be spending all their days fitting out their warships, target-shooting with their cannons, and marching about their parade square wearing armor. Either he's took it in mind to invade Mexico, or he's coming here.

"And if he comes, it'll be in the spring. He ain't fool enough to try laying siege in an Acadian winter, more's the pity. But once spring comes, he'll want to move quick, before the people of the country come back out from their winter camps. I don't know if even Keeshetech would take up his hatchet in a war between two Frenchmen, but d'Aulnay won't want to chance it."

He uncoiled his long legs, grimacing when his knees cracked, and settled into the chair beside hers. " 'Tain't near so bad as it seems. He'll only ruin himself trying to take this place—provided we have enough men and arms and provisions to stand a siege. *Les Bostonais* are fond of us now—or of you, at least. I don't doubt they'll allow us to buy arms and provisions, maybe even to hire men. But one of us will have to go to Boston to do it."

"Why not both of us?"

He shook his head. "It's miracle enough no one's deserted us. If we look to be deserting *them* . . . You'd likely do a better job of it in Boston than me. If you could get there. I know the *Renard Noir* and the Baye Françoise well enough d'Aulnay would never catch me. You'd be safe here till the spring. And I'd be back long before then; with enough supplies that we can sit snug behind our guns till the Sieur d'Aulnay rots, or the *sagamos* decide to help us rid their country of him, whichever comes first."

"It sounds to me as though you've already decided who'll stay and who'll go."

He reached his right hand across and settled it onto the back of her left. She could feel the pattern of callus that fitted his sword. He said: "What I'd already decided was I'd likely have to take a quick sail back and forth at the end of the winter to fetch a few necessities. Enough necessities to stand a siege will take a lot more persuading. And now the only time I have is till the spring. If you can think of any other way . . ."

She looked down at the gnarl-knuckled hand overlapping hers like a blanket covering Claude and shook her head, then looked up into the weather-honed features in their raggedy frame of mottled hair. It suddenly struck her that the odd pelt his hair had first reminded her of hadn't been a wolf after all, but a fox. She turned her hand over so they were palm to palm and said: "No fear, La Tour; when the hounds run us to earth, they'll get a rude surprise."

"Well . . . I'd best go scour the warehouse for anything of any value, to remind *les Bostonais* they have more reasons than Christian charity to help us keep Jemseg."

She sat alone for a moment, running her thumbnail back and forth across the canine tooth that the good God had intended for a larger head. Then she pushed off from her chair and climbed the boxed-in staircase between the sitting room and bedroom. Claude was still happily ensconced in his parents' bed, but no longer sleeping. He had wrapped himself up in the fabulously extravagant, marten-skin bedcover and was rubbing his cheeks with the fur. "Claude hungry, *maman*."

"Go down and ask Lorette to give you something to eat."

"Thank you, *maman*."

He leaped off the bed and charged for the stairs. She shouted after him: "*Don't* run down the stairs."

"No, *maman*."

She went to the sewing basket she'd had to dust off when the seamstress/maid La Tour had hired for her was dispatched back to France as a needless expense. Among the spools of thread and papers of pins was a sharp-nosed little tool for picking apart seams. She sat down on the bed and began to turn the bedcover back into individual marten pelts.

It was a bright, cold day when the *Renard Noir* embarked. La Tour waited until everyone else had been loaded on board and then turned to her on the dock. She arched up onto her toes and stretched her arms to reach his neck. He stooped and wrapped his long arms around her back. Claude wrapped himself around his father's leg and began to wail.

La Tour let go of her to crouch in front of Claude. "Now, Claude, Papa won't be gone long. Nowhere near so long as you and *maman* were gone from me the last time. I'll bring you something back from Boston." He stood again. "And I'll bring *you* back something more than something."

"Adieu, La Tour."

"*Au revoir*, my Françoise."

She watched the boat carry him out to the *Renard Noir*, watched the ship weigh anchor and the tide carry her out of the harbor, watched the mainsails unfurl and come to life as the wind carried her past the headland into the ship channel past Partridge Island. Then she wiped her son's eyes and her own, took a grip on his hand, and walked back up the path to the fort, with her silky-haired watchdog Rainville following behind.

It didn't take her long to discover to her sorrow that it hadn't been an empty courtesy when La Tour announced that she would be in command while he was gone. She hadn't imagined how many matters he'd been called upon to resolve while apparently ambling his way through the day. If it wasn't the apothecary and the surgeon at each other's throats, it was the harbormaster asking whether the floating dock should be dragged on shore immediately or whether he should chance there might not be a flash thaw to send ice floes roiling down La Rivière St. Jean.

It didn't help that a so far mild winter suddenly turned so

cold that cheeks and noses would be burning after just a quick scamper from the main hall to the cookhouse. So much snow fell in one day that it took three weeks to clear the paths. Nerves that were already fraying around the edges unraveled with being housebound for so long.

Françoise was passing by Lorette's room and heard weeping. She tapped on the door and pushed it open. Lorette was sitting on her trunk, wrapped in a blanket, shivering and snuffling, twisting a sodden handkerchief in her hands.

Françoise said: "It is cruel on all of us, Lorette, but the cold *will* go away again, I promise."

"It is not that. It is Gaspard. The Recollets have forbidden him to keep company with me, because I am not a baptized Catholic."

Françoise threw her cloak on and stomped out along the maze of pathways cut through the head-high snow—head-high to her, at least. Old Père Montagne was in the rectory. She said: "What is this nonsense about Lorette and Gaspard?"

"It is not *me*, Françoise. I have lived in Acadia long enough to believe that any bit of warmth that helps one soul—or two—through the winter is a blessing. But perhaps I have lived in Acadia too long. If my father superior says it is a sin for a son of the church to keep company with a woman who is not of the faith, I must be obedient."

"Where is the father superior?"

"In the chapel. But you must not—"

Françoise was out the door before she heard what she must not do. The father superior was overseeing Père Montagne's confrere and a Micmac altar boy polishing the altar vessels. The father superior saw her coming down the aisle and said: "I did not see you genuflect."

"And you *will* not. What is this nonsense about Lorette and Gaspard?"

"You call the edicts of God nonsense?"

"This is not an edict of God; it is an edict of you."

"Is that what they taught you in Boston—that an ordained priest knows no more of the will of God than any other man?"

"I have never interfered with the practice of your religion or anyone else's. But I will not have you interfering in life outside the walls of your church."

"*You* will not have . . . ?"

"All the people in this fort have been placed in my charge. It is difficult enough to keep them from chewing each other to pieces before spring, without you making their lives more miserable."

"I am not answerable to you; I am answerable to God."

"So long as you live under my roof and eat my bread, you are answerable to me. If you can't stomach that, I will provide you with a boat and you are free to go." Which would make Père Montagne his own father superior.

"Go? Go *where*?"

"You can go to the devil as far as I'm concerned."

CHAPTER 41

D'Aulnay sat in his dining hall entertaining his guests from across the bay—and seeing to it they were entertained royally, with overflowing platters of all the best that the cellars and kitchens of Port Royal had to offer. There were eleven guests, freshly arrived in a leaky old pinnace—two priests from the Recollet mission at Jemseg and nine deserters from among La Tour's *engagés*.

One of La Tour's ex-*engagés* said, around the lump of mutton he was masticating with his mouth open: "When the good father said that all who served the rebel heretic were excommunicate, we decided that no bonded contract meant shit next to our duty to God."

"Of course." D'Aulnay nodded. "Any true son of the church would do the same."

"Besides," another gravy-bearded lout put in, "we've had no wages for half a year now."

"Your back wages will be paid to you." D'Aulnay waved the matter away airily, as though trifles of money meant nothing to the Governor of Port Royal. "You were, after all, contracted by La Compagnie de la Nouvelle France, and the work that you did for La Tour will turn to La Compagnie's benefit once Jemseg is ours again. In the meanwhile I will have you billeted with my men-at-arms, and my armorer will fit you out."

D'Aulnay turned to the Recollet father superior. "Would it be fair to say, Father, that your troubles with that woman only began after her sojourn among the heretics of Boston?"

The father superior took a swallow of Bordeaux to wash down his latest mouthful of smoked salmon. "I suppose it would, my son."

"I have no intent to put words in your mouth, Father, but when I report the matter to the Hundred Associates and the Conseil du Roi, would it be agreeable to you to witness a statement that the reason the woman drove you out into the wilderness in the dead of winter was because any true son of the church has become anathema to her since her conversion to the Puritan blasphemy in Boston?"

The father superior took another thoughtful sip of wine and nodded. "It would."

"And what of La Tour himself? Did he take an active part in this or merely sit by and allow it to take place?"

"La Tour?" The father superior looked confused. "La Tour has been gone for a month and more."

"Gone? Gone where?"

"To Boston to procure more arms and supplies."

D'Aulnay had to take hold of the edge of the table to keep from jumping out of his chair. He took a couple of slow breaths to forestall any unseemly show of emotion from distorting his voice. "Then who is in command of the fort?"

"That woman. That is why we had no recourse but to leave."

"*She* is?" Once again d'Aulnay had to pause to maintain the unrufflable tone befitting a son of René de Menou. "How many men-at-arms did he leave with her?"

"Well ... less the crew of the *Renard Noir* ... and the servants who sailed with La Tour ... and these nine true sons of the church who came with us ... I would say there might be fifty men all told left at Jemseg, perhaps not quite that many."

D'Aulnay stood his walking stick up to lever himself to his feet. "If you gentlemen would be kind enough to excuse me ... Monsieur Le Creux will see to your billeting." On his way across the corridor to his office, he despatched a footman to summon the sergeant at arms and the captain of the *Grand Cardinal*. The *Grand Cardinal* alone could carry twice as many troops as La Tour had left behind to guard his wife.

Over supper d'Aulnay mentioned to his wife: "I shall be sailing the day after tomorrow."

"Where to, Charles?"

"Only across the bay. Once the good Recollet fathers and their companions have recovered their strength, I think charity demands that they be employed to give their friends still at Jemseg one last opportunity to escape the rat's nest they are trapped in."

"You will be careful of yourself, Charles ... ? What seems to you like an opportunity for charitableness may seem to a man with no honor to be an opportunity for treachery."

He had to smile. He would've been hard-pressed to say which was the more touching: her genuine concern for his welfare, or her notion that she could advise him on matters of arms and ambuscades. He said: "You need have no fear for me, my dear. I am not such a fool, nor so bloodthirsty, as to engage in combat unnecessarily."

As the outgoing tide carried the *Grand Cardinal* down Port Royal basin, d'Aulnay stood on the half deck smiling and humming to himself, bouncing the tip of his walking stick on the deck. He set a course north by northwest, to a point north of Jemseg, then drifted down the western shore to anchor where a headland hid his masts from La Tour's fort.

As the ship's boat was being lowered the Recollet father

superior said to d'Aulnay somewhat nervously: "If she imprisons us or offers us harm, you *will* sail in to rescue us?"

"Of course, of course, Father. I would never leave mice in a rat trap." The good father didn't appear to see the humor.

CHAPTER 42

"Madame?" Françoise looked up from her book at the *engagé* in the sitting-room doorway. "There is a boat coming into the harbor."

She jumped out of her chair. "La Tour?"

"We think not, madame. It is only a small shallop, but not *les sauvages*."

Françoise reached down her cloak and went up the stairwell to the bedroom. She glanced at the bed on her way past to make sure Claude was still sleeping, then continued down the corridor through the officers' and *engagés'* quarters to the gatehouse and the hatchway up to the parapet.

Rainville was standing at the parapet with his spyglass. The shallop had almost reached the field of mud bordering the shoreline at low tide. He said: "It is the Recollets and the other deserters."

"Where could they have got the shallop?"

He shrugged. "Perhaps from d'Aulnay?"

"Well, if they have changed their minds they are welcome to come back. Open the gates."

"Do you think that wise, when we do not yet know what they intend?"

"What harm can eleven men do us? Open the gates. I would go down and do it myself, but I misdoubt I could lift an iron bar as long as I am tall."

Rainville smirked. "Oh, perhaps even a finger's breadth longer than that, madame; perhaps even as long as *I* am tall." Even after two ocean crossings in each other's company, and countless giddy nights in the officers' dining hall, her lithe little stepbrother-in-law still insisted on calling her "madame," as though to keep a curtain of courtesy between them.

Rainville shouted down to the gatekeeper. A moment later Françoise heard the cold clang of the bar and then the groaning of the hinges. The *engagés* chopping wood in the courtyard came forward curiously and then began to shout. By the time the men from the shallop reached the gates, every citizen of Jemseg except Françoise, Rainville, and Claude was waiting in the courtyard to greet them.

Françoise watched the Recollet father superior and his ten companions disappear beneath her into the passage through the gatehouse, then turned to look down into the courtyard to see what would happen when they emerged. What happened was an orgy of backslapping and handpumping and jovial voices. She smiled at Rainville. "Shall we go help welcome the prodigals home?" and started down the ladder.

But as she came out of the gatehouse she heard a patchwork of the words those voices in the courtyard were trumpeting: ". . . paid me every sou La Tour owes me! . . . the Sieur d'Aulnay will welcome any man who . . . beef and mutton overflowing from his table! . . . hanged, drawn, and quartered is the fate of rebels, and excommunicates shall not be shriven . . . one last chance to save your necks and your souls!"

Françoise pushed her way through to the father superior and demanded: "Why have you come here?"

"On an errand of mercy."

She shrieked: "Get out of here!" and pushed her hands against his chest. "Go back to your master!"

Out of the corner of her eye she saw Rainville loosening his sword in his scabbard and the master gunner cocking a pistol. The father superior saw them, too, and began to back toward the gates, bellowing: "This is a house of the damned! Save yourselves while there is still—"

Françoise shouted to all and sundry: "D'Aulnay will

promise you anything now," easily drowning out the father superior; a voice adapted to reaching the back pews of reverent congregations was no match for one that had spent twenty years filling tavern courtyards temporarily converted into theaters. "But what will d'Aulnay's promises mean when he no longer has a use for you?"

They went on that way all down the slope to the shoreline, with the father superior and the deserters yelling to their "sons" and friends to come away with them, and Françoise yelling back anything that came to mind. Her forty-some remaining *engagés* were shouting as well; some of them that "Charlot" would fix the deserters when he got home, some of them that they had as much right to leave freely as the nine who'd deserted with the Recollets.

As the melee approached the landing stage, some of the forty elbowed their way forward to try to join the eleven. Françoise could see that once they all got mixed together it would be difficult to separate them without it turning into a brawl or worse. She shouted at Rainville: "The chain!" and pointed at the chain for anchoring the landing stage, coiled in the snow. Rainville snatched up one end of the chain, the master gunner took the other, and they stretched it out as a cordon between the men who'd come out of the fort and those who'd come in the shallop.

Françoise was in the no-man's-land between, up to her ankles in sorbetty mud. As the deserters climbed back into their boat and prepared to shove off, the father superior pointed his finger at her and intoned: "Must all these men die for your pride?"

"Speak to the Sieur d'Aulnay of pride! He has only to leave us alone and no one will die."

Once the shallop's bow oozed off the mud, Rainville and the master gunner lowered the chain. Once Françoise was back in the sitting room, wiping the mud off her shoes, she summoned the quartermaster and suggested that tonight would be a good time to serve out full measures of the wine they'd been rationing so carefully.

But before night came down, the *Grand Cardinal* appeared

in the mouth of the harbor. Françoise ordered the men to stand to arms, but the *Grand Cardinal* came no farther. In the morning the *Grand Cardinal* was still there, and the next day. Some days the *Grand Cardinal* would tack back and forth out on the bay, some days she lay anchored off Partridge Island, some days she would be joined by the *Vierge* or one of d'Aulnay's other, smaller ships would join her.

Whenever Françoise climbed up to the parapet, there would be at least one of d'Aulnay's ships hovering in sight. But despite all the cannons on the *Grand Cardinal*, d'Aulnay never sailed in past the harbor mouth to use them. Finally, Françoise muttered to Rainville: "What the hell is he waiting for?"

"For Charlot."

CHAPTER 43

D'Aulnay sat looking out his ornately carved cabin windows as the *Grand Cardinal* tacked back and forth between Partridge Island and the headland. He hadn't seen his wife and children for a month and more. As if to frustrate him, when the *Grand Cardinal*'s patrolling carried her farther out into the bay, on a clear day he could just make out the shore-line of Port Royal.

Today was decidedly not a clear day. He was beginning to wonder if they *had* clear days on this side of the bay. Sheets of gray sleet gusted down into the gray waves, misting his windowpanes. Although the calendar said April, the black shore rocks still wore patches of snow. At Port Royal, the meadows would already be a sparkling green speckled with wildflowers.

Out of all the injuries that La Tour and that woman had

done him, perhaps this was the worst—condemning him to spend his days cruising back and forth through wintry waters within sight of his home. But, if he kept up his vigil until La Tour came sailing unsuspecting into the guns of the *Grand Cardinal*, his life would be his own again from that day forward.

"A sail!"

D'Aulnay wrapped his cloak around him, clapped on his hat, and went out on deck. He tugged his hat down tighter against the wind slanting the sleet and called up to the crosstrees: "What sail?"

"A small sail, monsieur! Coming up the bay and bearing for the ship channel!"

D'Aulnay turned to the captain. "We shall intercept her. Have your men stand to their guns." Then he loosened his sword in his scabbard and took a grip on the stern rail as the *Grand Cardinal* sprang to life out of her sluggish half sail. He also took a grip on the unreasoning thrill he felt at the prospect that this might be the day he'd waited for for so long. It seemed highly unlikely that the lookout would describe the *Renard Noir* as a small sail, but given the diminution of distance . . .

It soon became apparent that the "small sail" was only an unarmed flyboat. D'Aulnay hailed her through the speaking trumpet. The shout that came back was in English. He handed the speaking trumpet to the captain, who had serviceable English, and said: "Tell them to come alongside or we will fire upon them."

Great, woven-rope bumpers were lowered against the larboard side of the *Grand Cardinal*. Weighted lines were tossed to the flyboat and she was hauled in like a harpooned whale until both hulls thumped against the bumpers. A Jacob's ladder was unrolled from the *Grand Cardinal* down to the deck of the flyboat.

By the time all that had been accomplished, the sleet had soaked through d'Aulnay's cloak. He sent Le Creux with a boarding party down the Jacob's ladder and followed after them, angling out his walking stick to keep his sword from

getting snagged between the rungs, acutely aware of the sleet-
slicked steps and the gap of waves between the two ships.
Once his boots were safely on the flyboat's deck, he asked Le
Creux to ask the Englishmen which one of them was the captain and what they were doing in French waters.

"They say they are seal hunters from Boston."

"Are they, now? What say we inspect their cargo, then, and
discover how many barrels of seal oil they have stolen from
me?"

There were no barrels of seal oil, only barrels of gunpowder,
flour, and salt pork, and pigs of lead and crates of cannon shot.
D'Aulnay told Le Creux: "Tell these seal hunters' captain that
his vessel is impounded and his crew are my prisoners."

The flyboat captain's sputtering reply was translated as: "He
says he has a perfect legal right to trade with Jemseg."

"Does he, now? Then why ever did he lie to me?"

"Monsieur?" a voice cut in from behind d'Aulnay.

D'Aulnay looked over his shoulder to see who had interrupted him. Among the boarding party was one of the deserters
from La Tour's fort. The fellow looked appropriately cowed
when d'Aulnay's eyes lighted upon him, but nonetheless went
on: "If you please, monsieur—*that* man is a servant of La
Tour's," pointing to a fellow trying to make himself inconspic-
uous among the flyboat's crew.

D'Aulnay stepped up to the accused and said in French:
"Where is your master?"

The man put on a confused face and began to respond in
English. D'Aulnay turned away from him with: "Monsieur Le
Creux, have that man's person and possessions searched with
thoroughness."

Tucked into the man's jerkin was a packet of letters from La
Tour: to the woman Françoise Jacquelin and to Godard de
Rainville and several other officers of Jemseg. D'Aulnay said:
"I shall peruse these before proceeding further. Monsieur Le
Creux, please to see that these 'seal hunters' are kept under
guard." Then he climbed back up the swaying ladder to the
Grand Cardinal and his cabin fit for an admiral.

The letters La Tour had written to his officers and to his

"Dear Françoise" all bore essentially the same message: he would be embarking from Boston soon, with enough men and ships and arms to put an end to the war between Jemseg and Port Royal. Other portions of the letter to the woman were disgusting: *I went to wash my face this morning and smelt you on my fingers. I thought I must still be dreaming, until I recalled I'd supped last night on buttered lobster.*

The letters weren't all from La Tour. There was also, most salubriously, one from Governor Endecott to "Madame La Tour." The governor of the Boston heretics expressed his hope that Madame La Tour was profiting from the religious instruction she'd received there, and continuing to hold fast to her new faith.

It was incumbent upon d'Aulnay, as Governor of Acadia, to make his more momentous decisions in consultation with a Conseil du Gouverneur. So he summoned to his cabin Nicolas Le Creux, the captain of the *Grand Cardinal*, and the Capuchin father who ministered to her crew. After revealing to them the germane portions of the letters, he said: "This faces us with a difficult decision, messieurs. Perhaps La Tour's Boston armada is only a fairy tale to encourage the defenders of his fort. Or perhaps he and *les Bostonais* have indeed formed a league of Protestants to destroy His Most Christian Majesty's colony of Port Royal.

"Until now it has seemed to me only Christian to avoid unleashing the guns of the *Grand Cardinal* on La Tour's fort: once La Tour himself would be in our hands, his fort would have no choice but to surrender, without any blood being shed. But if La Tour *is* coming with a fleet large enough to win past us to his fort, he and *les Bostonais* will have a secure base from which to launch attacks upon Port Royal.

"I can't but speculate that La Tour would not have chanced sending provisions and munitions ahead on an easily captured flyboat if Jemseg fort weren't even more scant on matériel than we'd thought. They may not even have enough gunpowder to fire even one volley.

"We have an easterly wind. I suggest we let it carry us into the harbor and destroy La Tour's fort before he can come to strengthen it."

The Capuchin chaplain cleared his throat. "It is difficult, monsieur, for a priest to counsel bloodshed. . . ."

D'Aulnay replied: "A little bloodshed now, Father, might well prevent a great deal more in the future—Catholic blood shed by Protestant swords."

"It is a hard choice, my son, but I cannot dispute you. 'Render unto Caesar . . .' And His Most Christian Majesty *has* instructed you to put down the traitor by any means necessary."

"Then we are agreed. Monsieur Le Creux; you will, if you please, select a prize crew and put yourself in command of the flyboat. I suggest you put the Boston crew ashore on Partridge Island and then lay at anchor there until matters have been decided."

Le Creux said: "Monsieur le Gouverneur; if you please, I suggest in all modesty that I would be of more use standing beside you on the half deck of the *Grand Cardinal*."

"Your bravery commends you, Monsieur Le Creux, and I do not question for an instant but that you would be of more *immediate* use standing beside me on the *Grand Cardinal*. But if some mischance should befall me—and to anyone who might be standing beside me—someone needs must shoulder the fortunes of Port Royal. I would have it noted by all present in this chamber that I prefer that person should be you.

"Well, messieurs, since we are all agreed, I suggest the captain beat to arms and the good father lead the crew in prayer. Who knows but that I may be wrong about Jemseg fort's stores of gunpowder?"

The Capuchin chaplain didn't appear to have any more sense of humor than the Recollet father superior.

CHAPTER 44

The gilt paint on Françoise's plaster Athène cuirass had finally dried, so she buckled it on and she and Lorette and Claude and her hand mirror studied the effect from various angles. The paint had a convincingly metallic sheen. Even buckled tight, the breast- and backplates were no more constricting than a corset, and they certainly squeezed her breasts less, since the breastplate had been molded around them. She and Lorette had had good fun shaping the plaster and shading the paint to suggest young, pert-nippled breasts and a concave, taut-naveled belly. Bald-headed ancient Caesars had given themselves athletic young torsos on their breastplates; why shouldn't she?

Claude handed her her scabbarded sword. The blacksmith had filed a broken sword blade to a point and fixed it to a handle she could get her fingers around. She slipped the baldric over her head, drew the sword, and flourished it. Claude and Lorette laughed and applauded.

A harsh clanging broke in on them: the iron tube and striking rod the blacksmith had hung in the courtyard to replace the signal gun. Françoise ran outside with her sword still in her hand. The courtyard was filled with running men. Rainville was on the parapet above the gatehouse. She shouted up at him. He shouted back: "The *Grand Cardinal* is coming in!"

She manipulated the blade back into the scabbard and scrabbled up the sleet-slick stone steps. The *Grand Cardinal* was through the harbor mouth and coming in fast, running before the wind. She said to Rainville: "What is he about?"

"I do not know, madame. Perhaps he has another proclamation to try to lure out more deserters."

"A red flag means go to the devil, does it not?"

"Or words to that effect."

"Run up a red flag."

The breastplate had become a cage her heart was trying to batter its way out of, but she had other things to concern herself with besides unbuckling her plaster armor and finding a place out of the way to set it down. The fleur-de-lis floating above the fort was replaced by a scarlet banner that could've been seen halfway to Port Royal, but the *Grand Cardinal* kept coming on.

The master gunner muttered: "He means to bombard us out of here."

Françoise said: "Can he?"

The master gunner shrugged. "The wooden bastions on our inland sides, one broadside from a warship would blow them to pieces, if a warship could get at them. That is why Charlot went to the trouble of building the front bastion out of stone and earthworks. But even stone and earth will crack with enough hammering. And Monsieur d'Aulnay will have two volleys to our one."

"How so?"

"Like so, madame: He fires his larboard guns and we fire our guns, and then we and his larboard gunners go to work swabbing out our guns so there will be no smoldering powder flakes left inside the barrel to blow up the next charge when we ram it home. But, in the meanwhile, he has turned his ship around to fire his starboard guns at us while his larboards are reloading. And so on."

It seemed obvious that the only sensible thing for her to do would be to tell Rainville and the master gunner that they were in command and then run down and hide until it was all over. But although she might not know anything of military matters, she did know something about human character, and neither Rainville nor the master gunner was the type to relish leading the pack—they were doers, who were accustomed to effecting what "Charlot" decided. And she remembered La Tour saying:

"Miracle enough no one's deserted us yet—if we looked to be deserting *them* . . ."

The *Grand Cardinal*'s majestic progress had reached the middle of the harbor. If anyone on the parapet was going to decide anything, it would have to be soon. Françoise said to the master gunner: "Would our front bastion withstand one full broadside from the *Grand Cardinal*?"

"Hmm . . . well . . ." The master gunner kissed his fingertips and squinted at the clouds. "Perhaps . . . likely . . ."

In between the pellets of liquid ice pelting against Françoise's eyes—not quite hail and not quite rain—she saw scraps of three sunny days when she'd followed La Tour and his gruff, military friend Gargot around the fort's defenses. She remembered Gargot inspecting the rack of wall guns: a handheld hybrid between a cannon and a musket, made for scattering shot among attackers swarming up the walls. She said: "Is he within the range of wall guns?"

The master gunner said: "Not yet, madame, but if he keeps on coming on as he is—"

"With the tide this high," Rainville cut in, "he could come within pistol shot—if he's confident enough that we can do him little damage."

"Bring out the wall guns and distribute them."

Rainville said: "*Oui*, madame," and went to do so, culling a crew from the men ranged along the wall.

"Master Gunner?"

"*Oui*, madame?"

"Would I be right to say our best chance is to let him have one volley at us, and then throw all we have at him at once while he is still close in and beam on to our guns?"

"I could not say you would be right, madame. But I would not say you would be wrong."

She suddenly remembered La Tour's abashed description of how d'Aulnay had crippled the *Renard Noir*, the summer she first came to Acadia. "Master Gunner, would it be possible to aim all your guns at his afterdeck and rudder?"

"Perhaps, madame. But if we are to wait until after his first broadside and then immediately fire all our guns, I will not have much leeway and the air will be filled with smoke. Better I should hit him *some*where than make a guess at where his rudder may be and shoot wide. But I will do what I can."

"I am sure no one could do more."

The master gunner climbed down through the hatchway to see to his guns: four long sakers and demi-culverins and a dozen stubby-barreled guns of varying sizes, some no longer than her arm. Rainville came back from distributing the wall guns and stood beside her looking out at the *Grand Cardinal*, still coming straight on under full sail as though d'Aulnay meant to ram the gatehouse.

Rainville drawled: "Whatever else may be said about the Sieur d'Aulnay et de Charnisay, no one can deny he is a sailor. I think he will not begin to come about to present his guns to us until he is so close in as would make another captain soil himself. And when he does come about, I suspect he will do it so neatly she will not be full beam on to us until the instant before she fires."

Françoise was astounded at Rainville's calmness. Except for a small flash of pallor along each cheekbone, he might be looking out at a fishing boat coming in to sell salt cod. But then she recalled ingénues telling her that they aspired to someday become as calm before performances as she, at moments when her stomach was performing acrobatic contortions.

She looked up and down the parapet at her musketeers and wall gunners. Here and there was an old, rusty breastplate or helmet, or a buff leather jerkin, but most of them stood to in their shirtsleeves, with sleet crystals sparkling in their hair. Many of them were crossing themselves and murmuring prayers.

She called out to them: "*Mes amis!* We are going to give him the first blow and then fire all at once! Keep down until you hear the order, and may the good God keep you!"

Rainville added: "And keep your matches and priming pans out of the rain, if you hope to have anything to fire back with!"

Now that all the decisions that could be made had been made, Françoise suddenly thought of Claude and Lorette. She turned around. They were in the courtyard below, Claude crying and Lorette holding him back from the steps to the parapet. Françoise shouted down at Lorette: "Take him into the well room! We will all be safe!" then turned back to the *Grand Cardinal*.

The prow was beginning to come about. Françoise could hear the orders shouted from the afterdeck, and see the sailors straining at the rigging lines to execute them. The elephantine ship arced in cleanly and smoothly, with the ports on her larboard gun decks springing open in unison and the black noses of her cannons poking out as she came beam on. The precision of commander and crew finding a harmony with wind and currents and canvas was beautiful to watch.

A hand grabbed Françoise's wrist and dragged her down. She crouched beside Rainville behind the parapet. She heard the voice of the Sieur d'Aulnay et de Charnisay roar: "Fire!" and dug her fingernails into the interstices between the wall stones.

There was a clap of thunder and the wall shuddered. She heard a splintering of wood from the courtyard behind her and a rumble of falling stones off to her right, followed by a voice howling in pain. Her mouth and eyes were filled with mortar dust and the smoke of gunpowder. She wanted to claw her fingers so deep into the mortar that no one could pry them loose again. But she rose to her feet, drawing her child-sized sword.

Right in front of her, above the smoke cloud, was a topmast with a sailor in the crosstrees aiming a musket at her. He had blue eyes. Instead of flinging herself down again, she flourished her sword and shouted: "Fire!"

There was a booming from beneath her feet and the parapet shook again. The banging of muskets and wall guns shattered both her ears. The smoke from the fort's guns mingled with that from the *Grand Cardinal* for a moment and then the cloud began to dissipate.

The blue-eyed sailor was no longer there. Nor was the topmast he'd been clinging to. The *Grand Cardinal* was drifting away from the shore. Her middeck was a tangle of fallen wood and canvas; her afterdeck was splintered wreckage. Looking down from the parapet, Françoise could see the torn bodies strewn across the decks and hear their screams. She swallowed fiercely to keep her stomach down, then flung her arms around Rainville's sapling neck and kissed him.

The master gunner, as soot-faced as a chimney sweep, appeared through the hatchway, so she kissed him, too. He blushed red enough to see through the black and said: "Shall we give them another volley, madame?"

"They are finished, are they not?"

"For now, madame. But still in range."

Rainville said: "You can see them furling their sails as though their lives depended. The wind that carried them in now keeps them from getting out."

The master gunner said: "Madame?"

She shook her head. "Why waste precious powder and shot when it is over?"

Rainville muttered: "We could finish him."

"You said he *was* finished."

"For now."

The *Grand Cardinal* had drifted near a point of land on the far side of the harbor and was lowering her boat. Françoise said: "What are they doing?"

"I would say," Rainville said, "they are trying to warp her ashore behind the point, to make what repairs they can while they wait for the wind to change or the tide to carry them out."

"Then it *is* over."

And then everyone was cheering: all her beautiful, ice-drenched, raggedy men—even the ones in the courtyard trying to douse the fire where a red-hot cannonball had come down through the chapel shingles. What they all were shouting was: *"Vive la belle Françoise!"*

CHAPTER 45

"Charles . . . ?" Jeanne said it tentatively, as she said all things to him since the *Grand Cardinal* had hobbled back to Port Royal. She knew he had it embedded in his heart that the twenty crewmen dead and thirteen wounded were all because he'd arrogantly overestimated his own strength and La Tour's fort's weakness. But she couldn't try to convince him he wasn't to blame, since he'd never said a word of it aloud, and if she broached the subject it would sound like an accusation. All she could do was try to find ways to distract him from brooding on it.

"Yes, Jeanne?" He turned his head to look at her over the back of his chair. But it seemed to her he didn't really see her. Those heavy-lidded, chestnut eyes—that had come home bearing even more weight than before—didn't seem to see much of anything anymore. Except something out there on the other side of the bay.

"Joseph has something to show you."

"Does he, now?"

"Yes." She pushed her son forward, whispering into his ear: "Show your father just as you showed me. There is no need to be afraid."

Joseph took a step forward and then stopped and looked back at her, with his hands still behind him clasping the willow wand like a tail. His father propped his elbow on the chair arm and his chin on his fist. "Well, Joseph?"

Joseph's shoulders hunched higher. Jeanne nodded at him. His mouth and eyes screwed down at the corners and he tucked his chin into his shoulder. She nodded more vehemently, then saw the click behind his eyes—the same click as when he'd stood on a shore rock of La Rivière au Dauphin with brown-skinned children splashing around him and finally decided to take the plunge.

Joseph bounced forward into a bent-kneed stance, left foot planted sideways beneath him and right foot pointed ahead, left hand cocked behind his shoulder. Using the willow wand for a sword, he snapped from parry to parry, calling out: *"Deuxième! Troisième! Cinq! Six! Carte!"* then held his stance with his willow wand trembling, waiting for his father's judgment.

The corners of Charles's mouth managed to turn up a little, but his eyes still drooped dully. Jeanne prompted him with: "Joseph had watched you and his uncle Nicolas so many times he learned by imitation. And then, while Nicolas was here and you were out on the bay, Nicolas came upon him practicing and taught him the names."

Charles said listlessly: "That is very good, Joseph—although your third position is too wide. Your uncle Nicolas is a good fencer and I am sure he will teach you more precisely, once he brings the *Vierge* back from . . ." and he turned his head away again to go back to staring out the window.

"Monsieur le Gouverneur?" It was the captain of the *Grand Cardinal*, standing tentatively in the doorway.

Charles sprang out of his chair. "Yes! How long?"

"Well, it is not only the tiller, monsieur. We find the rudder shaft has a crack that may open up at any time. And the hole in the aftercastle may be below the waterline in a high—"

"I did not ask you for an enumeration of the damages, I asked you: 'How long?' "

"Perhaps ten days, monsieur."

"Ten days is too long. If La Tour comes back from Boston in more strength than Monsieur Le Creux can stave off with the *Vierge*, the crew members you have lost will have died for nothing."

"Monsieur, we have only so many carpenters, and they can do only so much work in a day—"

"Then have them work at night as well. I am not asking

them to build a bit of frippery to decorate my parlor, I am asking them to refloat a ship that all our lives depend upon. I pay them well enough to loll around through the winter—now they can earn it. If the *Grand Cardinal* is not ready to sail within the week, I will put the carpenters in a longboat and discharge them back to France."

"Yes, monsieur."

When the captain had gone, Charles turned to Jeanne. "If you will excuse me, I had best parade the men-at-arms who will sail on the *Grand Cardinal*, and see what needs to be done to make them fit to face the enemy in a week."

Jeanne saw Joseph's eyes glint and said: "The children would like to watch you parade the troops."

"You may bring them out onto the portico if you wish."

She waved Joseph to follow his father outside and went up to the nursery to gather those of his brothers and sisters and cousins who were old enough to stand and watch without fussing. She could hear the shouted orders from the courtyard, and the clatter of arms and boot heels.

When she herded the children onto the portico—actually only an extended front step with a roof over it—the courtyard was already filled with gleaming ranks of men encased in polished steel. Charles was prowling up and down the ranks with the sergeant at arms trailing behind him. He stopped to clang the head of his walking stick against a breastplate. "Rust. Sergeant at Arms, this man will come to me before the end of the day wearing a cuirass with all traces of corrosion scoured away."

A little farther along the line was a young pikeman wearing a helmet a bit too big for him. Charles stopped in front of him and said: "Draw your dagger." The young man looked in confusion from the pike propped in his right hand to the long dagger on his left hip. Charles began to whack his walking stick against the pikeman's breastplate and helmet, saying crisply: "Draw your dagger. There is a swordsman too close in to employ your pike—draw your dagger!"

The helmet brim sloped down across the part-time soldier's eyes. He pushed it back clumsily, threw down his pike, and drew his dagger. As soon as the point cleared the scabbard, Charles's walking stick cracked across the pikeman's right wrist. The dagger spun away. The walking stick whipped down against the back of the disarmed man-at-arms' knee and he went down backward.

Jeanne watched her husband plant one foot on the downed boy's breastplate and poke the tip of his walking stick against the exposed throat. Although Charles didn't shout, his voice carried clearly across the courtyard: "You are dead, do you understand me? The point of a sword has just gone through your Adam's apple and severed your throat and crunched through your neckbones as it pinned you to the earth.

"Sergeant at Arms, you will conduct pike drill through the afternoon. I will take the musketeers out to the meadow and see whether they have any better notion of how to handle their weapons than this dead oaf."

As Jeanne watched her husband march his musket men toward the fort gates, their images blurred and began to swim. She crinkled her eyes against the tears threatening to escape. She knew he was only being fierce against sending unprepared soldiers into battle like lambs to the slaughter, but she wondered how many of them knew that.

At supper it was the turn of Madame de Brice and her sons to share the governor's table. Besides Madame de Brice's two sons at the Capuchin mission, her third son was now at Port Royal as well, employed as assistant to Charles's intendant. From what Charles had said, Brice de Saint Croix was doing such a good job of assisting the officer employed to manage the governor's estates and businesses that the intendant was beginning to seem like an overpriced figurehead.

As the fish course was being whisked away Madame de Brice said to Charles: "Monsieur?"

Jeanne saw Charles's mustache curl inward. He swallowed his latest mouthful and turned agate eyes on Madame de Brice. His lips parted with a pop to say: " 'Monsieur *le Gouverneur* . . .' "

"Of course." Madame de Brice ducked her horsey head. "Monsieur le Gouverneur. Forgive me. . . ."

"Of course." Charles smiled. "We all require forgiveness. What is it you wished to call my attention to, Madame de Brice?"

"Some of my girls—some of my best students—are being taken away by their families, as *les sauvages* come out of the woods to hunt shellfish. If they wander with their families all spring and summer, when they come back they will have forgotten all I have taught them through the winter. What am I to—"

"Whip them."

"Pardon me? Monsieur le Gouverneur?"

"Any girl who expresses a desire to go, whip her soundly and tell her never to come back. The willow shoots along the river are better than the alders, more pliable. After three or four have been whipped and cursed, the others will gladly stay. Steward, where is the next course?"

"It is coming, Monsieur le Gouverneur."

"Coming? You take one course away and tell me the other is 'coming' someday?"

"Here it is, Monsieur le Gouverneur."

"If you cannot manage your subordinates to pick up a full platter when they carry out an empty one, I shall have to find me a steward who can."

The next morning, as soon as Charles went out to inspect the progress on the *Grand Cardinal*, Jeanne went up to the nursery where Anne was helping the nursemaid amuse the tribe of small Motin-d'Aulnays and Motin–Le Creux. After admiring the new ball gown Nicole had made for her doll—more like a peasant's smock, actually—Jeanne said to Anne and the nurse: "Might you step out into the hallway with me a moment? It will only be a moment—not long enough for the children to do themselves mischief."

Jeanne closed the nursery door behind them, looked to left and right to make sure there were no servants in the corridor, and lowered her voice. "I think it would be well, for the next while, if the children could be kept away from Charles—Monsieur le Gouverneur—except when he deliberately comes to the nursery to visit them."

Anne and the nurse looked at each other. Jeanne twisted her fingers together and explained: "It is only, you see, that he has so many matters weighing on his mind at present, you understand, and it would not be fair to trouble him with children. . . ."

Chapter 46

"Charles?"

La Tour replied warily: "Yes, Françoise?" She never called him Charles unless he'd done something he should've thought about first. He turned manfully to face her, and found the setting somewhat odd. He was still in the room Major Gibbons was putting him up in, but one wall was missing and the harbor of La Rivière St. Jean was visible through the gap. Françoise was sitting naked in a chair, despite the ice floes bobbing beyond her shoulder. On second look, though, she had the marten-pelt bedcover draped around her, so it was all right after all.

"Charles, what is your religion?"

"Religion?" There was an off chance that if he echoed the word as if he had no idea what she meant by it, she'd specify which particular corner he had to squirm out of this time.

"Yes, religion. Sometimes you represent yourself as a good Catholic. At other times you allow people to believe you are a Protestant, if that happens to be more convenient. What do you believe?"

"What do I *believe* . . . ?" Nine times out of ten, simply repeating someone's question back at them would induce them into a long tangent about their own answer to the question, giving a pretty fair idea of what to say that would be agreeable to them.

Françoise, damn her, wasn't so easily baited into helping him wriggle off the hook. She said only: "If you believe anything."

"What I believe . . ." La Tour latticed his fingers behind his head and leaned back to study the ceiling and buy time while he guessed at an expedient answer. The ceiling disappeared, disclosing a bright blue, cloudless sky that seemed out of place over La Rivière St. Jean. But then again, he was still in Boston, so that was all right.

Much to his own astonishment, he decided to tell the truth. "What I believe—not that I think about it much—is that all religions agree on one thing: that we were put on this earth as a trial and those of us as do it right get rewarded in the next world. But it do seem unlikely to me that the good God would set us a test and then tell us how to pass it. So then what we are supposed to do is pay attention to this world, instead of sneaking guesses at how to get above it. And that way, if all religions turn out to be wrong and there is no next world, at least we've enjoyed this one."

"I wish I could be so certain."

"Did I say I was certain?" He lifted the edge of the bedcovers. "Why are you sitting all the way over there when you could come in here with me?"

She brought the marten blanket with her and snuggled in beside him. Things were just getting interesting when the Voice of Judgment shouted: "Mr. La Tour!" and hammered thunder on the rim of the world.

It did seem odd that the Voice of Judgment should call him in English. It was Major Gibbons, banging on the door of his room. La Tour sat up in his lonely bed, rubbed the sand out of his eyes and croaked: *"Entrez."*

Major Gibbons burst in with an excessive amount of energy for this early in the morning. "Mr. La Tour, the captain is back!"

"Captain? What captain?"

"The captain of the flyboat you sent to Jemseg. Only he did

not come back in his flyboat, but in a leaky shallop he was given by d'Aulnay."

"D'Aulnay . . . ?" The world had been making more sense a few minutes ago when walls and ceilings were disappearing.

"Mr. d'Aulnay intercepted the flyboat and impounded its cargo."

"*Merde.*"

"Worse than that, d'Aulnay then sailed his warship in to attack your fort."

"*Françoise?*"

"She is unharmed. According to the captain, Mrs. La Tour and her garrison killed twenty of the attackers and crippled their ship so badly it could barely limp back to Port Royal."

La Tour sank back against the pillows and sighed. "Oh, my beautiful darling."

It didn't take him much more waking up to realize that his darling was even more beauteous than that. Despite the encouraging letters he'd sent on the flyboat, the truth was he hadn't been able to sway the nervous assemblymen of New England beyond grudgingly allowing him to charter the supply boat. He'd been hoping to convince them to allow him to hire enough militiamen and ships to make sure Port Royal no longer posed a threat to anyone, but he hadn't been having much luck. But once *les Bostonais* learned that d'Aulnay had unleashed cannons on their beloved "Sister La Tour . . ."

At the next assembly La Tour kept his mouth shut while Endecott and Winthrop galvanized the meeting hall by thundering red-faced against any tyrant who would attack a defenseless woman. If the good burghers of Boston wanted to believe Françoise Marie Jacquelin defenseless, La Tour wasn't going to argue with them.

As the oak trees started to bud La Tour took a short jaunt inland to the nearest village of Abenaki cousins to the Maliseet, and asked that any hunters or fishing parties that happened to be traveling north bear a message for him. Past experience had proven that a message sent that way would reach its destination faster and more certainly than any letter handed to a ship captain. A family of Abenakis digging clams on Penobscot

Bay might encounter a boatload of Maliseet seal hunters whose next shore camp might be at a river mouth where a passing Micmac canoe was on its way upstream to a portage to La Rivière St. Jean and down to Jemseg.

Past experience had also taught him, though, that a message sent that way had to be simple enough to not get mangled out of recognition in the passage through so many mouths and ears. This one had the bald simplicity of truth: "La Tou is coming with *les Bostonais*."

CHAPTER 47

Françoise was rambling on the hill behind the fort with Claude, breathing in the scents of new green growth. It was Good Friday, so most of the fort's population were at Mass. She and Père Montagne had adopted a working compromise: he wouldn't bother her and she wouldn't bother him.

"Look here, Claude. They call these little trees staghorn sumacs. Look at the new branches here, with the velvet on them. Are they not just exactly like the velvety new antlers on the stag Papa brought in last summer? Or, no—it must have been the autumn before. You would have been too young to remember."

"I remember, *maman*. They were just exactly the same, all pointy and furry like so."

She broke off two many-pointed fronds and handed them to him. "Here, Claude, now you can be a stag, too."

He held them to his forehead and ran about pawing his feet on the ground and snorting. She laughed and twisted off two more branch ends and fisted them against her hairline. She got down on her knees and she and Claude butted heads gingerly, tangling their antlers together, snorting and stamping and bugling.

Claude backed away ten paces and came on at a run with his antlers lowered to meet hers. At the last instant she twitched her head aside, so that instead of their foreheads crashing together, his chest hit her ample padding. They fell and rolled about giggling in the moss.

A clanging came from below. Françoise looked down at the fort and the minnow-sized men cascading out of the chapel, then looked out across the harbor.

A few whisps of smoke stood above the Maliseet village on the far side of the harbor: the cooking fires of the first returnees from the deep woods. Beyond the strands of smoke were the sails of the *Vierge*, as they had been since the day after the *Grand Cardinal* hobbled away from Jemseg. Coming in toward the *Vierge* was a much bigger ship and two smaller ones.

Claude said: "Papa?"

She wanted to tell him it was, but the three ships were approaching to the north of Partridge Island. Any ship coming from the south would've taken the ship channel southwest of the island. The big ship was the *Grand Cardinal*.

"Give me your hand, Claude. We must get back quickly. But carefully—the path is steep."

By the time they got back inside the fort, her raggedy men were all standing to their guns. Rainville was on the parapet above the gatehouse, sweeping the harbor mouth with his spyglass. She said: "What are they doing?"

"Riding at anchor. They are landing boats on either point. . . . Ah." He lowered the telescope and snapped it shut. "Cannons. I expect they mean to drag them inland and set up gun emplacements to make a cross fire against the rear of the fort, where the walls are only log pickets."

It was exactly the same plan La Tour had told her he would've used to take Port Royal, if *les Bostonais* had been willing to join in the attack. She cursed La Tour in her mind for not strengthening his own fort against just such a possibility. But perhaps it would've taken resources he didn't have, and it was too late to rail about it now. She said: "Can we stop them from setting up their guns?"

The master gunner said: "I misdoubt we have the means. The only guns we have of any range are the sakers and demi-culverins in the front bastion, facing out to sea. The little guns in the rear redans were only meant for scattering grapeshot in case the Mohawks came a-raiding."

"Can we move the sakers and demi-culber . . ."

"Demi-culverins."

"Can we move them to the redans?"

"We could, madame, but it would take time. And it would leave us precious little in the front bastion should they attack us by sea as well as land."

Françoise looked at Rainville and the master gunner waiting for her to decide what to do. She said: "Which have the longer range, the sakers or the demi-culverins?"

"The demi-culverins."

"Then we will move the demi-culverins to the redans, one on each side—so you will have at least one gun to fire back at each of their gun emplacements—and leave the sakers in the front bastion."

They both nodded as though that sounded sensible, so maybe it was. She added: "But first, I suppose we should assemble everyone in the courtyard and I should speak to them. It is only right that they should know as much about what is coming as we do."

Rainville lowered his voice. "Before you do, madame . . ." He winked. "Put on your breastsplate."

"My what . . . ? It is only slats and painted plaster!"

"I know that, and so do they," nudging his head to indicate the men lining the parapet. "But they like it."

She went down into her room, where Lorette had taken charge of Claude. "Now, Claude, Lorette is going to take you down into the well room again. You will have a blanket and a book and a lamp, and a loaf of bread if you get hungry. And if you are thirsty, why, there will be the well right beside you."

"What if I have to make piss?"

"Lorette will bring along a bucket. You remember the last

time you had to hide in the well room? There was a great deal of noise of cannons, wasn't there? But none of it could touch you. And when it was safe for you to come out, no one had been hurt by all that noise—except that poor man who the stone fell on his leg, and he is almost mended now."

"I will try to be brave, *maman*."

"So shall we all, my dear." She kissed Lorette and Claude to send them on their way, then buckled on her "breastplate," lifted the sword baldric over her head, and slid open the drawer containing the little flintlock pistol she hadn't carried since she was a traveling player.

Her hands were shaking so much she could hardly load it. But she managed, then slipped it into the pocket of her skirt and went outside.

The forty-eight men of her garrison were standing murmuring in the courtyard. She put her hand on Rainville's thin shoulder to boost herself up onto the plinth La Tour had stood her on when he'd first introduced her to his "ruffians, louts, and knaves." They stopped their murmuring and gathered around her.

She could easily have dredged up a stirring battle speech from one of the best poets in France. But she couldn't bring herself to ply her trade on them. She said simply: "*Mes amis*, d'Aulnay is bringing cannons ashore to fire on our back walls. We are going to move two of our long guns to the back redans to fire back at his guns. But that will take time. If he can breach our walls in the meanwhile, he may try to storm the fort."

She saw Rainville's plumed hat nodding, so her guess had some validity to it. She went on: "You know that Charlot will come with *les Bostonais*, but we do not know when. If we can hold these walls until he comes, he will finish d'Aulnay once and for all, and then the Counseil du Roi will have no choice but to grant us pardon or have no one who knows Acadia to govern for them.

"If we cannot hold out, we are all already condemned to death. All our lives are in our own hands, and the good God's. Rainville."

"*Oui*, madame?"

"Run up the red flag."

They roared, *"La Tour!"* and *"La belle Françoise!"* and *"No surrender!"* and anything else to encourage each other. Even the two Swiss mercenaries La Tour had left behind joined in. Françoise had wondered at times whether Desjardins du Val had done La Tour any favors by enlisting foreign mercenaries. They went about their business dutifully enough, but to them it was a business.

The demi-culverins were each twice as long as she was tall, made for hurling medium-sized cannonballs long distances. The carriages they were mounted on had only vestigial wheels for rolling back and forth across a smooth floor. They would never manage frost-heaved flagstones and patches of spring mud. The fort carpenter solved the problem by knocking the wheels off and sawing a couple of seasoning logs into rollers.

Françoise stood by trying to look helpful as the master gunner set a crew to work pushing and dragging, and another crew shifting the rollers from the back to the front as the big gun rolled over them. They had barely gotten the first demi-culverin out into the courtyard when a distant boom came from the east. A geyser of flagstone chips and mud went up next to the cross in the courtyard and the ground shook.

Françoise stood staring at the steaming cannonball half-embedded in the earth. It was no bigger than Claude's head when he came out of her.

The master gunner was shouting: "Come back, damn you!" Françoise looked up from the cannonball and saw the gun-moving crew all running for the safety of the gatehouse, leaving her and Rainville and the master gunner in sole possession of the courtyard. Another cannonball came in and punched a hole through the roof of the main hall, scattering shards of her lovely, lunatic tiles.

Françoise shouted at Rainville and the master gunner: "If you can drag it, I can move the rollers!" The two of them took hold of the rope and heaved. She picked up the log that rolled free from under the back of the gun carriage and carried it around to the front. Her hands were trembling so violently now

that she could barely set the roller down straight in line, but if
they couldn't get the demi-culverins moved, they might just as
well surrender now and get it over with.

Lorette's Gaspard appeared beside Françoise, setting down
the next roller. One of the Swiss mercenaries came shamefaced
out of the gatehouse and joined Rainville and the master gunner on the towrope. Soon the master gunner had his crew back
and Françoise could step back and look around.

When she did, she thought it might've been better if she
hadn't. There were more gaps in the roof tiles now, and a hole
in the wall of the rectory. The surgeon and the apothecary were
carrying a screaming man toward the infirmary. He usually
worked in the cookhouse when he wasn't doubling as a man-
at-arms. At the moment he had a jagged shard of lumber sticking out of his back.

Most of the cannonballs seemed to be directed against the
west wall. Some of its point-topped logs were as thick as her
waist, but the whole wall shuddered when a cannonball hit,
and splinters flew. She could see it starting to buckle inward in
one place, but there was nothing she could do to stop it. So she
found an open space on the demi-culverin rope and helped
pull. Not that she expected the strength of her pudgy little arms
would make much difference, but it kept her from watching
the west wall getting gradually battered to pieces.

The demi-culverin inched close enough to the arrowhead-
shaped redan that Françoise could see the fort carpenter inside
it, sawing out a new gunport. Then someone shouted from the
parapet: "They're coming!"

She dropped the rope and shouted back: "Where?"

"The west wall!"

She drew her sword and bellowed: "*Mes amis*—all to the
west wall!"

There was a gap in the wall now, where three logs had been
shattered to stumps. Françoise planted herself there, with
Rainville and a few others, while the rest swarmed up to the
firing ledge with their muskets and wall guns.

Through the hole in the wall she could see a troop of shining steel men marching along the shore. The thump of a drum

joined the lapping of waves and the gulls' cries. It all seemed
very distant to her, like watching a play when she didn't know
any of the actors. It occurred to her that the Maliseets across
the harbor must think the white men very dull indeed to beat
a drum so unimaginatively.

The front rank halted and the ones behind began to spread
out in a wide line facing the fort. Françoise had counted
enough audiences in her time to gauge that there were upward
of a hundred of them—a good take for a country town. Some
of them carried muskets, some pikes, some scaling ladders.

Rainville said by her ear: "I think they will fire one
volley—from too far off to do much damage if we keep our
heads down—and then come on at a run."

She called up at the firing ledge: "*Mes amis!* As before, we
will let them waste their powder and shot with a volley at our
walls, and then fire back when they are closer in! Remember
they are armored, so we must wait until they are *very* close in!
Wait for my order!" She added in a much lower tone to
Rainville: "Does that sound right to you?"

"I can think of nothing that would sound more right, madame." Then Rainville stepped away from her, swept off his
hat, and scaled it across the courtyard. He Xed his arms across
his chest, drew his sword and dagger simultaneously and stuck
them in the ground, stripped off his sword baldric and jerkin,
and took his weapons up again, wiping the earth off their
points.

The line of armored musketeers were raising their weapons.
Françoise shouted: "Keep your heads down!" and skipped
sideways against the wall. There was a crash of gunfire and a
swarm of leaden bees drove their heads into the other side of
the wall. She stuck her head out through the gap again. They
were running forward, roaring, with pikes and scaling ladders
sloped toward the parapet. In time with the thudding of her
heart, she muttered: "Wait—wait—wait—wait—wait—wait—
now. *Fire!*"

The wall guns, packed with everything from deershot to
rusty nails, tore broad holes in the line, but they kept on com-

ing. The men around and above her were throwing down their muskets or wall guns and drawing swords or hefting pikes.

Françoise reached her left hand into her pocket, drew out her pistol, and cocked it with the heel of her right hand still fisted around her sword handle. Rainville pushed the back of his sword arm against her plaster chest, saying: "Keep back, madame, if you please," and stepped into the gap in the wall: a cornsilk-haired little slip of a man in a loose white shirt and pantaloons, with a sword in his left hand and a long dagger in his right.

A jagged, many-pointed halberd head thrust through the hole in the wall. The doll-like mannequin in white parried it with his sword, trapping the ax blade part of the halberd and sweeping it downward so violently that the man holding the haft was pulled through the gap to meet Rainville's leaping dagger in the throat.

But there were many more pikemen and swordsmen behind the halberdeer, clambering over the stumps in the gap and slashing indiscriminately, while the defenders had to aim for unarmored places. A mustachioed face under a gleaming helmet appeared in the sky above Françoise, and a leather-clad arm raising a bloody sword. The fierce features around the mustachios went confused for an instant and she took that instant to fire her pistol into them.

Rainville was trying to fend off two swords with his sword and dagger. She stooped under the swords and drove the point of her sawed-down Athène prop up under the bottom of a breastplate, through the pantaloons. There was a scream and her sword was torn out of her hand as the man it was stuck in fell writhing on the ground.

She was thrown onto her hands and knees, with her stomach trying to tear itself out through her throat. She was tossing in a hurricane of animal howlings and clanging blacksmiths.

And then the hurricane was gone and men were cheering. She pushed herself up onto her knees, expecting to see the remnants of her men laying down their arms and d'Aulnay's men cheering. What she saw, through the gap in the wall, was men in armor running away.

Not all the voices filling the courtyard were cheering. The man with her sword stuck in his groin was still writhing and screaming. Rainville reversed his dagger, said: "Misericord," and ended the screams.

Françoise looked around her. Lorette's Gaspard was lying nearby, coiled uncomplainingly around the pike embedded in his midriff.

Rainville offered her his hand to help her to her feet, wiped her sword on his pantaloons, and handed it back to her. The master gunner came up wiping his own sword and said: "I think, madame, we will hear no more from them today. Soon their gunners will lose the light. If we can work through the night, tomorrow morning I can start to show Monsieur d'Aulnay's cannoneers the difference between blazing away with endless stores of shot and powder or sighting carefully."

Rainville said: "Some of their dead that they thoughtfully left behind are musketeers wearing bandoliers of ammunition. And they have left us a good deal of armor, for anyone as cares to wear it."

Françoise said: "It might be wise if *you* did."

"A meager gamin like me, madame, cannot bear the weight of a cuirass and a sword at the same time. I would suggest that if we still have enough men left to spare a crew to plug up that hole in the wall while the demi-culverins are being moved, we should do so."

Françoise nodded and turned to address the troops, but discovered she was no longer able to address them as *mes amis*. "*Mes frères*, our master gunner promises that if we can get our guns in place before morning it will not be *we* that eat cannonballs for breakfast. Let us bury our dead and carry on."

They came down off the parapets handing their wounded brothers down the ladders and helping them hobble to the infirmary, reassuring each other with jokes about their clumsiness with weapons and calling boisterously for the steward to get busy in the cookhouse. She saw the fort carpenter slope his pike over his shoulder and stoop to pick up his saw to go back to work, and the master gunner scratching his beard beside the demi-culverin, gauging weight and distance. She had to wipe her eyes and nose before she could whisper to Rainville: "How can they be so brave?"

He squinted at her strangely, then looked away and said with some apparent difficulty of his own: "How could they not, *'ma' général'*?"

"I suppose you are right—they have nowhere to run to."

CHAPTER 48

D'Aulnay had elected to stay with the main shore battery while Nicolas Le Creux led the assault on the fort. Since he was more expert than Le Creux in siegecraft and gunnery, and Le Creux a competent enough field commander, it only made sense.

What did not make sense, though, was what he was seeing through his telescope: the wave of bright steel carapaces that had rolled like a tide up the wall of the fort was flowing back. It could hardly even be called a retreat; many of them were running. Once they had distanced themselves from the fort, they formed up again into something resembling ranks and began to march back along the shore toward the base camp, where their comrades were still occupied in erecting tents and clearing brush.

D'Aulnay snapped his telescope shut and strode forward to meet them. Le Creux was marching in front, setting a slow pace for the benefit of those who were using their halberds as crutches or lending their shoulders to the wounded. "Monsieur Le Creux, what is the meaning of this?"

"Charles—Monsieur le Gouverneur—you must understand . . . I have fought battles on land and sea, from behind fortifications and in front of them, and I have never seen men fight like that. A cornered rat can kill a dog five times its size. If I had not called a retreat when I did, it would have been a rout."

"I understand perfectly, Monsieur Le Creux. You attacked a fort with a sizable breach in its walls, whose defenders you outnumbered more than two to one, and you failed to carry the day. Tomorrow, *I* shall lead the assault. See to your wounded."

D'Aulnay had himself rowed back out to where the *Grand Cardinal* rode at anchor, leaving orders with both shore batteries to begin the bombardment again as soon as the sun was up. He'd always had difficulty sleeping the night before he went into battle. After a light supper he wrote a letter to Jeanne and the children, in case he should fall in the fighting. His aide-de-camp brought in his helmet and cuirass from repolishing them, and had done it right this time.

After the letter had been sealed and locked in his strongbox, and the key delivered to the captain of the *Grand Cardinal*, d'Aulnay sat up reading Cervantes and drinking a little wine to make himself drowsy. When the wine was gone, he called his aide-de-camp again, to assist him in disrobing and donning his nightshirt.

He lay in his wave-rocked bed listening to the murmuring of the night watch overhead. He couldn't say unequivocally whether or not he slept, but his eyes were open when the casements began to turn red. He waited for the red to brighten to yellow and then called for his aide-de-camp.

The back- and breastplate fit a bit too snugly, even with the buckles on the last notch of the straps. Either he was going to have to start resisting heavy cream confections or pay a visit to his armorer next time he was in Paris. Then again, he didn't expect to ever have to don armor again after today. Unless La Tour could inveigle *les Bostonais* into still helping him fight when there was nothing left to fight for.

D'Aulnay took only a cup of wine and a heel of bread for breakfast. He was just finishing the wine when the shore guns began to boom. He would've thought the light was still a bit too indirect for long-range sighting, but if his master gunner wanted to go to work early there was no shortage of powder and shot.

There did seem something odd, though, about the sound of the guns: individual shots rather than salvos. D'Aulnay put on his helmet and went out on deck. The captain looked back over his shoulder and said: "It seems odd, monsieur."

"What seems odd?"

"That they did not fire yesterday and are today."

"They . . . ?"

"The fort, monsieur. You can see the powder smoke above their rear redans."

"If you would please to lend me your telescope."

Through the glass, d'Aulnay could clearly see a puff of smoke appear out of the northwest redan, then heard the boom of a medium-sized gun echoing across the water. He swept the telescope around the harbor. From the low range of white hills that were the tents of his men-at-arms, half-dressed men were pouring out, running in the opposite direction from the fort. There appeared to be a new valley opened up in the hill range.

D'Aulnay handed the glass back to the captain, saying: "I suppose I'd best be going ashore."

"The boat crew are waiting at their oars, monsieur."

The *Grand Cardinal* had permanent boat stairs fixed onto her sternworks, so d'Aulnay didn't have to negotiate a Jacob's ladder in armor. Nonetheless, he was more than glad to plant his boots on dry land—or mud, at least. But he was less than glad to see his master gunner coming down to the shore to meet him. D'Aulnay said: "Why are you not at your post?"

"We had to abandon it, Monsieur le Gouverneur."

"*Abandon* it?"

"It was all we could do to save the guns, monsieur—those that are left. One culverin was hit square on. Two of my crew are dead and another near so. Our gun emplacements, monsieur, are only hastily thrown-up earthworks. By the time we might hope to effect any damage on his redans and silence his guns, he would have blown us to pieces. Our battery on the other side of the harbor is in the same state as we, and I am told there are five dead in the camp. We must move back beyond the range of his guns."

D'Aulnay held his composure, since it was hardly encouraging to troops to see their commander cursing ineffectually. And, after all, the damage wasn't that great and wouldn't be repeated once the fort had been stormed.

The men who'd run from the camp were sitting in their shirtsleeves looking like a flock of seagulls blown into the woods. D'Aulnay called: "Monsieur Le Creux, your men-at-arms do not appear to be armed."

"Monsieur le Gouverneur, canvas walls do not hold out cannonballs."

"Well, no more cannonballs appear to be coming down now, do they? I suspect he has not enough powder and shot to continue bombarding our camp. Nevertheless, while I am leading the next assault, you are free to employ those men I leave in reserve to break down the camp and move it back out of range. First, though, all of you will follow me back to the camp to collect your arms and those of your comrades who could not or would not run."

D'Aulnay led the way with some trepidation, not at all as certain as he'd sounded about the bombardment being ended. But either he'd been right about the fort's shortage of munitions or the woods obscured their progress back to the tents, because no more cannonballs fell.

The hundred men he meant to carry the fort with were all fresh troops. He saw no need for a greater than two-to-one advantage, so the ones who'd fought yesterday could rest today. As the assault force was forming up, Nicolas Le Creux said dubiously: "*Mon gouverneur,* I fear our gunners had not time to open a new breach in the wall this morning."

"Then I suppose we shall have to use the old one."

"God keep you, Charles."

"And you, Nikki."

There was no gunfire from the fort as d'Aulnay's column approached. Just out of musket range he signaled the drummer to cease his marching cadence and called the sergeant at arms forward. "If you would please, Sergeant at Arms, to form your men in two skirmish lines—pikemen and scaling ladders in the front line, musketeers behind. The front rank will advance at a slow march toward the wall. When the enemy rises above his parapets to fire, the musketeers will fire upon him over the heads of the front rank, and then we charge en masse. I will wait with the musketeers and give the order."

Once the ranks were formed, d'Aulnay walked along the aisle between them until he came parallel with the breach in the wall. Overnight it had been partially filled in with earth and broken timbers, but the barricade was no higher than what an active man could clamber over. There was no sound from within the fort, no sign of life except the red flag fluttering above.

D'Aulnay crossed himself and said: "*Mes braves,* yesterday your fellows tried to take that wall against a force less than half their numbers and failed. Shall we show them how it is done?"

They shouted back: "*Oui,* Monsieur le Gouverneur!" and d'Aulnay signaled the drummer to begin beating a slow march. The pikemen and halberdeers started forward. D'Aulnay gestured the musketeers to take aim at the rim of the parapet, then waited.

The lines of pikes and scaling ladders reached the halfway point of the clearing between the forest and the fort, and still no heads appeared above the parapet. Then a muffled, high-pitched voice shouted: "Fire!" and there was a ragged crash of gunfire as smoke puffed out in a line halfway up the wall; they were firing through the chinks between the logs.

D'Aulnay noted several of his pikemen falling as he swept out his sword and shouted: "Fire!" His musketeers fired back in perfect, useless unison. He shouted over the echo: "*En avant!*" and began to run forward, with the weight of his back-and breastplate bouncing up and down on his shoulders.

He heard an ugly crash off to his left, and screams. He glanced in that direction. The enemy had mounted a small gun in the back angle of the front bastion to enfilade his men, and had cut down about a dozen of them. He looked ahead again. The gap in the wall was about ten paces away. The pikemen who'd gotten there before him were thrusting their weapons through and trying to climb over. Metal clanged overhead from the parapet. A scaling ladder teetered and fell beside him with a crunch of steel-encased flesh.

He reached the breach, but it was clogged with the backs of pikemen and halberdeers. He lunged his sword over the shoulder of one of them to skewer a wild-eyed man swinging a felling ax. The halberdeer whose shoulder he'd lunged over suddenly fell backward. The deadweight knocked d'Aulnay off his feet. He dragged his legs out from under the halberdeer and looked around.

The barricade across the breach had grown half again as high with piled corpses. Two armored swordsmen were making motions as though trying to climb over and in, but it was clear to d'Aulnay that they didn't really want to. The men at the tops of the scaling ladders were only trying to defend themselves against the blades and torn-up flagstones coming down at them. The sergeant at arms was yelling: *"En avant, mes braves!"* while backing away.

D'Aulnay bellowed: "Retreat!" and crawled back up to his feet to trail behind the bright-armored backs pelting headlong for the woods. From behind him came the sound of whooping laughter.

The sergeant at arms formed ranks on the shore for the march back to camp. D'Aulnay had lost his helmet and wished for his walking stick. The ranks took their time forming, but d'Aulnay didn't quibble; he needed time to regain control of himself.

By the time they'd marched back to their new camp, d'Aulnay had stiffened himself sufficiently to be able to say in relatively even tones: "It appears you were correct, Monsieur Le Creux. Within the hour I want you and the rest of the Conseil du Gouverneur convened upon the *Grand Cardinal.* And bring along with you those men who left La Tour's service for ours this winter."

D'Aulnay managed to keep himself in a frozen state all the way across the harbor and up the stern steps of the *Grand Cardinal* and down into his cabin. He closed the cabin door behind him, sat down at his table, and picked up the pewter pitcher of wine that his aide-de-camp had obediently set out for him. He studied the pitcher for a moment, noting how its interestingly burnished, grainy, condensation-beaded surface reflected the belled-out, distorted features of the Sieur d'Aulnay et de Charnisay, son to René de Menou. Then he proceeded to smash the pitcher down on the tabletop until the handle broke off in his hand.

His face was wet. He wiped it with his hand and tasted a slightly oversweet Bordeaux tinged with salt. He called his aide-de-camp in. "The pitcher had a flaw in it. The handle broke off in my hand. Clean up this mess."

"But, Monsieur le Gouverneur . . . Your hand is bleeding."

"Oh, so it is. I suppose a sword cut . . . Give me your hand-kerchief."

D'Aulnay sat up on his bed squeezing the handkerchief in his hand while his aide-de-camp cleaned up. The cabin was in decent order again by the time Le Creux appeared with the captains of the *Vierge* and the *Grand Cardinal*, trailing the Capuchin and Recollet chaplains and the half-dozen surviving ex-*engagés* of La Tour's.

D'Aulnay pointed at the deserters from Jemseg and said: "Why did you lie to me?"

"Lie, Monsieur le Gouverneur?"

"You said there were no more than forty-nine men left in La Tour's fort."

"But . . . Monsieur le Gouverneur . . . That was no lie."

"That was no forty-nine men I faced today."

"Well . . . perhaps . . . Monsieur le Gouverneur . . . Perhaps some of *les Bostonais* snuck up here through the woods. Or perhaps, *les sauvages* . . ."

D'Aulnay hadn't considered that. It was possible. He said: "Who is in command there?"

"Françoise Marie Jac—"

"*Don't* play the fool with me. I know La Tour left his slut in charge of his fort. I meant, who is in command of the fort's military defenses?"

"Well, Monsieur le Gouverneur . . . La Tour did not take his master gunner with him on the *Renard Noir*. . . . And Godard de Rainville also stayed behind. . . ."

"Rainville . . . I would not have thought he had it in him. . . . Well, regardless, tomorrow before dawn I want the crews of every one of our ships armed and ferried to the shore, leaving only a skeleton watch on board. Every man-at-arms at our command is to be ready to march at dawn. Tomorrow morning we finish this."

Nicolas Le Creux cleared his throat. "Is it wise, Monsieur le Gouverneur, to leave our ships defenseless? If La Tour should appear while we are all onshore . . ."

"Your caution commends you, Monsieur Le Creux. But there is a time for caution and a time to seize the moment. If we fling forward all the forces at our command, I have small doubt we can overwhelm the fort in less time than it would take La Tour to sail up the ship channel, even were he anchored in the lee of Partridge Island at this moment."

One of the Recollets said: "But, Monsieur le Gouverneur, tomorrow is Easter Sunday. . . . We must hold Mass."

"We can wait Mass till midday. That way you will be able to save your breath by holding Easter Mass and Victory Mass at the same time."

CHAPTER 49

Françoise lit a stub of a candle and went down into the well room to try to comfort Claude a little. He had been in there for two days and a night now with rarely any company besides Lorette, who'd done nothing but weep since Françoise told her of Gaspard. Perhaps it would have been safe to let Claude come out at night. So far the attacks had only come in daylight. But Françoise didn't want him to hear the screams from the infirmary, or to see the cannonaded wreckage of his home or the stacked corpses waiting for the torchlit work crew to find enough unrubbled space in the courtyard to dig another common grave.

She saw a crack of light beneath the well-room door, from Claude and Lorette's fish-oil lamp. So as soon as she had her hand on the door latch, she blew out her candle so as not to burn away any more of it than necessary.

She felt the air change as she stepped across the threshold; cooler and fresher, without the stench of gunpowder and ashes. The sound of dripping water echoed up the stone-lined well shaft and off the thick stone walls.

Claude jumped up from his blanket-nest sanctuary between two empty casks and ran forward to clunk against her. She'd forgotten she was still wearing her breastsplate. She unfastened it and sank down on the floor to hold him against her body.

He cried for a while, then found enough voice to say: "I was frightened you were dead, too."

"How could any harm come to me when I have so many brave men to protect me?" She didn't tell him there weren't nearly so many anymore. There were barely thirty left who could still stand to. And some of them wore bandages that seeped blood whenever they had to pick up a weapon again.

"Why, *maman,* do those bad men want to hurt us?"

"They do not want to hurt *you*, Claude." Although she wondered if even that was true. "I think you are too young yet to understand how this has come to pass. When you are older, I will explain it to you."

First she would have to explain it to herself. She was quite sure that if her mind were still capable of thinking of anything beyond the moment, it would've been able to follow back along a series of steps that had brought her and Claude to be huddled on the floor of the well room while d'Aulnay loaded his guns for tomorrow's assault. But that wasn't necessarily an explanation.

Lorette crouched down on the floor beside Françoise and Claude, and Françoise put her free arm around her. Françoise sat with them a few moments longer and then struggled to her feet, saying: "Well, I must go to see to ... things. . . ." She picked up her breastsplate. "Lorette, if you will help me with the fastenings . . ." The plaster was crumbling under the armpits and along the spine from sweat, but Rainville had said they liked her to wear it.

Claude said: "Will you sleep with us tonight, *maman*?"

"If I sleep, my dear, it will be with you."

She lit her candle stub from the wick of Claude and Lorette's lamp and started for the door. She was heaving her leaden foot over the threshold when Lorette called after her: "Françoise . . . ?"

Françoise stopped and turned. Lorette came up close and whispered: "We are all going to die, aren't we?"

Françoise lifted her hand to Lorette's tear-chafed cheek and said: "Someday, my dear, we are all going to die. But tomorrow's sun may well see La Tour's sails coming up the bay, and then we will not be the ones to die soon."

Françoise moved off down the corridor, supporting herself with one hand against the wall. Over the last two days it had become habitual to her to walk like a veteran drunkard: automatically reaching a hand out to skate along a table rim, or bouncing a shoulder along a wall.

She wondered after the fact how she could've responded so offhandedly and stoically to Lorette's question. The most surprising part was that it had been a perfectly honest reply. It did seem odd that she wasn't more afraid for herself. But when there were so many other people to be afraid for . . .

Not that she still didn't expect to feel the urge to burrow into the courtyard the next time the muskets began to crack and the halberd heads poked over the stockade. But she'd already lived a life's worth in France and then been given a second life when that one was done, and a son.

Or perhaps her surprising sangfroid had nothing to do with anything but being numbed by exhaustion and by the bloodstains on her skirt from men chopped like hogs at sausage-making time. She giggled giddily at the likelihood that if she were ever in her right mind again, she would recollect her current state as less stoic than stupefied.

The floor of the dining hall was dotted with snoring men

who'd fallen asleep the instant they didn't have to stand up any longer. Torchlight shone through the hole in the window and the shards of panes around it. She went outside.

It was a soft spring night. A fog was creeping in off the bay, carrying the tang of salt and kelp. Rainville and the master gunner and a half-dozen other men were leaning on their shovels, dozing, while Père Montagne intoned the names of their friends under the fresh mound of earth: ". . . and their fellow sons of God interred here with them."

Père Montagne closed his book and came over to her. "Madame, tomorrow is Easter Sunday."

"Is it? Tomorrow is Sunday?"

"*Oui*, madame. I know you are not of the faith, but so many of the men are. . . . If you could see your way, madame, to allow me to say Mass to them tomorrow . . . I know they must man the walls in case of attack, but I am sure it would be safe. I am certain the enemy camp will be holding their own Mass."

"Are you so certain? But even if you are wrong, I think you could still hold Mass without jeopardizing our defenses. If the enemy approaches during the Mass, we can man the walls in an instant, *if* you would be agreeable to our men keeping their weapons beside them in the chapel."

"Under the circumstances, madame, I think the good God would understand."

" '*Nos morituri* . . .' "

"Pardon me? Forgive me, madame, but I would not have thought you had any acquaintance with the language of Holy Mother Church."

"It may be the same language, Father, but I fear it is decidedly not of the church. '*Ave Caesar, nos morituri salutatamus.*' "

"Are you so certain of that?"

"No. And I intend we shall do all we can to keep it uncertain. To that end, to make certain we are not taken by surprise while you are saying Mass, we need only post sentries on the parapet to give the alarm in case you overestimate the piety of the men from Port Royal. Our Swiss mercenaries would no sooner go to Mass than their own funerals, so we can appoint them to—"

"Pardon me, madame, but there is no 'them' anymore. Only one of them has not yet attended his own funeral."

"Oh. Well, it only takes one voice to raise an alarm."

"For that matter, madame—if you will permit me to suggest—you could help keep watch yourself, since you are not of the faith."

"There are faiths and faiths, Father. After these last two days, there is nowhere my brothers go where I will not go with them."

"Even to a papist Mass?"

She reached up and twisted his ecclesiastical ear.

CHAPTER 50

D'Aulnay landed on the shore in the first graying of dawn. And *gray* it was: during the night the fog had thickened. He wouldn't have known which direction the shore was if not for the dim glow of the watchfires where his men-at-arms were camped. If it weren't for the creaking of oarlocks and the ghostly bobbing of bow lanterns, he would have had no way of knowing there were other boats besides his plying back and forth ferrying sailors carrying muskets and cutlasses.

As soon as his boots were on land, d'Aulnay called out: "Monsieur Le Creux?"

Le Creux's voice came back from the direction of the watchfires: "Monsieur le Gouverneur?"

"I am on the shoreline."

D'Aulnay stood waiting as shadowy figures stumbled and mumbled around him trying to form ranks with their fellows, who kept disappearing. Le Creux called from closer than before: "Monsieur le Gouverneur . . . ?"

"Here, Monsieur Le Creux."

One of the shadowy figures coalesced into an armored Nicolas Le Creux. Le Creux said: "Shall I have the men stand down until the fog lifts?"

"Nothing of the sort. You know as well as I that when the fog descends on the mouth of La Rivière St. Jean it can stay for days. Or perhaps it will dissipate by the time the sun is up. In either case, the Conseil du Gouverneur decided yesterday that we put a finish to this matter today, and so we shall."

"We cannot fight in this. You could stuff a pillow with it."

"What a rustically charming phrase, Monsieur Le Creux. But that does not alter the fact that you and I can see each other perfectly clearly, can we not? And we are certainly no closer in than men fighting hand to hand, are we? Besides which, this should relieve you of one of the worries you expressed yesterday; so long as this fog covers the harbor approaches, La Tour will not be arriving to take our ships by surprise."

"La Tour could navigate these waters with a sack over his head."

"Then all the more reason we should take his fort immediately, lest we find ourselves trapped between two enemy forces. I have always valued your counsel, Monsieur Le Creux, but the morning of a battle is not the time to quibble about what has already been decided. Now, if you would please to form your men into marching order. A single file seems best under the circumstances. I will take the lead."

As soon as there was enough light for d'Aulnay to be able to see where the shore rocks ended and the low-tide mud began—at least for as far as a pace in front of his boot toes—he set off along the shore with three hundred armed men strung out behind him, marching without drums. It turned out to be a long walk, stumbling over spray-slicked, uneven ground.

But the longer the march took, the longer the sun and breeze had to work on the fog. D'Aulnay found he could see up to two paces in front of him, then three, then ten. By the time they were within two musket shots of the fort, there was nothing left of the fog but a gentle haze and a few thicker shards still drifting here and there. So much for old woman Le Creux.

Just out of musket range d'Aulnay called a halt to deliver his orders. He was going to spread out his three hundred in an arc around the rear and side walls of the fort. He had no doubt that it was what he should've done on the first day, instead of allowing Godard de Rainville to concentrate his forces on one wall.

D'Aulnay had just begun detailing which troops were to be distributed where when Le Creux interrupted him. "Monsieur le Gouverneur—look there on the fort wall. Do you see it?"

D'Aulnay turned to look. Above the pointed parapet an arm was waving a piece of white cloth, perhaps a handkerchief. But the red flag still flew over the fort.

Le Creux said: "Shall I go see?"

D'Aulnay shook his head. If the white cloth were only a bit of petty treachery to lure an envoy into musket range, better it should not be his most competent officer. So he sent a sergeant instead.

The sergeant advanced cautiously toward the fort. But no gun fired, not even when he'd reached the base of the wall and stood there with his head cocked up toward the fluttering white cloth. The sergeant came back at a trot. "Monsieur le Gouverneur, the man on the parapet says he is a Swiss mercenary who was tricked into La Tour's service. He says all the others are at Mass and he was left to stand sentry alone. If you will grant him clemency, he will not raise the alarm."

D'Aulnay looked at the wall again. It could be a trick to lure his entire force forward and shoot them down at close range. But he couldn't forgo the chance that the tale told to the sergeant might be true. He ordered that a hundred men form a skirmish line and began to walk forward in front of them, leaving Le Creux in command of the reserves. He could have stayed behind and sent Le Creux, but it seemed that if anyone was going to take the chance of walking into a trap, he should do it himself.

Grass stalks and tree shoots pulled at his boots as though to urge him to turn back. He selected a tall blue weedflower a few paces in front of the wall and told himself that if the parapet didn't erupt gunfire by the time he reached the blue flower, it wasn't going to. His boot came down on the weed and still nothing happened.

Scaling ladders blossomed up on either side of him. He stepped to the nearest one and climbed hand over hand to the top, then gingerly levered his legs over the sharpened stakes to bring his boots down on the firing ledge beyond.

A hollow-eyed scarecrow in a dented breastplate thrust itself upon him, sputtering in fractured French: "Gouverneur Monsieur, clemency I have?"

"Yes, yes, clemency." D'Aulnay pushed the creature away so he'd have room to raise his arm to signal Le Creux and the bulk of his army. When he saw them starting forward, he turned to look down at the interior of the fort he seemed to have been staring at the outside of for half his life.

The courtyard was a shambles of shattered bits of buildings, twisted bits of metal, and humpbacked mounds of fresh-turned earth. Through the holes torn in the chapel came the wispy sound of an old priest saying Mass, and hoarse male voices singsonging responses. D'Aulnay drew his sword and started down the steps.

CHAPTER 51

Françoise sat in the front pew of the chapel with Claude in her lap, Lorette on her left, and Rainville on her right, half listening to the ritual cadences of Père Montagne. Her eyes drifted to one of the holes in the chapel walls and she saw that she'd made a mistake. She had thought it would be safe to bring Claude out for a respite from the well room, since the fort was so blanketed with fog he wouldn't be able to see the wreckage. But now there was barely a trace of mist left.

She set her mind to thinking up some close-your-eyes game she could lure Claude into when it came time to take him back across the courtyard. Instead, her mind wandered off on the fact that she could hardly have been expected to assume the fog would lift so quickly. Her first encounter with Jemseg fog, in her first autumn in Acadia, she'd grouchily asked La Tour after three days of it if it was ever going to lift. La Tour had replied: "Don't be ungrateful to our fogs, they are a wondrous softener of the complexion. See?" and he'd taken hold of her hand to rub it up and down his shoe-leather cheek.

Her memory was interrupted by a roar from the back of the chapel: "They're in over the walls!" The congregation snatched up their weapons and ran for the door.

Françoise and Lorette were the last ones through the doorway, Françoise clutching Claude screaming in her arms. There were armored men all over the west wall. The men of Jemseg were firing their muskets at them and knocking a few down. Françoise shouted: "To the gatehouse!" and ran. Her only thought was to get Claude into the safety of the stone gatehouse, with its rabbit warren of corridors and tunnels radiating out to the rest of the front of the fort.

Françoise flung open the gatehouse door and scrambled inside, gasping for breath. Lorette had followed on her heels. Françoise pried Claude's arms from around her neck and thrust him at Lorette, shouting: "Take him to the well room and bar the door!" then went to the window.

Half a dozen of her raggedy men had also followed on her heels. Rainville and the rest were stretched in a thin line across the courtyard, backing step-by-step toward the gatehouse as they fought against the oncoming tide with their swords or pikes or clubbed muskets. The point of a sword came out through one of the ragged-jerkined backs. Another in the line went down under a halberd.

Françoise shrieked at the men who'd followed her inside: "Can we do nothing to help them?"

"When they get a little closer, madame."

Half the line had fallen by the time they'd backed within a corpse length of the gatehouse. The men inside thrust their pikes out through the window, over their friends' heads, and into the helmeted faces. Françoise fired her pistol out the doorway. The attackers wavered for an instant, which was all Rainville and the others needed to dive inside.

The steel tide tried to pour in after them. Pikeheads clanged against pikeheads poking in through the window. Rainville stood planted in the doorway, cutting and thrusting, with blood streaming down one leg and seeping from a line across his forehead.

Françoise heard a rumbling behind her and whirled to look. The master gunner was wheeling forward one of the stubby little guns that flanked the gates. He faced it toward the doorway, blew his smoldering match aglow, then looked toward the doorway again and hesitated.

Françoise jumped toward Rainville, grabbed the back of his shirt with both hands, and flung herself sideways and down. They hit the floor hard. She felt one of the struts in her breastsplate snap. Or perhaps it was one of her ribs.

A clap of spring thunder went off inside her ears, filling the room with acidy smoke. She was coughing and wiping her eyes and amazed not to find herself buried; it seemed impossible that the thunderclap hadn't burst the wall seams and brought the ceiling down. But it had torn pieces out of the door frame and blown the door off its hinges. Outside, inhuman voices were shrieking and howling.

Through the smoke stinging her eyes to tears, Françoise saw a blurred picture of the master gunner ramming in a fresh charge and another bag of jagged scattershot without bothering to swab out the barrel. The howlers in the courtyard apparently considered it impossible for anyone to reload a gun that fast, because a horde of them came boiling through the doorway just as the master gunner was yanking his ramrod out.

The head of the ramrod hadn't quite cleared the mouth of

the barrel when the gun went off. Mingled with the thundercloud this time was a shower of warm, wet droplets and flakes of flesh.

When Françoise could see again, the barrel of the gun was flared out and twisted into a warped, split trumpet mouth, as though inch-thick iron were wet clay. She grunted up onto her hands and knees and crawled to where the master gunner lay. From his groin to his forehead there was nothing but red pulp.

She started to push herself up to her feet, but only got as far as her knees before slumping backward. Her shoulders thumped against the wall. For a moment she assumed the second thunderclap must have struck her deaf. Then she realized that there were no more clangs of steel or roaring voices or musket cracks to hear. There were only low groans and murmurings, gasped intakes of breath, and soft scuffing sounds.

She saw something on the floor that shouldn't be there. It seemed ridiculous to think that any particular object shouldn't be there on a floor covered with broken bits of wood and masonry, cracked weapons, and a coating of dust flecked with blood. But this decidedly shouldn't be there. It was the master gunner's arm.

Rainville was sitting on a table with his lips pulled back from his teeth as the surgeon cut away the leg of his white pantaloons which had turned pink. Françoise croaked at him: "They will come at us again in a moment, will they not?"

Rainville said: "I expect so. If they have any sense they will also get up on the parapet above us and come down through the hatches. Or perhaps they will simply roll the demi-culverins back out of the redans and turn them against us."

"I want you . . . I want you to take out a white flag and tell him I will surrender if he swears to give quarter to my men."

Rainville slitted his periwinkle eyes at her and tightened his mouth. "And what of *you*?"

"He is bound by law to take me back to France for trial. Once I have been given the opportunity to explain to the Conseil du Roi what has happened here, I think they will not judge me so harshly."

Rainville shook his head. "I will not do it."

"You *will not*?"

"I *can*not do it. Nor can any other man here. We all of us swore an oath that we would die before seeing you in his hands."

"You also swore an oath to serve La Tour, did you not?"

"Not in so many words, but yes."

"And La Tour left me in command of this fort, did he not?"

"Yes, but—"

"Monsieur de Rainville, I am giving you an order. Obey it."

"*Oui*, madame."

CHAPTER 52

D'Aulnay was reordering his troops for the next assault when a piece of white cloth fluttered out of the shattered doorway of the gatehouse. Godard de Rainville stepped out into the open waving his shirt over his head, leaving his scrawny torso naked to the crisp spring air.

D'Aulnay said: "Monsieur Le Creux, if you would please to go discover what this may signify. Sergeant at Arms, have a squad of musketeers train their weapons on that man in case of any sign of treachery."

Le Creux returned from speaking with Rainville wearing an oddly pinched-in expression. "Monsieur le Gouverneur, they are offering to surrender—if you will swear to give quarter to the men of the garrison, who only fought as foot soldiers obeying their orders, and are not responsible for the course their commander chose to take."

D'Aulnay looked out across the piece of ground between where he was standing and the gatehouse. He could barely see the floor of the courtyard for the mounded wreckage of twisted halberd heads, broken pikestaffs, embedded cannonballs, and entangled corpses. At a rough guess, there were three bright-armored corpses-at-arms or butchered sailors for every dead Jemseg tatterdemalion. And the rebels would fight even more fiercely if their last desperate hope for mercy were taken away. Logic dictated that there had to be at least fifty of them still left in the gatehouse, to have withstood his last assault. Given the arithmetic, half the men he'd brought from Port Royal would have to die to finish them off.

"Monsieur Le Creux, inform the rebel Rainville I swear my oath that the garrison will be spared if they surrender. Sergeant at Arms, bring that red rag down off the flagpole and run up the lilies of France." Besides signaling the return of order, the fleur-de-lis would also serve to signal the captains of the *Grand Cardinal* and her sister ships to ride in on the tide.

D'Aulnay led his army forward across the slaughter yard to form a cordon in front of the gatehouse. One by one, starved-looking, bleeding men in rags staggered out to pile their weapons in front of him—everything from crack-stocked matchlocks to kitchen cleavers. Eighteen of them came out, and then no more.

D'Aulnay waited for the rest of them to start appearing. When they didn't, he said to Rainville: "The terms were that every man of you was to surrender."

"The two men still inside cannot walk. And the surgeon stayed behind to attend them."

D'Aulnay felt his gorge rising at the way he'd allowed himself to be duped. He could have overwhelmed eighteen walking wounded with a snap of his fingers, and without losing one man. He said tautly to Rainville: "Where is your sword?"

"I left my weapons behind when I came out under a white flag."

"It is customary for a defeated commander to surrender his sword to the victor."

"I was never in command here."

"Then who was?"

Rainville just turned and pointed. Standing on the gatehouse steps was La Tour's diminutive whore, in a bloodstained skirt

and a crumbling, gilded plaster cuirass that still showed traces
of an obscene design. The eighteen ragged remnants of the
rebels somehow summoned up the strength to cheer: *"La belle
Françoise!"* Despite the croaking and cracking of their voices,
d'Aulnay could discern more than a trace of laughter.

The woman came down off the step and approached. She
stopped in front of him, drew a toy sword, and proffered it to
him hilt first.

He slapped it out of her hands and turned to his sergeant at
arms. "See that these men and this woman are incarcerated se-
curely in separate places. Detail gravediggers to see to our
dead, and to dig a pit to dump the rebel dead.

"Monsieur Le Creux, we will convene a meeting of the
Conseil du Gouverneur in my cabin on the *Grand Cardinal*.
You there, open the gates." The two men-at-arms nearest the
gates ran to lift down the great iron bar.

D'Aulnay went down to the shore to await the *Grand Cardinal*. Nicolas Le Creux and several of his other officers followed him. They made a few attempts to speak with him, but
he was in no mood for idle conversation. He could feel the hot
blood rising into his cheeks, so he employed a device he'd invented as a child: imagining himself rubbing an icicle up and
down his face so the flush wouldn't show.

The *Grand Cardinal* finally dropped anchor in front of the
fort and sent her boat ashore. Once on shipboard, d'Aulnay
said to Le Creux: "The council will attend me in a quarter of
an hour," and repaired to his cabin.

He summoned his aide-de-camp to pour out a flagon of
wine, help him off with his cuirass, and lay out a fresh suit of
clothes. With his face and hands washed, his hair combed, and
his body attired in clean linen and brocade, he felt more himself again. But there was still a queasiness that wouldn't go
away. One moment he felt overwarm, the next chilled to the
bone.

His brother-in-law arrived with the ships' captains and chaplains. D'Aulnay seated himself at the head of the council table
and said: "Messieurs, as my advisers I hope and trust you can
help me find a solution to the grave difficulty I find myself

placed in. As the last three days have proven, La Tour had garrisoned his fort with men who are more like wolves. What are we to do with such men?

"If we set them loose, they will go straight to La Tour. But it is not safe to take them into our service. They would not hesitate to cut our throats in the night at a word from La Tour. And if the arch-rebel should reappear to lay siege to Port Royal again, we would have a contingent of his fellow rebels already within our walls.

"Over and above those considerations is the indisputable fact that the king himself has already sentenced these men to death. I am duty bound to execute that order. I see no alternative."

"You swore your *oath*!" The unseemly shout came from Nicolas Le Creux, and the splashing of wine and rattling of crockery came from Le Creux's hands slapping down on the table.

D'Aulnay said calmly: "You are quite right to be so passionate, Monsieur Le Creux, over the oath I swore to obey my sovereign. If, however, you are referring to the oath I gave to abide by the terms of surrender, you are overstraining your nerves over a bagatelle. The terms they offered were a lie. I only agreed to them to prevent further slaughter among our men. The woman knew I would never consider granting clemency if I knew there were so few rebels left, so she tricked me into believing otherwise. No man can be bound by an oath to a lie.

"Regardless, clemency is not mine to grant. The decree sealed by the king's hand is explicit that once La Tour or his woman are in my hands, I am to transport them to France for judgment; all other rebels I am to put to death immediately.

"Perhaps you of my Conseil may see some alternative to either disobeying my king or immediately hanging the dogs who disobeyed him. I myself see no choice."

There was a silence. The captain of the *Grand Cardinal* licked his lips and said hoarsely: "But, Monsieur le Gouverneur . . . Among all of our complement of men, there is not one I know of who has ever served as an executioner. It is a terrible duty to impose upon a common sailor or *engagé*."

"Oh"—d'Aulnay smiled and almost gave away the surprise he had in store—"you need not trouble yourself on that account, Captain. I believe I have the perfect solution for that awkward detail.

"Well, messieurs, it appears that my Conseil approves of this course of action. Or at least sees no alternative."

Nicolas Le Creux said: "I do not approve."

"Duly noted, Monsieur Le Creux. That is the way of Conseils, after all: one councillor may be of one opinion and all the others of another, and so the matter is decided. Well, best we be getting ashore again and dispose of this unpleasant matter as soon as possible. I suggest that all the Holy Fathers acompany me; I expect there will be more than a few elaborate last confessions to attend to."

His Conseil rose up out of their chairs with him and all started for the door. All except Nicolas Le Creux, who said: "Monsieur le Gouverneur, if I might have a word with you . . ."

"A brief word, Monsieur Le Creux."

Le Creux looked over his shoulder at the last backs disappearing from the cabin, then slid the door shut. "Charles, I beg of you, do not do this thing. Think of your soul."

"That you are married to the sister of my wife, Monsieur Le Creux, does not entitle you to speak of my soul. It is good of you to be concerned, but if three Capuchin fathers could hear me say what I must do and not dispute me, I think my soul is not in jeopardy."

"The Capuchins would not dispute you if you said you planned to sell a conventful of nuns to *les sauvages*; they are too fond of the profits you earn them from Acadia."

"If that is your opinion of the holy fathers, perhaps you had best be apprehensive for your own soul."

"What do you intend to do with Françoise Jacquelin?"

"Exactly what my sovereign decreed: the dogs shall die here, the bitch in France. Now, if you please, we have grave matters to attend to."

The sergeant at arms had placed the male prisoners in the officers' dining hall, with guards at the doors and windows and at the larger holes in the exterior wall. The guards flanking the doorway smartly uncrossed their halberds as d'Aulnay approached. He stepped inside and stood with his left hand on his hip and his right hand cocked on the head of his walking stick.

The prisoners' groans and mutterings died down as all eyes gradually turned toward the doorway. When d'Aulnay was certain he had all their attention, he said: "By order of His Most Christian Majesty, you are all condemned to death for treason. The sentence shall be carried out as soon as those of you who still claim to be true Christians have been shriven." He was quite aware that all of them could be denied last rites as excommunicates, but it seemed only merciful to allow them a chance at God's mercy.

There was silence for an instant and then the room erupted with noise. Some of them cried out in terror and some of them cried out in rage, flinging themselves toward him. The guards' halberds came down in front of him to stop them.

D'Aulnay smiled over the halberds and unveiled the surprise that the captain of the *Grand Cardinal* had almost tripped him into giving away. "Not *all* of you, though, will die. We needs must have a hangman. Whichever man of you volunteers to perform that service will be spared. After all, the executioner can hardly execute himself."

Then he waited to see this so defiant band of brothers turn on each other. Not that that had been the point of the idea, of course. It was simply the most pragmatic solution to the thorny problem he'd identified long before the captain of the *Grand Cardinal* had raised it.

They cast silent, sidelong glances at each other from under matted hair or filthy bandages. D'Aulnay waited patiently for it to sink into their heads that if one of them didn't volunteer to save his neck, there was bound to be at least one man in all Port Royal's forces who would be willing to take on the duty for a healthy amount of money.

"I'll do it!" A grizzle-whiskered scarecrow jumped up and forward, away from the clutching claws of the rest of the pack.

"*I* will!" a peach-fuzzed fellow shouted.

"Too late." D'Aulnay waggled his finger at the peach-fuzzed boy. " 'He who hesitates . . .' Come along, hangman. The rest of you: the holy fathers will help you use what time you have left to best advantage."

"Monsieur d'Aulnay!"

D'Aulnay stopped on the threshold and turned back. La Tour's silky lapdog of a stepbrother, Godard de Rainville, had risen to his feet, awkwardly balancing his weight onto the one leg left to him that had more than a blood-soaked bandage to cover its nakedness. Rainville's sharp little features had become gratifyingly pallid, but perhaps it was only the loss of blood. D'Aulnay corrected him: " 'Monsieur *le Gouverneur* . . .' "

"Would it not give you more satisfaction to take your sword in your hand, and give me back mine?"

"I do not soil my sword with the blood of gallowsbait."

"I had not thought you such a coward." D'Aulnay had to laugh at such a transparent attempt to bait him into granting the hobbled, chin-high excuse for a man a quick death. "But if so it must be, I can only thank you for giving back our honor in exchange for yours. By breaking your sacred oath, you allow us to keep ours."

CHAPTER 53

Françoise sat huddled on her bed with Claude and Lorette on either side of her. She knew she should wash herself and change out of the blouse and skirt she'd been wearing for three days and two nights, but she couldn't bring herself to move.

Since d'Aulnay's men had shut them in the room, the only
words spoken had been when Claude said: "Is that man going
to hurt us?"

"No, my dear. He is going to send us back to France."

"And Papa?"

"I do not know, my dear."

She could see the sky through the hole in the roof. It had
turned into a day of gray, soft cloud cover, but fortunately the
clouds weren't weeping. If d'Aulnay intended to keep Claude
and Lorette there for any length of time, she would have to ask
him to have the hole patched. It seemed little to ask, given that
his minions had already found time to nail planks across the
mouth of the staircase down to the sitting room.

The door opened and d'Aulnay was there. "You will come
with me, madame."

As she started to rise up off the bed, Claude squealed and
clutched her tighter. She disengaged his fingers gently, murmuring: "Shh, Claude. There is nothing to fear. I shall not be
gone long," and then turned to d'Aulnay. "Will I?"

"Not so very long. It is dependent upon factors not entirely
in my control."

There were two men-at-arms waiting in the corridor. They
took hold of her arms and walked on either side of her behind
d'Aulnay. She had to hurry along to keep up with the long
strides of their boots.

They brought her downstairs and out into the courtyard. The
corpses had been cleared away, but the rest of the tangled
wreckage had been left where it lay. Men-at-arms and sailors
stood in ranks around the edges. For some reason, someone
had rolled a barrel out of the storehouse and stood it on its
end.

Françoise's escort picked their way across the rubble to the
barrel and stopped there. One of the men-at-arms tied her
wrists behind her back. D'Aulnay held up a length of thick
rope knotted into a hangman's noose. He necklaced the noose
over her head and tightened it, then draped the slack around
her shoulders. She prayed Lorette was keeping Claude away
from the window.

They lifted her by the waist and set her on her feet on top of the barrel. She could see over the lines of helmets now. One of her raggedy men—grizzled André Bernard—was busying himself with something in front of the warehouse, as though he weren't a prisoner after all.

High above André Bernard was the projecting beam and pulley for lifting goods into the loft. A long rope had been threaded through the pulley, with a noose at one end.

Françoise found it confusing. If they meant to hang her, why didn't they just use that rope? For that matter, the one draped over her shoulders was too short to hang even her.

D'Aulnay called: "Bring them out," and Rainville and the rest of her little garrison stumbled into the courtyard, all with their arms bound behind them. They were marched along an aisleway formed by two lines of men-at-arms with drawn swords. The aisle ended at the pulley and the noose.

Françoise screamed at d'Aulnay: "You gave your oath!"

"The king sentenced them to death long ago."

André Bernard whimpered to his recent brothers-in-arms: "Forgive me. I have a wife and children in France." Some of them murmured good Christian formulas of forgiveness; some cursed and spat on him; some looked through him as though he didn't exist.

Françoise wailed at them: "Forgive *me*!"

Some of them shouted feebly: "*La belle Françoise!*" Some of them called back: "There is nothing to forgive," but she didn't believe them.

Rainville stepped forward to be the first. André Bernard had set up two of the trestles for extending the table in the dining hall on feast days, with a plank across them. He fitted the noose around Rainville's neck and two men-at-arms balanced Rainville up onto the plank while André Bernard went to adjust the anchoring of the rope's other end.

Rainville held his eyes on hers across the shining line of helmets. She could see his thin little throat working as he tried to swallow through the noose. He said: "I look upon you for the last time, milady," and then turned to d'Aulnay. "But *you*, I will be waiting for in hell." D'Aulnay kicked out the trestle.

Françoise clamped her eyes shut. But something hard and pointed jabbed her in the ribs, popping her eyes open. D'Aulnay was poking her with the tip of his walking stick. He said: "You will *see* all that you have caused. Or by the good God I will have them all broken on the wheel so you will *hear* it."

Rainville was gyrating in the air. His blue eyes and tongue bugged out of his purple face. A brown sludge was seeping down from the cut-short leg of his pantaloons and over the bandage on his thigh. It took a long time before d'Aulnay's surgeon pronounced him dead.

The next was the boy Bellerose, who'd had to ask Desjardins du Val to advance him the price of a pair of shoes when he'd signed on in Paris so he could walk to La Rochelle. Next came the fort carpenter, who liked to assert that any man who hadn't lost a finger or two during his apprentice days couldn't truly be called a craftsman. Then came the fort surgeon, who as far as Françoise knew had never shed a drop of human blood except with his lancet.

Some of them climbed the trestle stoically, or with Rainville's bravado; some of them wept for mercy; some cursed d'Aulnay. Those who were too badly wounded to stand, or who fought and thrashed too hard to be lifted onto the plank, were simply hoisted into the air by the pulley. André Bernard was no hangman. Even among those who stood on the plank for the drop, not one had his neck broken: all died of slow strangulation.

Night came down and still it wasn't over. D'Aulnay ordered a bonfire built from the plentiful scrap lumber in the courtyard. By that time Françoise hardly knew whether she was watching her men die by firelight or sunlight. It was all the same man twitching in the air in front of her, although his distorted features shifted indiscriminately from the quartermaster's to Rainville's to the master gunner's to La Tour's to her first Scaramouche's.

Her face was coated with a sticky mucilage that had seeped out of her eyes and nose and dribbled out her mouth when she gasped for breath. After standing so long with her arms bound tightly behind her, her rib cage felt like it was squeezing her lungs flat and about to pop loose from her sternum. But she still stayed on her feet. She had decided that d'Aulnay would have to roast her alive before he saw her on her knees.

The man twisting in the air was lowered down and no one was hoisted up to replace him. Hands lifted Françoise down off the barrel and a knife cut the cords around her wrists. Two men took hold of her arms and walked her toward the main hall. The coarse hemp around her neck and the knot weighing down between her breasts had chafed her skin raw, but still they wouldn't take it off.

They walked her up the central staircase and down the corridor to her room, opened the door, and nudged her forward across the threshold. She sagged to the floor. Lorette and Claude came to her. Both of them were crying. Lorette loosened the noose and lifted the rope off, then tried to help her to her feet. Lorette was a strong girl, but still, all that she and Claude could manage between them was to support her on her knees toward the bed.

Françoise climbed up onto the bed and Lorette and Claude curled up against her. She closed her eyes, but the man in the air was still there.

There were mornings after that, and days and nights, but Françoise hardly noticed their passage. D'Aulnay was building a new fort on the other side of the harbor. When it was finished, she and Claude and Lorette would be transported to Port Royal and from there to France. Until then she had the freedom of the fort, as long as she didn't try to pass the sentries guarding the gates and the breach in the wall.

Not that she had the desire to wander about much, or the desire for anything else. But sometimes she would walk around the courtyard with Claude and Lorette—trying not to look up at the warehouse block and tackle—or stand with them on the gatehouse parapet to watch the tides.

D'Aulnay was usually at the site of his new fort, or on the *Grand Cardinal*. The few times he was at the battle-shattered fort he never spoke to her. But sometimes she felt an eerie fancy that red-brown eyes were watching her from a shadowed window.

Micmacs or Maliseets drifted through the fort occasionally, to gaze uncomprehendingly at the damage the white men had inflicted on each other. One of them approached her as she was stumbling aimlessly around the courtyard, and made a leg like a French courtier. "Madame La Tou . . ."

It took her a moment of blinking at him before she placed him. "Keeshetech . . ." She wouldn't have imagined that a face painted in violet sun rays could look so sad.

Keeshetech said softly: "Tomorrow, maybe next day, I take my boat south. Maybe so south as Boston. Have you any word to carry to La Tou?"

It hadn't occurred to her that it might not all be over. She stepped in closer to Keeshetech and whispered: "Tell La Tour his family still lives, but he has not much time before they take us back to France."

After Keeshetech had gone, Françoise wandered along the parapet for a while in the company of ghosts. When she got back to her room, Lorette and Claude were mixing henna in a basin. Claude was actually chortling as the red juice stained its way up his arms. Lorette said brightly: "You have left your hair for far too long, Françoise. The roots are showing gray."

Françoise docilely allowed them to sit her down and spread a cloth around her shoulders. Anything that might give them a moment's buoyancy, no matter how ridiculous, was worthwhile.

They'd barely gotten started, though, when the door flew open and d'Aulnay strode in with a man-at-arms at his heels. D'Aulnay said: "I should have known better than to trust a painted slut. You take advantage of my leniency to conspire messages to the traitor. From now on you will be confined to this room, alone. Guard, remove the brat and the scullery maid."

Claude wrapped himself around Françoise's leg and shrieked: "No!" She snatched him up in her arms and jumped to her feet, with henna dripping into her eyes.

D'Aulnay had already turned and started for the door. Françoise shouted at his back: "Where are you taking them?"

He came to a halt and slowly pivoted around the axis of his walking stick, then pronounced: " 'Where are you taking them, *Monsieur le Gouverneur.*' "

She whispered: "Monsieur le Gouverneur."

"We are taking them ... away from *you*, until such time as you and they can be placed on a transport ship where you can cause no more mischief. They will be kept safe until then."

"Do I have your *word* on that, Monsieur le Gouverneur?" He stiffened, but then just gestured at the guard and turned on his heel.

The guard stepped forward. Françoise peeled Claude off her breast, kissed his streaming eyes, and handed him to Lorette. As the man-at-arms herded Lorette toward the door Françoise called after her: "Lorette—take good care of your little brother."

Lorette's eyes cartwheeled back over her shoulder and over the top of Claude's head. And then the guard had ushered her across the threshold and slammed the door.

Françoise sat back down and stayed there, looking out the window while the henna in her hair and on her forehead dried to a crust. Sounds began to emanate from the wall behind her—a woody and metallic malleting and drilling. It took a while for the sound to define itself to her: they were fixing a bolt to the door.

The sun went down and still she sat there, moving only to shift her head so she could look at the stars through the hole in the roof. The fort grew so quiet she could hear the tide coming in.

There came a soft thumping of a pair of boots approaching slowly down the corridor. Her first thought was that it must be the morning watch coming to replace the night watch. But the ragged patch of sky through the hole in the roof tiles was still a spangled black. And, when she thought back on the sound of the boot falls, they hadn't had the thumping cadence of a man-at-arms demonstrating that he was performing his assigned duty.

There was a low murmuring of male voices beyond the door. And then a barely audible, clicking, snicking sibilance. It was the iron tongue of the bolt slipping out of its mouth. She looked to the door. The latch was moving.

The door swung open slowly and then carried on of its own weight to thud softly against the wall. D'Aulnay was standing on the threshold, with a man-at-arms behind him holding a lantern high to light the room. D'Aulnay was hatless and swordless, though he did have his elegant walking stick, and he looked as though he was up much later than he was accustomed to. He said nothing, just stood with his hand propped on his walking stick, staring at her. There was something of disgust in his expression, perhaps even self-disgust.

Françoise said: "What do you want?" D'Aulnay still said nothing, but it seemed to her she could see something in the red-brown eyes besides disgust, something she had seen in a lot of other male eyes before.

She realized that she was sitting with her knees up and her feet wide apart. She reached down to the front hems of her skirt and shift, yanked them up above her knees, and said: "Is *that* what you want, pig?"

D'Aulnay crossed the room in two strides and swung his walking stick down between her knees, forcing her skirts back down, then shoved the tip into her belly like a sword point. The man-at-arms behind him said hesitantly: "Monsieur le Gouverneur . . . ?"

D'Aulnay pulled the walking stick back out again. His blubbery jawline shuddered, as though swallowing something bitter. He said: "Had it not been decreed you be returned to France, I would give you to the troops."

The door closed behind D'Aulnay and the guard, and Françoise could hear the bolt rattle home again. She stayed sitting where she was, absently rubbing the spot where d'Aulnay's walking stick had stabbed into her belly, until the sky began to lighten. Then she moved to the chair by the window. She was afraid to close her eyes. Without Claude and Lorette to distract her, the man twitching in the air had come back again.

The guard opened the door to place a plate of bread and cheese and a pitcher on the floor. She ignored it. The idea of putting food in her mouth wasn't something she could imagine ever having done. Knives twisted in her stomach, but her stomach was very far away and the smell of the bread made her gag.

She sat looking out at the ruined courtyard and the pulley above the warehouse and the hole in the wall where the pike had come through to impale Lorette's Gaspard. Perhaps if she'd surrendered when the *Grand Cardinal* first sailed into the harbor, they would all still be alive.

She hadn't known she'd been sitting there for a long time until the guard brought in her next meal. He protested from the doorway: "But, madame, you must eat and drink!"

She knew he was there, and yet he wasn't there. There was a thick wall of puffed wool wrapped around her. He didn't seem to be aware of it, but she was.

The guard went away. The sky began to darken again. She could feel her lips and the lining of her throat slowly cracking. She decided she couldn't sit up any longer and started for the bed. But her legs were wooden and full of splinters. The floor came up to meet her.

She woke up in her bed, dressed only in her shift. D'Aulnay's surgeon and his assistant were hovering above her. The surgeon was explaining to the apprentice that lack of nourishment had allowed the evil vapors in the sea fogs to enter Madame's body. She supposed that would explain why she was shivering and sweating at the same time.

They held her nose and poured some kind of cold broth down her throat, but her stomach threw it straight back out at them. Eventually, they went away. At least her throat didn't feel cracked anymore, but torn, from the force of the broth being expelled.

The next face she saw was a priest—not Père Montagne, but one of d'Aulnay's Capuchins. He dabbed a damp cloth across her lips and said: "You must not do this, my daughter."

She croaked: "Do what?" It hurt her lips and throat so much to move, and her tongue was so swollen, that she decided to carry on the rest of her half of the conversation in her mind. After all those years of filling her rib cage and orating, it was almost a pleasure not to be able to speak.

"Suicide is the one unforgivable sin."

She replied in her mind: You are mistaken to think I intend to starve myself to death. I can no longer intend to do anything.

"Think of your soul."

She said in her mind: I have no soul.

"Think of your son."

It didn't seem possible that water could come out of her eyes when she'd put none in her body for so long, but it did. She knew there was nothing she could do for Claude and Lorette anymore. She had no doubt that d'Aulnay would deliver them safely to France. He had no legal excuse not to, and d'Aulnay never did anything without a legal excuse. A cook as inventive and hardworking as Lorette would easily find a position in France, and Lorette would take good care of Claude. If Françoise went back with them, all it would do for them was force them to see her hanging from a gibbet as a convicted traitor.

She drifted away from the priest into a place that wasn't quite sleeping and wasn't quite not sleeping. She was brought back to her shatter-roofed bedroom by a different priest shaking her shoulder. He held a crucifix toward her and said: "Do you heartily abjure all the sins you have committed in your life?"

"No." She had managed to say it aloud. He went away.

Now that she'd been dragged into wakefulness, she discovered that the painful throbbing on both sides of the base of her spine had grown vicious while she'd been gone from her body. She wrestled herself over onto her stomach to try to ease it, and lay there gasping.

She began to hear a deep, rhythmic thumping. With her ear and her chest both pressed to the mattress, her heart had become a bass drum. It was too loud and too persistent and she wished it would stop so she could sleep. Finally, it did.

CHAPTER 54

Jeanne Motin de Menou d'Aulnay et de Charnisay sat in a field of wildflowers, munching cold roast capon and watching the tide surge up La Rivière au Dauphin. Madame de Brice had brought the pupils of her girls' school out for a picnic and Jeanne had decided that since her own children and Anne's were also pupils of Madame de Brice, they should come along as well. Charles didn't like his sons mingling too much with Madame de Brice's Micmac girls. But if one of the children happened to spout about the picnic after Charles got home from building his new fort, Jeanne could always say it was only once.

"Maman!" Joseph shouted. "The *Vierge* is coming in!"

Jeanne didn't bother to stand up and look for herself. At nine years old, Joseph was already showing an uncanny ability at recognizing ships at a distance, especially his father's ships. She handed her capon leg to a servant, wiped her mouth with her napkin, and said: "Come along, children, it may be Papa."

The children bounded ahead through the banks of wild roses while she and Anne followed arm in arm, the pregnant supporting the pregnant. By the time they reached the landing stage, the *Vierge* had anchored and lowered a boat. Anne squealed: "It's Nikki!" and let go of Jeanne's arm to run for the end of the wharf, with both hands cupped tight around her gourd-ripe womb.

Nicolas Le Creux climbed up onto the dock wearing a face of molded plaster. He kissed his wife and children coldly and said stiffly to Jeanne: *"Bonjour."* He didn't seem like Nikki at all.

339

Jeanne said: "Is Charles still . . . ?"

"*Monsieur le Gouverneur* will return within the week, once the last details of the new fortification have been completed to his satisfaction. I have been sent ahead to see that the *Vierge* is fitted out for an ocean voyage. Once Monsieur le Gouverneur returns, I am to sail the *Vierge* to France and deliver Françoise Jacquelin for judgment. The *Vierge* will sail back to Port Royal before the end of the season, bearing a cargo of supplies. But I will not be on her."

Anne gasped. "What?"

Nikki said: "The time that it will take to fit out the *Vierge* should be more than enough time to pack up our possessions to move back to France."

Anne sputtered: "Move back . . . ? Why?"

"Because I am your husband! It should be enough for you to know what I have decided!" Jeanne had never heard him speak in such a tone to Anne—or to anyone, except a lazy man-at-arms. He softened his voice considerably to add: "I will explain it to you in good time, Anne. Until then, please take it on faith there is good reason."

Over supper Jeanne tried to ply him to say more, but all he would say was, "Better you should ask your husband."

She interrupted Anne's packing to try to pry it out of her, but all Anne could say was, "He has told me nothing except that he will tell me once we've weighed anchor for France, and then I'll understand why we must go. What else am I to do but take him at his word?"

Jeanne waited for an opportunity when Nikki wasn't on the *Vierge* overseeing the refit, when Anne was in the nursery occupied with the younger children, and the older children were all at their lessons with Madame de Brice. She found Nikki in Charles's office with Port Royal's chief fur traders, going over the list of imports they wanted brought back on the *Vierge*. She said to the traders: "Monsieur Le Creux and I would talk awhile. You may leave us."

The traders looked at Nikki. Before he could either nod or shake his head, Jeanne said: "I *said*, 'You may leave us.' "

The traders filed out. Jeanne closed the door behind them

and turned back to her brother-in-law, who was looking rather uncomfortable, with his hands splayed like flattened crabs on her husband's desk.

Jeanne said: "You are taking away my sister. And my nieces and nephews. And my children's beloved uncle. Why?"

"Jeanne, I . . ."

"Why?"

She was crying and he nearly so. He got up and came around the desk and put his arms around her and leaned her head against his chest. He said thickly: "Jeanne, it is not for me to say. What I judge for myself is not the way all others have to judge. And you do not have the choice."

"What choice?"

"Jeanne, after ten years and more, do you think I'll not miss you, and Acadia?"

"And we you. *Why?"*

"You must not ask me that again, Jeanne. Please. And it were best for all of us you not ask Charles until Anne and I are gone. And then it will be up to you to judge whether I do right or wrong. Or not judge me at all, as I would never judge you. I can only judge myself."

"I will always trust you, Nikki, to do what is right."

"And I would always trust you. That is a rare and precious commodity in this world."

"What will Charles do without you?"

His voice grew cold and distant. "That is also not for me to say."

It was four more days before the *Grand Cardinal* appeared. In the boat that rowed Jeanne's husband ashore were also a scoured-looking young woman and a sealed-mouthed boy about four years old. The young woman's right hand and the boy's left appeared to be glued together as firmly and permanently as the boy's lips.

When Jeanne asked Charles who they were, he replied offhandedly: "La Tour's whelp and a kitchen maid. They shall be transported to France on the *Vierge*."

"And what of the lady?"

"What lady?"

"Françoise Jacquelin."

"Oh. The shock proved too much for her. We gave her a Christian burial, which was more than she deserved."

PART IV

A MAN OF ABILITY

"... in order to restore the said country ... together with the forts which the said Charles de Menou, Sieur Daulnay Charnisé has seized upon, it is necessary to send there a man of ability, versed in the knowledge of those parts. ..."
—Royal Decree, Given at Paris,
Thirtieth of January, 1654

CHAPTER 55

Nicolas Denys sat in his orchard behind his establishment on the beautiful Acadian isle of Miscou, looking out over the Bay of Chaleur. He was aware that some people might call it overoptimistic of him to call it an orchard, but he could always point out to them that his fruit trees were already nearly as tall as any tree on the island. But then, it had been only two years since the cannoneer who'd thought he could smoke tobacco while drying gunpowder had succeeded in burning off every tree on the island.

It suddenly occurred to Denys that the heat from that fire might have encouraged the sprouting of the nuts he'd put in the ground, carefully saved from every peach or nectarine or clingstone plum he'd ever eaten. Botany was an art that interested him, but he'd never had much chance to practice it. Now he could.

He wondered if any of the vegetables in old Claude La Tour's garden on Cape Sable had reseeded themselves while the forest grew up among them. Or whether the climbing roses Françoise Jacquelin had planted still grew among the ruins of La Tour's fort, while the lady herself lay in an unmarked grave somewhere along La Rivière St. Jean.

That brought Denys to ruminating on Charles La Tour. La Tour had escaped to Quebec, or so Denys had heard. Apparently the Governor of Quebec considered a little peccadillo like treason no reason to deprive himself of the services of a man so adept at dealing with *les sauvages*, both friendly and unfriendly. Some said that La Tour's way of getting to Quebec had been to murder the captain of a Boston pinnace and maroon her crew. Denys prided himself upon not putting too much stock in the wagging of idle tongues. But it wouldn't come as a shock to him if someone came up with proof that La Tour had tried on a bit of piracy; he'd tried everything else in his life.

Denys still found it hard to picture a man well over fifty guiding missionaries through the Quebec wilderness and fighting Iroquois. But no one had to tell Nicolas Denys that if a man begged off because of age before he'd built a secure place to grow old in, he would spend what was left of his life begging for his bread. Denys well knew that if it hadn't been for doggedness and a couple of seasons' clear sailing, he might well still be running errands for La Compagnie de la Nouvelle France, instead of musing in his own orchard beside his permanent fishing and trading establishment, gazing at his own ship riding at anchor.

Another ship was coming in, through the passage to the Gulf of St. Lawrence, but Denys didn't pay it much attention. Many foreign fishing vessels came in to anchor in his harbor, for storm shelter or to refill their casks from the marvelous spring of fresh water that came up through the seawater at low tide.

As this ship came in closer, though, he saw that it was bigger than any fishing vessel. A little closer still and he saw it was the *Grand Cardinal*.

The *Grand Cardinal* trimmed her sails and dropped her anchor about three hundred paces out from Denys's establishment. Oddly, she then lowered a stern anchor as well, as though to keep her larboard on to the fort. Odder still, she then opened all her larboard gunports and ran out her guns.

Denys got up out of his chair, stepped over his row of peach trees—or perhaps they were nectarines—and started for the landing stage. The longboat of the *Grand Cardinal* was coming in, with the sun gleaming on her giltworked bow and on the saltwater-patinaed oar blades dipping in and out in perfect unison. Between the rows of oarsmen sat a portly, dark-haired man in black velvet and a blue-plumed hat.

Denys wasn't sure whether to wave or not. He settled for

folding his hands across his beard and waiting. The boat crew brought her in smartly and two of them jumped out to hold the lines as their master stepped out onto the wharf. Denys said: "*Bonjour*, Monsieur d'Aulnay."

D'Aulnay cocked his head at him, cocked his arm out on the fulcrum of his walking stick, and pursed his hatbrim-shaded mouth, as though considering whether to correct someone. Instead, he smiled. "*Bonjour*, Monsieur Denys. Allow me to congratulate you. You appear to have established yourself well here."

"Early days, but I believe the endeavor will prosper, the good God willing."

"Unfortunately, it is an illegal endeavor."

"Pardon me?"

"You have not obtained permission to plunder the riches of Acadia."

"I have a concession from the Hundred Associates!"

"I do not doubt it. But they and their Compagnie de la Nouvelle France are a mere mercantile concern. The king has recently commissioned me Royal Governor of Acadia, so it is my duty to act as the representative of His Most Christian Majesty in all matters Acadian. I and my Conseil have decided there is no present need for permanent establishments in Acadia, beyond my own.

"I am sure you understand your moral obligation, Monsieur Denys, to obey the decrees of your sovereign over those of tradesmen. But if not, the guns of the *Grand Cardinal* are willing to persuade you."

Denys found it difficult to work his tongue. "But . . . you cannot simply sail in here and—"

"I have. I realize it is not a simple matter to fit out a ship for a voyage back to France, and to load all one's goods and people aboard her. So I will wait for three days. But only three days, mind—I have other duties to attend to beyond sailing up and down my coast evicting interlopers. Any of your possessions you have not got on board by then will have to be left behind, for you *will* sail for France within three days."

"But . . . I cannot load up all I possess here! It cost me five

hundred *livres* at the least to erect the buildings and the stockade, and I cannot carry them away! There is not room in the
hold for all the trade goods I stocked up for the fur season. . . .
And even if there was, there is no market for them in
France. . . ."

"*Oh*, Monsieur *Denys—now* I understand why you seem so
distressed. You are under the impression that my intention is to
uproot you unceremoniously and cast you adrift. Nothing could
be further from the truth. My intention from the beginning was
that you would be fully indemnified for every sou it cost you
to build this place. After all, you are hardly to be held responsible for the Hundred Associates encouraging you to believe
that they still rule Acadia, or for the fact that matters have
changed since they granted you your concession.

"As for your trade goods, what profit is there in carrying
them back to France? I came here intending to pay you full
value for them, and take them back with me to Port Royal. I
will even undertake the risk of bottomry, so if some mischance
should send them to the bottom between here and Port Royal,
it is none of your concern."

"Well, well, Monsieur d'Aulnay, that changes the matter entirely. You understand, of course, that I would prefer to stay
here. But if this venture has cost me nothing but a little time,
and I am not returning to France destitute, I can always start
another venture elsewhere."

"Just so. Now, I know you for an honest man, and we have
only three days, so rather than you and I prowling your store
shelves with clerks peering over each other's shoulders, all you
need do is take an inventory of all the goods you will leave behind and of all the debts you incurred in erecting this establishment. You need merely present the total to me and I will sign
a promissory note payable next year."

"Next year?"

"But of course. You do not imagine I import strongboxes
full of gold to hoard at Port Royal? The matter will have to be
arranged through my bankers in France. Now, I will take up no
more of your time when you have so many matters of detail to
attend to. Boatswain, prepare to cast off."

CHAPTER 56

The Governor of Acadia stepped out of his new-built manor house toward his waiting sedan chair. The house had cost him a few new twists and turns in his labyrinth of debt. But since La Tour and *les Bostonais* no longer posed any threat to Port Royal, and *les sauvages* were largely Christianized, there seemed no longer any need to house himself and his family within the walls of the fort. So he'd had a new château built behind the strip farms along La Rivière au Dauphin, a residence more befitting a royal governor.

The sedan chair—made of carved tropic woods trimmed with Spanish gold—had cost him nothing. It had been intended as a present from the Viceroy of Mexico for the viceroy's sister back in Spain. But the ship carrying it to his sister had encountered privateers from Boston. The Assembly of New England had presented it to the Governor of Acadia as a token of their regret for any injuries they may have done him in the past.

D'Aulnay paused on the portico to kiss his eight children *au revoir* in order of age, beginning with gawky-limbed Joseph and ending with the infant in its nurse's arms. Then he turned to his wife.

It struck him that the less frequently he had to bid her *au revoir*, since those years when La Tour was making it necessary for him to be constantly putting out to sea, the more difficult it became. She gave him a tranquillity that he found nowhere else. There had been that untranquil period when she'd insisted on knowing why Le Creux had taken it in mind to take his family home to France. D'Aulnay had done his best to make her understand that there are unpleasant necessities that go with governing a province, as with raising a child. Fortunately, he hadn't had to go as far as to point out to her that all the laws of God and man decreed that she had no choice but to cleave to her husband, regardless of the squeamishness of Nicolas Le Creux or anyone else. He suspected that if this fact had actually been spoken aloud, he would have wondered ever after whether the only reason she gave him a tranquil home was that she and the children had nowhere else to go. As it was, the question didn't exist, which was as it should be.

He and his wife kissed each other on both cheeks and she said: "God keep you."

"And you, my dear. I expect I should be back within the week; the return downstream should be much swifter than the journey up." He climbed into his waiting sedan chair and rapped his walking stick against the roof to signal the porters. They hefted their poles and carried their governor down toward the landing stage and the waiting flotilla of canoes.

D'Aulnay was going on an expedition to find more farmland. The farmers at Port Royal were prospering well enough to make the colony nearly self-sufficient, but there were hardly enough of them to call it a *seigneurie*—nor, for that matter, to produce enough exports to put a scratch on their master's debts. According to the missionaries, farther up La Rivière au Dauphin the floodplain widened out enough to settle hundreds of immigrants, even thousands. So d'Aulnay was going to see for himself.

He stepped out of his sedan chair on the landing stage and found all was in readiness, as it should be. There were five Micmac canoes, all manned by sturdy converts. The flotilla was to carry the governor's chef and aide-de-camp, the two men-at-arms who formed the governor's escort, the oldest and most experienced husbandman of Port Royal, and Father Ignace de Paris, who had recently become the governor's spiritual adviser.

The governor himself traveled in the lead canoe. As Port Royal dropped farther and farther astern, and there grew to be no sounds but those of the forest and the river—the wind, birds, and squirrels in the trees; the sibilance of flowing water and the hissing of knife-hewn paddle blades—d'Aulnay grew more and more ill at ease. Through fifteen years and more of living in the Acadian Wilderness, he'd always been buffered by the sounds of other civilized humanity—a ship's crew, or a troop of *engagés*, or the populace of Port Royal. . . . The sounds he could hear now seemed formless and uncontrollable, like echoes in a cave.

The two men-at-arms in the canoe behind his were apparently feeling something of the like sensation, because they began to sing a barracks song to fill the void. The paddlers of d'Aulnay's canoe tried to sing along, chanting tunelessly and wordlessly. The one in the bow kept grinning back over his shoulder, as though to show off the fact that he had no front teeth and a nose like a goiter. But the neck thong of his sheath knife also dangled a wooden cross, so d'Aulnay reminded himself that even this misshapen child of the forest was also a child of God.

The song the men-at-arms were singing took a bawdy turn. D'Aulnay glanced back at the canoe behind his, to remind them that Father Ignace de Paris was riding in the canoe behind theirs. They stopped their singing abruptly, then began again a little later with a tune more appropriate.

The forest grew dark before the river. D'Aulnay pointed toward the shore. While his aide-de-camp set up his tent and his chef set to work with mutton and shallots, d'Aulnay said to his spiritual adviser: "Might I make confession, Father?" Barely a day in the last six months had passed without him making confession. And this would be the first day since his spiritual reawakening that he wouldn't spend two hours on his knees in the chapel, attending Mass and the litanies of the Virgin.

Father Ignace de Paris said: "Of course, my son," and followed him into the woods. They didn't go far. The spaces between the trees were tortuous with vines and brambles, and the ground treacherously uneven. Father Ignace sat down with his back against a tree trunk, d'Aulnay on the other side.

"Forgive me, Father, for I have sinned."

"How have you sinned, my son?"

"Today, as we were traveling, I found myself praying that

the reports of the country upriver will prove true; so that my *seigneurie* in Acadia might become as great as any in France."

"Prayer seems no sin to me, my son."

"But do you not see, Father . . . ? My prayers had no thoughts in them of the good that it would do to increase our colony of true Christians in the New World. I was not thinking of the greater glory of God, but of my own."

"Ah. Pride is the most pernicious sin of all. All men must struggle against it every day. Say three Hail Marys and two Our Fathers."

"Thank you, Father."

As the expedition pushed farther upriver the hills on either hand spread farther apart and the valley floor became a leagues-wide meadow that the river coiled through like a lazy, blue snake. D'Aulnay ordered an early halt and waved the canoes in to shore. The old farmer in the last canoe leaped out onto the land and rooted about breaking off grass stalks to inspect, scooping up earth to compress in his palm and sniff at, squinting upriver to see no end to the valley, and exhaling all the while: "Magnificent! It is magnificent!"

A hand slapped down on d'Aulnay's shoulder and a coarse voice chortled thickly: "Damn good country, huh?"

D'Aulnay looked down at the grimy, brown, crack-nailed hand beside his chin, and then up at the gap-toothed, bulb-nosed, grinning face behind it. He twitched his shoulder so that the hand fell away.

The gap-toothed Micmac squinted at him, then down at his offending hand, then back up at d'Aulnay. The black eyes slitted, the grin closed and curled up at one corner, and the *sauvage* wiped his hand on his loincloth.

D'Aulnay swung his walking stick hard against the side of the thick, brown neck. The Micmac stumbled sideways, recovered his balance, and drew the sheath knife dangling around his neck. But the sword of a man-at-arms barred his way.

D'Aulnay whipped his walking stick across the knife wrist and then brought it down repeatedly on the naked shoulders and back. There were no shrieks of pain or cries for mercy, only low grunts and the continuing whipcracks of the walking stick. The Micmac sank to his hands and knees and slowly lowered his head. When it was low enough, d'Aulnay stopped and stepped back and recovered his breath.

D'Aulnay straightened his hat and announced to the rest of his entourage: "I believe we have seen enough of the country to make it unnecessary to make a farther camp beyond this one. Tomorrow morning I shall proceed upriver for half the day, to see for a certitude if the valley does not close in again soon, and then return to you by evening so we may start back toward Port Royal the next morning.

"Father Ignace, while the chef is preparing to attend to our temporal needs, perhaps you will attend to my spiritual . . . ?"

"Of course, my son."

Father Ignace walked out across the meadow to a copse of willows and sat down on one end of a fallen tree. D'Aulnay sat down on the other end, with trailing willow fronds providing an effective confessional screen. "Forgive me, Father, for I have sinned."

"How have you sinned, my son?"

"There was . . . a woman I once knew . . . a woman ripe with sin. . . . Last night I found myself having carnal thoughts of her. . . ."

"I see. Have you committed no other sins since your last confession?"

D'Aulnay pondered on that a moment. "Not that I can call to my mind, Father. Although perhaps it is my own forgetfulness which—"

"Did you not but a moment ago beat unmercifully a simple-minded *sauvage*?"

It seemed an odd question. But d'Aulnay dutifully replied to it. "The man was a servant in my employ. Does not the church teach that humble obedience is what we all must learn . . . ? The child to the parent, the wife to the husband, the servant to the master, and all of us to God?"

There was a pause. Then Father Ignace said: "Say three Hail Marys and two Our Fathers, for the sin you have confessed."

In his moonlit tent d'Aulnay lay half listening to the river and the creatures of the night, wondering about Father Ignace's strange hesitation before giving him his penance. It seemed that the priest had been trying to tell him something about the incident with the ugly Micmac, but what?

Perhaps there was some clue in Father Ignace's choice of words: "beat unmercifully." Mercifulness was demanded of all Christians. But then, d'Aulnay knew he would have been, and indeed *had* been, merciful—as soon as the insolent Micmac's posture had shown that he'd submitted to his place in the order of things.

After all, without order in this world, were men any more than beasts? The Holy Scriptures began with God creating order out of chaos. Anyone who doubted the importance of that message only had to look at England, where the gradual collapse of order over the past ten years had culminated last year in the English cutting off the head of their annointed king. What more proof could anyone need that the human appetite for unholy madness would grow larger with each bite, if rebellion wasn't crushed at birth. La Tour and other wild animals in the shape of men were still loose in the world, and would gleefully return all into chaos if they could.

D'Aulnay came to the realization that the reason for Father Ignace's strange hesitation had been to suggest that he meditate upon the fact that the struggle between order and chaos never ended. With his question resolved and his set task completed, he slid into sleep.

When he embarked in the morning, his aide-de-camp accompanied him, in order to serve out the cold luncheon his chef had prepared the night before. As the paddlers transported them deeper into the valley, the air grew thicker and damper, like a hothouse made for propagating gold out of earth.

Through a haze rising off the river, the walking-stick-welted back in front of d'Aulnay's eyes bent and rose in rhythm with the paddle. But today there was no noxious grinning over the shoulder to show off the hole where other men had front teeth. D'Aulnay had debated whether to take a bow paddler from one of the other canoes, but decided it were better to demonstrate that once a mistake had been corrected, the matter was over.

The prow nosed into a narrow bend where the current

surged more strongly. The bow paddler suddenly flung up his arm and shouted something in Micmac. D'Aulnay looked ahead and saw the roots of a waterlogged deadfall just breaking the surface, coming straight at their larboard beam.

The stern paddler swerved to starboard, but d'Aulnay could see that the canoe wasn't going to clear the sharp end of a root poking toward its thin, bark skin unless the boat heeled over to starboard. He leaned his torso over the starboard gunwale and the canoe heeled over too far.

There was a brief splash and then he was sinking through a green-gray, cold world, with the sun rippling distantly above him. The dull boom of the overtopped canoe cupping the surface came to him after the fact. There were muffled thrashing and splashing sounds and legs kicking above him and a torrent of silver bubbles.

He breached the surface, gasping, looked to his right and left, and struck out for the nearest shore. The current was stronger than it looked. The corner of his eye showed the bottom of the canoe sweeping downstream with his hat close behind.

The riverbank didn't look that far away, but all his kicking and arm scooping didn't seem to be bringing it any closer. His thigh-high boots were filled with water, his sword was entangled between his legs, and his puffy layers of velvet and wool and suede leather had become sodden layers of lead.

He told himself that if he gave in to the panic that he would die by drowning, he would. He reminded himself that he wasn't wearing armor and that he'd been a strong swimmer in his youth.

He tried to kick his boots off, but they wouldn't budge without a servant to tug on them. He managed to pull off his gloves and unknot his cloak, but sloughing off their weight made little difference. It seemed that whenever he tried to take advantage of an instant when his mouth or his nose were above the surface, by the time he inhaled he breathed in water.

He heard a blubbery "Monsieur!" and saw his aide-de-camp dog-paddling furiously toward him. But the fellow was a long way off and not making much progress.

Then out of the ether a strong hand wrapped itself in d'Aulnay's hair and a strong voice shouted: "I got her! No 'fraid! Safe now!" D'Aulnay just had a glimpse of the face beyond the arm before he started being towed. It was the blessed, gap-toothed, Christian *sauvage* he'd taught obedience to the day before.

D'Aulnay relaxed his body to let his rescuer take him. He could hear the guttural voice still shouting: "She safe! No 'fraid! I got her!" As a reward, d'Aulnay would see that the man was tutored by Madame de Brice on gender and other mysteries of the French language.

But in his urgency to save his master, the Micmac wasn't noticing that he was holding him facedown. D'Aulnay held his breath and batted at the wrist above his head, but the wrist and hand stayed rigid. D'Aulnay arched his neck to bring his head up, but the hand pushed it down again.

D'Aulnay's lungs started to collapse in fire. He struck at the body swimming in front of his, but his blows had no effect. His lungs burst his mouth open and water seared his windpipe. He reached back to draw his sword, but the baldric was twisted around the hilts and his fingers were turning to wood. He struggled to free his sword and struggled to overpower the muscles in the paddler's forearm with the muscles in his neck.

Up from the reddening depths came swimming a grinning little blond-haired man with a sword in his left hand. And then Charles de Menou, Sieur d'Aulnay et de Charnisay, Royal Governor of Acadia, ceased to struggle.

CHAPTER 57

Jeanne was brought into the sitting room of the *château du gouverneur* to hear her husband's will read. Ranged about the room were Father Ignace de Paris, Madame de Brice, and Madame de Brice's three sons: the two Capuchin missionaries and the temporally oriented one, Brice de Saint Croix. Jeanne couldn't imagine how she could have stumbled her way through the last three days—or was it four?—without Madame de Brice's arm in hers on the walk to and from the funeral, without Madame de Brice to see to it that the children were fed properly and did not become hysterical.

All that Jeanne knew of what was in the will was what Father Ignace had had to bring out before the funeral: Charles's wish to be interred beneath the steps of the church, "entreating all those who pass by to have pity on a soul who merits only the thunderbolts and chastisements of a justly angry God."

Father Ignace coughed and said: "Shall I begin, madame?" Jeanne nodded and he began to read aloud. Her eyes drifted up to the portrait of Charles above the mantel: the later portrait, not the young chevalier. She could almost see Charles's neatly mustached lips moving as Father Ignace read out his words.

The arrangements Charles had made for his worldly goods and dependents were simplicity itself. His sole heir was his father, René de Menou. He commended into his father's hands the future welfare of his wife and children. And then Charles added, to help his father understand and appreciate the widow now in his care, a summation of the character of Jeanne Motin:

357

"She has not the necessary qualities to be a woman of the world, but is a very humble and modest little servant of God."

Jeanne was aware that Father Ignace was still droning on, but her eyes stayed nailed to the portrait, and all she heard was Charles's voice pronouncing: "She has not the necessary qualities . . . a very humble and modest little servant . . ." For fifteen years she had thought she'd had some inkling of what those chestnut eyes were seeing when they looked out on her.

She realized that Father Ignace de Paris had finished reading. Her eyes slid off the portrait to Father Ignace. She said: "Thank you, Father. You were so devoted to my husband, I would like you to have the portrait of him hanging there."

"Oh no, madame, I could not possibly . . . !"

"Believe me, I want you to have it."

"I can well understand, madame, how you would not wish to be so painfully reminded every time you step into this room. But in time the pain will soften, and then you will wish you had his portrait back again. But if you wish, I will put it into the hands of the Capuchin rectory, until such time as you ask for it to be returned.

"I trust, madame"—Father Ignace smiled as he folded the will back together—"that this puts your mind at ease as to your future and your children's. One could not ask for a more astute or powerful guardian than René de Menou."

"René de Menou," Brice de Saint Croix drawled matter-of-factly, "has the mind of a toasted cheese."

"Monsieur Saint Croix!" Father Ignace exclaimed. "I will thank you not to speak so of your betters!"

"No doubt he was my better in his day," Brice de Saint Croix replied flatly. "But that day is gone. Last year he begged an audience with the queen regent, and counseled her at length on what part she should take in a contretemps between her husband and Cardinal Richelieu—both of whom had been dead seven years and still appear to be.

"It matters little to Madame, though, whether or not her father-in-law is capable of managing his son's estate. Because our late governor's estate consists entirely of debts."

"What?" Jeanne recognized her own voice after the fact.

"Had you no idea, madame," Brice de Saint Croix turned to her, "of the state of your husband's finances?"

"I knew the war with La Tour cost him a great deal of money. But since then Port Royal has been prospering, and we have had the income from Jemseg as well, and . . ."

Brice de Saint Croix shook his head. "For all his other qualities, madame, your husband was not the magnet for *les sauvages* and their furs that La Tour was at Jemseg. And Monsieur d'Aulnay was an inveterate builder; as soon as some of Port Royal's tenants became able to pay him the rents he was counting on to pay off his debts, he would use the money instead to import new immigrants—who then had to be supported until they were established. The accounts are a mare's nest that will take some unraveling, but I would estimate the total debt as somewhere near three hundred thousand *livres*."

Jeanne felt the floor tilting under her chair. Three hundred thousand *livres* was more than her father had earned in his lifetime. She looked at the portrait again and said to it in her mind: I *trusted* you. She felt like the fool of the world at remembering all the times she'd hugged to herself their unspoken compact: that he would trust her to manage the hearth and she would trust him to manage matters beyond the threshold. And all the while that she'd been counting sous to make sure that each year ended with no more money expended on the household than they'd agreed upon at the beginning of the year, he'd been airily signing commitments for tens of thousands of *livres*. She tried to remind herself that managing a war wasn't quite like managing a château; a responsible commander didn't put off buying a new cannon until next year if the enemy was coming this year. But it didn't help much.

She took her eyes off the portrait again. Everyone else in the room had their eyes on the floor. Except Brice de Saint Croix, who was looking at her. Like it or not—and she decidedly didn't—it was obvious that if anyone was going to navigate her and her children and all of Port Royal out of this sinkhole, it was going to have to be a certain "very humble and modest little servant of God."

She said: "Monsieur de Saint Croix, I shall have to have an

intendant to keep my accounts. Would you have any interest in such a position?"

"I would be honored, madame."

Fortunately, he proved to be not only honored but meticulous—although there were times she wished he weren't quite so meticulous, as when he dredged up ten-year-old debts for leasing warships or buying church bells.

Someone had to approve and finalize the annual list of supplies the *Grand Cardinal* was to fetch from France. Jeanne put it off for as long as possible and then took herself by the scruff of the neck and sat down with Brice de Saint Croix and the quartermaster and the sergeant at arms and the stack of tenants' requests. She was amazed to discover that projecting a year's needs for the entire colony wasn't all that more complicated than doing it for her household—one simply added two or three zeros to every number.

With no governor at Port Royal, and a new one not likely to be appointed until at least next year, there was no one to settle disputes. Even the pettiest dispute could build disaster in a wilderness community that would be snowed in and living in each other's pockets from December to April. It devolved upon Jeanne to decide whether it was only by mistake that Beliveau's sons had mown off half the common pasture to stock his barn, or whether it was appropriate for the sergeant at arms to drill his militia on Sundays, or whether the traders should be allowed to bribe the *sagamos* with brandy. The responsibility terrified her at first, until it dawned on her that it was just like raising children; one could only try to be as fair and consistent as possible and hope that when they grew up they would understand that even their mother was human.

As for her own children, they accepted being fatherless with a swiftness that astounded her. All except Joseph, who was just a shade too old to benefit from the good God's gift to His most helpless of creatures—the resiliency of all soft, pliable things. One day Jeanne found him out behind the château with a mallet and chisel, carving his name onto a thin slab of raw, black rock shaped roughly like a gravestone. She said tentatively: "Why are you doing that, Joseph?"

He shrugged and mumbled: "So people will know I was here."

"Oh. Well . . . Be careful of your fingers with the mallet. And that chisel looks very sharp. . . ."

"Oui, maman."

By the time winter came on she was feeling quite comfortable in the role of Madame le Gouverneur, although she knew it would only last until the new governor arrived. She was also feeling something else that she thought perhaps she should mention at confession but didn't. She wasn't sure it was exactly a sin, but it felt suspiciously like one: she was beginning to feel that widowhood wasn't an entirely tragic condition.

In the spring she was in the quartermaster's office in the fort when the signal gun boomed. She went out into the courtyard. The sentry on the western bastion called down: "A sail!"

"What sail?"

"I do not know, madame. But she is a large ship, flying the fleur-de-lis."

"Sergeant at Arms."

"Oui, madame?"

"If you please, perhaps an escort party should be marched down to the landing stage. It may well be our new governor."

"Oui, madame."

She escorted the escort party down to the landing stage. The ship looked even larger than the *Grand Cardinal,* and her captain appeared unfamiliar with La Rivière au Dauphin, since the place he'd chosen to anchor would be a sandbar when the tide went out.

A boat was lowered and approached the wharf. The only people in the boat who weren't either rowing or steering were a man with dun-colored hair—wearing clothing that was neither exactly gray nor exactly brown—and a vibrantly dressed youth perhaps a year or two older than Joseph. The boat docked and the colorless man helped the peacock boy up onto the dock.

Jeanne approached them and curtsied. "I am Jeanne Motin de Menou d'Aulnay. Are you our new governor?"

She had addressed the man, but it was the boy who replied.

"I neither know nor care who your new governor may be. I am Alexandre Le Borgne de Belle Île, son to Emmanuel Le Borgne. This is my intendant. René de Menou has signed a paper acknowledging that two hundred and sixty thousand *livres* are owed my father by the estate of Charles de Menou. We are here to collect it."

The colorless intendant nodded ponderously and intoned: "It is by the form of the king's law."

From then on Jeanne was confined to her house and gardens, unless she wanted to watch the boy Belle Île parading her men-at-arms about or leading his intendant from farm to farm to take inventory of anything that might be transmuted into Emmanuel Le Borgne's precious *livres*. Brice de Saint Croix could only shrug at her painfully. "I am sorry, madame, but the instant René de Menou signed that paper everything your husband left behind became the property of Emmanuel Le Borgne, until such time as the accumulated income or selling off amounts to 260,000 *livres*."

Belle Île appeared at her door one afternoon with his intendant, whom Jeanne had never heard pronounce two words beyond his ubiquitous, "It is by the form of the king's law."

Belle Île reeked of wine and seemed unsteady on his feet. He said: "Your husband was barely in his grave, madame, before Nicolas Denys and his brother took advantage to erect new, illegal establishments in the north of Acadia. We have a paper for you to sign." He cocked his hand over his shoulder without bothering to look back at his intendant extending the rolled-up paper. "Since Acadia still has no governor, it is up to you to sign the accusation of those who trespass on your late husband's domain so that the Denys brothers may be legally seized and transported in chains to Quebec for judgment."

"Two small establishments on the Bay of Chaleur can hardly affect us here!"

"So you would say; since the income they are robbing from Acadia means nothing to you so long as it would go only to pay the debt you owe my father. You must sign the order."

The intendant nodded. "It is by the form of the king's law."

"And what if I refuse? You would have no form of law to evict the Denyses."

"If you refuse"—Belle Île smiled—"I will have to start taking possession of your household possessions, as I have a perfect right to do. I have only let you keep them out of charity."

The intendant said: "It would be by the form of the king's law."

Jeanne signed. She hoped Messieurs Denys would understand.

While she was putting the younger children to bed that night, Madame de Brice came scratching at the door with her three sons. Madame de Brice whispered: "It cannot go on like this, madame. My girls and the boys at the Capuchin school are slipping away to go back to their families in the woods. What choice do they have, when we are not supplied with provisions to feed them, because the mission schools are not an expense Emmanuel Le Borgne agreed to support?"

"What choice do *I* have," Jeanne asked, "when everything done in the name of Emmanuel Le Borgne is done 'by the form of the king's law'?"

Brice de Saint Croix looked over his shoulder and said carefully: "Other papers besides the one signed by René de Menou can be created to fit the form of the king's law. But they cannot be arranged from Acadia. Were I in France . . ."

The next day Jeanne was summoned to the fort. Belle Île said: "Is it a fact, madame, that last night you instructed the captain of the *Grand Cardinal* to fit out for a voyage to France?"

"It is."

"You have no right! The *Grand Cardinal* is my father's property!"

"But, Monsieur Le Borgne de Belle Île," Jeanne said meekly, "if the *Grand Cardinal* does not make a voyage to France to bring back supplies, Port Royal will have no goods to trade for the furs that would help pay back the debt owed to your father."

Belle Île looked uncertain. His intendant pronounced: "It may not be precisely by the form of the king's law, but I believe your father would understand that a garden that is not manured and watered grows no cabbages."

When the *Grand Cardinal* was ready to sail, Brice de Saint Croix whispered to her on the wharf: "I misdoubt, madame, that I shall be able to accomplish much before the *Grand Cardinal* must start back on her return voyage. I shall likely have to remain in France throughout the winter. But, by next summer—if you can hold out here for that long . . ."

"I can—if I know there is hope."

Jeanne began to doubt there was hope as the summer passed with incidents such as half of Port Royal's men-at-arms and *engagés* being loaded onto the *Vierge* to be discharged in France. The *Vierge* herself was to be added to the merchant fleet of Emmanuel Le Borgne, and her holdful of plunder from Port Royal sold at auction—including the gold-trimmed sedan chair the Viceroy of Mexico had had constructed for his sister.

The hills framing Port Royal were turning gold by the time the *Grand Cardinal* came home. Sailing alongside her was an unknown, sleek-looking fregate also flying the cross-and-lilies of France. Jeanne and just about everybody else at Port Royal trooped down to the landing stage to watch the ships come in. Belle Île came down from the fort with an escort of musketeers.

Whoever was in command of the fregate certainly knew these waters, because the fregate had already lowered her anchor and her boat while the *Grand Cardinal* was still cautiously edging around Goat Island. As the fregate's boat set off toward the landing stage, Jeanne shaded her eyes with her hand and squinted. Lounged back lazily between the oarsmen was a man wearing worn leather clothes and salt-rimed seaboots. It seemed impossible that a man with so much gray in his hair and such deep lines in his face could look so long and lean and hard.

Belle Île said: "Have you any notion, madame, of who that man may be?"

Savoring a sense of wickedness, Jeanne said softly: "Oh yes. I most certainly do."

"Could you tell me who he is?"

"I most certainly could."

"Well . . . ? *Would* you?"

"Oh. Certainly. You are about to meet . . ." She could never have imagined a circumstance when she might pronounce that name with pleasure. "Charles de Saint Étienne de La Tour."

Belle Île squealed: "Sergeant at Arms! Sound the alarm! Have your men look to their priming!"

The boat docked and La Tour swung up onto the wharf nimbly—although a twitch of his naked features made Jeanne hear the grunt in his mind from his aged hinges. He wore no sword, but carried a rolled-up parchment under one arm.

Belle Île waved his musketeers forward and cried: "You have no business here! Be off with you! You are a convicted felon and a traitor!"

"What I *am*, puppy—if you can read"—La Tour unfurled the parchment with a snap that threatened to dislodge the seals and ribbons appended to it—"is Governor of Acadia."

CHAPTER 58

La Tour stood on the plunging deck of his new frigate, watching the harbor of La Rivière St. Jean open up in front of her prow. The frigate's captain didn't need instruction to find the safe channel between Partridge Island and the headland: he'd been the captain of the *Renard Noir* until *les Bostonais* claimed her against La Tour's debts.

Although all the men between La Tour and the bow had their backs to him, he could pick out at a glance which of them had sailed with him on the *Renard Noir* and followed him from Boston to Quebec, and thence to France when the sad news came of d'Aulnay's death. While the men new-come from France bustled and gabbled, pointing out sights on the shoreline to each other, the old hands stood silently staring at the ruined fort on the point. Among the silent ones was Godard de Rainville's younger brother, whom Rainville used to berate for stealing all the inheritance of height and bulk that should've been divided equally between them.

D'Aulnay had built his new fort on the opposite side of the harbor from the old one. La Tour anchored his new ship in front of the new fort and climbed down into the bobbing boat with his rolled-up parchment under his arm. He didn't quite know what kind of reception to expect, but it seemed best to proceed as though obedience to the new decree were a matter of course.

An armed party trooped down from the fort to meet him. He stepped up onto the wharf and said: "Who is in command here?"

A neatly clipped officer said warily: "I am. What do you want here?"

"I am the new Governor of Acadia." They gaped at him. He unrolled his parchment and let them have a glance at it, then rolled it up again. "Unmoor your boats and ferry the crew and cargo off my ship. I have something to attend to, then I will inspect the fort and take inventory."

He climbed back into the boat and sat back down, then looked up at the men from the fort still standing idle. He said to the neatly clipped officer: "Well?"

"Unmoor the boats! Fetch down twenty men to row them! Assemble a crew of porters. . . ."

La Tour signaled the boatswain to push off. As they neared the fregate he said: "Pass her by and take me across the harbor."

The old landing stage was gone. Either d'Aulnay had floated it across to the new fort, or six springs of cascading ice had carried away every trace. La Tour stepped out of the boat into the mud, said: "Wait for me here," and climbed the slope of the sandy point.

The front gates were lying rotting in the weeds. Some of the timbers of the gatehouse had fallen in. There were a few poplars growing in the courtyard, but there wasn't much room for them to sprout between the twisted, rusting halberds, broken muskets, and embedded cannonballs. La Tour stood looking around at the wreckage that was still discernible as the work of men rather than decay, shaking his head at the evidence of how fierce the fighting had been.

Here and there among the rubble was a rose-pink glint from a shard of one of Françoise's ridiculous roof tiles, and the air smelled faintly of roses from the last blooms of the season on Françoise's climbing rose vines. They had taken well, but trailed along the ground with no human hand to fasten the new growth to the wall.

The postern gate in the back wall was sagging open. La Tour stepped through it to the meadow beyond. A few self-seeded grain stalks stood among the wildflowers and the advance troops of the forest reclaiming its own. It occurred to him that this might well be where Françoise and the others were buried. He might be standing on her grave.

He sat down, with his back against a moss-covered rock ledge and his hands between his knees bouncing the end of the rolled-up parchment on the ground. He unfurled the parchment and said: "See, Françoise? Now you are Queen of Acadia," and then began to weep.

When he was done, he stood up and wiped his eyes, blew his nose with his fingers, and went back to the boat. The tide was going out and the boat crew were having some difficulty staying moored to a shore that kept receding. He climbed in and pointed his parchment baton across the harbor.

Long before they reached the wharf, La Tour could hear a mob-voiced roaring from within the new fort. As he climbed the hill toward the gates he began to hear the ringing of steel.

Two men were clashing swords in the courtyard. It was no sportive fencing bout; one of them had blood dripping out of a slash in his shirtsleeve.

It took no great leap of intuition to guess what it was about: one of the swordsmen was the neatly clipped officer d'Aulnay had left in command of the fort, the other Rainville's younger brother. It also didn't take much guesswork to discern why the shouting watchers weren't ringed around them, but were in two groups lined up on opposite sides of the courtyard. The ones on one side were the men of the fort, those on the other the men who'd just come off the ship. Some of the men on both sides were fingering their own sword hilts or holding pistols.

The sentry above the gate had turned to face inward, thumping his musket butt on the firing ledge in time with his hollering. La Tour bellowed up at him: "Throw me down your musket." The man looked down at him and hesitated. "Now!"

The musket dropped. La Tour caught it and checked the pan to make sure the cover hadn't opened and spilled. Then he started toward the two swordsmen with his musket set to fire from the hip. The mob on both sides of the courtyard went silent, which made it much easier for La Tour to make himself heard. "Drop your swords or I kill you both!"

How exactly he was planning to kill two men with only one shot was another question. He decided the most sensible thing would be to shoot his stepbrother first. One of the other old hands was bound to step in and finish off the veteran of d'Aulnay's service before La Tour had to do too much sword parrying with an empty musket.

The duelists edged away from each other and turned half toward him, both still keeping one eye on the other's poised sword. Rainville's younger brother muttered out of the side of his mouth at the man who'd watched his brother die: "Don't doubt he will do it. Take my word for it."

La Tour said: "Or perhaps I'll only kill the second man to drop his sword."

Both swords fell in relative unison. La Tour stepped back and swept his eyes around the courtyard. "Whether all of you like it or not, I *am* the Governor of Acadia now. Any of you as can't swallow that are free to return to Port Royal. But you may not like how matters stand there these days."

A few of them took his offer, but most of them had already heard enough stories about the regime of Le Borgne de Belle Île and his intendant. La Tour settled in to make himself as comfortable as possible before winter. The trading post d'Aulnay had built was nowhere near as substantial as the old fort. For that reason and others—not the least of which was the skeletal ruin leering across the harbor—La Tour would've preferred to winter at Port Royal. But until the matter of d'Aulnay's legacy of debts was resolved, Emmanuel Le Borgne had first claim there. It seemed that every time Port Royal came within La Tour's grasp, some new complication jerked it away.

As the news spread among the people of the country that he was back, more and more Micmacs and Maliseets began to drift in and out of the fort. One of them had violet sun rays around his eyes. "So, La Tou, you some big *sagamo* now."

La Tour surprised himself by replying flatly: "For what that's worth, Keeshetech."

CHAPTER 59

Jeanne passed the winter at Port Royal with no great physical discomfort. Belle Île allowed her to draw what provisions she wanted from the fort stores, and her château was snug and warm.

But there were other kinds of discomforts. She had little company except the children and Madame de Brice. She lay awake nights worrying about the children's future, or lack of one: four girls who would have no dowries, four boys who would have no inheritance to get them started in the world. Not even her home was secure. At any moment Belle Île could exercise his father's legal right to take possession of her house and send her penniless back to France. Her aged parents were in no position to take in a widow with eight children.

And there was more to "home" than her château. The

possibility of being sent back to France made her realize it would be exile. She had lived more than half her life in Acadia now, and Acadia was where she belonged.

When spring came, she looked anxiously for the *Grand Cardinal*. Last autumn the *Grand Cardinal* had sailed back to France as soon as her cargo was unloaded, to spend the winter plying European trade routes for Emmanuel Le Borgne. As soon as the winter gales were passed, the *Grand Cardinal* was to sail for Port Royal with this year's supplies. Jeanne expected Brice de Saint Croix to be on board, with news of whether he'd managed to loosen the chains around her neck.

The apple trees were in bloom when Joseph came running from the river, calling: "*Maman!* The *Grand Cardinal* is coming in!"

She dropped the cloak she was patching and hurried down to the wharf, but Brice de Saint Croix wasn't there. He'd sent a letter, though, with the captain, who slipped it to her surreptitiously before going up to the fort to report to "His Little Majesty."

It was all Jeanne could do not to rip the letter open on the wharf, or not to break into a run on her way back to the château. As soon as she was inside, she broke the seal.

Chère madame,

I fear you may be angry at me for overstepping the bounds of my authority as your intendant, but it seemed to me you would not want me to hesitate to seize the opportunity that came to hand. Using the power of attorney you granted me, I have made an arrangement with the Duc de Vendôme. In return for two *seigneuries* in Acadia, the duc has agreed to assume half your debts, and stand as your sponsor for the rest. The matter is now no longer between you and Emmanuel Le Borgne. It is now a matter between the lion of Vendôme and the rodent of La Rochelle. . . .

Jeanne jumped in the air and shouted for the kitchen boy to fetch a bottle of wine from the cellar.

"What kind, madame?"

"Any kind! The first bottle you can lay your hands on! And bring along a cup for yourself!"

Although she was just the opposite of angry at Brice de Saint Croix, she expected Belle Île would be furious. She found out just how furious when a troop of men-at-arms marched past her château toward the cluster of school and dormitory buildings behind the church, and marched back escorting Madame de Brice, the father superior of the Capuchins, and the father superior's assistant.

Jeanne went out to intercept them. "What is the meaning of this?"

The sergeant in charge of the escort replied uncomfortably: "I have no choice, madame, but to obey what I am ordered. Monsieur Le Borgne de Belle Île has took it in mind that the holy fathers and Madame de Brice hatched the plan that her son played out in France. So they are to be imprisoned in the fort, where they can cause him no more mischief."

Jeanne turned to look at the fort, sighed resignedly, and said to the sergeant: "If you would be so good as to tarry here a few moments before carrying on so I may go into the fort before you . . ."

"What do you intend to do, madame?"

"I intend to inform Belle Île that these three had no part in what took place in France. My intendant was merely obeying my orders."

The sergeant became more than a little distressed. "If you please, madame, what good would that do? He has already made up his mind about these three, and will not change it. If you force him to blame you as well . . . He would never dare when he is in his right mind to offer any harm to you, but he is not always in his right mind. The garrison is at each other's throats as it is—if he were to order you imprisoned . . ."

"Very well." But her feeling of relief as she stepped aside made her wonder whether she was thinking of the good of Port Royal or just her own.

Overnight the rest of the Capuchins at the mission disappeared, apparently feeling safer in the camps of *les sauvages* than at Port Royal. All their pupils disappeared with them.

Jeanne had her cook prepare a basket of cheese, cold meat, bread, and wine and carried it over to the fort and down into the dungeon her husband had had built. Madame de Brice was in the same cell where Jeanne had tried to bandy words with Charles La Tour twelve years before.

Madame de Brice said: "I know you, madame—you will think you are responsible for this. No so. Belle Île has been searching for any excuse to lock up my mouth. You see, he is no different from any other young man, except that he has been thrust into a position where there are no checks upon his appetites. But in my years in Acadia I have learned that the ignorant women *sauvages* could teach Christians a thing or two about chastity. A female Micmac would no more go with a man other than her husband than jump from a mountain—except when she is drunk, when she will do anything. So I have been telling all my girls that Belle Île pisses in his wine casks.

"And I am not so uncomfortable down here, at least until the winter. Only one thing keeps me from being at peace. I worry for my books, being left in a deserted building where there is no one to see that the roof above them has not sprung a leak or that the mice and moths do not get at them. Would it be possible, madame, for you to have my books moved into your house until I am released?"

"Of course. It is the least I can do."

"It is the most anyone here can do, madame. But I have an intuition that even now, in France, the Duc de Vendôme is having words with Emmanuel Le Borgne that Emmanuel Le Borgne would rather not have."

As Jeanne was starting across the courtyard with her empty basket over her arm, a voice behind her bugled: "Madame!" She stopped and turned. Belle Île was hanging out of one of the upper windows of the château, with his shirttails hanging out of his pantaloons. "You did not obtain permission to visit the prisoners!"

Looking up at him, Jeanne could see that Madame de Brice was right; he was only a boy whose father had sent him out to carry a man's load. She said, in the same tone she would use to one of her own sons, "Monsieur Le Borgne de Belle Île, it is truly not demanded of a *seigneur* that he control every footstep of every tenant on his *seigneurie*."

For an instant it looked as though he might actually be about to respond as one human being to another. Then he pointed his finger at her and shrilled: "I will make it known among the guards that any one of them who allows you to see the prisoners without first obtaining permission from me will find himself on the other side of the bars!" and slammed the casement.

On her way back to her château, Jeanne visualized the books on Madame de Brice's shelf and decided that she and Joseph and the kitchen boy could carry them all. She sent the kitchen boy down to the cellar to fetch three empty flour sacks. But no matter how many times she called or how many rooms she looked into, Joseph was nowhere to be found. Finally, Marie said: "*Maman* . . . he is out in the woods behind the garden."

"Well, why did you not say so to begin with? Go and fetch him in, please." Marie hesitated. "Is there some reason you should not?"

"I am afraid."

"Afraid of your own brother?"

"Not so much . . . but perhaps a little, just today . . ."

Jeanne went out to look for him herself. She heard him before she saw him: a grunting and gasping and twig snapping, accompanied by a whistling sound. The whistling sound turned out to be his father's sword. He was fiercely dueling an unseen opponent, slashing and parrying and stretching his lunges out to the point where it looked like he would split up the middle.

He saw her and stopped, wiping the sweat out of his eyes. She said: "What are you doing?"

He panted: "Practicing, *maman*, as I do every day."

"Not like *this* you don't. And not with a real sword."

"I must accustom myself to a sword instead of just a practice foil. I may have to use one soon. If Belle Île tries to imprison you, or insults you further than he has already, I shall have to call him out."

"You will do nothing of the kind!"

"I would have no choice. You have no one else to protect you."

"I am perfectly capable of protecting myself. And Belle Île would never dare do anything that would rebound against his father in France."

"Would he not? He has said Nicole and Marie should be put to work in his scullery to earn their keep."

"What he says and what he will do are two different things. Now come along and help me do something practical." But she understood now why Marie was afraid.

The girls' school had already taken on the eerie, mouse-skittering feeling of a building no one lived in. Madame de Brice's books were on shelves at the front of the classroom. Jeanne pointed Joseph to the door of Madame de Brice's private quarters and said: "She may have left one or two in there as well," then she and the kitchen boy started filling their sacks.

Joseph came back looking confused. "*Maman*, the door appears to be locked."

"Locked?"

"Bolted from the inside."

She went to the door and tried it. It wouldn't budge. She nudged it with her fingertips and heard the bolt jiggling in its housing. She rapped on the door and called: "Who is in there?" There was no reply. "This is Madame d'Aulnay. There is no one from the fort with me."

The door opened slowly. In the curtained dark beyond, Jeanne could just make out Madame de Brice's assistant, the half-Micmac Jeanne La Tour. "Please, madame . . . I am doing no harm here. I stay inside in daylight so no one knows. You see, it is one thing for the holy fathers and the children to escape among the people of the country, but I would only be seen as an unmarried Micmac woman who knows more of books than of how to make herself useful around the camp."

"Why did you not go to your father?"

"That is what I will do, madame, when I can find a boat to take me across the bay. Until then I am hurting no one by staying here."

"Excepting yourself. How will you eat?"

"I have a little flour, madame. And in the night I sneak down to the river for water."

"There is no need for you to live like a mouse. We have plenty of food in our house, and plenty of room. Tonight instead of sneaking down to the river, you will sneak across to the château and stay with us. If you stay inside the house during the day, no one will know you are there any more than they know you are here."

"Oh, madame, I could not put you in danger so—"

"You will not be putting us in danger. It is only until you can find a boat. And you will help me to not feel so sinfully wasteful that the leftover food from our table could feed another family."

That last part had some truth in it when Jeanne said it, but not by the end of the day. The cook went to the storehouse in the fort as usual and came back more red-faced than usual. "Madame, they say we are now on rations, the same as any other fort dependents. And only a half ration for each child."

"*Child?* Joseph and Nicole have more appetite than most grown men!"

"I know that well, madame. But the intendant has declared that all those who still live in their mothers' houses and do not earn their bread are perforce children."

There were enough pickled oysters and other oddments in the cellar to fill out the table for a while, if Jeanne and the cook exercised their imaginations. But only for a while. Jeanne had little doubt that the arrangements Brice de Saint Croix had made were having their effects in France, but it wouldn't be until next year's supply ship that any formal decree found its way to Acadia. She also had little doubt that if she tried to depose Belle Île with nothing more substantial than a letter from Brice de Saint Croix, she would precipitate a civil war in Port Royal. She did her best to disguise from the children that their mother was seeing the ground they'd run and played on all their lives as very thin ice.

Mademoiselle La Tour had only been with them a few days when Jeanne saw her suddenly cock her head as though someone were calling her name. Jeanne listened, but heard nothing that didn't fit into the usual evening murmur of the draughts board and the girls humming over their needlework and the songbirds' vespers.

Mademoiselle La Tour said: "If you will excuse me, madame, I must go out into the garden for a moment."

"But of course."

Jeanne watched through the window. Mademoiselle La Tour appeared to be conversing with the lilac hedge. She came back bubbling, her brown cheeks flushed brightly. "It is my uncle Keeshetech! He brought his boat to take me home! When the tide begins to flow back out tonight, he will come for me."

Jeanne forced a smile. "I'm glad you will be able to escape."

"Oh, I wish you could as well, madame. I feel I am deserting you."

"Not at all. This is my home," but the word stuck in her throat.

Mademoiselle La Tour added conversationally: "Keeshetech says the Beard is at Jemseg just now, too."

"The beard?"

"Oh, that is what the people of the country call Nicolas Denys: the Beard."

"Your uncle must be confused. Nicolas Denys and his brother were taken in chains to Quebec."

"But no, madame—that is, yes, but the Governor of Quebec set them free. Among the people of the country it has been known since the spring that the Beard is back at his place in the north. And now there is no one to drive him out again, since the Governor of Quebec said he is breaking no law and the Governor of Acadia is his friend."

Jeanne said suddenly: "How big is your uncle's boat?"

"Not so big. A fishing boat he found."

"Is it big enough to carry my children and me, as well as you and your uncle?"

"Maybe ... I think so. ... Packed tight."

"Children"—Jeanne clapped her hands—"Hurry upstairs and pack together some of your clothes and—"

"Why, *maman*?" Marie interjected. Marie always had to know why.

"There is no time to ask questions. Each of you just take enough of your clothes to make a bundle you can hold in your lap. And not your nicest clothes, but the warmest and strongest. Nicole and Joseph will help the youngest ones decide. Hurry along now, there is not much time."

She followed them upstairs and went from room to room to make sure the clothes they were picking out weren't too many or too insubstantial. When they came back downstairs with their bundles, Jeanne extinguished all the lights in the house except one candle in the sitting room, as though the household were settling in for the night. She and her children sat waiting in the light of the lone candle, the younger ones dozing in their brothers' or sisters' arms, while Jeanne La Tour sat waiting in the dark in the garden. After what seemed like a long time, Mademoiselle La Tour stole back in and said: "My uncle says his boat can carry us all, but we must hurry to catch the tide and we must go quietly. He will meet us at the river."

Mademoiselle La Tour led Jeanne and her brood through a diked cornfield peeping with crickets and frogs. When they reached the dike, a deep voice whispered from the other side: "*Bonjou*, madame. Quick aboard. No talk till I say, if you please."

Jeanne settled onto the midboard bench with Marie and René wedged in on either side of her and little Louis in her lap. The boat pushed off and the surge of the tide carried them away from Port Royal.

Morning found them out on the Baye Françoise, with Mademoiselle La Tour's uncle holding the tiller in one hand and the rope to shift the sail in the other. It was a gray, drizzly day, with a wind that kept changing. What with the drizzle and the spray from the waves, Jeanne's cloak was a damp rag and the children were miserable. She wondered if she was putting them through all this for the sake of a ridiculous impulse that would come to nothing.

The sun was going down again when they entered Jemseg harbor, although the only way Jeanne knew it was sunset was by the reddish tinge to the fog. The only way she knew they were entering the harbor was by a darker gray to left and right amid the general blur.

Everyone in the boat had to shift around carefully so Keeshetech could break out his oars. As he rowed he called out: "La Tou!" The reverberating echoes suggested to Jeanne that somewhere in the fog must be rocky hills cupping the harbor.

Moving lights appeared ahead of them, like hazy fireflies, and then the side of a wharf with waves lapping against it. There were several men standing on the wharf, among them La Tour and a man with such a long pelt hanging from his jaws he must be the Beard.

The instant the boat kissed the wharf, Mademoiselle La Tour sprang out and ran to her father. Even through the fog, Jeanne could see the fear melt out of Jeanne La Tour as soon as that long, gristly sword arm settled around her shoulders.

Jeanne could hardly get out of the boat, her legs were so cramped and cold, and the children were almost as bad. La Tour didn't ask why they'd come to his fort and he spent no time on *politesse*, just said: "You look like drowned rats. Come up by the fire." The reference to "drowned" seemed even more heartless than she would expect of La Tour.

Once the whole boatload were settled in front of the hearth in La Tour's dining hall, with dry blankets around them and cups of tea or mulled wine warming their hands, La Tour insisted on introducing himself to the children one by one. When he said, "And you are?" to Joseph, Joseph replied stiffly: "I am the eldest son of Charles de Menou, Sieur d'Aulnay et de Charnisay."

Jeanne had never before been in an establishment run by Charles La Tour. It was difficult to tell the servants from the gentlemen, and a pack of hunting dogs seemed to think his dining hall their kennel. But she hadn't come there to observe La Tour's domestic life, or to bandy any more words with him than absolutely necessary. As soon as she'd stopped shivering enough to speak evenly, she turned to Nicolas Denys and said: "Monsieur Denys, I have come here to beg a very great boon

of you. It seems more than presumptious of me, after you were
taken off in chains in my name, but—"

"I never thought for a moment, madame, that your name on
the order meant it was your doing. It was Le Borgne."

"It is very generous of you to have seen it in that light."

Nicolas Denys wrinkled his forehead, as though she'd said
something he couldn't fathom, and said: "It was not generous-
ness, but the truth."

"You may say what you like, Monsieur Denys, but you do
have a reputation for generosity. I have come here to impose
upon it, if I can." Her words sounded clumsy and overformal
in her ears. It was difficult to speak when she kept hearing the
echoes of "she has not the necessary qualities. . . ." She
couldn't stop thinking that Françoise Jacquelin would've
known exactly what to say and how to say it. But Jeanne had
no tongue but her own to speak for her and her children, so
she bulled on through the echoes. "If you know that that order
was only signed because I had no choice, you have some idea
of how matters stand at Port Royal these days. . . ."

La Tour said: "We all have some idea of that."

Jeanne wanted to say: I was not talking to you—but that
would've been rather impolitic. La Tour's pale eyes had been
fixed on her disconcertingly since she'd started to speak. For
her part, she wanted her eyes to touch as little as possible on
the man who'd burned the mill at Port Royal, killed or
wounded many men of Port Royal, and caused the war that
had eaten up her children's inheritance.

Pretending La Tour hadn't spoken, she continued to Nicolas
Denys. "Belle Île and his intendant dare not do any harm to
me. But I fear that this rankles them and they will find some
way to take it out on my children—as they already have upon
others around me. But if I take the children away with me to
somewhere safe, Belle Île and his intendant will take advantage of my absence to move into my château, or strip it clean,
and claim that we have abandoned all rights to Port Royal."

She had intended to proceed through several further logical
steps toward her conclusion, as she'd worked out on the way
across the bay, but instead she blurted out: "Monsieur Denys,

could you find it in your heart to take my children back north with you where they will be safe?"

The younger children were crying softly, as were some of the older ones. She'd explained it to them at length on the boat, but that didn't make it any easier. She might well have been crying herself, if it weren't that she could feel La Tour's eyes on her.

Nicolas Denys said: "But of course, madame. My own children will be delighted to have new faces to play with."

"I am afraid I cannot pay you for their keep until—"

"Madame"—Nicolas Denys shook his head gravely—"this is Acadia, not France."

She wasn't sure exactly what he meant by that, except that it was somehow intended to convey that she needn't worry about such trifles as feeding eight children for an indefinite time. And it also meant the matter was settled.

Before she could begin to try to express her gratitude to Monsieur Denys, La Tour imposed himself with, "It do seem like all Acadia is still stumbling from one sinkhole to another. Being governor of her inherits more than a few rats' nests. But I think I know of a way, madame, to resolve both our troubles—or the worst of them, at least. I should put it to you in private, though. Your children look in need of dry beds. My steward will show them where to lay their heads."

A slovenly-looking sloucher who'd been sucking on a lemon pushed off from the wall and said: "Come along, children."

As Jeanne kissed her children good night, nodding at Joseph to assure him he needn't stay behind to protect her, La Tour said: "If you'll excuse us, Denys . . ."

"Where are you going . . . ? Oh! But of course, time I was abed, too."

La Tour put his fingers in his mouth and whistled. The dogs leaped up and the various groups of pipe smokers and cup nursers around the hall looked toward him. He pointed at the door and said: "Out."

When she and La Tour were alone, he leaned back in his chair, scruffed his fingers through his mottled hair, and said:

"You see, madame, my problem is that it is not possible to simply wipe away fifteen years of rancorousness and war—at least *I* have not found it possible. The men here who once served under your husband still think of my old officers as enemies, and versey-vicer. I can keep them off each other's throats, by whacking their bottoms with the flat of my sword, but that ain't the same as men serving together by choice. And in the eyes of your people at Port Royal—who will be part of my province once Le Borgne is out of the way—I am still seen as nothing more nor less than the pirate who burned their mill and killed their friends.

"As for you: Your problem is that you are at the mercy of your husband's creditors, so long as you are seen in the eyes of the law as nothing more nor less than his widow."

"That problem is already being solved in France."

He nodded. "The Duc de Vendôme."

She almost spouted: How did you know that?—but caught herself in time. She didn't want to give him the satisfaction and didn't wish to know any more about La Tour or his works than she already did.

"Brice de Saint Croix," La Tour went on, "is a clever lad, but young. I have learned over the years—sometimes to my regret, sometimes to my good fortune—that written agreements can change. Emmanuel Le Borgne is a bulldog, and he loves a good lawsuit almost as much as he loves gold. Perhaps the Duc de Vendôme can frighten him off, perhaps not. If not, you are still stuck in your problem. But I think there is a way to kill your problem and my own with one stone."

"What stone is that?"

"Marry me."

It took her a moment to convince herself he'd actually said that. Once she had, she said: "You're mad."

He threw back his head and barked a laugh like the village idiot. "You'll get no argument from me on that—nor from anyone as knows me."

She said in a colder voice than she'd thought she had in her: "Will you not be satisfied until you possess everything that once was Charles d'Aulnay's?" He slitted his eyes and closed his mouth and sucked his teeth. "I wouldn't marry you if you were the last man in Acadia."

"The way things have been known to go in Acadia, madame, that do seem a possibility. Well, since you don't want to leave your château at Belle Île's mercy for too long, I know Keeshetech'd be willing to take you back to Port Royal immediately, but—"

"You can't know that."

"I do. Because I know Keeshetech. But, it would be swifter and more comfortable if I ferried you back on my ship."

"I would feel safer traveling in an open boat with a man of *les sauvages*. Now, if you will be so good as to excuse me, I must say good-bye to my children."

The one offer she did accept was to start back across the bay that night, but that wasn't really accepting anything from La Tour, but from Keeshetech. The *sagamo* didn't seem in the least perturbed to climb back into the boat he'd just spent a day and half a night in. But no matter how lullingly the waves of the Baye Françoise rocked Jeanne's floating cradle, or how many layers of blankets she curled around herself, she couldn't sleep. It had been sixteen years since the last time she'd lain down without being in hearing distance if a child of hers began to cry.

Keeshetech grunted: "Good wind," lashed the sail straight, lounged back with the tiller under his armpit, took out his firebag, and coaxed his pipe alive. "La Tou, he a good man."

"He is a rogue murderer."

"Huh. By what you mean La Tou murder faster than them that try murder La Tou. You man murder La Tou woman."

"She died of natural causes!"

"Huh. That you call 'natural,' huh?"

"La Tour would have murdered my husband if he could."

"La Tou not alone there. La Tou alone now. You alone. Alone ain't no damn way to be."

"I have no money to pay you, Keeshetech, for all that you have done for me and my children. But anything you see in my house that you like, you may have."

"Oh, I was going this ways anyways."

The house felt hollow. By the end of the summer Jeanne's eyes in the mirror looked as haunted as she imagined Jeanne La Tour's would've grown if she'd kept on being the lone ghost haunting the mission school.

In the autumn Belle Île and his intendant decided to sail back to France before winter made it impossible, to find out what had come of the arrangement with the Duc de Vendôme. Jeanne strongly suspected that what they'd really decided was to loot as much as possible from Port Royal before the next supply ship brought a decree that the Le Borgnes no longer had any right to Port Royal.

From an upper window of her château Jeanne watched through Charles's old spyglass the boats and porters loading the cargo onto the *Grand Cardinal* against a background of fluttering gold leaves. They appeared to be taking half the colony's winter food stores as provisions for the voyage. Most of the contents of the powder magazine were going, and all the wine and brandy, along with anything else portable that might fetch a sou or two in France, even bedsteads.

Jeanne debated trying to put a stop to it. But with no official verdict yet delivered from France, the men-at-arms Belle Île had brought with him and the Port Royal folk who were intimidated by his claims would line up on one side, the ones who were loyal to her would line up on the other, and the ones who weren't sure would be caught in the cross fire. And the important thing was that as soon as Belle Île and his intendant were gone, she could instruct the captain of Port Royal's one remaining ketch to sail north to bring her children home.

Once the *Grand Cardinal* had disappeared beyond Goat Island, people began to seep out of the fort and from the farms and fields along the riverbank, washing up like a tide in front of Jeanne's house. She went downstairs and out onto the portico. The men-at-arms and *engagés* who'd chosen to stay at Port Royal despite no immediate hope of wages turned their eyes on her. So did the Acadian farm families who had no homes in France to go back to. None of them said a word, but their eyes all asked her the same question: What do we do now, madame?

Chapter 60

La Tour had plenty enough to keep him occupied during his second winter in the cramped little fort d'Aulnay had built. There were furs and hides to be haggled over, seventy men to be kept victualed and away from each other's throats, Micmac and Maliseet visitors to entertain and be entertained by, moose hunts to go out on. . . . But none of it managed to take his mind off the woman across the bay.

He was willing to admit that his proposal seemed mad at first blush, but it was less mad than the two of them living out the rest of their lives alone, with the hazy line of each other's coasts on the horizon. A marriage would make perfect sense in terms of politics and finance. Not to mention that lithe-looking, not-yet-forty, bed-warming body that voluminous skirts and high-necked blouses couldn't entirely disguise.

If all he'd wanted was his bed warmed, he could easily have found himself a bouncy young bride among the people of the country. But he'd grown too old to fancy spending the rest of his days and nights with a woman who didn't think in the same language he did, given she were old enough to think at all. His brief conversation with Jeanne Motin had made it abundantly clear that she was no longer the fiberless little broodmare d'Aulnay had imported from France, if indeed she ever had been.

La Tour had no doubt that if he took a trip to France next summer he could easily find a woman willing to trade civilization for a rich old man. But there'd be little joy in a bride who looked on living in Acadia as a penance. The fact that Jeanne Motin hadn't gone back to France, even after the death of her

384

husband and the harassment from Belle Île, proved that she had become Acadian. Outside of tenant farmers and a few *couriers de bois* and the people of the country, there were only two of them, sitting on opposite sides of the bay.

It wasn't difficult to keep himself apprised of how she was getting on at Port Royal. He knew she'd had her children returned to her. He knew that her farmers and fishermen had provided almost enough for the colony to make it through the winter on short rations, but they had little or no wine. He knew from experience that it was difficult enough to keep a snowed-in garrison from turning surly, without adding wine deprivation to the bargain.

A week before New Year's, La Tour and his quartermaster did a careful inventory of the cellar and decided they could easily spare three barrels of a serviceable Rhenish and a small keg of brandy. He debated delivering them to Port Royal himself, but in the end just sent them across in his fregate with his compliments to Madame, along with two kegs of gunpowder for good measure.

His fregate came back with several beaver pelts as payment for his gifts. He didn't know whether she'd intended to insult him or whether d'Aulnay had kept Port Royal so sealed for all those years that she hadn't understood when Denys said: "This is Acadia, not France."

Either way, La Tour told himself, you've primed the pump, just sit back and wait for the winter to do its work.

It turned into a satisfactorily harsh winter. His meat hunters ranged far into the forest and were lucky to come back with a brace of rabbits. Fortunately, Jemseg had more than enough stored provisions to live comfortably through a winter when the game disappeared. But he knew that wasn't the case at Port Royal.

In the depths of February a pinnace came scudding across the bay, bearing a draft marriage contract between Jeanne Motin de Menou d'Aulnay and Charles de Saint Étienne de La Tour. La Tour called for a bottle of wine, dumped the dog off his chair, and sat down to read it.

The preamble of the contract made it abundantly clear that

the sole reason for this marriage was to accomplish *the peace and tranquillity of the country, and concord between the two families.* The elaborations that followed the preamble essentially came down to: "What's mine is mine and what's yours is yours." Except for a gift of twenty thousand *livres* the groom was to make to the bride. He crossed it out and wrote in thirty thousand.

As his fregate entered Port Royal basin La Tour retired to his cabin to change into the new-fashioned finery he'd bought in France to help convince courtiers he was the best choice for the new Governor of Acadia. The costume wasn't exactly practical: knee-length velvet coat and thigh-length brocade waistcoat, tight breeches, buckled shoes, and a hat with its vestigial brim pinned up in three corners so as not to keep the rain off the wearer's shoulders. It seemed ridiculous for a man to dress himself up in a style that required him to take his coat off before he could wield his sword unconstrictedly. But that was the fashion.

The most ridiculous part of the costume was the sword that went with it: a stubby little rapier no longer than his arm. A sword blade should be half a man's height if he meant to do anything useful with it. But La Tour had discovered by experiment that if he tried wearing his old sword with his new clothes, he wouldn't get ten paces before the scabbard got entangled in his coattails and put him on his face. Ah, well, it was only for special occasions.

As soon as he'd stepped up onto the wharf, the boat turned around to start ferrying ashore the casks of salt fish and other largesse he'd brought along to allay any second thoughts the lady might be having. She was waiting for him in the great hall of Port Royal fort, with three Capuchin priests and two statue-imitating halberdeers. She sat corset straight, with her hands clasped in the lap of an apricot-colored gown that had seen better days. The scythe-sharp halberd blades crossed behind her chair provided an interesting contrast to her soft brown eyes. She looked thinner than when he saw her last.

She said: "It has occurred to me since this contract was drawn up that there is a matter it does not resolve and should.

The contract speaks of what share my children will inherit, and the children born to you by your Micmac wife, but makes no mention of the son Françoise Jacquelin bore you. If the marriage contract does not make clear what inheritance is due to him and what is not—"

"He is dead. Or vanished beyond finding. I have not heard a word from him or of him since he was transported to France. If neither he nor the woman that went with him have sent a word to me in eight years—and for one of those years I was very visibly in France—they either cannot or will not."

"I'm sorry." Remarkably, it sounded like she genuinely was.

"It was not your doing. But, there *are* children this contract don't refer to and should."

"Which children are those?"

"The children that will come from this marriage."

She went redder faster than any lobster he'd ever dropped in a boiling pot. But she said nothing, just read through the draft clause he'd brought along to resolve the matter, handed it to the priest waiting with his quill and inkpot, and nodded.

When the contract had been signed and witnessed, La Tour said brightly: "Well, madame, since we have your priests on hand already, shall we see to the posting of the banns?"

She didn't go red this time, but white. She said: "If you please, Monsieur La Tour, I would prefer to wait a little while. . . . The signing of the second marriage contract of my life—something I never expected to do—is dizzying enough to me without plunging further. If you would allow me just a little time . . . I hope you can understand."

It cost him some effort to smile. "But of course, madame."

He went back to Jemseg and waited. He waited long enough to begin to wonder if he shouldn't have saved his largesse until his wedding day. The holdful of provisions he'd brought with him to Port Royal might be just enough to get them through until news might come from France that her problem had already been solved.

Spring brought a flurry of annoying reminders, in the form of nesting birds and salmon swimming upstream. Out on the bay even the lumbering, thick-hided, sieve-mouthed whalefish were singing in pairs, but the Governor of Acadia was alone.

He was still waiting when his supply ship arrived in June. In the odd corner of the hold not taken up by the cargo he'd commissioned, there was a paltry smattering of useful articles Brice de Saint Croix had been able to pay the freight on, to be delivered to Port Royal on the way back to France. The most useful article was in the captain's strongbox: a letter from Brice de Saint Croix to his mistress.

La Tour made a plaster cast from the seal on Brice de Saint Croix's letter, sent for a Maliseet he knew who was a genius woodcarver, and broke the wax. The letter regretfully informed Madame that Emmanuel Le Borgne and the Duc de Vendôme had become as thick as thieves and Le Borgne was on his way to Acadia.

La Tour hummed to himself as he melted sealing wax. The wooden reproduction of Brice de Saint Croix's seal wasn't perfect, but La Tour doubted Madame would study the impression closely before cracking it apart. He handed the letter back to the supply ship's captain, along with a gold *livre* to keep his mouth shut, bade him a cheery bon voyage, and waited.

He didn't have to wait long. Four days after the supply ship sailed out of Jemseg harbor, a pinnace sailed in bearing the message that the banns had been posted in Port Royal church.

The day before the date appointed for his marriage, La Tour sailed his fregate across the bay and spent the night anchored within sight of Port Royal. When he walked into the church in his wedding finery, he found himself feeling as wine-softened and queasy-bellied as any boy who'd never knelt beside a woman before.

His bride was wearing a purple velvet gown with her breasts masked under a chignon that was happily gauzy, and a Spanish veil in her hair. When he put the ring on her finger, and she on his—blacksmithed, melted-down *livres* until he could make arrangements with a proper goldsmith in France—he felt for the first time the difference between her hands and Françoise's. Jeanne Motin's fingers were longer and wider, without Françoise's sudden taper at the ends, but they seemed adept in their own way. When the kiss came, he wrapped his arms around her back and pressed her to him. Her lips stayed slack and submissive. Perhaps that was how d'Aulnay had liked it.

The people of Port Royal and the crew of his ship followed them back to her château, throwing wildflowers and gamboling. The feast laid out on her lawn, and the barrels of wine he'd brought from Jemseg, provided La Tour with a good many jolly pictures of people from both sides of the bay enjoying themselves and each other. But the festivities did mean that his bride was constantly disappearing to consult with her steward to give some instruction to her cook.

When the sun went down, the fiddles and tin whistles came out and a bonfire was built. La Tour watched the dancers for a while, then went looking for his new wife. She jumped when he touched her bare shoulder from behind. He made a pantomime of yawning and said: "Do it not seem past time, Jeanne, we were abed?"

A servant was waiting in the hall to light their way upstairs. Her bed was already turned down and a candle burning in the sconce beside it. Although La Tour had no doubt there was no end of facets he had yet to learn of Jeanne Motin, it was already obvious that she managed her household like watchworks.

When the servant had bowed his way back out the door, she went directly to the bed, reached under it, and dragged out a feather mattress with blankets and bed linen folded on top of it. She maneuvered the mattress into a far corner and said: "If you prefer the bed, I will sleep here, or 'versey-vicer.'"

He looked from the bed to the mattress on the floor to her. She was already disappearing behind a tapestried dressing screen in another corner.

Despite the celebratory cacophony outside, La Tour could hear distinctly the rustling of layers of fabric beyond the screen, and the soft snicking of rows of hooks and eyes. He crossed his arms, walked to the gap between the screen and the wall, and raised one foot off the floor to cross his ankles as his body fell sideways until his shoulder hit the wall to prop him up.

She was facing him but was pulling her shift off over her head, allowing him a good view of the arched breasts and downy triangle that belonged to him now. As the hem cleared the top of her head, she shook her hair out of her eyes and saw him. She squawked and turned her back, draping one arm and the tail of her shift across her buttocks as an afterthought. But he could still see the horseshoe curve of her hips stretching the cloth, and the naked back V-ing down to merge with them. Her back was more stretched out and angular than Françoise's, though not skeletal by any means. At the moment it was quivering, like a hare finally run to ground.

He said: "By all the laws of church and state, it is my right."

She said to the corner in front of her: "I cannot prevent you from taking what is your right."

He thought about it for a moment. Even if she put up a fight, the noise outside would drown out anything short of a barrage of cannon. But if all he'd wanted was a fleshy orifice, all he would've needed was a bottle of brandy and a few Micmac girls.

He twitched his shoulder to spring his aged bones away from the wall, walked back to the mattress on the floor, and sat down on it. She came out from behind the screen in her nightdress, knelt to say her prayers, and then climbed into her bed. She picked up the candlesnuffer and automatically reached it toward the flame, then caught herself and said: "Do you still want the candle?"

"The game ain't worth it."

She snuffed it out. It took him a long time to get to sleep and even longer to wake up. The room was empty and far too bright with sunlight. He put his wedding clothes back on and went downstairs. She was sitting with her children eating breakfast. Her oldest son cast him an even eviler eye than usual. She pointed at an empty chair and said: "A place is set for you."

"I'll breakfast on my ship. Adieu."

Idiots grinned at him from their gardens on his way down to the landing stage. He waved at his ship and stood waiting in plain sight an unmercifully long time while the boat came to fetch him. The oarsmen seemed to think something amusingly jolly had taken place. So did the captain. La Tour took hold of the quarterdeck rail and said: "The tide is going out. Don't lose it."

As the anchor winched up and the fregate swung her nose around, La Tour could see that the captain and his crew had lost their laughter, which wasn't right. Old fools were meant to be laughed at.

Chapter 61

A month after Jeanne's paper husband sailed out of Port Royal, the *Grand Cardinal* sailed in. Jeanne didn't go down to the landing stage, but watched through the spyglass from an upper window. While the boats plied back and forth and various porters and functionaries made their way up the path to the fort, a round-shouldered man in a fur-trimmed cloak came straight from the wharf toward her house. Emmanuel Le Borgne.

Jeanne put down Charles's old telescope and went downstairs. Le Borgne squandered no time in niceties. "Well, madame, you have led me a merry chase, but now it is over. I have here a paper for you to sign, acknowledging once for all what is owed me."

"Why do you persecute me?"

"Persecute you? It is I who is persecuted. I am nearly ruined with financing your late husband's schemes in Acadia and receiving nothing back but promises. You of the nobility are all the same; you think because your escutcheons give you honor, you can bleed a poor man dry and feel no shame."

"Where in God's name did you get the notion I was of the

nobility? You did business with my father, and he was a plain man of La Rochelle the same as you."

"You should have held more to the principles you learned in your father's house, madame, instead of following your husband's airy ways. I am still owed 206,286 *livres* and I intend to have them."

"How? I do not have them to give you."

"There are still furs coming out of Acadia, and fish and timber. I mean to exercise your late husband's trade monopoly until Acadia has paid me what I am owed. Now, if you will be so good as to sign this accounting . . ."

She tried one last bolt-hole. "It is not up to me to sign that. My husband's debts are now in the hands of the Duc de Vendôme."

"I am acting in the interests of the Duc de Vendôme. When I explained to him how he'd been duped, he engaged me to see to it that his *'seigneuries'* in Acadia come to be more than names on a map. I must thank you, madame, for arranging matters so that I would make the acquaintance of so powerful a patron as the Duc de Vendôme. Now, if you will please to sign this accounting . . ."

She saw no choice. She had no doubt that the figure he'd named was accurate, or at least provable to anyone who cared to wend through the rabbit warren of ten years' accumulated dealings between Charles and Le Borgne.

Flapping the paper to dry her signature, Le Borgne said: "It is not true, madame, that you have nothing of value to pay against the debt. You have this fine house and gardens. I am a man of business, not a thief. I shall of course make an inventory of all the furnishings and fittings before I take up residence, and reduce your debt by the value of the property."

"But where am I to go? And my children . . . ?"

"I am a man of business, madame, not a brigand. I would not have dreamed of taking your home against the debt had you nowhere else to go."

"Where?"

"Why, to your husband, of course."

"My husband is dead!"

"Your *new* husband, madame. In three days' time my ship will carry you and your children and *personal* possessions across the bay to your husband's establishment. I will not add the cost of your passage to the debt—I am a man of business, not a ragpicker."

When she told the children, Joseph went white and said: "I will not go."

She put her face in her hands and whispered: "Please, Joseph . . . We have no choice. . . ."

"You made me believe, *maman*, that you had no choice but to become the wife of that man, but that it was only to be a marriage of convenience. Now we are to live under his roof?"

"We have no—"

"Perhaps you have no choice, but I do. By the time my father was my age he was already an officer in the king's marine. I believe my grandfather still has enough influence to procure me a commission."

She wanted to tell him he was too young, but he'd already parried that. She said: "If that is what you choose, Joseph, your father would have been proud. But you still must live somewhere in Acadia until you can find a ship to France. If you are going to be a soldier, you will have to learn to endure without complaint."

In her bed that night she lay awake wondering whether a woman of the world like Françoise Jacquelin would have managed to find a way to baffle the beaters and the hounds. All Jeanne could say she'd managed to do was not to mention to Le Borgne the thirty-thousand-*livre* wedding gift La Tour's bankers were holding in her name. Three years ago she would have considered that dishonest.

On the day appointed she walked down to the landing stage holding Louis's hand in her right hand and toddling Marie Hélène's in her left. The rest of the children followed her, with Joseph bringing up the rear like a sheepherding dog.

She didn't look back until she was on the deck of the *Grand Cardinal*. When she did she discovered that the foot of the wharf and the dikes and banks on either side of it were all lined with men and women and children in homespun clothes and wooden shoes or no shoes at all. The fort battlements were dotted with points of light, where the sun gleamed on the helmets of Port Royal's remaining garrison.

One of the tenants standing on the dike reached up and tugged off his raggedy straw hat. Then another did so, and another, tugging their sons' sleeves to tell them to do the same. The women raised their kerchiefs to cover their heads. The gleaming points up on the parapet disappeared as the men-at-arms took off their helmets.

Jeanne raised her hand to wave good-bye to them, but found she couldn't wave, just stood at the rail with her hand held at her shoulder, palm toward them. They were all still standing there when the tide carried the *Grand Cardinal* beyond Goat Island.

As Port Royal disappeared behind her the captain of the *Grand Cardinal* muttered: "It's a devil of a world, madame, when a man like that can drive out a lady like you."

When the *Grand Cardinal*'s boat delivered her and her children to the landing stage in Jemseg harbor, La Tour was standing there with his arms crossed, looking wary and self-contained. When she'd explained why they'd come, he merely shrugged. "It is your right—the marriage contract gave you the *siegneurie* of La Rivière St. Jean for your lifetime."

"I do not know how matters stand here for housing, but we shall need three rooms, if that is possible—one for the girls, one for the boys, and one for myself. Or, if needs must, the girls and I can —"

"It is possible."

It took her and the children a while to adjust to roughly furnished living quarters. It took longer to adjust to the more rugged landscape and rougher climate on this side of the bay, and the even rougher population. For the first few nights the children found it hard to sleep through the sounds of coarse singing and laughter coming up from the dining hall, or of drunken men stumbling past their doors. But in time they grew assured that even the drunkest of La Tour's retainers would still regard them as pets.

The only demand La Tour made on Jeanne was that she sit

beside him at the evening meal, or when a visitor was being entertained. At first she thought he wanted to display her as a symbol of his triumph over Charles. But then she began to get the strange impression that what he wanted was for her to participate in his life. Nonetheless, whenever she announced that it was time she retired, La Tour would merely nod. *"Bonne nuit."*

It was an odd assortment of visitors she found herself playing chatelaine to. One of them was a raffish-looking *courier de bois* named Groseilliers. Jeanne had no idea why La Tour was waxing so adamant to their guest that "the big salt water to the north" had to be the same bay Henry Hudson disappeared in: "You can tell Major Gibbons I said so—Gibbons is a practical man who don't let the past get in the way of future profits—but it do seem unwise for you to mention my name to the Winthrops and Endecotts and such."

"I expect not," Jeanne put in dryly. "Not after you murdered that Boston ship captain, marooned his crew, and stole his ship." The pale blue eyes went cold and wolfish and turned on her. "Is that not how the story goes?"

With his eyes still fixed on hers unwaveringly, La Tour said: "Do the story include that if *les Bostonais* had told me when I got there that they were too afraid to help me, I would've turned the *Renard Noir* around and I would've *been* here . . . ? Or that when they finally did work up their courage to loan me ships and men, they kept dithering until it was too late . . . ? They cost me my wife and my son and my home and then took my ship and left me stranded in Boston.

"I rotted in Boston for a year before they finally allowed as how I might be useful to guide a trading expedition in that gimcrack little pinnace. I would've been perfectly content to set that fool of a captain ashore peaceably, as I did his crew, if he'd had the sense to allow me.

"Besides"—the wolfish eyes crinkled and twinkled with the oddest humor Jeanne had ever seen—"I didn't kill him. I did put a pistol in his face and pull the trigger, but he moved too fast."

The autumn brought another visitor, and a more unpleasant

one than she'd yet had to entertain at La Tour's table. She was in the girls' room, discussing with Nicole and Marie and the fort carpenter the advantages of chests of drawers over blanket boxes, when another of La Tour's retainers appeared in the doorway. "There is a ship in the harbor, madame. Charlot asks that you join him in the dining hall to make welcome her master."

"Who is it?"

"Emmanuel Le Borgne."

Jeanne went downstairs with her hand on her throat, as though trying to loosen a snare. It had never occurred to her that Le Borgne might pursue her even to here.

La Tour was sitting alone in the dining hall, with his feet up on the table and his hands behind his head. She said: "What does Emmanuel Le Borgne want here?"

"I have no more idea than you. Perhaps he's just come to pay his respects to the governor."

When Le Borgne was ushered in, La Tour welcomed him jauntily, pointing him into a chair and calling for cups and wine. So jauntily, in fact, that Jeanne wondered if he and Le Borgne hadn't come to some secret arrangement about her thirty thousand *livres*.

Le Borgne told La Tour: "By law, you must deliver up to me all the furs in your possession."

La Tour laughed. "It do seem to've slipped your mind, Le Borgne, that I am Governor of Acadia."

"Be that as it may, I am the heir of all the rights of the previous governor, including his monopoly on all Acadian trade, until his debts to me are paid. By law, you must deliver up to me all the furs in your possession, plus any other articles you mean to ship to France for profit."

La Tour leaned forward across the table and smiled. "You are a man of business, Le Borgne, not a *courier de bois*. All the clerkish tricks you pull in France mean shit to me. If you knew anything about Acadia, you would know not to come into another man's fort and threaten him with laws and debts. All manner of accidents can happen to a businessman walking up and down a rough path on a steep hill.

"Take what you can out of Port Royal—*until* the debt is paid out. If you do that and no more, I will not interfere with you. But, for the sake of my soul and your skull, please do not interfere with me."

Jeanne gaped from the rounded, fur-trimmed back scuttling out the door to the tide-etched, bare face of her convenient husband. She wasn't sure which she found more difficult to believe: that any man could threaten another man's death without even a pretext of legal or moral justification, or that it could actually be that easy to shake off Emmanuel Le Borgne. She said to La Tour: "Even if an accident happened to him, there are still his sons and heirs in France to pursue the debt."

"There are accidents enough to go around. Failing that, I suppose I'd have to fall back on something legitimate, like the queen regent's seal on my commission. *Merde*, I told René and Marie I'd take them down to the fish weir when the tide went out, and I can hear it's past ebbing. If you'll excuse me . . ."

La Tour took such obvious delight in her children that they had all fallen into calling him "Charlot." All except Joseph. One evening after Jeanne had spent another afternoon shepherding the younger children around the gorge to watch the water flow up the falls, La Tour kept grimacing and clutching his chest whenever he reached for something on the supper table. Joseph snickered companionably at every grimace, and at one point Jeanne saw him actually winking at La Tour.

Her amazement must've shown, because La Tour turned to her and explained: "Bruised ribs. Your son's a devil of a fencer. I came across him practicing by his own self this afternoon, and like a fool I suggested he needed an opponent if he hoped to learn anything but how to dance."

"Charlot is showing me," Joseph spouted, "the difference between wielding a gentleman's rapier and a soldier's sword."

Jeanne said: "How?"

"How else, *maman*"—Joseph looked at her as though she'd asked a woman's question of a man—"but with swords?"

For a change, Jeanne tarried in the dining hall after the last of the children had gone to bed so she could ask La Tour:

"Swords? I would've thought, if you put a real sword in his hand and stood in front of him, he would try to kill you . . . ?"

"He did. At first. Well, it was getting damned embarrassing, the way he was picking me apart with the foils. . . ."

There came a winter's evening not apparently different from any of the evenings Jeanne had spent on La Tour's side of the bay, ending as always with Jeanne rising from her chair and La Tour settling in with his pipe and his pitcher of wine. It struck her that the purpose for the pitcher was to numb him to the point where he might flop immediately to sleep after fumbling his way up to his bed.

As always, he didn't embarrass her by trying to hold her back when she stood up to go to her bed. But he did, as always, look like the prospect of the rest of the evening was something to try to put the best face on. Like the rest of his life. Like the rest of hers.

She fully intended to say good night and turn straight toward the staircase, as always. But this time she found herself putting her hand on his shoulder and saying something she seemed to remember saying many times before, in another life: "Is it not past time, Charles, we were in bed?"

EPILOGUE

Nicolas Denys stood on the afterdeck of his ship, anxiously twining his snow-white beard around his fingers, trying to keep one eye on his helmsman and the other on the rocks bordering the entrance into the harbor of Port La Tour. The English fort at the head of the inlet fired a cannon, but Denys wasn't alarmed. He had no doubt it was only a signal gun announcing an incoming ship. He and the English left each other alone. In fact, although it might be a treasonous thought, it was only since the English took the southern half of Acadia that he'd been able to prosper peacefully in the north.

La Tour hadn't been so lucky. Although he hadn't seen La Tour in years, Denys knew that once the English had finished making La Tour pay off his debts to *les Bostonais* and the other Englishmen, all La Tour had left was the little *seigneurie* at Cape Sable. And the only reason he'd been allowed to keep even that was that he was a baronet of New Scotland.

There was another ship flying the fleur-de-lis already anchored in the harbor, one Denys didn't recognize. He anchored next to her, lowered his boat, and pointed the tiller toward the landing stage as the rowers bent to their oars.

A man with a peg leg stumped out onto the landing stage. Denys squinted to focus his age-fuzzed eyes. Everything about the peg-legged man except his face and hands—his clothes, his hair and beard, even his peg leg—was black. Denys found it hard to believe that Gargot's beard could still be black after all those years, but that was who it appeared to be. Denys hadn't seen La Tour's military friend Gargot since that chance encounter on the quai at La Rochelle, when Gargot had been escorting poor Françoise Jacquelin to France and Denys's leased fishing ship was sitting on the bottom of the harbor.

Peg leg or no, Gargot nimbly caught the bow-and-stern lines, tied them off, and skipped over to give Denys a hand out of the boat. Gargot didn't say *bonjour*, just growled: "Why, Denys, what the devil's happened to your beard?"

"My beard?"

"It's gone all white!"

"We are none of us getting any younger, Gargot. I thought you were in a Spanish prison."

"That was years ago."

"I mean again."

"They let me go again."

"Oh. Is that where you lost your leg?"

"No. Left it in my other pair of breeches."

Denys reminded himself that Gargot had always had an

eccentric mode of expression, so he just said civilly: "How did you get here?"

"Didn't *swim*. That'd be my ship you anchored beside. Aren't set *foot* off her more'n two days since April. Brought two ships to Newfoundland—I'm Governor of French Newfoundland now; fair trade for my leg. Left one there—ship, that is—and sailed on to Quebec to deliver the new bishop. Lucky I did; when we stopped in at Plaisance en route I found the *engagés* had killed their governor and chaplain and were busying themselves trying to kill each other."

"What did you do?"

"What else? Took the ringleaders to Quebec, put a raft out on the river, and hanged one where everyone could get a good view and a good example. What brings you to Cape Sable?"

"I came to ask some advice of Monsieur La Tour. And you?"

"The king's minister of marine instructed me to seek advice from the treasonous outlaw La Tour."

By that time Gargot had walked Denys past the English fort and along a cart path to a garden gate with a thatched log cottage beyond it. Gargot opened the gate. Kneeling in the flower border beside the path to the house was a bare-legged, earth-streaked servant woman of a certain age, with her very ample breasts threatening to fall out of her low-necked peasant blouse. Something about the servant woman made Denys look twice. "Madame d'Aul—La Tour!"

"Why, Monsieur Denys, what a pleasant surprise." As she rose to her feet Denys saw why her breasts were so ample: she was more than mildly pregnant, and making not the least attempt to disguise the fact with corsets.

She took his arm to walk him up the pathway. A blue-eyed, brown-haired boy about as tall as her shoulder was drawing water from a well in front of the house. She called to him: "Jacques, this is Monsieur Denys."

"Bonjour, Monsieur Denys."

"Bonjour."

As Denys stepped across the threshold with her, she called out: "Charlot! Look what Gargot found on the wharf!"

Out of the shadowed interior came: "Hmm? What's that?"

Madame La Tour whispered to Denys: "He's growing a little deaf."

"I'm growing nothing of the kind. She mumbles. Denys!" As Denys's eyes adjusted from the sunlight he saw La Tour rising from a chair and disentangling himself from a toddling girl occupying his lap. Although La Tour's hair had gone whiter than Denys's beard, his face was brown with sun and his hands were obviously still steady enough to wield a razor—and strong enough to clasp uncomfortably tightly on Denys's shoulders. "Sit down, Denys, sit down. We'll have some wine. I'll have to find another cup. . . ."

"*I* know where they are," Madame La Tour put in. "Sit back down and stay out of my way."

La Tour did as he was told and gestured at the other chairs around the room. "Sit down, Denys, sit down."

Denys started to, but Gargot growled from behind him: "That one's mine." Denys shifted to a different chair, and saw why when Gargot sat down: Gargot's chair was placed so that his peg leg stuck out toward the wall, instead of into the room where someone might trip over it.

Madame La Tour brought cups and a pitcher of wine. La Tour poured and said: "You're a long ways from home, Denys."

"I was fishing down the coast, and decided—since I had come that far as it was—I might just as well come see how matters fare for you at Cape Sable. And . . . there is a difficulty I thought you might advise me on. . . ."

"Matters not faring well at Cape Bretonne?"

"No, no—very well. I have three establishments now, and all are prospering. Excepting, of course, for the debts I incurred to build and man them—"

"It do seem"—La Tour laughed—"I ain't the man to advise you on debts."

"For my part," Jeanne d'Aulnay de La Tour said lightly, "I have had nothing but the best of luck with debts and husbands."

"No, no." Denys shook his head. "My debts are not the

difficulty—that is, they *are* a difficulty, but not the one I came to . . . The difficulty is, you see, La Compagnie de la Nouvelle France has gone and granted to a new man a concession that is part of the concession they have already granted to me."

La Tour laughed louder than before. "They *will* do that, Denys."

"I have no fear," Denys went on despite La Tour's non sequiturs, "that I will have to drive the new man out. He knows nothing of Acadia and within two years will ruin himself or starve. But he may grow desperate enough to try to drive *me* out. I came here hoping to get your advice on how best to arrange the defenses of my fort and the few little pieces of cannon I have."

"Gargot's the man to tell you that better than I. It's good luck you came when he happened to be here. Before you both sail, Gargot will sit down with you with a burnt stick and birchbark. Won't you, Gargot?"

"I might."

The conversation widened from Denys's troubles to events in the Old World that were bound to affect the New: the redefinition of Quebec and New France by the new minister of finance; the coronation of Charles II of England, driving the last nail into the coffin of Oliver Cromwell; the wildly fluctuating markets for beaver pelts and cod. . . . But most of the conversation had to be between Denys and Gargot, since Monsieur and Madame La Tour would only roll their eyes at each other and laugh, as though the doings of kings and ministers and financiers were nothing more than a comedy arranged for their entertainment. Denys found it quite disconcerting. Even the rumors that Nova Scotia might soon become Acadia again, given the debts Charles II owed to his cousin Louis XIV, seemed only grist to the La Tours' mill of laughter.

Looking around at the room he was in—with its crude kitchen fireplace, rough-cut furnishings, and walls bare of ornament except the occasional wolf pelt or wooden candle sconce—Denys couldn't help but feel it was a shame that a man of La Tour's ambition, and a woman who'd once been chatelaine of Port Royal, should come to such an end.

A boy a little younger than the one Denys had met at the well, and a girl a little older than the one who'd been in La Tour's lap, came running in, chattering something about an otter and declaring they were hungry. Madame La Tour said: "Go and watch the otter a little longer, dears, and I will have a meal on the table."

Denys said: "Where are Joseph and Nicole and all my other foster children of the isle of Miscou?"

Madame La Tour said: "All gone to France, one by one. The boys are all soldiers now, and the girls in holy orders. Marie is canoness of Poussay Abbey."

Denys clucked, "My, my," trying to put a bright face on this further evidence of fallen fortunes. The fact was, the dowry a girl needed to become a bride of Christ was a fraction of that required to make an earthly marriage. And any penniless young man could be a soldier.

Madame La Tour said: "But that still leaves me with more than enough hungry mouths to feed, including you three helpless men." She heaved her ripening body out of her chair and moved toward the hearth.

La Tour set his cup down and said: "I must show you my garden, Denys."

"*Your* garden . . . ?" came from the hearth.

La Tour shrugged. "Well, I dig where she points me."

It seemed to Denys that La Tour walked stiff-jointedly, but became somewhat sprier once they were out in the sunlight. Gargot followed them out the door, saying: "I'll watch from the path while you're showing off your cabbages, La Tour. A peg leg's as good as any leg, except in tide mud or tilled ground."

La Tour replied jauntily: "You ought to carve yourself a wooden foot to stick on the end of it."

"You ought to carve yourself a pair of crutches against the day your legs give out—next week or the day after."

"Do you see, Denys, that house on the other side of the trees there . . . ?"

"Yes," although all he could see of it was a chimney tip.

"My daughter Jeanne lives there, with her husband. I

suppose it's just as well she got herself married and changed her name. Two Jeanne de La Tours was confusing. But I still find it hard to approve of mixed marriages."

Denys said confusedly: "Is your daughter not herself the product of a mixed marriage?"

"Mixing French and Micmac's one thing—she went and married a *Basque*. But, he do occasionally lend his father-in-law small sums of money, for the sake of family harmony."

La Tour stopped by a trellis of blown-out climbing roses and cupped one blossom in his hand, empurpled pink petals falling off into his palm. "Pity you couldn't have seen these a week ago, Denys. I grew them from cuttings from the border my Françoise planted at Jemseg. . . .

"The more time I have to think on it, Denys, the more it seems to me old Governor Razilly had a plan for the three of us—you, me, that pig of hell d'Aulnay. . . . I think Governor Razilly planned to will Acadia to us equally, with no need to draw borders. After all, you were always mostly interested in the fishery and timber, I in the fur trade, and d'Aulnay in planting a *seigneurie* in the floodplains. If Governor Razilly hadn't died before he expected . . . But then, who don't?"

La Tour glanced back at the house and lowered his voice. "Did you notice, Denys, there is a shelf of books beside my chair?"

"I did." Anyone who had the least acquaintance with La Tour would be bound to notice the incongruousness of a shelf of books beside his chair.

"I was never much one for books. They were hers. Books of plays. D'Aulnay brought them back to Port Royal as part of his booty from Jemseg, and donated them to Madame de Brice. Madame de Brice had her doubts they were suitable for schoolgirls. So they came into Jeanne's hands, and thus to mine.

"There is no need Jeanne should know this, but, when I read them I can see Françoise. I know from what Françoise told me they are not the kinds of roles she would have played. But I can see her . . . and hear her. . . ."

Gargot growled: "She was some woman."

La Tour plucked a rose that miraculously still had some living petals on it and said: "So is my Jeanne."

In a snowed-in little stockade in the north of Acadia, Nicolas Denys took his beard out of his mouth, picked up his quill, and jabbed into his inkwell. The ink was frozen. He thawed it over the candle and began to write: *The entrance of the Rivière St. Jean is dangerous. . . .*

AUTHOR'S NOTE

If piecing together a story out of history is like puzzling out the doings of nocturnal creatures by the tracks left to the morning, the civil war that founded Acadia is a few smudgy pawprints in melted snow. Nicolas Denys, John Winthrop, and several others left contemporary accounts. But they tend to be rather sketchy, as the writers all had other axes to grind.

One detail that most accounts agree on, though, is the event the rest of the story revolves around. Françoise Marie Jacquelin (often misnomered "Marie La Tour") held Jemseg Fort against overwhelming odds and only surrendered on the Sieur d'Aulnay's promise that her remaining men would be shown mercy. Then d'Aulnay stood her on display with a decorative noose around her neck and hanged her men one by one in front of her eyes. The ingenious notion of offering a pardon to whichever rebel volunteered as hangman wasn't my invention but d'Aulnay's.

Some accounts say Françoise lived for several weeks after that, some several days. Some say she died of a broken heart, some say d'Aulnay poisoned her to keep her from telling her story in France, some hint at darker things.

D'Aulnay left his own account of the feud, and it's about as self-serving as La Tour's would be if he had been inclined to write things down for posterity. D'Aulnay's account isn't only unreliable for political reasons. He mixes up more than a few utterly apolitical details that get wiped away by a glance at the logs of his ship captains. The captains wrote their logs day by day; d'Aulnay was dredging up memory years later. I did,

406

though, check and weigh as many of d'Aulnay's details as possible, so you can be reasonably assured that this story isn't entirely unbalanced (as opposed to the storyteller).

You might be disappointed, though, that d'Aulnay's unreliable account is the only source for the suggestion that Françoise came from the *demi-monde*, which later generations have taken to mean she was an actress. But there's plenty of other reasons to believe that. For one thing, it's generally accepted that she was almost forty years old when she married La Tour. She did *something* for the first twenty years of her adult life; there is no suggestion she was a widow, and she sure as hell wasn't lolling about in a convent. Her recently discovered marriage agreement makes it abundantly clear that she knew her way around a contract, and that she wasn't a charity-case spinster willing to settle for whatever terms she could get. And even skeletally recorded incidents—ranging from her dealings with Captain Bailly to charming the pantaloons off the Massachusetts Assembly—paint a picture of a woman who'd been around the block once or twice.

Speaking of pictures, there are two surviving portraits of d'Aulnay but not even basic physical descriptions of Charles La Tour, Jeanne Motin, or Françoise Marie Jacquelin. A seventeenth-century painting in the New Brunswick Museum was long purported to be a portrait of Françoise, but it's been pretty much discredited. That painting of a dimpled woman in a "breastsplate" did make me realize, though, that there was no need to make her the stalwart Amazon featured in some representations of the final battle scene. It isn't difficult to come up with examples of renowned male military leaders who weren't exactly imposing physical specimens. Besides, I've written about too many tall women already (in several splendid volumes available from Ballantine Books or through your neighborhood bookstore).

Let's see, what else might you want to know about veracity. . . . It's impossible to say whether I've exaggerated the contrast between La Tour and d'Aulnay. But there's no question that by comparison d'Aulnay was a properly starched aristocrat and La Tour a rough-edged *courier de bois*.

Jeanne Motin left little to go on besides three facts that were interesting to add together. The first is d'Aulnay's patronizing description of her in his will. The second is that when she found herself and her children buried in an inheritance of debts, she didn't roll over and play dead. The third fact is that her "marriage of convenience" to La Tour resulted in five children.

There is no evidence whether Nicolas Denys was or wasn't the messenger who delivered La Tour's proposal to Françoise. But he was in France at the time, and his description of her last days makes it clear he'd met her enough times to form a strong admiration. The pickle I've placed him in at the beginning of Part II, with his leased ship sinking in La Rochelle harbor, is one I borrowed from someone else's life. But Denys's life was such an unrelenting chain of disasters that one or two could've easily slipped his mind.

Many of the secondary characters, such as Rainville, Le Creux, and Desjardins du Val, left no historical record beyond the occasional signature on a contract or name on a passenger list. There is no record of whether Le Creux was appalled at what his brother-in-law did after Françoise surrendered, but Le Creux did disappear from the annals of Acadia around that time and reappeared in France. As for Rainville, there were two Godard de Rainville brothers, François and Jacques, as I mentioned toward the end of the story. I figured it'd be easier on all of us if I concentrated on one of them. One of the brothers co-signed Françoise's marriage contract and escorted her on her second voyage to France. It's generally assumed that at least one of the brothers was beside her in the final battle.

Keeshetech, or Quichetech, is recorded as the name of one of the Micmac *sagamos* who accompanied La Tour to France in the 1630s. But whether he was the one who did the outrageous performance with the deer in the Paris park, or whether he was still around when the events in this story took place, no one will ever know. Many of the sayings and doings I've attached to Keeshetech *are* recorded, but only as anecdotes of anonymous Micmacs. In the same vein, the records of many of the incidents I've placed Rainville in refer to him only as "an officer of La Tour's."

Some of the people who were kind enough to read this book in manuscript expressed disappointment that I let d'Aulnay off too lightly, with a mere death-by-drowning. Unfortunately, the only leeway I had was to pick the most satisfying recorded version of his fatal boating accident. But if you like a good revenge—and who doesn't?—there is a codicil to this story that's so diabolical I couldn't've invented it.

It would work only on someone as fanatically proud of his ancient bloodline as d'Aulnay was. D'Aulnay's four daughters all went into holy orders, and his four sons all died in the military without producing heirs. So all the descendants of Charles d'Aulnay's wife—and there are thousands of them, scattered from New Brunswick to Louisiana and other compass points—are actually descendants of his enemy, Charles La Tour.

Inexplicable little coincidences can happen when you're trying to put yourself in the skin of people whose skins went back to dust hundreds of years before you were born; coincidences that almost seem like someone's trying to reassure you when you're on the right track. I'll mention two that happened during the writing of this book.

Despite the fact that most seventeenth-century French ships were named after saints or holy sentiments, I got the weird idea that La Tour was the kind of guy who would name his ship after some sleek, swift, wild animal. So with no supporting evidence whatsoever, I christened his ship the *Otter*. It was only much later that I came across an ancient harbor record listing La Tour's ship as the *Renard Noir*—the Black Fox.

The other funny coincidence came up in the Epilogue. I wanted Gargot there, since I wanted some things said that just wouldn't fit in Denys's mouth. But Cape Sable was several hundred miles out of the way of any route Gargot might conceivably take to or from Newfoundland on business. So I dug up some more detailed information on Gargot, just to prove to myself that the scene wasn't feasible. Turned out that around the same time Denys was having trouble with interlopers,

Gargot received specific instructions from France to seek advice from La Tour on another matter.

Port Royal is now Annapolis Royal, Nova Scotia. One corner of d'Aulnay's fort has been excavated, but most of it lies under the Fort Anne Historic Site, and the preserved eighteenth-century fort would have to be demolished to get down to the seventeenth-century fort. One artifact that has been dug up, though, is a rough slab of stone with the name of d'Aulnay's son Joseph carved into it. It was first assumed to be a property marker, but then the curators realized that Joseph left Acadia to go soldiering and had never owned property at Port Royal. So the stone remains a mystery. Or maybe not.

The mouth of La Rivière St. Jean is now the city of St. John, New Brunswick. The site of La Tour's fort became an archaeological dig when the promontory was leveled for a freeway. The original courtyard was still littered with broken pikes, swords, and cannonballs. I have given the fort a few more pieces of artillery than were found on the site, since it seems logical that d'Aulnay would've taken any useful guns to arm his new fort across the harbor. One of the guns that *was* found on the site is a stubby little article whose mouth of inch-thick iron was twisted and torn like wet clay. It now resides in a display case in the New Brunswick Museum. Sitting beside it is a rose-pink ceramic roof tile.

Apparently there's now a permanent sign identifying "Fort La Tour Park," which will save future visitors my delightful experience of scrambling up and down sleet-drenched embankments trying to guess which overgrown vacant lot was the place. They tell me it's full of wildflowers in the summer.

Françoise's grave has never been found. Good chance it was inadvertently bulldozed for some project or other. If you're ever passing by a certain scruffy-looking wildflower meadow in St. John Harbor, give her a wave for me. It will probably never be known for certain whether she was or wasn't a Parisian actress adept with the joint stock companies of the day. But, given what *is* known about her, I'm expecting to hear from her attorneys regarding royalties.

ALFRED SILVER

THE ADVENTURE AND ROMANCE OF HISTORIC AMERICA.

KEEPERS OF THE DAWN

In 1750, the Mohawk Valley was a haven of peace and plenty to both Indians and Englishmen. But with the American Revolution, the Iroquois had to choose sides. As the bitter war turned son against father, the Iroquois made the fateful choice to side with the British. This is the story of the beginning of the end.

WHERE THE GHOST HORSE RUNS

Cuthbert Grant, known as the "Chief of all the Half-Breeds," dreamed of an Eden for his half-Indian people of the Nothern Great Plains. Marie McGillus had long admired Grant, but when she married him, she discovered he was a very human husband. And she held the family together as Grant pursued his long-sought paradise.

Published by Ballantine Books.
Available at bookstores everywhere.